Praise for

Blonnie Wyche's storytelling transported me to a world with personalities from the past that seemed very real in the present; a time I didn't want to leave and a place I really visited. I'm amazed at the richness of the work.

- Mike Taylor
Director, Pender County Public Libraries

———————————

In *Cecilia's Harvest*, author Blonnie Wyche recreates the turbulent times of the American Revolution on the North Carolina coast. Cecilia sparkles as a colonial girl becoming a woman while she struggles through the fires of adversity to take her place with other memorable fictional heroines. Cecilia Moore Black and Jo March of Alcott's *Little Women* are cut from the same cloth: feisty, spirited, rebellious independents. It's a rousing yarn with characters you will remember long after the story ends.

- Nan Graham
Commentator for WHQR Public Radio in Wilmington, NC
Author of Turn South at the Next Magnolia *and* In a Magnolia Minute

CECILIA'S HARVEST

A Novel of the Revolution

by
Blonnie Bunn Wyche

Blonnie Bunn Wyche

Whittler's
Bench
Press

Lines from the poem "Daughter" by Kathryn Stripling Byer, from *The Girl in the Midst of the Harvest*, ©1986, Texas Tech University Press. Reproduced by permission of the publisher.

Cover art by Margaret James

First Edition 2009
Published in the United States of America by Whittler's Bench Press,
an imprint of Dram Tree Books.

Publisher's Cataloging-in-Publication Data
(Provided by DRT Press)

Wyche, Blonnie Bunn
    Cecilia's harvest : a novel of the revolution / by Blonnie Bunn Wyche.
    p. cm.
    ISBN 978-0-9785265-6-6
[1. North Carolina - Fiction. 2. Wilmington (N.C.) - Fiction. 3. United States --History--Revolution, 1775-1783 --Fiction. 4. Fear, Cape (N.C.) --Fiction. 5. Historical fiction. I. Title.]

PZ7. W9695 Ce 2009
[Fic] - dc22

Volume discounts available.
Call or e-mail for terms.

Whittler's Bench Press
P.O. Box 7183
Wilmington, N.C. 28406
(910) 538-4076
www.dramtreebooks.com

Potential authors: visit our website or email us for submission guidelines.

DEDICATION:

For my sons
David James Wyche and Graham Clark Wyche

ACKNOWLEDGMENTS

Writing's solitary endeavor must leave its isolation if the words are to be read. My first readers are the diverse, critical and supportive members of my writers group: Sue Atkinson, Vonnie Fry, Linda Martin, Carolee Morris, Rebecca Petruck, Maria Ross, Peggy Sheehan and Barbara Teachey. My overwhelming thanks to each of them for their championship of my writing.

My thanks to other helpful readers: Ellyn Bache, Joyce Cooper and Brooks Preik. Margaret James, illustrator extraordinaire, brings life to the characters who live on the story page. Special thanks to Meg Sheehan for her meticulous research on colonial period cheesemaking. Tim Boyd, from the Moores Creek Battle Ground Historic Site, instructed me, with marvelous patience, about colonial firearms. Bert Felton, historian and sailor, helped with the identification of sailing vessels. Judy Ward knows her colonial and early statehood sheriffs, sharing names with me. Barbara Baker loaned me books from her collections and knows where bodies are buried. Members of the Pender County Historical Society shared much information about colonial families who had plantations along the Cape Fear River. The helpful staff at the New Hanover County Public Library brought out resources of maps and documents for research. Brenda Bryant and her staff at the Brunswick Town / Fort Anderson State Historic Site gave valuable assistance on the local colonial period. Steve and Sue Bilzi keep my computer going, which at times is no small task. Heartfelt love to my sister, Frances, who is always there. And to my sons and their wives, who bestow constant support, I give my love. Any misinformation of the period is my responsibility.

IGRAMS:

While the earth remaineth, seedtime and harvest, and cold and heat, and summer and winter, and day and night shall not cease.

Genesis 8:22
King James Version

*When I look up the future's a field for me.
I am the girl in the midst of the harvest.*

From the poem: "Daughter"
From: *The Girl in the Midst of the Harvest*
by Kathryn Stripling Byer,
North Carolina Poet Laureate

CHAPTER 1

Cecilia Moore pulled the wagon to a stop at the edge of the tavern yard. She stared at the bustle of activity and swallowed an unexpected knot of fear. "War," she whispered.

The setting sun slanted across men camped on the grounds of The Anchor and all along the street leading to the Brunswick docks. Cooking fires burned at several sites. A piglet, skewered on an iron rod, roasted over embers near Mister Ashe's house. Nearby a man turned a brace of rabbits on a makeshift spit. At another spot a kettle simmered, the fragrance of onions and herbs drifting through the air.

"War," Cecilia repeated. "I hate the thought that fighting is on the way here. Lexington and Concord are far away. This is right at home. Those men are cooking our own peas and corn that they've picked right out of our fields. Timmie, those are the crops we are supposed to take back to Wilmington."

Timothy Charles, her ten-year-old brother, spoke up. "Cecilia, they're militia. They need the food."

"There's the group that passed us on the road today." Donny Smith, Timothy's friend, squirmed around on the wagon seat, counting. "There must be thirty men here."

Every muscle of Cecilia's slender body hurt. Her arms ached from driving the horse all day on the rutted, sandy roads. She could feel, even through her leather gloves, a blister forming on the palm of her right hand. She slapped the reins across Natty's back, guiding him toward the barn.

The boys unhitched the horse and led him into an empty stall. "Plenty of oats. Make sure you water him," Cecilia said, as she pulled a burr from the horse's mane and began to brush him off with handsful of straw.

"I know how to feed a horse," Timothy said.

Donny laughed. "Timmie, she knows you know. She just has to tell you. My big brother Ricky is the same way. 'Donny, do that. Donny, do it like this.' "

Cecilia took off her mobcap and used her fingers to brush her straggling brown hair back from her forehead. The heat of the July afternoon pulsed through the barn. She dampened a corner of her apron in the horse's water bucket and wiped her face, then pulled the cap back on her head. For a long moment she stood staring out the barn door. She didn't want Timmie and Donny to sense her fear. Now, prepared to make her way from the barn to the tavern, she said, "Let's see what Mister Richards has on the hearth."

"I'm ready to eat," Timothy informed her.

As she walked into the stable yard a knot again narrowed her throat. She willed herself to stay calm. She'd grown up here in the tavern in Brunswick before she and her sisters opened their tavern, Three Sisters, in Wilmington. She was used to men coming and going, smoking their pipes and cleaning their muskets, sharpening their knives and rolling out blankets to sleep for an hour or two by the hearth. She couldn't yet decipher the mood of these militiamen, but she could feel, in her bones, a different temper. The climate across their camping grounds was like a gentle breeze blowing from the ocean that could build, without warning, into the winds of a hurricane.

Eerie shadows crisscrossed the grounds as she walked through the campers, but the torch outside the door of The Anchor shed a welcome light. Mister Richards, the man her sister Polly had hired to operate the tavern, did not give a welcome. He frowned across the width of the room at her. "What brings you here today, Miss Cecilia?"

"Errands and supplies, Mister Richards. Just now we need refreshment. Anything you have in the stew pot. Then we can talk business. Polly did send a long list."

Mister Richards looked around the room filled with men eating, drinking, playing cards, cleaning guns, talking in low tones. Some were dressed in everyday attire. One wore a leather shirt with fringed sleeves and Cecilia wondered if he'd come down from the mountains.

"No time for you just now, ma'am."

Cecilia walked behind the long counter, retrieved three wooden bowls from a shelf and set them on the hearth. She ladled stew in each bowl, handing the boys their servings. When she had finished eating her portion, she again went behind the counter to draw ale from a cask into a pitcher.

Mister Richards glared. "Ma'am, you stay from behind my counter. Your sister may own this place, but you can't just help yourself. How'd you learn how to draw ale?"

Cecilia sat on the edge of a bench beside her brother and Donny before she answered. "Mister Richards, I was born in this tavern. I know more about this house and this little town of Brunswick then you can imagine."

"Mister Richards is acting strange, Cee," Timothy whispered. "What's going on?"

"Timmie, I'm not sure."

A man sitting across the table from them spoke up. "You are a feisty one, ma'am. My name's Bennet."

Cecilia nodded at him. "Cecilia Moore from Wilmington."

Donny spoke up. "Have the British landed yet? We've heard about the ships gathering at the mouth of the river."

"Governor Martin moved from Fort Johnston to one of those ships. He's scared enough of what's coming that he's boarded the sloop-of-war *Cruizer*."

Bennet drank from his mug before he continued. "Guess he thinks he can run the colony from the deck of a ship. He's sending messages for the Tories to rally. 'Fight,' he says. 'Put down this rabble.' " Bennet laughed. "Calling me rabble! Not a rabberly bone in my body."

"We'll hold the fort," someone said.

"Or we'll burn the fort." A voice behind her took up the theme. "The British won't have the luxury of firing our own guns at us. We're joining up with Colonel Howe."

"Robert Howe knows Fort Johnston. He'll know what to do about defending it," a man sitting near the door commented.

About the tavern room most nodded in approval. "Bet we'll find John Ashe when we get there," someone said.

"And Cornelius Harnett. Harnett's always in the thick of things."

"Amen," someone shouted.

Mister Richards tightened his lips. Cecilia wondered exactly where the man's allegiance lay. She looked through the open tavern door to the yard.

A young man lounged against a fence post. Firelight haloed his black curls and silhouetted his tall frame. His face was clearly visible in the torch light and he was, most truly, the most handsome man she'd ever seen. He watched her with a strange intensity, as if he would like to probe out her inmost thoughts and hold them in his hand. She felt a blush creep up her neck and quickly turned her attention back to the room.

All was orderly, but excitement bounced from the walls. Was it the thought of fighting that intoxicated the men with this unseen but tangible fervor, palpable enough to quiet voices and quicken the very air about them? No one was drinking heavily, but they were spirited in a way foreign to her.

She spoke softly to her brother, "Timmie, we'll camp in the barn loft tonight."

CHAPTER 2

Cecilia could not sleep for the worry that nagged at her. How was she to get the supplies they needed? She could see dozens of hogsheads filled with tar and turpentine sitting on sleds near the barn. Polly's list included tar and turpentine, to be loaded on a barge or sloop, and sent upriver to Wilmington. Could she and the boys get a barrel in the wagon? No. Even if they could, Natty, strong as he was, wouldn't be able to pull that kind of load. But she had to have gun powder and she knew where to find it.

She waited till the moon started moving toward the west before she shook Timothy awake. "Gather up your stuff, little brother. We're leaving."

"Donny," she said, pulling at his arm. "Get up. Get Natty hitched to the wagon. Make sure he's fed and watered."

"Cecilia, it's the middle of the night," Timothy protested. He buried his head back into his hay pillow.

"It's the middle of the night and everything around here is going to explode at any time. Now wake up and help me."

Stretching and grumbling, the boys climbed down the loft ladder.

Cecilia searched through the yard of sleeping men to find the quietest way to thread through their ranks. Dying camp fires gave enough light that she could see Timothy and Donny lead Natty from his stall and back him into the wagon traces. Several soldiers turned to watch as Cecilia walked the horse toward the road. A man pulled himself to his feet and began to rearrange his packs. Another pushed a log on his camp fire and lifted a pot to hang over the coals. The handsome, black-haired man sat up to give them a half-salute.

She nodded back, but even as she moved away she could feel his eyes following her. No one in the camp spoke or tried to stop them.

"We're just going home?" Timothy asked as they walked, leading the horse.

"No, we're going to the Russellborough house. Mister Dry owns it now."

"Why? What's at Russellborough?" was Donny's question.

"Gunpowder." Cecilia patted the horse's neck. "We can't get the supplies Polly wanted. There's no one to hire to move barrels or load a barge to go up river. The soldiers have picked the gardens clean. There are no beans. No potatoes. They've eaten most of the corn crop. It would be a waste of time to even try to salvage anything from the gardens or fields. But we have to have the powder."

"Don't the soldiers need the powder, too?" Timothy asked.

"Of course they do. That's one of the reasons they have to take Fort Johnston. For the guns. The cannon. Any powder stored there. That is, if the soldiers and sailors off the British ships haven't gotten it first." Cecilia kicked a pine cone ahead of her on the road as the bright moon slid behind a cloud. She couldn't see where the cone landed. "If we don't have gun powder, we can't hunt. If we can't hunt, we can't keep the tavern running."

"My brother Ricky's been looking for powder for the sheriff," Donny said. "There's powder at Russellborough? You know this?"

"When I was a little girl the Tryons lived here. Margaret was my very best friend in the world. We played upstairs and downstairs in that big house. I think I could walk through the rooms blindfolded." She watched Timothy catch a pine cone on the toe of his boot and kick it well in front of them.

"Mister Dry bought the house when Mister Tryon moved to New Bern. There's a tunnel from the house to the wharf. One day, when they were having a meeting at the tavern, I heard Cousin James Moore tell Mister Dry to hide all sorts of stuff there. We're going to appropriate some."

"We're going to steal it," Timothy exclaimed.

"No, Timmie. I'll leave a note for Mister Dry. He'll know who took his powder."

Without another word she led the horse down the slope to the edge of the water and tied him to a railing on the small dock. She groped her way into the entrance to the tunnel, the boys following close behind.

As soon as they were inside, she took a candle and flint kit from her pocket and handed them to Timothy. When the boys had the candle burning, she lifted a lantern from a hook on the wall and lit it as well.

"Wow," Donny said. "Look at the wine bottles. That whole wall is covered with wine bottles."

"And kegs of rum," said Timothy. "They've never been tapped. Cee, the tavern could serve rum from here till tomorrow next year and never run out."

"Powder, Timmie. Look for hogsheads marked gunpowder," Cecilia said. "That is all we're going to take."

Donny lit a candle in another lantern and moved ahead up a slight slope farther into the long tunnel. "Corn meal," he called back. "Dress goods. More whiskey."

"Think I've found your powder," Timothy called.

"Young man, just what do you think you are doing?"

Cecilia whirled around at the sound of a man's voice. "Mister Dry!"

"Indeed, yes. I know who I am." Mister Dry stood in the middle of the tunnel. His long dressing gown circled about his feet, making patterns on the dirt floor. He folded his arms. "I've had my slaves keeping watch. I expected a raid from those men camped at Brunswick. I thought some of Robert Howe's men might try to loot my stores. I didn't expect a girl and two boys. Who are you?"

"Oh, Mister Dry, I'm Cecilia Moore."

"Henrietta's daughter? Polly Moore's sister?"

"Yes, sir." Cecilia felt as if she should curtsy. Instead she pointed toward the boys. "My brother Timothy Charles. His friend Donny Smith."

Mister Dry slowly unfolded his arms and sat on the edge of a packing case. "You are here for what reason." He wasn't asking a question.

"To appropriate gunpowder, sir."

"As honest as your sister." The man chuckled. "There are other terms for the word 'appropriate,' you know."

"Yes, sir. I wasn't stealing. I was going to leave a note. And coin." Cecilia pulled a small leather bag from her pocket and held it in her hand.

"This powder will be for a good purpose, I suppose."

"I want it for hunting, Mister Dry. I'm the hunter in the family."

Timothy spoke up. "I'm learning, sir. I'm pretty good with a musket. Cee is best with a rifle. She can bring down a running deer."

Mister Dry nodded at him, then looked Donny up and down. He turned again to Cecilia. "James Moore and Robert Howe want these supplies. Their men will need everything stored here."

"Yes, sir."

"How were you planning to transport this contraband?"

"Sir, we have a horse and wagon on your dock. Polly sent me to Brunswick for supplies, but the soldiers are camped out there. They've eaten or taken the food we were supposed to take back to the Three Sisters tavern in Wilmington. Mister Richards was not at all cooperative about other things I was supposed to get. I don't think he's very friendly to the continental cause. Sir, I wasn't going back to Wilmington empty handed."

"Interesting." Mister Dry stood, shook out the skirt of his dressing gown and called back into the tunnel. "Monk. Tinker. Come on out. We're going to load a wagon."

In short order the slaves lashed two hogsheads of gun powder on the wagon and covered them with sail cloth to hide the contents. A box filled with bolts of linen material and a crate of wine, packed in saw dust, came next. When one of the slaves headed for a barrel of rice, Cecilia spoke up.

"We ordered rice at Orton. You are being most generous, Mister Dry, but the foreman there is sending rice to Wilmington by barge."

He carefully inspected the load on the wagon and checked the lines on Natty before he turned to take Cecilia's hand in a firm grasp. "You go safely. Give my regards to Polly. She was always a shrewd one to bargain. She's raised her equal in you."

"Thank you, sir."

As she led the horse up the slope to the road, Mister Dry called out to her. When she looked back he pointed south. A glow rose above the top of the tall pines as if to mirror the sun just beginning to rise in the east. A harsh odor of fire lifted through the trees.

"The fort!" Cecilia blurted. "Oh, Mister Dry, it has to be. Fort Johnston is burning!"

"July 19, 1775, Cecilia. The war has started here in our corner of the world." He bowed his head, as if in resignation. "It's started."

CHAPTER 3

In the late afternoon Cecilia crossed the Cape Fear River on the ferry from Eagles Island into Wilmington. As she guided the horse up Market Street toward Three Sisters, the boys jumped down to run ahead. Polly met them in the stable yard, stopping her work to listen to tales of their journey.

"Soldiers were everywhere," Timothy said. "On the road. In Brunswick."

Polly reached to hug her sister. "I didn't realize I was sending you into danger."

"You weren't. Not really. I couldn't get most of the supplies you wanted but I did get gunpowder. Where shall we put it?"

Polly set Timothy and Donny to dig a trench near the fence that hid the stable yard from Second Street. She called Rollen and Travis, the indentured boys, to heat tar and waterproof several small barrels.

While her sister was busy with those duties, Cecilia unharnessed the horse, rubbed him down and made sure he had hay and oats. She looked up to find Polly watching her.

"I'm sorry about the beans and corn," Cecilia said. "The men had gathered most of the crops and were cooking our vegetables in their pots." She reached up to scratch Natty behind the ears.

"I wish I had your way with animals," Polly said. "I never learned to like a horse."

"Horses are wonderful," Cecilia said.

"As soon as the tar cools, Rollen and Travis will fill those smaller barrels with powder, then we'll bury them. There's petty pilfering everywhere. Food for the tavern is always an invitation for thievery. If anyone knows we have the gunpowder, we'll be more of a target than we are now."

"Have we lost much?"

"A ham hanging in the smokehouse walked away last night," her sister said. "If you're through taking care of the horse, go on in and get some of Leah's mutton stew."

Cecilia barred the stall opening, scooped up her cat to cradle in her arms, and started across the yard toward the tavern. Polly called after her. "Cecilia, you did a good job."

"Good job? Oh, Polly, you have no idea how much I hate this tavern. How much I hate all the work. How much I hate -"

She held the cat up to her face. "I am going to marry a rich man, Daisy. I am going to be the one to tell the servants, and everybody else, what to do. When to fetch a bucket of water. When to bring in the wood for the fires."

Daisy nestled in Cecilia's arms and purred comfort.

"I knew you'd understand. Now I have to face Mama."

As Cecilia stepped into the huge room, her mother called to her. "You look so bedraggled. Do fix your hair. It's tumbling out of your mobcap. Your apron is just filthy. What have you done with yourself?"

Cecilia nodded to the women in the sewing circle with her mother. "Cousin Margaret. Mistress Harnett. I'm just back from Brunswick. I'm sure I look a sight."

"Tell us what you know of Fort Johnston," Mistress Harnett said. "There was a man in here at noon who said there was a fire there last night."

Cecilia nodded. "A rather large fire, from what I could see. The news I heard on the road today confirmed that most of the fort burned. Robert Howe and his men made sure the British won't be able to use it."

"Our men? And the British ships?" Mistress Harnett asked.

"I know nothing of our soldiers, except many of them were camped in Brunswick. The ships are still blockading the entrance to the river. Governor Martin is still aboard the *Cruizer* and giving orders from there."

"Cecilia! You camped with soldiers!" Henrietta fanned at her face. "Oh, mercy."

"Mama, I'm fine. Really, I am. Now I'm going to get some stew that Polly said was on the hearth. I'll fix my hair. I'll change my apron. I'll do my chores."

Cousin Margaret spoke up. "Henrietta, leave the girl alone. It's no easy task driving a wagon from here to Brunswick and back."

"But I want her safe," Mama wailed.

"None of us is safe," Mary Harnett said.

Cecilia ladled stew from the pot as she listened to Mistress Harnett. "The loyalists want the patriots to shut up. The patriots want those who support the king to change their minds. The neutrals want both sides to go back to the way things have always been. It's no longer safe to express an opinion. It's no longer safe to venture out. It will get worse."

Margaret Moore Hill shook her head. "Mary, you really believe that? You really believe the situation will get worse?"

Mary Harnett folded her quilt squares and packed them in her sewing basket. "Yes. It will get worse. The Safety Committees have been warning us. Every letter I get from Cornelius confirms the unrest. Our Congress members are planning for war, just as I'm sure our royal governor, Josiah Martin, sitting on his ship in our river, is planning for war." She nodded to Cecilia on her way out onto Market Street.

In the days ahead, news and messages from Fort Johnston, and the surrounding countryside, filtered into Wilmington. Men, taking a break from a store or tannery or blacksmith forge, ate at the long trestle table in the middle of the tavern. Because of the unrest, with military action all about, frivolity was outlawed. Playing a game of cards, considered very frivolous indeed, was canceled. Men still shuffled a deck and made their bets under the table. They drank rounds of beer, saluting causes. And they talked, trading any information they had.

"The British moved the guns of the fort out of reach," one man said. "We sure could use those cannon."

"Had a grand time burning the sheds near the fort," boasted another.

"Governor Martin's calling for men to take up arms for the king," said one. His hushed voice led the listeners to lean toward him. "He's sending messages everywhere for men to join up with him. Special invitations are going to the Scots up at Cross Creek. Mark my word. There will be bloodshed."

Cecilia listened while she helped Leah peel potatoes, stir the stew, baste a ham. She caught the ragged ends of tales as she brought in water from the well and wood for the hearth. "War," she muttered under her breath. "War and work. Work and war. There's no end to either one of them."

An old man, tamping tobacco into his pipe, chimed up from the chimney corner. "My grandson's with Colonel Howe. Sure miss my boy. I haven't heard from him in two weeks now."

"Howe is a most capable leader, I've heard," someone said.

"Bobby Howe?" Henrietta asked Polly. "Cousin Bobby Howe?"

"Yes, Mama. He led the raid against Fort Johnston."

Henrietta wrung her handkerchief. "What is going to happen to all of us?"

To quiet her mother, Cecilia sat beside her. "Are you sewing something from that linen Mister Dry sent? Do show me what you're working on."

From across the room, Polly nodded her approval.

A September blow lifted shingles from the tavern's roof. Two sloops and a brig, on the winds of the storm, slipped around the British ships moored at the mouth of the Cape Fear River and anchored near the foot of Market Street. Polly and Cecilia left the repairing of the roof to Rollen and Travis, and went down to the docks to see what they could buy.

"Molasses! Sugar! Cloth! What marvelous treasures!" Polly exclaimed as she bargained with the ship's captain.

"I have sulfur, Miss Polly," the captain of the brig said.

"Sulfur is needed for making black powder." Polly nodded. "I'll take a barrel. I'll let our newly formed Continental troops know that sulfur is available."

On their way back up Market Street from the docks Cecilia saw the man who had regarded her so intently from the tavern yard in Brunswick. His curls were hidden under his hat, but she remembered the steady gaze of his blue-green eyes as they had fastened on her. Today he sat astride a great black stallion. Her breath caught in her throat at the beauty of the animal.

The horse moved toward her until his chin rested on her shoulder. Cecilia patted his nose and scratched between his wide black eyes. "You are a winner," she said. "A beautiful black champion."

"That he is," the man answered. "I've never before seen Big Boy go up to anyone like that." He swung from the saddle. "If I may be so presumptuous, ladies, I'll introduce myself. My name is Kenneth Black."

Polly asked, "Judge Theodore Black's son?"

He took off his hat and gave a short bow. "Yes, ma'am."

"I'm Pauline Moore, kin of Judge Maurice Moore. He has spoken of your father. I believe you and he are neighbors near Rocky Point. This is my sister, Cecilia. May we offer you refreshment at Three Sisters?"

Kenneth and Big Boy followed the sisters up the street.

In the tavern he charmed Henrietta. "Your daughter must take after you, ma'am. She captivated the attention of each and every man gathered at Brunswick."

"Mercy me." Henrietta actually simpered.

Kenneth turned to Polly. "Word of your delicious meals is spread far and wide."

"Thank you," Polly said, handing him a mug of ale. "But we haven't seen you here before now. Have you been away?"

"I've been staying with my mother's Swann relatives in Carteret County. My father requested I return because of the political climate." Kenneth looked at Cecilia with that same fierce stare he'd worn in Brunswick. "It is very good to be back."

"The Swanns are a fine family," Henrietta said, as if a problem had been solved. She busied herself with her knitting.

Cecilia felt too shy to ask questions or make polite conversation, but she knew, from the way they were talking, that Mama and Polly both liked Kenneth Black. He was, then, acceptable as a beau for her. She glanced across the room to see Leah, sitting at the hearth, shake her head.

CHAPTER 4

K enneth visited a few days later, bringing Henrietta two skeins of butternut colored yarn. "You knit so beautifully, Mistress Moore. I thought you could put it to use."

"Where did you find such beautiful thread?" Mama asked.

Kenneth didn't answer, but he sat with her, holding the lengths while she wound the yarn into balls for her knitting.

On his next visit he brought Polly a cloth packet of spearmint seed. "I've seen how you care for your herb bed, there by the garden wall," Kenneth said. "Perhaps the mint will add to your collection."

Polly spilled a few of the tiny black grains in her palm. "Thank you, Kenneth. Plants from these seeds will be a welcome addition for my garden."

Kenneth brought Cecilia a lace handkerchief. "For those times when you do not have to work so hard," he said. He caught her hand and twirled her about, as if there were music for dancing.

Cecilia felt giddy with his attention. Her brain didn't want to keep up with her feet as he clasped her hand.

After he was gone she sat on a stool by the hearth to catch her breath. Leah said, "Miss Cecilia, that man be bumptious. Downright bumptious. He courting you mighty hard. You takes care."

Not even Kenneth's visits or the news of war stopped the constant chores. On a cold November morning Cecilia pulled her shawl closely about her shoulders and leaned her head in the cow's flank as she milked. The sounds of shouted orders from the large field just up the street, where Cousin Jamie's Continentals were learning to form lines, the paradiddle of a drum and the shrill of a Donny's fife playing off-key, set her teeth on edge. Daisy rubbed against her ankle, meowing.

"Do you want some warm milk, ma'am?" Cecilia sent a stream of milk toward the cat and watched as the animal boxed the air to catch droplets.

"Now that's a pretty picture."

Cecilia twisted on her milking stool and looked up at Kenneth. He came so often that his sudden appearance didn't surprise her. Her heart pounded an extra beat as she said, "You are out early this morning."

"You are working early this morning." He lifted a stool from its peg on the wall and sat beside her.

"Why aren't you marching? I would have thought you'd be on the parade grounds. Cousin James is still recruiting." She stood to set the milk pail on a shelf out of reach of the cow's feet and the cat's tongue. "Colonel James Moore, of the Continental Line, appointed by the North Carolina Congress -"

"No marching for me. I will not fight." Kenneth stood and pulled her to him. "I've had nothing but fighting in my life from as long as I can remember. I won't take on another foe."

Cecilia gazed up at him. She really did want to understand. "Who have you been fighting, Kenneth? And if you won't join the militia, or the Continentals, what were you doing in Brunswick back in the summer?"

"I was there to enlist two slaves in the militia. One for my father. One for me. The law allows for that."

She picked up Daisy and stroked her fur, trying to give herself a moment to still her confusion over this piece of information. A slave to serve in his stead? A slave for his father? She didn't know what to say. If he wouldn't go to war, how could he send someone in his place?

The warmth of his arms about her waist made her shiver. Then he leaned down to kiss her forehead. "Marry me. Marry me, Miss Cecilia Moore. Marry me and help me."

His words sent bewildering apprehension coursing through her. She looked at him, unable to speak.

The thoughts of marriage - especially marriage to Kenneth - set her heart pounding so hard her ears pulsed. A sudden panic welled from her stomach. Marriage to a rich man was a fantasy she's had since she was a little girl. Marriage to get away from the tavern and the work, from the constant coming and going of sailors and trades people and old men with their pipes and stories, had been a dream for as long as she could remember.

She pulled herself from Kenneth's arms to slump on the milking stool, her throat tightening. What did he mean about helping him. She swallowed as hard and fast as she could to force an answer. "We'll have to talk with Polly."

"Polly? Why Polly?"

"Because Polly is the head of the house. She has been since our father left. Polly makes the decisions. I trust what she says. When our sister Charlotte married it was Polly and Cousin Maurice who made all of the arrangements."

"Then let's go ask Polly. What's the sailor's song? 'His hair was black, his eye was blue, his arm was stout, his word was true. I wish in my heart I was with you.' And, dear Cecilia, I want to marry you!"

She was beginning to think that maybe, just maybe, she could love him. She forced a laugh. "I think the next verse says something about the girl selling her spinning wheel to buy her love a sword of steel. Kenneth, you don't want a sword."

"No sword. Cecilia, I want you." He reached for her hand and pulled her to her feet. "You. Just you. Let's go see Polly, if that's what we have to do."

Cecilia skipped to keep up with Kenneth's long strides as they headed across the stable yard toward the tavern. She did care for this tall, black-haired, sometimes strange man. Didn't she? Maybe he was the answer to her dreams of having a place of her very own. She managed to ask, "Kenneth, will you let me ride Big Boy?"

He stopped abruptly. "What? Cecilia, you're so tiny I don't think you can handle Big Boy. Besides, girls don't ride stallions." Still holding her hand they went into the tavern.

Leah sliced bacon into a pan sizzling on the coals. Polly stirred mush bubbling in a large iron pot. Timothy sat at the end of the long table restlessly turning pages of a book. Her brother, always glad of interruptions to his studies, looked up as Cecilia and Kenneth came in.

"Polly?" Cecilia hadn't realized how excited and scared she was until she spoke.

Polly swung around. "What's wrong?"

"Good morning," Kenneth said. "Nothing's wrong. At least I do hope not. I've asked Cecilia to be my wife."

"What!" Polly and Leah exclaimed together.

Mama, coming down the stairs from her bedchamber, added to the chorus. "What?"

Timothy chose the opportunity to escape his books. Snatching a handful of bacon from the platter, he ran outside.

Polly waved her hands as if to shoo him out of the door. "Well, Timmie's gone for the morning." She sat at the table and closed the book he'd been pretending to read. "Cecilia, you and Kenneth sit with me. Tell me this important news."

Cecilia sat on the bench at the side of the table. Kenneth paced the length of the room before he came to stand behind her.

Polly waited.

"I will care for her," Kenneth said. His voice was so stern that Cecilia twisted around to look up at him. "I will look after her. I will keep and protect her."

Was he angry about something? Was he upset that he had to ask for her hand? Cecilia's thoughts swirled. Had he said he loved her?

Polly was talking and Cecilia sat up straighter to focus on her sister's words.

"Kenneth, I know of no reason why you and Cecilia should not marry. We will send word to Cousin Maurice -"

He interrupted. "Why Judge Maurice Moore?"

"He's our guardian, Kenneth. As a judge, he can sign the marriage agreement and talk about the dowry. I'm assuming you and your father will want a marriage portion."

Henrietta was crying. "Cecilia is much too young. She's only fifteen."

"Mama, I'll be sixteen in March. Charlotte got married when she was sixteen."

"Jonathan Reynolds took her away to Charles Town. I haven't seen her since. I can't lose another baby." Mama sank into her chair, rocking back and forth as if the action could take her back in time.

Kenneth, ignoring Henrietta, spoke only to Polly. His voice was now gentle, almost pleading. "I want to marry Cecilia. I will care for her. We will live on my father's farm near Rocky Point. It is a fine farm with a large house where any woman would be pleased to live and entertain."

He put his hat on, tilting it at a swaggering angle. "When you reach an agreement, let me know." He strode out.

Polly watched him leave before reaching for Cecilia's hand. "Sister, do you *want* to marry Kenneth?"

"Polly, what is love?"

"I'm not sure I'm the one to ask."

Leah sat down beside them. "Ain't nobody knows more than you, Miss Polly. Lawdy, child, you love that Daniel. The stars went out when you turn him down."

"Leah, that was so long ago. Cousin Maurice had taken our papa away so he wouldn't end up in a British court for his gambling and stealing. Timmie was an infant. Cecilia and Charlotte were still little. Mama was so sick. If I had married Daniel I could not have looked after them."

Worry lines etched Polly's forehead and she shook her head. "Leah, I did the only thing I could do. I would not change a single act. Cecilia has choices. She can support herself. She does not have to marry."

"Polly, I want to." Cecilia pulled her hand from her sister's grasp. "I will be the mistress of a fine house. I will be able to give the orders." She got up to twirl about the room. "I can dance the night away with my husband." She dropped a curtsy. "I think spring would be a grand time for a wedding."

CHAPTER 5

Into the grind of daily duties and the chill of winter that wrapped an icy glaze about everything, news of increasing unrest filtered into town. The few papers that reached Three Sisters had reports that were weeks, sometimes even months, old. That did not keep those who came into the tavern for a drink or a meal from reading with interest and commenting on each article. Local events - fires, deaths, storms, marriages, goods exported, prices, and ships entering and clearing the port - were reported with great brevity. It was Polly who tried to keep up with all the information about shipping so she could plan for supplies for the tavern. For the most part, the British blockade at the mouth of the river was doing its job quite effectively.

The Committee of Safety outlawed all merriment. There should be no frivolity while the country was at war. No parties to be held. No horse racing or gaming allowed. Men went outside of town to hold card games. The beach sands south of Wilmington furnished a natural race track and many took advantage of the course. Betting on horse racing was hushed, but money still exchanged hands for a favorite to cross the finish line. The rowdy taverns on the waterfront had a steady business, as they always had. As far as Cecilia was concerned, Three Sisters Tavern served as many people as ever.

Usually, during a storm, a ship could maneuver around the small fleet of British ships anchored at the mouth of the Cape Fear, so some vessels came upriver to the Brunswick and Wilmington ports. That November of 1775 one ship docked to unload not only cargo, but a large group of Scots who had come to settle at Cross Creek.

" 'Tis Mistress Flora herself," one man reported to others in the tavern. "Come on the *George*, she did. The gracious Mistress Flora MacDonald with her family."

"Governor Martin'll be pleased," someone commented. "He's been trying to rally the Scots. Wants 'em to fight the patriots to redress grievances, though I ain't yet figured what's a grievance to be redressed."

"Thought 'twas the patriots wanted to talk 'bout grievances." The old man in the chimney corner spoke up. "As for things to grieve about, there's always something."

James Moore, now commissioned a colonel in the Continental Army, put out another call for the five hundred men he had been promised. Every white male, from the age of sixteen to old men of sixty, was obliged by law to join the militia. Cecilia listened as Cousin James explained about wanting the best of the best for his continental troops. He and Cousin Maurice, meeting at a table in the tavern, held strategy meetings.

Before he left with his troops for Virginia and the defense of Norfolk, Robert Howe conferred with them. Cecilia served ham and sweet potatoes, beans and rice, apple pie and winter collards, to John Ashe and Alexander Lillington, as they added their expertise to the conversations. Colonel Richard Caswell, with a group of his officers, rode in from New Bern to huddle in the conferences. The patriotic leaders talked and ate, studied maps and ate, stretched, walked about the tables, and ate.

"So many men to feed," Cecilia complained. "In here they talk of nothing but war. Outside in the courtyard their aides talk of nothing but war. And I have to go out there to take their rations. Can't they meet somewhere else?"

"The British sympathizers are everywhere, so our leaders are safer here," Polly said. "Men meet in taverns. They sit and drink an ale and talk. No one can reasonably report their meetings are political. I served many a planning meeting at Brunswick during the time of the Stamp Act."

"Polly, I remember. I didn't like the work then anymore than I like it now."

The news came by rider that Cornelius Harnett was elected president of the North Carolina Provincial Congress and commander-in-chief of the patriot forces. Reports of Congress were brought by riders, through letters to the wives of men in the area, from broadsides tacked to fence posts. When Mister Harnett could be in Wilmington, he, too, met with the other men as they laboured over plans to counter Governor Martin's schemes of raising a loyalist army in North Carolina.

Mary Harnett brought loaves of bread, dried fruit pies and roasted chickens to help serve the men as they studied maps and worked on strategies.

Polly hugged her each time she came. "Mistress Harnett, thank you so much for your kindness."

"I want to help," she said. "It's also a way to see Cornelius. He's never home these days. When he is, he has his nose in papers."

Kenneth, riding Big Boy and seeking shelter from icy winds blowing off the river, sought out Cecilia in the barn, where she was mucking stalls.

"You'll not have to do that kind of work when we're married," Kenneth stated. He waved his arm at the stalls which still needed cleaning. "Your slaves should be doing this."

"We don't have slaves here at the tavern," Cecilia said.

"You have Leah."

"Oh, Kenneth, Leah is free. She's always been free. She grew up with Mama.

She's been more a mother to me than Mama ever has been. Without Leah -" Cecilia caught her breath. "My goodness, Kenneth, without Leah it would be impossible for Polly to run the tavern."

"I don't want to argue with you, dear Cecilia. Oh, March is such a long time to wait." He pulled her to him, kissing her lips as if he could not satisfy his longing for her.

Cecilia felt a passion rising up through her stomach, but a strange tug of fear overlaid it. She pushed her hands against Kenneth's shoulders. "There is so much to do to get ready for a wedding. Spring will be here quickly. Just another month. I'm sorry your mother is gone. She must have been a wonderful person. She could have helped with the planning and the sewing and everything else. I would like to have known her."

She knew she was babbling. She couldn't seem to stop. "Kenneth, when will I get to meet your father? Before the wedding? Will we visit the farm? Your farm? Have you been cutting wood and seeing to the fields? Staying busy with all the chores you must have to oversee?"

Kenneth had taken a step away from her as she talked. "I must attend to business now. I'll be back soon." He settled in his saddle, pulled Big Boy's reins close and trotted out of the stable yard.

Cecilia leaned against the door frame and watched him leave. Why would he never answer her questions? When they were married she would ask him again. Maybe she would find answers to her many questions. She did so want to understand. He hid so much from her. Her nagging fear didn't have a name any more than the excitement she felt when Kenneth kissed her. Perhaps when she was married she would understand. She sighed and went back to work.

Clouds threatened rain the cold February morning Mistress Harnett hurried into the tavern. She took Polly's hands in a tight grip before she made her announcement. "Our men have marched out for Cross Creek."

"That's why I didn't hear the drums on the parade grounds this morning," Cecilia said.

She hated those paradiddling drum beats that kept time for the march. She hated watching Timothy Charles, who had grown into a sturdy eleven-year-old frame as tall as most of the men, parade with them, through she had to admit Timmie could keep up with the best. Donny marched, too, playing his fife as if the tunes he tooted would keep left and right feet in time. He was getting better, but he still lost the melody at the oddest times. She hated the commotion that filled the streets and tavern when the men were dismissed from duty.

Now, a dire silence filled the tavern. Cecilia hugged her arms about herself.

Mistress Harnett continued with her news. "Caswell and Lillington are on the move from New Bern. They're taking an inland route to meet with James Moore and his force near Cross Creek. King George has declared us in rebellion. For once the king is right."

Leah, who had just come in from the yard, stopped short. "Is we gonna have fighting here, Mistress Harnett?"

Mary Harnett looked out through the window toward the Cape Fear River. "We'll have fighting. Oh, yes, it will come here. Wilmington's port is too important not to be a focus of attention. For both sides. We'll have fighting."

"Oh, Lawdy, ma'am."

"Lawdy indeed, Leah."

Ricky Smith had followed Leah in from the yard. Now he interrupted them. "Cecilia? Polly? Have any of you seen my brother Donny?"

"And where is Timothy?" Henrietta asked.

"I bet they've both gone with the troops," Cecilia said. She sank to the floor and clutched her stomach. This fear she could name. "Be safe, Timmie. Stay safe."

"May they all be safe," Mistress Harnett prayed.

CHAPTER 6

Five days later there was still no word of Timothy Charles. There was no word of Donny Smith. Ricky stopped in every day to ask if anyone had seen his brother. Cecilia knew the rainy weather added to the pain Ricky always seemed to have in his misshaped leg, but he never let his rocking gait stop him from his duties with the sheriff.

"You will let me know if you hear," he said. "Mother's most worried."

"Ricky, so are we all," Cecilia told him. "Wouldn't it be wonderful to go back to climbing trees and shooting marbles, like we used to do." She handed him a piece of dried apple pie before he went out again into the rain.

Several groups of men who had marched with Cousin James came through town. They brought news of a battle at a place called Moores Creek. They brought notes for wives and sweethearts. One man brought plunder from a pillaged house and bragged about forcing the family to run for their lives. None of the men had seen two eleven-year-old boys marching with the troops.

Cecilia leaned her head into the soft flank of the cow and sobbed while she milked. A soft rustling at the door of the barn made her catch her breath and turn. Her brother stood there and all she could do was stare at him.

"Are you all mad at me?" Timothy asked.

Cecilia threw the contents of the half full pail at him. Cow's milk soaked his clothes and ran down into his shoes. He dropped the bundle he was carrying and gasped.

"Cecilia!"

"*Mad* at you?" She stomped her foot. "We were supposed to be *mad* at you?"

Leah appeared behind Timothy. "I seen you come in the yard, Mister Timothy. You be worrying us most to death. But Miss Cecilia done give you a good baptism." She put her hands over her mouth and struggled with laughter.

Timothy was sputtering, pulling his wet shirt from his chest, glaring at Leah and his sister. "You didn't have to do that, Cecilia."

"Yes, I did." Her giggles broke into guffaws and she doubled over with merriment. When she could speak she turned to Leah. "Go tell Mama that the prodigal has returned, but I don't think she'll want him inside as dirty as he is."

"Yes, ma'am," Leah said. "I'll tell 'er. After she scolds him she'll want all the news. Mister Timothy, did Mister Donny come home with you? His brother be here most ever day looking for him."

Timothy nodded. "He's gone home. 'Spect he'll get the same words I'm gonna get. Maybe he won't get baptized."

Leah shooed Timothy off to the wash house. Cecilia went back to work with a lighter heart than she'd had in days. But when Kenneth came that afternoon Cecilia sobbed in his arms, telling him about Timmie running away with the troops.

"See, Cecilia? If I went off fighting you would have to worry about where I was and what I was doing. I settled that because I will not go to war. Do you understand any better now?"

Cecilia nodded. "I'm trying to. Kenneth, I'm really trying to understand you. I'm trying to know what you want. I'm trying."

"You really soaked him with a pail of milk?" Kenneth asked.

She grinned up at him. "I did. Served him right, too, for scaring us so."

"What would you do if I ran away?"

Cecilia stepped back and looked up at him. "Would you run away from me?"

"Never. I will never leave your side. And you will never, ever leave me." For a moment his hands gripped her shoulders. Then he reached to take a small leather bag from his belt. "Hold out your hand, my dear wife-to-be." He shook the contents into her outstretched palm.

The sparkle of the tiny diamond earrings felt warm against her skin. "Oh, they are so beautiful."

"They were my mother's," Kenneth said. "I know she would want you to wear them. Put them on right now. Let me see how they look."

She fastened the gems in her ears.

"They are lovely." Kenneth gave her a courtly bow. "You are lovely. In fact, with or without war and battles and boys running away, the whole world is lovely because you are going to be my wife."

Kenneth stayed for supper. As soon as the last patron was gone that night the family gathered about the big table in the main tavern room. Polly, as usual, sat at the head and Cecilia, with Kenneth beside her, sat at the foot. Leah settled on a bench across from Timothy and Mama. Rollen and Travis, finishing up their chores, took their seats, too.

"All the way to Rockfish Creek we marched," Timothy bragged. "Cousin Jamie didn't know Donny and I were with them until well into the second day. He said he couldn't send me back then by myself. So I stayed."

As he got into his story Timmie jumped up to pace about the room. "We got word that Scotsmen from Cross Creek were already on the road, marching for Wilmington. They thought they were going to meet British troops coming up the river. When we got word they were on the march we turned back east. We met up with Caswell and Lillington's men from New Bern at Moores Creek. The battle was over when we got there."

Timothy stopped his frantic pacing and slumped in his chair. "There were dead men on the field. There were dead men in the creek. We only lost one man in the fight. The dead were all Scotsmen."

Timothy began to pace again. "Some of our men started to dig graves. Some cleaned their muskets. Some of them started their cooking fires. I never before saw a grown man cry."

Henrietta reached out and caught at his hand, but Timothy pulled away.

"Cousin Jamie started routing after the Scots to take prisoners. Donny and I were sent out as scouts 'cause we could crawl through the brush and get reports back to camp. We worked relays, watching and running the messages. Cousin Jamie said we did a good job of it. Then he said it was safe for us to travel back to Wilmington."

"Oh, lawdy," Mama and Leah chorused.

"I'm going to scout for the militia, Mama. You can't stop me."

Henrietta began to cry. Polly looked as if the breath had been knocked out of her. Leah chanted, "Lawdy, lawdy, lawdy."

"You had to know where I was. I didn't hide how I felt about fighting for the cause. Right, Polly? Mama? You knew I had to fight. I've been marching. I've been cleaning my musket. I've been getting ready to go since the call for men first went out."

Kenneth whispered in Cecilia's ear. "I'm glad your brother's home. I have to go now. Good night, my dear."

Cecilia watched him leave. She didn't know which hurt more: Kenneth walking out of their family meeting or Timothy's announcement of scouting for the troops. She felt her heart would tear apart with the battles of questions that raged inside her. She longed for her wedding day, now so very close. When they were married Kenneth would talk to her and answer all her questions.

She pushed her fear deep. For now, she had to plan her wedding. And, at least for now, Timmie was safe home.

CHAPTER 7

"It's my wedding day! My wedding day!" Cecilia chanted. She twirled about her bed-chamber, spreading her blue petticoats in a great fan. She peered in her mirror to settle her new mobcap on her head. When a horse whinny from the stable yard drifted up to her, she raced to the window and caught a glimpse of Kenneth leading his stallion into the barn.

"He's here," Cecilia whispered. She tucked a stray wisp of brown hair under her embroidered mobcap and tiptoed for the stairs. At the bottom of the steps she peeked into the huge tavern room. Polly lifted pies from the brick oven with a long-handled wooden shovel. The aroma of apple and cinnamon spilled out across the room. The spicy fragrance of herbs and peppers wrapped the air about the suckling pig and haunches of mutton roasting on the hearth. Leah turned the spit, her hands wrapped in thick rags to ward off the heat. Carrots and potatoes simmered in the juices from the meat, dripping in the pans set in the hot coals.

Cecilia waited until she knew Polly and Leah were both too busy to look up before she scurried across to the door and let herself out into the yard. A brisk March wind from the Cape Fear River flirted with her petticoats and tugged at her cap. "Kenneth?" she called.

Brushing the front of his coat, he came out of Big Boy's stall and barred the opening before he turned to her.

The sight of him - his curly black hair that always escaped the queue he tried to keep tied so neatly, his eyes so blue-green they sometimes looked violet, his trim waist that held his shirt firmly in his breeches - almost took her breath away. "You're early!"

He held out his arms and she snuggled for a moment against his chest.

When she pulled away, Kenneth took both her hands in his. "You are so lovely with your dimpled cheeks all rosy and your blue eyes twinkling like stars."

Cecilia felt the blush that crept across her face and neck. No one but Kenneth had ever told her she was lovely.

"Cecilia?" Polly stood at the barn door. "I thought you were in your room and here you are with Kenneth."

"Good morning, Polly," Kenneth said. "It's all my fault. I wanted to give Cecilia her birthday present before the wedding. It *is* an important date, turning sixteen."

Kenneth reached in his saddle bag, hanging from a post next to Big Boy's stall, and took out a small cloth-wrapped package which he placed in Cecilia's palm. "This belonged to my grandmother, who gave it to my mother on her sixteenth birthday. Mother gave it to me before she died. Will you wear it today for me?"

Cecilia unwrapped the cloth and held up a slim gold chain from which dangled three small pearls. "Kenneth, this is beautiful." She clutched the necklace to her bodice. "Of course I'll wear it. We can pretend your mother knows."

"I think my mother knows about today," Kenneth said. He took the necklace from Cecilia, turned her around to reach the back of her neck, and fastened the clasp in place.

"Such a lovely birthday gift," Polly said. "Kenneth, will your father be here today?"

"No."

Kenneth was always so abrupt when his father was mentioned. Sometimes it frightened her. "I'm sorry," Cecilia said. "Is he so sick, then?"

"My father does have his problems, Cecilia. Now let's go inside. I think I can smell yeast bread even from here and I've had no breakfast. I want to see how you've decked out that big tavern room for our wedding."

Notes drifted out to them from the violins tuning up in the tavern. "They're too early," Polly said. "I'd best go see about this."

"Let's try a dance with the music," Kenneth said. He caught Cecilia's hand to lead her in fancy steps across the yard as they followed Polly inside.

By noon Three Sisters Tavern was filled with well-wishers. Cousin Margaret sat with Mama, both of them knitting away as they talked. Mary Harnett helped with the cooking, and Cecilia saw her sift a sprinkle of some herb into the stew when Leah's back was turned. Mistress Harnett did love adding herbs and spices. Cecilia laughed at the chicanery.

The Ashe family moved about the room, greeting other guests. Mister Swann and his wife had driven in from Rocky Point and were discussing the horrible condition of the Post Road. Mister Dry told a joke, which led one man to slap his knee and another half a dozen men to burst into chuckles. When she saw her Cousin Maurice come in the door, Cecilia ran to greet him.

"Little Miss Cecilia, all appareled in colors of blue," Cousin Maurice exclaimed. "How nice you look."

"How good to have you here. Who is your guest?" she asked, indicating the young man at his side.

"My son Alfred. He's just returned from Boston, where he's been for the last several years, so I understand why you didn't recognize him," Cousin Maurice answered.

"I should have, he looks so like you," Cecilia said. "Welcome to our home, Alfred. Welcome back to North Carolina. You will have to tell us all the news of Boston. The British quartered there. The Battle of Breeds Hill."

Before Alfred could answer her, men were gathering at his side. "Are conditions as bad as the newspapers indicate?" asked one. "The battles will surely come to the Cape Fear, with our shipping and our supplies of naval stores," said another. Cecilia left them to their war stories.

Polly was rearranging flowers she'd used to decorate the long table in the middle of the room. "Cousin Maurice is ready for the ceremony," she said to Cecilia.

Kenneth and Cecilia stood in the center of the large tavern room, Mama and Polly by her side. A frowning Timothy Charles stood with Kenneth.

All the guests turned toward them as Cousin Maurice opened his prayer book and began to read. " 'Whither thou goest I will go . . . and where thou lodgest I will lodge . . .' . . .Kenneth, son of Theodore and Emma Black, do you take Cecilia for your wife?"

"Yes, I do." His voice was clear and sure.

Cousin Maurice smiled at her before he said, "Cecilia, daughter of Phillip and Henrietta Moore, do you take Kenneth for your husband?"

"Oh yes, I do," she whispered.

Kenneth slipped a thin ring of silver on her finger and lifted her hands to his lips. She was tingling from the soft kiss as Cousin Maurice concluded the service. "I pronounce you husband and wife. May you live in peace."

The violins Polly had hired began to play *In Dulci Jubilo*. Mary Harnett softly sang with the voices of the strings. "Now sing with hearts aglow!"

Then the violins swung into a lively tune. Everyone was talking at once and reaching for plates to serve themselves from the table. Several couples formed a dance circle. With his arm about her waist, Kenneth drew Cecilia into the group.

At sundown Polly went about the room lighting candles. Cousin Maurice motioned Cecilia and Kenneth to join him at a table in a corner of the room. "We haven't signed the contract. Kenneth, if you'll put your name here. Cecilia, write your name beside his."

Mama sat with them as the quill scratched across the paper. Cousin Maurice scrolled the date - March 6, 1776 - and his signature at the bottom of the page. By his name he dripped wax from a candle and pressed his ring into the warm tallow for the seal.

"Kenneth, it is a shame your father couldn't be here today," he said, waiting for the wax to cool. "I know he's unwell, but still, I think he would have enjoyed himself."

"Judge, you haven't seen my father in some time. You have no idea what he would or would not enjoy."

"True," Cousin Maurice answered. "It is my fault entirely. Politics and business have taken precedence too often lately. The priority of friendship has been much neglected."

He took Cecilia's hand as he continued. "Know that you are welcome at my home at any time. Although it's set well back from the road, Theodore Black's farm near Rocky Point is only a mile south of mine. If old Theodore and Kenneth don't have time or inclination to visit, you can ride that distance in short order."

"Thank you. You have always been so kind to us. Kenneth and I will be staying in Wilmington for a few days before we go out to the farm," Cecilia said.

"That will be nice for you." He stood and settled his hat on his head. "Now to war. The British seem determined to demand our attention. It's not as if we haven't been trying to demand theirs for the last several years. Dumping tea. Letters of protest. Petitions to address wrongs."

As Cecilia watched him stride out of the tavern, Kenneth whispered, "He seems to be constantly prying into my business. Knurly old man."

"Kenneth! Cousin Maurice is my kinsman. He has been my guardian since I was a little girl and my papa left us. My business *is* his business."

"Well, I am now your husband. Your business is mine." He thumped the contract. "I have the signed paper to prove it. I have the dowry money. I have you."

Ricky Smith limped up to them to offer best wishes. "Still play a winning game of marbles, Cee?" Ricky asked. He put his hand on Kenneth's shoulder. "She's one mean shooter, Kenneth. Used to knock all my best marbles out of the circle."

"Ricky," Cecilia said, "do you have any idea what your brother and my brother are hatching up? One of them getting notions about running away with the troops is bad enough. The two of them together can concoct major plots."

"Cecilia, your little brother is always in trouble," Kenneth said.

"Kenneth," Cecilia exploded, "you're acting like an im -"

Ricky interrupted. "Cecilia, be happy." The staggering gait of his short leg took him toward a laughing group of men.

Kenneth slipped his arm about her waist. "What is it I'm acting like, dear wife?"

"An imbecile," she blurted. She moved so she could hold both his hands in her own. "Kenneth, what is wrong?"

"I *am* acting badly." He kissed her on the forehead.

Cecilia leaned into her husband's chest and fingered a button on his coat.

He pointed his toe, the better to show off his new leather shoes. "I do like the buckles you gave me." Then he pulled her into a dance circle.

It was full dark when the guests began to leave. "It's been a wonderful wedding party," Mistress Swann said.

"The Moore girls do know how to feed folk," said Mister Dry.

Polly beckoned Cecilia upstairs. "You and Kenneth will be leaving in a few minutes to walk up to Cousin Margaret's house. Before I start cleaning up I wanted to ask if there is anything you need."

"Polly, you're always working. Now that I'm married to Kenneth I shall direct the servants. My hands will be smooth and my nails trimmed. My apron will be spotless." Cecilia turned in a dance step. "On my feet will be my prettiest cloth slippers, worn just for my Kenneth. He will twirl me about and catch me in his arms to hold me safe."

"My dear little sister, you paint a pretty picture. But no work?" She patted Cecilia's arm. "I do have one bit of advice for you."

Cecilia made a face, but sat on the edge of the bed and folded her hands.

"Dare to think for yourself."

"That's your advice?"

"Cecilia, do be happy." Polly crushed her in a hug and then pushed her away. "I'm being so silly. You will be at Margaret Hill's house tonight and back here in the morning for breakfast." Polly opened the door. "Go be with your husband."

Cecilia ran down the steps to Kenneth.

CHAPTER 8

As March moved into April, Cecilia and Kenneth were still living at Three Sisters Tavern. Kenneth would not talk about going to the farm. "Father is looking after things," Kenneth said when she asked what they were going to do.

He left the tavern each morning without a word. Sometimes he came back to eat a late supper. Other times he'd slip into their bed late at night, take her in his arms, and be so tender she could only say how much she loved him.

When he wasn't there, she worried. One morning, as she lay cradled in his arms, Cecilia pushed for an answer. "Kenneth, we can't live in the tavern forever. If we're going to stay in Wilmington, we have to find a house."

Kenneth yawned. "We have a house at the farm."

"Are we going to live in it?"

He frowned at her and without a word, got up to dress.

"Kenneth, why won't you talk with me? Please answer my questions."

He walked out. She listened as he made his way down the steps and toward the stable. She heard him ride Big Boy out of the yard. He didn't come back for two days.

"He gambling, Miss Cecilia," Leah told her one morning as they were gathering eggs. "He be down at that tavern on Front Street. The Whale Tale they call it. Nothing but riffraff goes to that place."

"How do you know this, Leah?"

"The mens talk. They always talking. They don't never think a old black woman got ears to hear nor a understanding 'bout what they say." She shooed at a hen and reached to pick up an egg. "He racing that great horse of his. He do seem to be winning. That Big Boy be one powerful animal."

Leah inspected an egg before putting it in her basket. "I don't know why anybody gamble, Miss Cecilia. Any more than I knowed why your pa gambled away most everything *he* had. Judge Moore got Mister Phillip out of all that by getting him away from Brunswick. You was so little then. Mister Timothy ain't even been born. The Judge be the one what put Miss Polly in charge so you and your sisters could have a roof over your heads and something to eat."

Cecilia set her basket of eggs on the ground and looked around the big tavern yard. "I remember Papa leaving. I remember watching him ride down to the ferry behind Cousin Maurice. I did so love Papa. I wanted to run after him."

"Just like you wants to run after Mister Kenneth now. Loving somebody sure can be hurtful. Gambling be a sickness, Miss Cecilia. It don't matter if'n it be playing cards or if'n it be betting on a fight or if'n it be racing a horse. Gambling be a pure sickness." Leah sighed. "Lawdy, we best get these eggs in and stir up the stew."

"I hate to go in," Cecilia said. "The only thing the men talk about is war."

British movements, Governor Josiah Martin's activities, and the taking of Fort Johnston at the mouth of the Cape Fear River, were subjects discussed with morning coffee and afternoon ale. The old man in the chimney corner burned the fort again and again, bragging on his grandson who had been the one, according to him, to spread the fire.

Tales of battling the Scots at Moores Creek brought men to their feet, swinging imaginary swords, swirling imaginary kilts, falling from imaginary bridge poles into the gun fire of Lillington and Caswell's militia. News of the committees in Halifax, where several of their Wilmington neighbors were meeting, came every few days from riders. Timothy Charles and Donny were two of the riders who ferried parcels filled with information, food and other necessities into the back country and brought packets of mail and news of the committees to Wilmington.

Mistress Harnett came often to share letters from her husband, Cornelius, who served as president of the Provincial Council. She was reading to Polly and Mama when Leah and Cecilia came in with the eggs.

" 'The people here are all for independence. I know of no dissenting voice.' " Mary Harnett nodded at Cecilia and continued. "'My committee assignment was to take into consideration the usurpations and violences attempted by the King and Parliament of Great Britain against America. Our report has been adopted unanimously by our 83 delegates present here at Halifax. We resolved that the delegates for this colony in the Continental congress be empowered to concur with the delegates of the other Colonies in declaring Independence.' "

Cecilia interrupted. "Is this the same as declaring to fight?"

"I think we've already done that," Polly answered. "We are at war."

Mistress Harnett said, "There's more. Cornelius writes here that a copy has been sent to Hewes in the congress at Philadelphia. 'Dear wife, when I have a moment to do so I will make a separate copy of the whole of the resolve and send it to you.' "

"My baby is caught up in the middle of it," Henrietta said. "Timothy Charles is eleven years old and he's in the middle of everything. Why can't someone else ride to Halifax? Why can't someone else ferry messages to Brunswick Town?" She dropped her knitting on the seat of her rocking chair. Moving like an old woman, she crept up the stairs toward her bedchamber.

"Polly, I always bring you the news because I know how closely you've worked with Maurice and Cornelius and William Hooper and the other men. You've performed tasks for the Safety Committee. You've sent out letters. You know all their plans. But if it's going to put your mother in such a fix, I'll stop coming."

"Mama gets upset whether you bring us the news or not," Cecilia said. "Do please continue to give us the latest information."

"Yes," Polly said. "Cecilia and I both want to know. The letters from Mister Harnett are the most accurate intelligence we have. There are so many rumors going around."

Mistress Harnett snugged her husband's letter in her pocket and began to gather her bread baskets. "Tell Henrietta I'm sorry she's upset. Polly, I will let you know whatever I hear from Halifax."

As soon as she was gone, Cecilia asked, "Polly, how can I get Kenneth to talk with me? He won't give me any answers about what he plans to do."

"Cee, I'm not the one to ask. I've never been married."

"But Polly, you talk with Cousin Maurice. You talk with the tradesmen who come to the door and you talk with the merchants at the stores. You talk with the ships' captains when they come into port. How do you get information from them?"

Polly gazed out of the window. "If a man is selling apples, I ask where he's from and get him to talking about growing apples." She leaned her head into the glass. "I ask a captain how his voyage was before I ask what he's carrying in the hold of the ship. At the shops I compliment something before I start asking price. I remember at Brunswick one of the women asked me how I got along so well with the trades people. I think I said I listen."

She turned from the window. "Cee, what does Kenneth talk about?"

Cecilia blushed. "He doesn't talk very much."

Now, on this bright spring morning, as a light breeze blew in from the southwest, Cecilia smelled the delicious scent of honeysuckle that twined its way up the outside wall near the window. She stretched, still caught in the glory of a beautiful night with Kenneth. He was sleeping, one arm flung above his head, the other gripping a pillow to his chest.

A faint odor of smoke filled the air. Leah wasn't even in yet to rake up the embers on the hearth and start the morning bacon. Smoke?

She heard running footsteps and a shout from the street. She pulled on a wrapper and hurried down the stairs. In the tavern room Timothy was packing his saddlebags. He took his musket from the wall before he looked at her.

"You're riding?" Cecilia asked.

"The messenger said Governor Martin ordered Captain Collett to march on Brunswick Town. The docks are burning there now. I can smell the smoke."

Cecilia nodded. The acid odor of burning wood was stronger than when she'd first noticed it.

Timothy pushed a pair of stockings into his bag. "We've heard Collett's been doing lots of piracy and robbery all about the countryside. Others have to be warned."

Donny Smith spoke from the door. "Ready?"

Timothy slung the bags over his shoulder and started out after his friend.

"Be safe. Ride safe. Timmie, be safe," she whispered to his back.

He looked at her from the door. "Thanks, Cee. Keep saying that."

Back in her bedchamber she fumbled with the ties on her bodice. Her fingers didn't want to work as she cobbled together skirts and apron. Scratching on Henrietta's door, she didn't wait for an answer from her mother or Polly. She stopped beside the bed. "Polly?"

Her sister sat upright. "What? Cecilia, what's wrong?"

"The British. Collett's left his ships and his camps on the islands. He's on the march. There is burning at Brunswick. Timmie and Donny are already gone. I guess they were called to scout."

Henrietta had not opened her eyes, but she began to wail. "Not Timothy. He can't go. My baby cannot go to war."

"Mama, hush," Polly said. "I will not take hysterics at this moment." She swung her legs over the edge of the bed. Cecilia knew her sister was getting ready for action. "The salt is hidden. The cellar doors are as well concealed as I know how to make them. The garden produce isn't yet ready for harvest, so we might as well leave it for later. If troops march into Wilmington probably none of it matters anyway. They'll take what they want to eat. They'll destroy the rest."

"Timothy Charles," Henrietta said. "Polly, what do we do about Timothy Charles?"

"Mama, we don't do anything about Timmie. Cecilia, go fix your clothes and help Leah with breakfast."

As Cecilia started out the door, Polly called. "If your husband is here, you'd best wake him. Perhaps he could help us today."

Back in their room Cecilia sat on their bed and touched Kenneth's cheek. When he opened his eyes, she began to tell him of the morning's events.

"It's time we went to the farm, dear wife. I'd like to leave by noon."

CHAPTER 9

Kenneth checked the straps holding Cecilia's trunk on the buggy, made sure Big Boy was tied securely to the back of the carriage, then climbed on the seat to wait as Cecilia said her good-byes.

Polly put her hands on Cecilia's shoulders, speaking so softly she had to strain to hear the words. "Cecilia, if you need me, for any reason, send someone for me. I'll come. Kenneth has told us about the reliable foreman and all the workers on the farm. There will be constant traveling from Wilmington. After all, it's only a two hour ride. We'll send letters and messages. Remember the things we packed in your trunk. You have resources."

Cecilia kissed her sister on the cheek, gathered her cat in her arms, and climbed into the buggy. Kenneth drove slowly, stopping to check a harness on the mare that Cecilia knew did not need attention, pointing out a lane that led toward the sound where the fishing was the best in the county, commenting on a flock of crows circling a corn field near the Post Road. In fact, he kept up a steady chatter. She listened, trying to understand this man she so cared for.

The sun was setting behind the trees when Kenneth turned up the long lane that led from the road to his father's farm. As the house came into view, Cecilia couldn't believe what lay before her. A shutter hung haphazardly from one of the windows of the house and a section of broken porch railing lay against the ballast stone foundation of what once must have been an elegant two-story structure built over a half basement. In bewilderment she stared at leaves from last fall scattered across the expanse of yard and drive.

"Doesn't anybody care for this place?" she blurted.

"I've tried all day to tell you," Kenneth said.

"Tell me what?"

"How I've lied to you. Cecilia, I've lied about the house, about the farm, about the slaves. About everything." He stopped the carriage near the front porch.

The mare stood quietly in the traces, but Big Boy, tied to the back of the buggy, snorted and pawed at the ground.

"He wants to run," Kenneth said. "I know the feeling. I've been trying to run away for a long time." He sounded tired. Or scared.

Cecilia looked across the vast fields that stretched for acres toward a thick woods. It was May and nothing had been planted. No corn. No beans. No peanuts. Pine seedlings and tangled vines grew across old corn rows that had not seen a plow in several years. As fear flared in the pit of her stomach, she swallowed to keep from throwing up.

Kenneth slapped the reins and the horse moved toward the rear of the house. The large barn loomed in front of them and he jumped down to lead the mare inside. Cecilia stepped down from the buggy and smoothed her skirts. She would have expected a slave to come running to unhitch the horse. No one came. Kenneth untied Big Boy to lead him to a stall, backed the carriage into an empty space and unhitched the mare.

She finally found her voice. "Kenneth, what can I do to help?"

"Feed the mare," he said. "I'm going to the creek for water."

She hugged her cat and set her on the barn floor. "Go be useful, Daisy." She watched the animal scamper away to explore before she scooped out a measure of oats in a bucket and carried it into the mare's stall. As she set the bucket down, Kenneth came back with the water, put the pail beside the oats and motioned her out so he could bar the stall opening. He stood for a moment with his hand on Big Boy's shoulder.

"We'll get your trunk later. Let's go meet my father," he said.

She took a deep breath so her voice wouldn't shake when she spoke. "Yes, Kenneth. I have been waiting to meet your father."

"Wait no longer, then. He's watching us."

Cecilia looked toward a man sitting on the spacious back porch. As she put her foot on the bottom step he raised his hand to his brow in a half salute.

"Cecilia, meet my father, Theodore Black," Kenneth said. "He's a drunk. He's a reprobate. You should be most wary of him."

"Come in. Yes, come in, my dear. 'Oh, how many torments lie in the small circle of a wedding ring!'" Mister Black did not rise from his rocking chair.

"My father loves to show off his learning by quoting obscure authors. He'll entangle passages from Shakespeare and the Bible, to see if you know the difference. As I said, be wary."

Cecilia gathered her courage. "I have been looking forward to meeting you, sir. I'm sorry you could not be at the wedding, but Kenneth explained that you have been ill. I do hope you are better."

Mister Black snorted. "More likely he said I was in my cups. Which I am, my dear. In my cups is where I spend most of my time." He waved a hand of dismissal. "My condition should not trouble you."

Kenneth led the way through the back door into a wide hallway. Cecilia could see the large dining room on one side of the hall and she went to the door. The neglect was as evident here as in the yard and fields. The room did not appear to have been cleaned in years. Dust motes wafted in the last rays of sunlight as she walked through the dining room and crossed the hall to the parlour. She sneezed and wiped her watering eyes with the back of her hand. She backed up to find Kenneth standing where she had left him in the hall.

"Seen enough?" he asked.

"Kenneth, why?" Anger begin to burn her insides and she pressed her fists into her stomach to smother the pain. "Why did you lie to me about all this?"

"I need you. Oh, dear Cecilia, you cannot know how much I need you. Want you. Long to have you here." He took her hand. "Come now, let me show you upstairs. We can talk about all of this tomorrow."

What did I long for? Cecilia thought, as she followed him. I wanted to get away from the tavern - that tavern always filled with men smoking their pipes and talking politics. I wanted to live in a grand house and be mistress of everything - the kitchen and the dining room and the parlour. I wanted to be on my very own, instead of always following behind my big sister. I wanted a man to love me. Does Kenneth *love* me? Would he have brought me into such a place if he loved me?

In the bedchamber, Kenneth gave her no time to ask questions as he held her close and began to kiss her forehead, her nose, her lips. Cecilia's last thought about the house, before Kenneth's determined passion overtook her, was how badly the bed sheets needed to be washed.

 **CHAPTER 10**

A rooster's crow brought Cecilia upright in an empty bed. She heard no other sounds from the house or yard. She groped about in the coverings for her shift and pulled it over her head. The door to Mister Black's room stood half open. His room was empty.

She called, "Kenneth? Mister Black? Is anyone here?"

Silence answered her.

Going down the steps she peered into both the large rooms on either side of the wide hallway. The quickening light revealed spider webs and dirt she had not seen earlier. The footprints of her felt slippers showed where she stepped yesterday through the rooms. There was no sign that anyone else had been there.

Pushing open the back door she went across the porch to the kitchen, built a few yards away from the house. She had thought the house dirty, but she knew a good cleaning could make it shine again. Here, in the kitchen, there was filth. As she moved across to the cold hearth, soot sprinkled down on the unwashed pots and pans scattered haphazardly in thick ashes. The table in the center of the room was littered with remnants of old meals, dirty plates and broken crockery. Empty wine and ale bottles lay on every surface.

Cecilia's stomach heaved. She ran into the yard, where she threw up bile. She sank down on the steps, too weary to wipe the mess from her shift.

"Oh, Kenneth, what have you brought me into?" she sobbed. "Where are the servants? Why has this house become a horror? Why does no one here *care*?"

Her need for water became paramount. She struggled from the porch steps and walked toward the path that Kenneth had taken to the creek.

An old black man, dressed in rags, stood near the barn. Then he simply vanished. When Cecilia ran to catch up with him, he just wasn't there. The buggy was parked where it had been left the night before. The stallion snorted from his stall. The little mare shook her head. Cecilia's trunk lay open, its contents spilled every which way across the barn floor. She picked up a shawl. Hugging it about her shoulders for comfort, she walked down to the creek. Cupping her hands to hold the water, she rinsed her mouth, then drank, hoping to still her empty stomach.

She walked back to the yard. Down a short lane from the barn, a thin spiral of smoke rose from a cabin chimney. She headed toward the log building, calling out, "Hello? Hello? Who is here? Answer me, please."

The man she'd seen at the barn opened the cabin door. There were others behind him in the room.

"Good morning." Cecilia took a deep breath, stepped up on the sagging porch and moved into the cabin.

The old man leaned against the wall as if all strength had left him. The two other men in the room came to attention, their hands behind their backs. Cecilia thought she hadn't seen such military precision even on the parade grounds when Cousin Jamie Moore was training his troops. A woman sat on a narrow board fastened to a wall opposite the hearth. She held a child in her lap.

"Good morning," Cecilia repeated. "I'm Kenneth Black's wife."

The woman gave a gasp before she clamped her hand over her mouth.

Cecilia pretended not to have heard the woman, but looked directly at her. "Call me Miss Cecilia, please. And what is your name?"

"Lula, ma'am."

"Is this your son?" she asked.

"Yes, ma'am."

"What is his name, please?"

"He be Little Mart, ma'am."

Cecilia looked at the boy. "Little Mart. That's a nice name. How old are you?"

The child peered up at his mother. "Answer the lady."

"Eight."

There were no chairs or benches in the room. Cecilia sat down on the floor in front of Lula and the child. "Eight years old. Little Mart, I have a little brother. He's a bit bigger than you, but I bet you're just as smart as he. Why, he just rode off on his horse to do some scouting for the army."

"He did? He really rode a horse?" the boy asked.

"Yes, he did." She turned to see the old man still leaning against the wall. "You are called by what name?"

He tried to stand erect. The effort was painful to watch. "Martin, ma'am."

"Is Little Mart your grandchild then?"

It was Lula who answered. "Old Martin be my uncle, ma'am."

"Lula, please call me Miss Cecilia."

"Yes, ma'am, Miss Cecilia."

She nodded to the older of the two men who still stood at military attention. "Your name?"

"Benjamin, ma'am. He be Simple. If you 'scuse him, he don't talk much."

Cecilia repeated the names before she turned again to Lula. "And the others?"

"Others, ma'am?"

"The foreman. The hands who work the fields. The house servants. Others."

"Ain't no others, Miss Cecilia. We it. 'Cept for Mister Black and Mister Kenneth, we the onliest ones on the place. Ain't been a foreman here in two, maybe three year. He didn't do no work even when he was here. Ever body what was here done been sold off some place else."

A buzzing started in her brain as she tried to sort this bit of information. Her stomach reminded her that she hadn't eaten since noon the day before. "Lula, is there any food?"

"Not much, ma'am."

Incomprehension mixed with the bile that churned in her stomach. First she needed food. Then she needed clothes. Then she would decide what to do next. She fixed her gaze on rabbit traps hanging on the wall next to a large sling shot. Someone had been bringing in small game.

"Lula, do you have a spring garden?"

"No, Miss Cecilia, ma'am. Ain't got no seeds to plant."

Cecilia squared her shoulders. "When I went down for water I saw a catfish gliding through the waters in the creek. I bet there are shad and bass there, too, swimming around in the eddies in that clear fresh water. Is there a fish hook anywhere on this place?"

"Yes, Miss Cecilia." It was Old Martin who answered. "We be fishing when we get a chance."

"Martin, go fishing. It sure would be nice if you caught enough for us all to have a noon meal." She stood as she spoke. "Can you do that, Martin? Can you catch us a good mess of fish?"

His toothless grin was her answer.

She had given an order. Well, that was what she'd expected to do. She just hadn't thought she'd be telling an old man to go fishing. She adjusted her shawl and looked at the other men.

"Benjamin, I want you and Simple to clean out the kitchen chimney. It obviously hasn't been used in some time and the last thing I need right now is a chimney fire. Lula, I want you and your boy to help me scrub. I cannot and will not live in filth."

"Miss Cecilia. Oh, please, ma'am." Lula's hands were shaking. "Mister Black ain't gonna like us up to the house. I be cooking his meals on my hearth for a long time now. Just takes the food up to him when he call for something to eat."

"Mister Black is not at home, Lula. I will deal with him when he gets back. We are going to clean that house. Now, all of you." She swept her arms in a wide arch. "All of you come me with me to the kitchen and let's get to work."

They followed her.

Benjamin and Simple found poles to ream the chimney. While they were at that task, she and Lula opened up the trap door in the kitchen floor and Cecilia went down with a torch to explore the cellar. A barrel of rotten potatoes caused her to gag, but she sorted through them as she fought back the vomit.

"There might be pieces we can plant," she said, handing a basket of the decaying mess to Lula. "It's not too late to try to have a fall garden. Take this out in the yard and come back with the men to lift this barrel out of here. It's still fit to use if we clean it."

Other foods stored in the underground room were too far gone to salvage. Benjamin and Simple carried load after load of debris up the ladder and into the yard. In a far corner of the cellar she discovered a keg of salt, which she told the men to take to the barn. Most precious were the metal boxes of lye soap and candles sitting on the floor under shelves which had long ago fallen from the pegs on which they had rested.

By noon, with all of them working, they had cleared out the cellar. Cecilia sent the boy to gather grape leaves from the edge of the woods. She wrapped the catfish, that Martin caught and gutted, in the foliage and covered it with coals from the fire she started on the hearth. She served each of them on bark that Simple stripped from a sweet gum tree. They sat together under a leafing maple in the yard and ate.

"Oh, that was good," Cecilia said. "Martin, I'm glad to know we have a fisherman here. Now do any of you know where there is any other food? Is there a smokehouse? A corn crib that might have corn still stored? You said there was no garden but what about herbs or mushrooms growing in the woods? Didn't I see rabbit traps in your cabin, Lula? There are lots of rabbits. I saw a large sling. Does someone hunt with a sling?"

Simple raised his hand.

"If you know how to set a trap or hurl a sling, Simple, please do. I think rabbit cooked on a spit would be most tasty."

He nodded, his hands already working at an imaginary contraption.

Benjamin showed her the empty smokehouse. "Ma'am, we ate the last of the pork some time back. We ain't had a hog on the place for a spell."

"No one went hunting?" Cecilia asked.

"No, ma'am. Don't know that Mister Black ever hunted. Though he did love to ride his horse." Benjamin creaked open the door to the corn crib. The movement sent mice scurrying. "Mister Kenneth never went hunting, neither."

She looked at the few ears of corn lying on the floor of the log crib. "Oh, I'm glad I have my cat. She's a good mouser."

"Cats is nice, ma'am."

"This morning I heard a rooster. Where are the chickens?"

"Chickens wondering 'bout in the woods, ma'am. They pretty wild."

"Build me a chicken pen, Benjamin. And a small house where the hens can roost. Put it in the lot behind the barn. Then we'll see if we can catch some of these wild fowl. That's a job to start on in the morning. This afternoon we're going to finish cleaning up that awful kitchen."

When she deemed the kitchen clean enough, the men brought her trunk from the barn. As she shook out the skirts and shifts, she knew she wouldn't be able to wear most of the clothes until they had been washed. Almost every piece of clothing had been dragged through stalls in the barn. Several of the hems were ripped loose.

Had Kenneth done this? Mister Black? Why? What were they looking for? Fear crept through her arms as she scrubbed her clothes and hung them on myrtle bushes to dry. Apprehension for tomorrow's unknown tasks bore into her stomach. She fought down the forebodings and went on with the tasks of cleaning.

Long shadows hung across the yard when Cecilia finally sat in a rocking chair on the porch. She straightened her back and stretched. "We've done a good day's work."

"Miss Cecilia, yous a working woman," Lula said. "I thought I could go at it, but you 'bout beat me out today."

Martin handed her a piece of fish on a bark plate. "I tried to fix it like you done, ma'am. All wrapped in them grape leaves. It don't taste the same, but it'll stop your stomach from growling."

Cecilia ate the fish standing alone in the middle of the yard. From his stall in the barn the stallion snorted. Where was Kenneth? Where was Mister Black? Had they meant to leave her here to go hungry? There were too many questions. There were no answers. Nothing was at all like she'd dreamed. She knew that it wasn't the way Polly would have done things. But she *had* taken charge. When Kenneth got back he would see that she could be a good helpmate to him.

She walked to the creek, filled the water buckets and came back to hang a kettle over the fire. She bathed, using the strong lye soap she'd found, before she slipped a torn but clean shift over her head.

At last light, Cecilia laid her head on her arms on the clean kitchen table and slept.

CHAPTER 11

Cecilia stretched awake. The rooster was again pleading with the sun, the clarion call closer to the house than when she'd heard it just yesterday. She longed to hear the bleating of goats in the barn. She longed for the sounds of Leah frying bacon at the tavern hearth and Polly calling to the indentured boys. Her dreams of being with Kenneth had never included sleeping in an empty kitchen, her stomach knotting with hunger.

She picked up a knife she'd found while she was cleaning. She dropped it in a basket, carrying it with her as she made her way to the creek. Yesterday she had found the necessary house to be falling down, the floor rotting. She cared for her personal needs by the edge of the path, then washed her face and drank her fill. Sitting on the decaying platform-like dock at the water's edge, she tried to think of what had to be done today. Food was still first. Maybe Simple really could trap rabbits in those contraptions she'd seen in the cabin.

Once, Timothy had caught a skunk in his rabbit trap. Cecilia giggled to herself as she remembered how long it took to clean away the horrible odor. Her happy laugh turned suddenly to a sob. She angrily scooped water from the creek and splashed it on her face.

She looked up at the sound of whirring wings and peered across the water. A pair of parakeets perched on a branch of a willow and cocked their bright yellow heads in her directions. "Good morning, pretty birds. I haven't seen parakeets since we moved from Brunswick," she told the pair. The birds flew into the deeper woods, their green-colored wings hiding them in the dense foliage.

Scouting near the creek she found dandelions. She gathered the leaves. Nearby were wild strawberries, which she plucked and spilled into her basket. The squirrels had left a few nuts under an old hickory tree. She added them to the trove.

She left the basket in the kitchen while she cared for the horses. She hobbled the mare and stallion in a stand of sweet grass near the barn. For a long moment she rested her head against the neck of the large black creature, thinking of the times Kenneth had ridden up to her, smiled down at her, held out his arms to her from the back of the horse.

She patted his neck. "You eat now. And behave. I don't want to go chasing you around the countryside."

Big Boy shook his head at her.

"You are most welcome," she answered him. "Now I have work to do."

She mucked one of the old stalls, piling the manure in a wheelbarrow. Gathering up hoes, she pushed her load to a patch of ground she'd spied behind the cabins. As she began to lay out rows in an old garden patch, she realized that Martin and Simple were working with her.

With the last of the rotting potatoes hilled in, she sent the two men to rake out the corn crib and bring every grain they could gather. It was late to plant corn. She had to try. At some point in the morning, Lula lead her to the shade of a tree and handed her a bowl.

"Fish?" She took a bite of the mixture. "But Lula, it's not catfish."

"No, ma'am. My boy done catch us some shad."

"You cooked it with the dandelion greens," Cecilia said. "Oh, Lula, this is good. I've never tried fish like this before."

Lula sat beside her. "What you want next, Miss Cecilia?"

She looked at the garden plot. "This is all we can do here. We'll start cleaning in the main house. The dining room first, I think. I do want everything nice for Kenneth when he gets home."

"Miss Cecilia, what you gonna do if Mister Black come back? That man do not like folks messing 'round in his house."

"I would like very much to see Mister Black." Cecilia handed the bowl to Lula and stood. "Yes, I would like very much to see Mister Black. I would like to ask him some very hard questions."

"Miss Cecilia, ma'am, he a hard man. He ain't gonna stand for no hard questions."

"Well, we'll just have to see about that."

On her way to the house she stopped to watch Benjamin's work on the chicken house and fence. She nodded approval at the way he'd constructed the board fence.

"Where did the boards come from, Benjamin?"

"Tore 'em outa that falling down cabin yonder. Can't nobody live in that place, it be so 'lapidated."

"Dilapidated. Benjamin, that pretty well describes everything about this place. How *did* it get so run down?"

Benjamin shrugged and picked up his hammer.

While Lula and Little Mart cleaned in the dining room, Cecilia invaded the attic. A dormer window gave enough light for her to see the same disorder she'd found everywhere else. She opened a trunk to find it packed with women's clothing. She shook out a black skirt and held it up to her waist. The material draped below her feet.

She left the trunk to open a box filled with books. Beside this box were other books and stacks of papers. Pegs set into the rafters held men's coats and cloaks. A trunk near the window held table coverings, napkins and towels.

Making a stack from this last find, she carried an armful down to the upstairs hallway. Back in the attic she took out clothes she thought she could wear and added them to the stash on the hall table. In the very bottom of the trunk she found cloth slippers and a pair of leather shoes.

She closed the attic door to stand in the hall, surveying her find. The woman who had worn the skirts and bodices was taller than she. The stitching was more elegant than Mama's work, and Mama was a grand seamstress. Embroidery on a set of pockets matched the design on an apron. The napkins were hemmed with such tiny stitches that they were almost invisible. Whoever had done this sewing was a master craftsman.

Mister Black had never remarried when his wife died. These things had to have belonged to Kenneth's mother. Cecilia held a shift up to her chest. She could tie pockets about her waist and blouse up the material to make it short enough. She could do the same with the skirts. With no needle or thread, she would have to make it work.

When it was almost dark she went down to the creek for water. At what she'd come to think of as a family cabin they ate frog legs and dandelion greens and wild strawberries.

"Had me a good time with them frogs," the old man said. "First time I be sticking a frog in the longest time. But I still knows how. Ma'am, I still knows how."

"You and Lula cooked them up just fine, too," Cecilia said.

"Thank you, ma'am. I was hungry." He leaned back against the wall. "Miss Cecilia, it be funny what hungry can make a fellow do."

Cecilia nodded in agreement as she thought back on what she'd done in the last two days. She walked back to the house, wondering what funny thing she might still have to do.

One of the men had cleaned off the outside of her trunk and brought it up to the bed chamber. She opened the lid and slid her fingers around the edges of the fabric lining. The stitches had not been disturbed. Pulling on the strings she and Polly had devised, the false bottom popped up. The small canvas sacks of coins were there, just as they had packed them.

Her birthday necklace had scraped against her neck all day. She couldn't wear it while she was working. She undid the clasp. She took off the diamonds that suddenly felt like a heavy burden hanging from her ears. For a long moment she held the jewelry in her hand, thinking of Kenneth's promises when he gave her these gifts. Was everything he'd ever told her a lie? Had the necklace with the dangling pearls really been his mother's? Had his mother worn the diamonds? Leah had talked about his gambling. Or had he won these lovely trinkets in a card game and lied about that too?

No, she would not, could not dwell on such thoughts. Kenneth loved her. She knew he did. He would explain everything when he got back from wherever he had gone.

Cecilia put the jewelry in the trunk and closed the lid. She looked at the rumpled bed clothing. She could not sleep where she had lain in this house that one night with Kenneth. Turning to the pile of linens she'd brought from the attic, she picked up a pillow and table cloth, then made her way to the barn. As she climbed the ladder to the loft the sweet smell of hay comforted her.

"Why? Oh, why?" she whispered to a dove who had made its nest in a rafter. The bird tucked its head under its wing.

CHAPTER 12

Ragged visions of cellars filled with rotting potatoes and attics filled with the clothes of a dead woman roiled through her sleep. The hooting of an owl roused her. Leah believed that an owl calling near a house meant death. When she heard the bird again it seemed far away. Cecilia stared out through a crack in the boards to see a few stars glittering in the darkness. She let her head fall back on the hay pillow.

The next time she woke, early light hazed through a wispy fog. For a moment she didn't know where she was. The rumbling of her empty stomach reminded her of the strange circumstances. She was at the Black farm and her husband was missing. He had said nothing of leaving. Certainly nothing of leaving her. He had lied about so much that she did not know how to think of the things he *had* told her. "A big working farm," he had said of the Black place. "Good servants," he'd said of the help she would have in keeping the house. He had called his father, Theodore Black, a drunk. The old man seemed more crazy than anything else she'd experienced from the men who came and went and drank at the tavern.

Big Boy was restless in his stall below her in the barn and she knew he needed to be fed. Her stomach growled at her. She had to find food for herself and those who now depended on her.

As Cecilia shook out the cloth she'd used for a sheet, the dove flew out of the barn door. She led the stallion and mare to a small pasture area and tethered them securely. At the creek she drank, easing for the time being the emptiness in her stomach. She went to the house, got the shoes she'd found and buckled them. Then, with her basket over her arm, she set out across the fields toward the woods. She knew there was food. She just had to find it.

The path she took led by the side of an old corn field where pines and scrub oaks invaded once productive crop acreage. Wax myrtle bushes grew thick under spreading gum trees. "Wax berries for making candles. Gum twigs for tooth brushes," she told a passing egret. The bird did not answer her.

Ahead was a grove of hickory trees. Squirrels might have left nuts from the autumn. Mushrooms might be growing there in the damp soil. She picked a honeysuckle blossom, dripping the sweet nectar on her tongue. This summer there might be a bee tree close by, she thought. There were certainly enough blooming vines and scrubs growing here for bees to collect pollen for honey making. She would remember to look for a honey tree.

She chopped at the thicket of honeysuckle vines growing up the nearest hickory tree, trying to clear her way into the grove. A loosened brier branch raked across her face. She turned as she slashed at it. Her foot caught on what she thought was a root and she bent down to see if mushrooms might be growing there.

A shoe? She pulled on the vines for a clearer view. A shoe attached to a foot? Again she pulled. The foot was attached to a leg, attached to a body, attached to a face that was . . .

A stillness washed over her. She stood for a long moment, looking at her discovery. Those silver buckles on the britches - britches covering legs that stretched out on the ground in front of her - were the ones she'd given Kenneth the week before their wedding. He had fastened the buckles at his knees and told her how proud he was of the fine workmanship. The day they were married she had admired his new shoes and teased him about those elaborate fasteners shaped like the letter B, even as he had teased her about the flowers on her mobcap and the new shawl draped about her shoulders.

She put her fingers to her mouth as if she would feel his kisses. She closed her eyes and remembered how he dismounted his great black stallion, how he smiled when he was happy, how he held her.

She wrapped her arms about herself, whispering, "Shhh. Shhh."

A squirrel, as if in answer, began to chatter somewhere above her. A mockingbird trilled, over and over, a three note tune. A soft breeze fluttered the leaves above her head. She looked up and up into the hickory tree, up above where loose fluffs of white lazed in the spring sky. A quail, scurrying through the underbrush, brought her gaze back to earth.

The body was there. She had not imagined it.

Now she saw the thick hickory limb that lay next to the still figure. She saw how the ground was scuffed, vines ripped from tree trunks, leaves scattered about, as if men had wrestled in some dog fight over a bone that wasn't there.

Her legs began to shake and she leaned against a dogwood to steady herself. Icy fear invaded her. Was there someone there, watching? Someone who was strong enough to slam that heavy limb into a man's head and leave him dying under a tree?

With the hem of her apron she wiped away the cold sweat that dripped from her forehead to blur her vision. She held the cloth to her checks as she forced herself to survey the woods. Just beyond her she could see that an opening had been hacked through vines and brambles from farther down the path leading to where she now stood. Someone else had been here. Someone else had seen this sight. Someone had caused it.

"Why? Why? Why?" she screamed.

The eery silence that followed the outburst alarmed her until she realized her own screams had caused the quiet throughout the surrounding woods. Timid animals freeze. She knew that. She was not timid.

Her fear turned into an anger that boiled up in her stomach, burning at her insides. The power of her rage shook her legs, shook her arms, shook her chest, till she felt as if her heart would thud through the fabric of her bodice. She welcomed the anger. If she were furious enough she wouldn't have to be afraid.

She untied her apron and wrapped it securely around a dogwood sapling poking its way through the vines and bushes. A slight breeze flipped the white cloth and she stepped back from the horrible revelation she had marked. She gathered her fear and anger into her chest, as if she would make the feelings into a tangible, containable bundle. *Now* she could think about what she had to do.

Sliding down the side of the tree she hunched, her chin on her knees. Only when a rabbit ran up to sit near her leg did she move. She needed help. She needed guidance. There was only one place she knew she could find both.

Cecilia pulled herself up and began to walk.

CHAPTER 13

Several men were sitting on Judge Moore's front verandah when Cecilia came up in the yard. One by one they stopped their conversation and turned to look at her.

"Cecilia?" Her cousin Maurice was the first to speak.

"You said I could come," Cecilia said.

"Yes, of course." As he came down the steps to greet her, he was asking, "But what has happened? What are you wearing? Your face. There are scratches all over your face. Have you been walking through bramble bushes? Where is your husband?"

Cecilia took a deep breath and laced her fingers at her waist. "Kenneth is dead."

Cousin Maurice reached to put his hand under her elbow. Cecilia moved away. "Kenneth is dead. Mister Black is gone. I don't know where. The fields haven't been planted. There's only Old Mart. He's really old." She stopped for a moment as Cousin Maurice again reached for her elbow.

Cecilia took another shuddering breath. She felt as if she were talking to herself but she could not stop telling her story. "Martin caught fish so we could eat. There's Lula and Little Martin and Benjamin. And Simple, who knows how to make rabbit traps."

She felt herself being led up the steps to the porch. "I tried to clean. Cousin Maurice, everything was so dirty. No one has tended the house in years. I found some salt in the cellar, but there isn't any food."

She heard Cousin Maurice bark an order to someone on the porch but she couldn't stop talking. She looked down at her clothes. "This skirt was in the attic."

Someone handed her a glass of water. She took a sip before giving the glass back. A plate of food, set on a hastily brought table, was put beside her. She lifted the spoon but put it down again. Then a man pulled his chair up in front of her. She knew she was supposed to know who he was, but her mind wouldn't give her his name.

"Sheriff Benning, ma'am," he said. "Tell me about your husband."

"How did you get here so quickly?" she asked.

"I was already here, Miss Cecilia, visiting with Judge Moore. Tell me about Kenneth Black and his father."

Cecilia felt as if the porch had started spinning about her and she swayed in the chair. Cousin Maurice put his hand on her shoulder. He was talking to her but she did not seem able to understand the words.

She wanted to scream but she bit her lip. She wanted to stomp her feet but she crossed her ankles. She wanted to hit this man who sat so close in front of her but she hugged her arms close to her chest.

Cecilia whispered, "Please take me back to Kenneth. Please, Cousin Maurice."

"Of course, Cecilia," he said. He began giving orders.

It seemed only minutes before everyone and everything was organized. Alfred drove the carriage that carried her. He talked on and on about his years in Boston. Cecilia knew he was trying to distract her. She tuned out most of what he said until he began to talk of the battle of Bunker Hill.

"The battle was really fought on Breed's Hill. I don't know if people will ever get the name right."

"We had news of that," Cecilia said. "Of the bravery of the men."

"Ah, another patriot we've raised," Alfred said. "The news closer to home is bad. Captain Collett marched his Grenadiers up to Brunswick. Much of the town is burned. The plantation house that William Dry bought from Governor Tryon was destroyed."

"I knew there was burning across the river. That's why we left Wilmington to come to the farm. But surely the British didn't burn Russellborough! That is such a beautiful house."

"You know the place?"

"Oh, yes. Little Margaret Tryon was a friend of mine. We played dolls together and listened to her mother practice on the harpsichord. My sisters, Polly and Charlotte, visited there as well when we lived at Brunswick. We were all sad when the Tryons moved to New Bern. Now they are in New York."

Sheriff Benning rode his horse up next to the carriage. Cecilia turned to him. "Sir?"

"You said there was no food on the place? How did you eat?" the sheriff asked.

"We fished. We gathered dandelion greens. We picked wild strawberries in the woods and found herbs growing by the creek."

Her fists clinched but she held her anger close. "Martin made a spear from a stick and gigged some frogs. Frog legs are much better fried than turned over a spit, but then we had no grease with which to cook."

She clinched and unclenched her fists, fighting the wrath building inside her. There was so much anger in her belly she thought she would explode.

Inside her head came Polly's voice. *Dare to think for yourself. Dare.*

Cecilia was shaking with the effort to be calm. "Sheriff Benning, the Black farm is a strange place."

The sheriff turned his horse to ride back and speak to one of the men. Maybe he was reporting what she'd said. Maybe he needed to confer with someone. She was too angry and too tired to care.

When the carriage turned up the lane to the house Cecilia asked Alfred to drive around to the back. As soon as he reined to a stop she jumped from the vehicle and started walking down the path toward the hickory grove. The hooves of Sheriff Benning's horse made padding noises as he followed behind her. She heard voices talking. Someone laughed. She had no idea how many men trailed behind her on the path. She concentrated on putting one foot in front of the other.

Then, ahead, she saw her apron hanging where she had tied it. Her basket, which she had not remembered dropping, lay on the ground next to a tree. She stopped and pointed. Her knees buckled and she leaned against a tree. The voices now seemed to buzz like gnats and no one was laughing. Hands under her arms supported her. She was being walked back toward the house. She knew Alfred was one of the men beside her and she made herself speak.

"To the kitchen."

"What?"

"Not the house. Don't make me go in the house," she pleaded.

"You want to go to the kitchen?"

Cecilia nodded. "I've cleaned the kitchen."

She saw Benjamin and Simple at the barn door, standing in that military formality they had used the morning she'd first seen them. Had it been only three days ago? One of the men went toward the slaves and began talking.

Inside the kitchen she stood, gazing out the window. Soon four men came into view. Each held the corner of what looked like sailcloth. She stared at the weight that caused the cloth to sag, almost scraping the ground. Cecilia knew that the men were carrying Kenneth's body and all she seemed able to feel was anger.

"Why?" she screamed, as she had done in the woods. "Why?"

Alfred put his arm about her shoulder, rocking her against his chest, pulling her away from the window.

When the sheriff and Cousin Maurice came to the kitchen a few minutes later, Cecilia looked at them for answers. "How did Kenneth die? Cousin Maurice, how did it happen?"

"He was struck on the head, Cecilia," the judge said.

"I think he died very quickly," Sheriff Benning added. "The blow was quite savage, from the looks of it. He fell back against the tree. He probably never moved again."

"Who? Oh, who could do this?"

The sheriff pulled up a chair and sat beside her. "Miss Cecilia, tell me what you know about Mister Black. Was he here when you and Kenneth got here from Wilmington?"

"Yes, sir." She closed her eyes, trying to remember what her father-in-law had said. "He quoted something about a marriage ring. Kenneth teased him about obscure authors." She opened her eyes. "I didn't understand what either of them meant, but they seemed to understand each other. I had never had the opportunity to meet Mister Black before that afternoon. Kenneth led me to believe that his father would welcome me. Everything here is such a mess. I was upset because the house was so dirty and the fields weren't planted. Nothing was as Kenneth had told me. When we got here he confessed that he'd lied to me. He had lied about everything."

Cecilia turned to again look out the window. "Where have you taken him? Where is my Kenneth?"

"We put his body in the parlour, Miss Cecilia," the sheriff answered.

She stood so abruptly that her chair pushed back. "Where's the scrub bucket? Where did I put my lye soap? I have to get everything ready. People will be coming."

But then she slumped, not able to contain the fear and anger that roiled inside her. Alfred caught her in his arms as she fainted.

 CHAPTER 14

Cecilia lay curled on a pallet on the kitchen floor, listening to the men, not understanding what they discussed. She slept and woke, aware that someone sat near her. She slept and roused, aware she was alone. The third time she woke to noises in the yard. In the dark she crept to a window and looked out.

A shadow, cast by a torch from a wagon, silhouetted a team of oxen against the side of the barn. A man on horseback followed. Behind him was another wagon. People jumped down and several walked toward the slave cabins. Cecilia knelt by the window and watched. Torches were now lit from the barn to the cabins, casting an eerie glow in the very early morning. The unyoked oxen docilely waited to be hitched to plows being lifted from one of the wagons.

Cecilia rolled up her pallet, placing it in a corner. She shook out her skirts and walked out to speak to the man on the horse, for he seemed to be in charge.

He jumped from his saddle. "Miss Cecilia?" he asked, jerking his hat from his head.

She nodded.

"Name's Mac Macdougal. I'm the assistant foreman for Judge Moore and he said I'm to look after getting things started here."

The man looked far too young to be an assistant anything. "Mister Macdougal, what do you mean by 'started?' " she asked.

The man turned his hat in his hands. "Ma'am, it is not too late for planting corn. If the weather holds, that is. The Judge said we might even try peanuts, though I don't think you'll get much of a crop. You're going to need a bigger house garden with beans, more potatoes and surely pumpkins. You need firewood for the house and slave cabins." He looked across the overgrown fields. "If you don't mind me suggesting-" He waited for her to speak.

"Suggest, Mister Macdougal."

"We start there," he said, pointing to the field just past the barn. "We cut the trees and plow. That's where we put in the corn. We work the acres deeper down in the woods for the peanuts. I'll look around for the best place for your house garden, unless you know where you want it."

Two men began unloading barrels, which they took into the barn. Other men cared for the horses that had pulled their wagons. Carrying a crosscut saw and ax, several men headed for the fields.

Cecilia planted her hands on her hips. "I've been invaded! James Moore's Continental Line couldn't be more efficient than this crew. Mister Macdougal, make war on this farm."

Lula stopped by a wagon on her way to the kitchen. "Miss Cecilia," she said as she came in the door. "One of them wagons is just piled with foodstuffs."

Lula threw her hands in the air. "My, my, but the Judge was almighty angry when he got home last night. Ain't heared him rant like that in a long time, them men out there be saying. They saying the Judge fuss on and on. 'Leaving little Cecilia no food. Leaving little Cecilia all alone with no help. What that man thinking to treat any woman that aways. Where Dorie Black gone off to with his son lying dead in the woods.' It won't no question he be asking, that for sure.

"Then Judge Moore call for Mister Macdougal and start giving orders. Then he call for Mister Alfred and start giving more orders. My, my, the orders flew 'round that house, the mens say." She smiled. "Miss Cecilia, you is in a *favor* with the Judge."

Cecilia left Lula there to put away the supplies and walked to the house. Standing at the door of the parlour, she looked at the cloth-wrapped shape lying on the table. "Oh, Kenneth," she moaned. "Why didn't you tell me about all the problems here? Why didn't you ask for help?"

From behind her a woman spoke. "Miss Cecilia, I be Ruthie. Ma'am, Judge Moore send me. It be my honor to wash and dress your man for the funeral."

Cecilia turned to see an old woman in the hallway. She had a bucket of water in one hand and a bag in the other. "Many and many a fine man I is had the honor to get ready for their service. You ain't got to worry none."

Cecilia nodded. She sank down in a chair in the hall, leaning her aching head back against the wall. Another woman came in to help and Cecilia listened to the quiet words they exchanged as they worked.

"Oh, Kenneth," she whispered, over and over. "Oh, Kenneth." Each time she said his name her anger grew. She held the strength of the feeling close.

Mama and Polly came the next day for the burial. Timothy Charles followed their buggy with a wagon filled with boxes and barrels and goats. Cecilia laughed at the sight of her little brother unloading the nannies who did not want to leave the wagon. The billy jumped from the wagon bed and tried to flee. She ran to help Timothy guide the bleating animals to a stall in the barn even before she could hug Mama. They were all talking at once.

Finally Mama stepped back from a hug. "I'm not sure we're acting with the best decorum. In the light of what has happened we should be prudent."

"Oh, Mama. Decorum! Prudence! Being careful will not bring my Kenneth back."

"Cecilia!"

Cecilia took her mother's hands. "Please don't quarrel with me. Please don't. If only you knew how much I've missed you. All of you."

Timothy Charles reached in the wagon and gathered up a puppy. "To keep you company, if you want her."

"A sheep dog!" Cecilia held the puppy close. "Does she have a name?"

"Not yet," her brother said. "You name her."

"Perhaps she should be our Prudence." Cecilia kissed the puppy on the nose. "See, Mama, now we have all the dignity you could wish for. Here's Prudence."

Cousin Maurice's buggy rattled into the yard. Alfred rode behind him and dismounted to help his father alight.

Sheriff Benning rode in with one of his deputies. He only shook his head when Cecilia asked if he needed her. He did spend some time talking with Cousin Maurice.

The slaves placed the coffin they had made on the back of a wagon and drove the team across the road from the house to the plot where Kenneth's mother had been buried five years before. Cecilia, using all the will she could muster, dressed in the blue skirt and bodice she'd worn for her wedding. Now she walked behind the wagon, trying not to think, trying not to feel, trying to control the angry energy that writhed inside her.

Henrietta took her hand, but Cecilia pulled away from her mother. She listened as Cousin Maurice read a simple service at the grave, but she had no idea what passage he read. Then the small group walked back up the lane to the house.

Lula, with the help of the women whom Cousin Maurice had sent, had been busy in the kitchen. They served ham and venison, potatoes cooked in cabbage, pans of cornbread and apple pies to everyone. Most of the men stood in the yard to eat, while Henrietta and Polly sat with Cecilia in the clean dining room and ate from Emma Black's china plates.

Cecilia's thoughts were so conflicted she did not know how to sort them out. Love for Kenneth and anger at his death mixed like gall inside her stomach. She didn't think she would have hurt any less if she had been delivered physical blows. She felt she should cry, but no tears came.

She made herself listen as Polly talked about the raid on Brunswick. "Cecilia, you were right about Mister Richards. He's gone over to the British lines. The tavern's burned to the ground. I'll be going over there soon to see if there is anything to salvage."

"Polly, no," Mama said. "You can't go riding off with everything that's happened."

Polly didn't answer her, but went on talking about Collett and his invasion. "We heard that Orton was spared. Many others were not so fortunate."

Cecilia tuned her sister out, wondering at the fickle twists of fortune.

In the late afternoon, as her mother and sister drove away, as Timothy waved from the end of the lane, as Cousin Maurice and Alfred left for home, she gathered Prudence in her arms and sat on the back steps of the empty house, waiting. What she waited for she did not know.

CHAPTER 15

Mister Black rode into the yard one early July morning while Cecilia and Lula were washing clothes. He climbed from his gray horse and handed the reins to Martin. "Put him in the barn," Mister Black commanded.

He looked past the women toward the fields green with growing corn. He surveyed the cropped grass and swept path that lead to the cabins. He peered up as if to check on the smoke that drifted from the kitchen chimney.

"Didn't ask for this," he muttered.

"Good morning, Mister Black," Cecilia said.

He shook his finger at her. "You stay away from me. Stay away." He weaved up the steps and disappeared into the house.

"Miss Cecilia, that man be drunk," Lula whispered.

"Yes," Cecilia said. "Go find Mister Macdougal and tell him we need him at the house now. Cousin Maurice wanted to know the minute Mister Black showed up."

That afternoon Judge Moore and Alfred sat with Mister Black on the porch, trying to find out where he had been. Cecilia wanted to hear everything. Cousin Maurice shook his head and waved her away. While Lula served sassafras tea and apple pie to the men, Cecilia hid behind the door to listen.

Mister Black demanded ale.

Cousin Maurice raised his voice. "There are no spirits. You took good care to strip this place before you rode off, Dorie."

"She's got the money," Mister Black shouted. "She can order what she pleases. Right now it pleases me to have a drink."

"What money?" Cousin Maurice asked.

Mister Black hurled his pie plate to the floor and headed for the barn. "Where's that boy? Boy, I want my horse. Come saddle my horse." He rode out a few minutes later.

Cousin Maurice shook his head. "I don't know where he's been. I don't know if he knows about his son. Cecilia," he called to her. "I know you're behind that door. Come out here. Do you understand what Dorie's saying about money?"

"No, sir." She walked out on the porch. "You and Polly wrote the dowry papers. I wasn't paying much attention."

"Dorie Black is not now the man I knew. When Emma was alive, he was altogether a different person. One of the best lawyers ever to practice. He could quote Shakespeare and Bible verses and complex law procedures in the same breath. Tell you chapter and verse anything he quoted."

Cousin Maurice took a sip of his herbal tea. "The awful manner of Kenneth's death is perplexing, to say the least. There is also the question of the money."

"I have to ask you. What money?

"The week before your wedding, when I signed the documents for the marriage, a parcel of seventy-five acres of land on the sound was transferred to Kenneth's name. He said it would be used for a salt works, which of course would make it even more valuable than it is now. I also gave him coin valued at two hundred pounds. Have you seen a chest that would hold that amount of money? The coins were in a small wooden chest."

"No, Cousin Maurice. We have scrubbed this house from attic to cellar. We have cleaned every cabin. We have cleared every outbuilding, from the corn crib to the smokehouse. We've even built a new necessary. There are no coins or chest here."

Cousin Maurice worried his chin with his hand.

Cecilia took a deep breath. "Could Mister Black have thought there was money packed with my clothes? My trunk was unpacked and plundered." She knotted her hands. "Cousin Maurice, do you think Mister Black killed Kenneth?"

"I don't know, child. I just don't know. But you let me know if Dorie comes back." He turned to his son. "Alfred, take me home."

Mister Black came back for supper. This time he brought his own supply of drink. Benjamin helped him up the stairs after dark and dumped him in his bed. Cecilia went to her own room while Benjamin was still with Mister Black. She got a quilt and covers. In the kitchen she made up a pallet for herself. She cradled Prudence in her arms to help ward off the fear that invaded her each time she thought of Mister Black. Daisy, who usually stayed in the barn, left her kittens to fend for themselves and curled up on the covers at her feet.

Caring for Mister Black meant keeping him feed, supplying him with ale or rum, and staying out of his way. He spoke so harshly to Lula that Cecilia served him. She bit her lips to avoid quarreling with him and pretended he was a patron at the tavern, to be indulged and endured.

Three weeks after her father-in-law moved back to the farm, Mister Macdougal, coming back from a trip into Wilmington, pelted into the yard. His shout brought Cecilia hurrying from the house garden. She pulled her mobcap from her head to wipe sweat from her face as she called out to the overseer. "What is it, Mister Macdougal? What has happened?"

He leaped from his horse and did a fancy two-step in the dust. "We have a Declaration of Independence, Miss Cecilia. We have a Declaration of Independence."

"Slow down please," Cecilia said. "A Declaration? Declaring what?"

The overseer stopped his wild dance. He lifted his hat from his head and held it between his hands. "Those men meeting in Philadelphia, like Mister William Hooper from Wilmington and Mister Franklin we've read about and Mister Thomas Jefferson -"

The overseer ran out of breath for a moment. More calmly he said, "Miss Cecilia, they have written it down. 'When in the course of human events, it becomes necessary for one people to dissolve the political bonds which have connected them with another -' "

He turned the hat in his hands. "Oh, I do wish I could remember it all. 'We hold these truths to be self-evident, that all men are created equal.' And there's so much more. Like when a form of government becomes destructive the people have rights to do something about it. Those words are saying that we are going to separate the colonies from England. It was signed in Philadelphia on the fourth of July. On the fourth of July, 1776. That was three weeks ago, Miss Cecilia. Three weeks for the news to reach Wilmington for us to know about it."

Mister Black, from his rocking chair on the porch, called out. "Young man, just where have you heard this foolishness?"

Mister Macdougal went to the steps and looked up at the old man. "I was in Wilmington ordering supplies, sir. The words were being read from the courthouse steps."

"You really heard such drivel as men being equal?"

"Yes, sir, I did. A decent respect to the opinions of people is written in there too. And there are times to reduce the absolute despot, which I guess means King George. Except I've found out that not all despots are kings, even when they try to act like they are."

Mister Black raised his fist and shook it at the overseer. "Get off my property. Get off my property now."

Mister Macdougal put his hat on his head. "I can't do that, sir. I'm here to stay till Judge Moore releases me or Miss Cecilia tells me to go." He gathered the reins of his horse, mounted and rode to his small house near the slave cabins.

The words that Macdougal had recited were moving. Men created equal? That was a heady thought. She'd have to dwell on it later though. She tucked her hair under her mobcap and went back to the garden.

The chores were so endless that Cecilia forgot time. The slaves Cousin Maurice had sent to help her were back at his plantation. She had Lula and her son to help in the house. Mister Macdougal had the three men working the fields. When they weren't hoeing peanuts or corn they were clearing trees or doing repair work.

The sun baked through her bodice as she picked beans. She reached the end of the row and bent to lift the basket when the world spun about her. Her legs gave way and she sat so suddenly that it was hard to breathe. She heard, as if from a great distance, Lula calling her name.

When Cecilia woke she was lying in the shade of a tree and Lula was wiping her face with a wet rag. "Well, I sees that you decided to come back to us," the woman said.

Cecilia pulled herself up to lean against the tree.

"You just stay quiet a time longer. Drink this water," Lula said.

"What happened?"

"Why, Miss Cecilia, you fainted."

"Nonsense, Lula. I don't faint."

The woman grinned. "You ain't never been in this condition afore, I guessing. Now you drink some more water. Then we gonna to walk to the house. Then you gonna rest. No more picking beans in the heat of the day.

"This condition?" Cecilia whispered.

Lula just grinned at her and suddenly Cecilia knew what condition! How was she going to feed herself and the others who now depended on her? How was she going to keep up with the work that had to be done. She pondered the words of the document that Mister Macdougal had recited from the Declaration. The words were written on a piece of paper that said men were equal. Had any of those men had a baby?

 16

Mister Black came and went. Cecilia never knew when he would ride in, demanding ale, or slump into a drunken stupor in a rocking chair on the porch. Although she ignored him when he ordered her about, she still kept her pallet in the kitchen, for she was truly afraid of him. She had too much work to do to let his trips interfere with getting ready for winter.

Through the late summer and into the fall Cecilia went deer hunting at least twice a week. Polly had taught her how to shoot as soon as she could lift and load a rifle. They had no cattle or hogs. The rabbits little Martin and Simple trapped and the deer Cecilia shot were their only source of meat.

This cold October morning she looked out the window when she heard Mister Macdougal yelling from the yard. "Miss Cecilia!" The overseer jabbed at the air with a pistol. "Merciful heavens, Miss Cecilia! Never seen a bigger one in my life. Never in my life."

She hurried to the porch. "Never seen a bigger what, Mister Macdougal?"

"Oh merciful heavens, Miss Cecilia, stay inside the house. It's a bear. He's after the goats."

She walked across the yard to the kitchen and lifted the rifle from the pegs above the mantel. She opened the cupboard and took out the shot and wadding. Quickly she loaded the weapon. With the basket of extra shot over her arm she walked back out to see Mister Macdougal peering toward the barn.

"Where is it?" she asked.

"Trying to bust through the door on the side toward the woods. But Miss Cecilia, what are you fixing to do?"

"I'm fixing to save my goats and have bear steak for supper, Mister Macdougal. Now stop waving that pistol around. Is it loaded?"

The overseer looked at the weapon in his hand as if he had not known he was holding it. Then he looked at her, a sheepish grin on his face. "No, ma'am."

"Well, put it down. Or at least stop waving it."

"Ma'am, I know you can shoot a deer. Are you good enough for bear?"

"Mister Macdougal, I guess we'll find out, now won't we."

Cecilia had been slowly walking toward the far side of the barn as she talked. Mister Macdougal fell into step behind her. As they rounded the side of the building she saw a black bear sitting on its haunches facing the door. As if it had gotten a whiff of their scent, it stood on all fours, turned its head in their direction and reared up, one paw stretched out to touch the barn door.

Cecilia checked the wadding, pulled back the hammer and set the rifle stock firmly against her shoulder.

"Miss - "

"Shut up, Macdougal."

The bear lifted its head and Cecilia shot. She did not wait to see what the animal would do. She was reloading and bringing the rifle again to her shoulder. The bear was still looking at her. She heard the man behind her take a jagged breath.

"Don't you move or speak, Macdougal," she whispered.

The bear went down on its forelegs. Cecilia did not lower the gun or change her stance. The animal fell to its side, stretched it legs out and was still. She did not take her eyes from the bear as she spoke.

"Mister Macdougal, we're going to butcher this bear just like we've done the deer. We just have more weight to deal with. We need ropes to tie it hind feet up, its back against the barn wall. We'll use the beam over the upper hay door to hang it on. We'll need every sharp knife on the place. We'll need every hand to work because I don't want to stop moving -"

"How did you learn how to carve up a bear?" interrupted Macdougal.

"You'd be surprised how many hog killings I've done," she answered. "I'll just think of this as a very large hog. I want every last piece of this bear cut up and either salted down to put in the smokehouse or cooking in the stew pot."

Cecilia brought the rifle to her side and turned to the overseer. "Well?"

"Ma'am, where did you hit it?"

"I was aiming for the mouth but I got it in the throat. I think the rifle sight is a little off. I do believe you were right, Mister Macdougal, about the size. I've never before seen a black bear this big. It must weigh over three hundred pounds."

"Is there anything you can't do, Miss Cecilia?"

"I hope not, sir. I do so hope not." She gripped the stock of the rifle so he could not see how badly her hands were shaking. No one must know how afraid she had been when she lifted that rifle to her shoulder.

She heard the curt tone of her voice as she shouted, "Get the men up here and get that bear tied up to the beam and get ready to work. I'm going to see how many pots and pans I can find in the house."

In the kitchen, out of sight of the overseer, Cecilia slumped down at the kitchen table. She gagged as fear crept through her and she swallowed hard to still her heaving stomach. "What if I'd missed?" she whispered. "What would have happened if I had missed?"

She folded her arms close to her stomach. This baby needed protection. No one must know that she had been afraid. She certainly didn't have time to be sick. She remembered bragging to Polly that she would sit back and tell others what to do when she was married. She really had thought that living with Kenneth, being his wife, would give her a life of leisure. Well, she had no time now to think about silly things like that. She'd just killed a bear. There was more work to do.

Cecilia and the men finished salting down the last pieces of the bear by lamplight. She had put the first haunch of the meat in the wash pot, stoked the fire under it and left it to cook throughout the day. As soon as the smokehouse door was closed and a slow hickory wood fire started to cure the meat, she called out to them all.

"We all worked for this meal. And I am tired of eating alone. Bring your bowls. We will give thanks and eat together."

Daisy twined about her feet. "You, too, you silly creature. You, too."

Martin ran out the next morning to shout to Alfred as he rode into the yard. "Sir, we done kill us a bear. A big bear. Yes, sir, the biggest bear in the whole world."

"What's this?" Alfred asked.

"Come in, Alfred," Cecilia called from the porch. "I can serve you bear stew and pour you a cup of sassafras tea sweetened with honey. And yes, we did kill a big bear."

"I came to bring you news, but you seem to have bigger news than I."

Seated in the parlor, with Prudence waiting at his feet for a handout, Alfred sipped the tea and tasted the stew. "Good, Cecilia. Very good. Tell me your story."

She finished her tale of the bear. "Your news, cousin. I would hear your news."

He slipped the dog a piece of bread before he wiped his hands on his napkin. "Father and I had a message that the committees in Halifax have been busy. Richard Caswell has taken the oath of office as our first State Governor."

"Mister Caswell of New Bern. He lead the militia to Cross Creek."

"Yes, he did. Good man," Alfred said. "Samuel Ashe was made speaker of the Senate and Abner Nash speaker of the House of Commons. Good men all. The problem is not the leadership but the fact that they have so little to work with."

He sipped his tea. "We have an empty treasury. There is no credit, and no commerce as basis for credit. We need the ability to tax or to use goods in lieu of money. We need to be able to make loans but we cannot do that with no credit. It is a weak economic state of affairs in which we find ourselves."

"I know that feeling well," Cecilia said. She watched a quail scratching for grain at the edge of the yard. "Cousin Alfred, it is hard to fly without wings."

"Philosophizing, Cecilia?"

Mister Black stumbled into the parlour and shook his finger at her. "You're the one who should fly away. Who are you? What are you doing in my house?"

Cecilia held Prudence close, wondering if she could ever stop being afraid of her father-in-law.

Alfred rose from his seat. "Sir, what is wrong with you? Surely you know Cecilia. You know me. I'm Alfred Moore, Maurice's son."

The old man stared at them both before turning on his heel and walking out.

"Cecilia, I'm not sure you're safe here," Alfred said.

CHAPTER 17

Only a few days later Cousin Maurice and Alfred, with Sheriff Benning and a deputy, rode in the yard. Cecilia invited them into the house.

"Where's Dorie Black?" Cousin Maurice asked. "And is he sober?"

"Sir, he's sitting in the parlour by the fire. This early in the day he's as sober as he ever is."

"Leave this meeting to us, Cecilia," he said. If he had wrapped his robes about him, ready to hammer his gavel on the court dais, Cousin Maurice would not have seemed more judicial as he led the men into the parlour.

Cecilia leaned against the door jamb in the hallway, making herself as small as possible while she listened.

Mister Black greeted the men. "Shakespeare said we should kill the lawyers."

"Yes, he wrote something like that in *King Henry*, I believe," Cousin Maurice replied.

"Maurice, you should not interfere here."

"Dorie, just what kind of interference is implied? A neighbor needs a helping hand. That is not interference."

Mister Black shifted in his chair. "If I'd wanted my fields plowed and planted, I'd have had it done. That girl is officious, poking her nose in my business. She will not even serve me ale when I call for it."

He raised his voice, "Girl, bring me drink!" He waited a moment. "See, Maurice? She does not answer."

Alfred and his father shared a glance before Cousin Maurice spoke. "You talk of killing the lawyers. Do you think our visit has something to do with the law?"

"My son marries, brings home a wife and leaves. That seems to bring the law." He sniffed. "And lawyers. Maurice, you used to be a friend."

The sheriff leaned forward in his chair. "Mister Black, you do understand that Kenneth is dead? We found his body here on your farm. We have to know how he was killed. Sir, he *was* killed."

Mister Black cried out, " 'Grief fills the room up of my absent child.' "

"Quoting Shakespeare won't help us," Alfred said.

"Is that what he's doing? Quoting again?" the sheriff asked. "Mister Black, when was the last time you saw your son?"

Mister Black pounded his fists on the arm of his chair, his voice raised in a scream. "He wouldn't give me the money."

Alfred spoke quietly. "Tell us about the money, Mister Black."

"The boy was supposed to bring the money, but he wouldn't give it to me."

"Judge Moore? Alfred? Do you know what money he's talking about?" the sheriff asked.

"Yes," Maurice said. "Part of the dowry that Cecilia brought. Two hundred pounds doesn't sound like that much to do murder over."

"Two hundred!" the old man roared. "It was supposed to be a lot more." He shook his fist in the air. "They traded land when they were supposed to give me money. I guess I showed them."

"Who did you show?" asked the sheriff.

"Those Moores. Those high and mighty Moores." He glared at Alfred. "You're one of them, you are. But I showed you."

"Mister Black, did you strike your son?" the sheriff asked.

"Of course I struck him. He wouldn't give me the money."

"Mister Black, did you lure your son into the woods? Is that where you argued with him about the money? Tell us what happened."

"He wouldn't give me the money," the old man yelled. He shook his fists at the men questioning him. "I needed the money for my Emma. I knew she'd come home if I just had the money." Then, as if his strength were depleted, he slumped back in his chair. "My Emma left. I needed the money to bring her home again."

Sheriff Benning held up a hand to stop the conversation. "Judge Moore, who is Emma?"

"She was Dorie's wife," he said to the sheriff. Then he took Mister Black's hands in his. "Dorie, Emma's been dead for more than five years."

"No," Mister Black sobbed. "No, my Emma went away to visit her mother. I know she'll come back. Maurice, you knew my Emma. You have to understand."

Cousin Maurice and Sheriff Benning huddled in conversation at the far end of the room. Cecilia could only hear bits of what they said. As their discussion heated she gathered that the sheriff and Cousin Maurice both wanted Mister Black out of the house. The sheriff wanted him arrested but Cousin Maurice just wanted him confined somewhere.

"The man's sick," Cousin Maurice insisted.

"The man's dangerous," the sheriff responded. "This is the first time we've found him sober enough to be questioned. I find his answers menacing. I need to lock him up."

Sheriff Benning's opinion won. Cecilia watched as he gave orders, placed Mister Black in a buggy with a deputy and sent them toward Wilmington.

"He wouldn't give me the money," Mister Black yelled as the buggy pulled out of the yard. "He wouldn't give me the money for my Emma."

The sheriff turned to Cecilia, who had followed the men out to the yard. "Do you know where the money is?"

"No, sir." The mist that had blocked out the sun for most of the day had now turned to cold rain. She moved to the porch to huddle close to the wall. The sheriff followed her.

"Sheriff Benning, I was told that there was two hundred pounds in coin. I was told that the coins were in a wooden box. I was told that it was part of my dowry." Cecilia rubbed her arms through her wool shawl. "Sir, I have not seen the box or the money. If I knew what had happened to that box of coins I would gladly tell."

She started to go in the house, but turned back to the sheriff. "Sir, what will happen to Mister Black?"

Cousin Maurice answered. "Cecilia, Dorie will be indicted for murder. He'll be held in the jail in Wilmington."

"And then a trial?" she asked.

"And then a trial," he answered.

She heard nothing more until Timothy Charles rode out to the farm in December to tell her that Mister Black would go on trial the next week for the murder of Kenneth.

"Oh, Timmie, I still don't understand any of this."

"Cee, nobody else does either. The gossip in the tavern says he's lost his mind. He mostly talks with his dead wife, Emma. He yells at everybody."

Cecilia nodded as she dished up a bowl of venison stew and placed it in front of her brother.

"Hey, this is good," he said, waving the spoon at her.

"Of course it's good. Polly and Leah taught me how to cook. Tell me what else you know about Mister Black. What other news is there from town? Have any letters come from Charlotte?"

"Well, Mister Black talks to Emma and tells her he had to kill Kenneth so she'd come home. That's what the gaol keeper said the last time he came to the tavern." Timothy scraped the last of the meat from his bowl, handed it to Cecilia and tilted back his chair.

"The last news from Charles Town was about fortifications being built on the islands. I don't know when Mama had the letter from Charlotte. Her husband Jonathan was in charge of something on the waterfront in town and she hadn't seen him for several weeks."

"Isn't Charlotte still living in Charles Town?"

"Jonathan sent her and the children out to their plantation, Mama said."

"To stay with Jonathan's mother! How Charlotte hates Mistress Reynolds. How she hates being out in the country. Oh, Timmie, she must be so miserable."

Timothy grinned. "Her last letter sounded miserable. Cousin James is sending me down that way soon. Maybe I'll have a chance to see her."

He let the legs of his chair down, stood and reached for his coat. "Oh, I almost forgot. Mama says you're to come into town by the first of the year."

"Why should I?"

Timmie stopped at the door, put his hands on his hips and imitated Henrietta's voice. " 'My Cecilia will *not* have her baby in that *lonely* place.' "

Cecilia sputtered with laughter. "Timothy Charles, what would Mama say if she heard you mocking her!"

" 'Boy, what *am* I to do with you?' " He leaped to his saddle and gathered the reins. "You'd best plan to have your baby at the tavern."

Cecilia watched her brother ride out of sight and sighed. The Black farm *was* a lonely place. She looked forward to going to Three Sisters and being with her family.

CHAPTER 18

Theodore Black was found guilty of the murder of his son, Kenneth Black. Cousin Maurice, sitting by the fire at the tavern, recited the events of the trial and the consequences following. Cecilia had heard all the gossip at Three Sisters. Theodore Black's trial was a main topic of conversation with the men drinking their ale and smoking their pipes. She knew Cousin Maurice was being both selective and kind in what he reported to her.

She shuddered as she listened.

"Cecilia, the man was ill. I don't think my old friend Dorie had any idea what he had done. He described in great detail about how he picked up a heavy limb and slammed it into Kenneth's head. He told exactly why he was fighting with his son. At the same time, even as the hangman tied the noose about his neck, he was pleading for his dead wife Emma to come home."

He worried at his chin, then let his head drop in his hands. "Cecilia, he had such a brilliant mind. He knew so much law."

She didn't remember ever seeing her cousin so troubled. "Cousin Maurice, I wish I could change things."

"Child, none of this was your fault."

"Yet I seem to be at the center of it. If I could change any of it, I would."

"You can't. At least now Theodore Black is not a threat to you. Or to your child."

"Cousin Maurice, Mister Black will haunt me for the rest of my life."

"The trial was just, Cecilia. The hanging was according to the law. He was my friend for many years, a man with an inquisitive mind and a thirst for learning. I repeat. He was ill. I do not think he really understood -"

She had never before seen Cousin Maurice at a loss for words.

After a moment he continued. "Cecilia, listen to me. Listen carefully. All those years ago, when I signed papers for Polly to take over The Anchor in Brunswick, I knew I was dealing with a strong young woman. I never doubted she was equal to the task. Your sister Charlotte is cut from a different pattern, but she has her own strengths. She will use them as she must."

He reached for Cecilia's hands, holding them palm up between his own. "You, my dear, may have the most strength of all. I've watched you carefully. You use what you're given. You work well with people. You have a kind heart. If I may paraphrase a scripture, strength and honor are your clothing. We've entered a new year. It's now the first month of 1777. Rest easy. Stop worrying. Have your baby."

As he left he patted the top of her head, as if to give her a blessing. In fact, Cecilia felt that was exactly what he intended.

Now, February winds blew across the river and sleet stung the window panes in the bedchamber where Cecilia lay. She listened to the noises in the great room downstairs. A burst of laughter erupted. Leah scolded at the indentured girl, Avey, who answered back that she was doing her best. They both called for Rollen to bring more beer. A door slammed and an explosion of noise was touched off by the men who came stomping in, calling for ale.

"How I've missed all this," Cecilia whispered.

"What did you say?" Henrietta asked.

Cecilia turned her head on the pillow to look toward her mother, sitting in a rocker by the bed. Before she could answer a grip of pain knotted her body and she groaned.

As soon as the pain let up, Henrietta wiped Cecilia's face with a damp cloth and pulled the covers up about her shoulders.

Cecilia pushed the sheet down and turned on her side. "Mama, just a year ago the men marched out for Cross Creek and Timmie ran away to be with them. We didn't know where he was and we were all so worried. Kenneth was here so we could plan our wedding. Just one year, Mama. How can so much hap -"

A contraction clamped her again and she screamed. She heard Mama yell for Leah to come. She knew the tavern had grown quiet. She felt hands doing something to her as waves of pain swept through her. It seemed a long, long time before she heard the squall of her baby.

"Yous got a girl," Leah said. "Lawdy, Miss Cecilia, yous got a little girl."

Cecilia felt Henrietta lift her shoulders to smooth the sheet beneath her and place a dry pillow under her head. Then Henrietta exclaimed, "Oh, Leah, I haven't seen that much black hair on an infant since Charlotte was born!"

Cecilia gazed at her baby as Leah wrapped her in a warmed blanket. "Mama, does she have ears and nose and fingers and toes? Is she all right?"

"Yes, Cecilia. More than all right. I could say she's perfect."

"Leah? Tell me, Leah."

"Miss Cecilia, your baby's fine as she can be."

Cecilia ran her finger down the baby's nose and across her mouth. She studied the blue eyes that peered back at her. She brushed the damp curls from her forehead. "Mama, her hair is like Kenneth's." Quiet tears spilled down her cheeks. "He'll never see her. My Kenneth will never see his daughter."

She crushed the baby to her chest as great sobs shook her. "Why? Why did my Kenneth have to die? Why did he have to die?"

Mama wiped her face and Leah poured her wine. They were talking to her at the same time.

"Stop that sobbing, Cecilia."

"Miss Cecilia, yous gonna hurt that baby do you hold her so tight."

She loosened her clutching hold, but she would not let her mother or Leah take the child from her arms. All through the night, when she knew someone was in the room with her, she faked sleep. When she knew she was alone she cried soft strangled tears that she had held at bay for so many months.

At first light she swung her legs off the bed and walked across the room to place the baby in the waiting cradle. She poured water in the wash bowl and bathed her swollen face. Then she turned her attention to her child. She changed the wet napkin and dressed her in a clean gown.

When Henrietta came in the room Cecilia was sitting in the rocking chair, the baby in her arms. "What are you doing out of bed? You should be resting, Cecilia."

"Mama, I've decided on her name."

Henrietta sat down across from her and folded her hands.

"My baby's name is Rory Grace, Mama. Rory is for that first Moore who came from his old home to the islands to make a better life for himself. And Grace is for God's blessings. Oh, what a blessing she is for me."

"Rory Grace," said Henrietta. "Well, it is a very different name, to be sure." She shook her head. "Rory Grace. My goodness, Cecilia."

As Henrietta was talking Polly came in the room with hot chocolate and fried apple pies on a tray. "Good morning, little sister. I hope your appetite corresponds to the magnificent labor you've been through. Do let me hold the baby while you eat." Polly set the tray on a table by Cecilia's chair and held out her arms.

"Did you hear what name she's chosen?" Henrietta asked, as Polly took the baby from her sister.

"I heard you say Rory Grace," Polly said. She gazed at the sleeping infant. "It's a strong name. Yes, little sister, a strong name for such a tiny baby."

Rory Grace opened her eyes and yawned.

When Polly brought the family Bible up to her room, for her to write the baby's name and birth date, Cecilia's hands shook so badly she handed the quill to her sister. There, under the date of the wedding, on March of 1776, Polly wrote Rory Grace Black, February 12, 1777.

Cecilia's finger caressed Kenneth's name on the page. "It's not fair, Polly," Cecilia whispered. "It's not fair that he is gone."

"Not fair at all, sister," Polly answered.

By the time the baby was three weeks old, Cecilia felt so back at home in the tavern that she'd taken on most of her old duties. First up this bright March morning, she'd rekindled the fire in the tavern room and brought in the water from the well. When Leah came in with a slab of bacon from the smoke house, she was ready to measure out grits for the pot.

Leah began to slice strips of pork to lay on the pans heating over the coals. "Miss Cecilia, yous been much missed here."

Rory Grace, from her cradle near the hearth, made a soft sleepy sound. Cecilia leaned over to pat the baby's hand. "I've missed being here, Leah."

"What you gonna do?"

"Do, Leah?"

"I means, is you staying here? Your mama sure do want you to."

Cecilia stirred the grits. "I have a child, Leah. I have a farm. I'm thinking about that."

She knocked the heavy wooden spoon against the edge of the pot and gazed into the fire. "Leah, do you ever look for pictures in the flames?"

"What kinds of pictures you talking 'bout, child?"

Polly had come in to set the milk pails on the table. " 'Sometimes we see a cloud that's dragonish. A vapor sometime like a bear or lion, a tower'd citadel.'" She pointed toward the ceiling, gazing up and up. " 'A pendant rock, a forked mountain, or blue promontory with trees upon't.' That's what Shakespeare wrote that some can see in the flames."

"Yes! Oh, yes, Polly. I knew you would understand. It's like looking for pictures in the clouds. A horse with a rider might sail across the sky. A wind comes along and takes the rider right out of his saddle. Or a scattering of small clouds might look like a herd of goats munching on meadow grass."

"You girls sees pictures like that in the fire? Miss Cecilia, what picture you looking at right now?"

"I'm not seeing very much, Leah. I'm thinking."

Leah and Polly left her there, staring into the fire.

CHAPTER 19

The fields were greening when she went back to the farm. On this trip she drove the lead wagon at the head of a convoy. Rory Grace, tucked in a basket on the boards between Cecilia's feet, cooed with the rocking of the horse-drawn wagon. Iron pots, frying pans and skillets for the kitchen, with a specially built tin bathtub, filled most of her wagon space. Linens and blankets, which Mama had hemmed, were packed in boxes.

Behind Cecilia, the indentured boy Rollen handled a team of oxen yoked to a wagon filled with two hogsheads of brandy and another of whiskey, boxes of raisins, linseed and olive oil in casks, and bottles of Florence oil. Hidden in the middle of his load, and marked "black molasses," was a cask of black gunpowder. When she thought of how she and Polly had pestered the captain of the ship to sell them the powder, she giggled. Oh, it was so much fun working with her sister.

Timothy Charles rode his horse between the wagon that Rollen drove and the one that Travis guided. This wagon was filled with crates of chickens and geese and ducks.

Timothy herded a cow and several pigs in front of him. He cracked his whip and shouted, "Stay in the road, you crazy cussed piglets, you."

Cecilia called back to him. "Shouting at the pigs will not make them behave."

"Shouting at these infernal, devilish-acting pigs sure makes me feel better," Timothy hollered back. "If these pigs get in the woods we'll never round them up."

Mister Macdougal rode out to meet them. He helped Timothy Charles guide the pigs into a corral he'd built for them and led the cow into the goat pen.

Prudence bounded to throw herself on her, as if she would wrap her paws about her mistress's waist.

"Oh, sweet Pru." Cecilia tousled the dog's ears. "How you have grown. Have you kept the goats together for me?"

The dog barked, as if she understood exactly what Cecilia said, and took off toward the barn.

Lula came running from the kitchen, her hands waving above her head. "Oh, Miss Cecilia, it be so good to see you. Where that baby? Where that baby girl I hear you got yourself back in Wilmington?"

Cecilia picked up the basket and handed it to her. Lula peered inside. "Oh, Miss Cecilia! She is a beauty. Oh, she is! Just look at those black curls peeking out her cap. Like Mister Kenneth's, those curls is. I could just stand here and look at her all day."

"Put her basket in the kitchen, Lula. We have all these wagons to unload and then we have to cook for these boys. Lula, these boys can eat."

"Oh, Miss Cecilia, you don't need to start cooking this minute. I got a big pot of stew going already, ma'am. Old Martin caught some catfish and I got them skinned and baking. I made a big pan of bread from the cornmeal you sent. We'll have enough food for today."

Cecilia watched as Rollen and Travis lifted a crate of chickens from the back of a wagon. "Lula, we'll have food beyond today." She hurried toward the barn. Daisy meowed a greeting and laid a dead mouse at her feet. She picked up the cat and stroked the fur between her ears. "So you missed me. Daisy, you keep on catching mice for me. You teach your kittens to catch mice,too."

She heard the geese honking a greeting for her home coming. The hens with their biddies scratched about in the chicken pen. It's a time of new life everywhere, she thought.

It was not yet full dark when a rider from Cousin Maurice's farm galloped into the yard. Cecilia hurried out to greet him.

He slipped from the saddle, but held the horse's reins with one hand, as if he would leap to the saddle if Cecilia spoke. "Sad news, ma'am."

She waited for his message.

He jerked his hat from his head and held it clutched to his chest. "Judge Moore is dead, ma'am."

Cecilia did not speak. She did reach out and touched the man's sleeve.

"Was a fever, Miss Cecilia. Judge Moore took a fever."

"When did he die?"

"About noon, his son said. Soon as Mister Alfred could decide what to do, he told me to come here with the news. Now I got to ride on into Wilmington to tell folks and then over to Eagles Island to tell Mister Alfred's new wife and her folks there."

"Will you come in for refreshment before you go?" she asked.

He shook his head and swung into the saddle. Without another word he was gone.

Cecilia sank down on the porch steps. Judge Maurice Moore - dear Cousin Maurice - her protector and guardian, was dead. She remembered him from the time they had lived at Brunswick. Cousin Maurice would come into The Anchor, sail his hat toward a wall peg, and call for an ale. He would inspect her dolls and listen to her tales about her kittens. He would laugh at Charlotte's antics. He would sit in conversation with Polly. Business and politics were their usual topics, but they could parley on any subject.

Once she sat in a corner and listened as Polly and Cousin Maurice discussed *Much Ado About Nothing*. It took Cecilia a long time to figure out they were talking about people in a play and not about folks in their little town of Brunswick.

Tears slipped down her checks and she wiped her face with a corner of her apron. "Oh, dear cousin, I shall miss you so terribly," she whispered. "So many, many people will miss you."

Rory Grace's wails pulled her up from the steps. "I'm coming, sweet baby. Your mommie's coming," she called. "I have a story to tell you about a great and good man. You will never know him, but you will know his story."

As she held the baby close she whispered. "This is the spring of 1777, Rory Grace Black. It's the year you were born. It's the year a good man died."

The baby seemed to be watching, listening to her words. "Cousin Maurice Moore was a patriot. He wrote letters to King George in England. He wrote pamphlets for the colonists to read. He confronted royal governors when he felt they didn't do right by the people."

She brushed Rory's hair from her forehead. "But, sweet baby, even more important than being a politician and a judge, he was a good man. He helped family. He helped your Aunt Polly and your Aunt Charlotte and me more than I can begin to ever tell you."

She searched her memory for a Bible verse Polly had made her memorize. "'His delight is in the law of the Lord; and in his law doth he meditate day and night. And he shall be like a tree planted by the rivers of water, that bringeth forth his fruit in his season.' That might well describe Cousin Maurice."

The infant had fallen asleep. "You come from good family, Rory Grace Black. Whatever you do in this life, don't you ever forget it." She put the baby in the basket and went to tend the hearth fire.

"Now my protector is gone," she whispered to herself. "I can't tell my baby that. I can't tell Rory Grace just how much on our own we are now." In spite of the warmth from the fire on the hearth, she felt a chill. "Oh, what will happen next?"

CHAPTER 20

Cecilia wasn't sure when the idea of making salt came to her. The price for salt was supposed to be fixed. The new state law said that it was, but she'd seen the price moving up. Her own supply was running low. She'd need a large quantity of salt for curing meat when fall came.

She collected every old iron pot and skillet she could find. The barn was filled with castoffs - a huge pot with a hole the size of a hammer bashed through one side, a small spider, its bottom worn thin and two trivets missing, a waffle maker with most of the prongs broken. Several misshapened harness pieces had been discarded in the tack shed and she added them to her trove of throw aways.

Then she went down to the slave cabins. Lula followed her as she poked through the abandoned buildings.

"Miss Cecilia, what you looking for?"

"Anything made of iron, Lula. Any old pot or pan."

"What for? I mean, I got my spider and my stew pot. Miss Cecilia, is you going to take my spider and my stew pot?"

Cecilia sank down on the steps of the cabin. "No, Lula, I am not going to take anything useful. I just want the old pieces. I'm going to take them to the blacksmith to make pans for collecting salt."

Lula sat down next to her. "I worked at a salt works one summer. It was where they let the sun 'vaporate the sea water." The woman let out a deep breath. "That was just about the hardest work I ever done in my life. Miss Cecilia, you ain't gonna make me do salt making, is you?"

Cecilia reached to take Lula's hand. She turned the palm up and patted it with her fingers. "Lula, I want you right here, using these hands to cook and clean. Most important, I want you using these hands to help me care for my baby."

Then she grabbed both of the woman's hands and raised them above their heads. "How wonderful to know you know about salt making. How wonderful to know I can ask you if I'm doing it right."

She jumped up to do a little dance in the yard. "I'm going into business, Lula. I'll be making something that everybody needs. We just might make some money, too."

Lula planted her elbows on her knees and sighed. "You *really* means that we got more work to do."

"Oh, posh, Lula. Who's afraid of a little work?"

Lula stood. "Miss Cecilia, if yous bound to do this salt thing, I do know where there be a pile of trash. There might be some old pots flung out there."

While they sorted through the trash, Cecilia asked questions and Lula told her everything she could about evaporation. "And it take buckets and buckets and *buckets* of that salt water to make a smidgen of salt. Ma'am, it do be hard work."

Cecilia asked, "Lula, how much is a smidgen?"

The woman held her hands apart.

"That looks like about the size of a ten pound cask. Good."

When Cecilia hitched the mare up to the cart the next morning, she had a goodly collection of old iron pieces to take into Wilmington to the blacksmith.

"Miss Cecilia." Mister Elliot greeted her even as he forced his bellows to blow across the fire in the forge.

"Good morning, sir. You seem to be busy."

The blacksmith lifted a glowing horseshoe from the fire and plunged it into a barrel of water. The sizzling of hot metal drowned out his answer. He lifted the shoe from the barrel, inspected it, threw it on the ground.

The action was so unexpected that Cecilia, about to climb down from the cart, settled back on the seat. "Mister Elliot, what's wrong?"

The man's tongs slipped from his hands to join the discarded horse shoe. He sat suddenly on a bench. "My wife's gone."

"Oh, Mister Elliot, I am so sorry. How did she die?"

"Die?" He looked at the fire. "Die?" He reached down and picked up the tongs. "She didn't die."

"Mister Elliot, you said your wife was gone."

The blacksmith picked up the shoe and began to toss it from one hand to the other. "She's gone off. Gone off with her clothes tied up in a shawl and all my savings in her pockets. She even took the ham roasting on the spit." He threw the shoe against the side of the forge. "I hope she chokes on it."

Cecilia bit her lip to keep from laughing. The man was either most distressed or most angry, she wasn't sure which. Laughing at him would never do. She stepped down from the cart, then reached back to take out one of the smaller frying pans. Holding it in front of her, she took a step toward him.

"Can you do some work for me, Mister Elliot?"

He took the pan from her, holding it at arm's length, turning it over and over. "You want this repaired? It's in pretty bad shape."

"No, I don't want any repair work. I want you to design pans to use for evaporating water to make salt."

Still holding the pan she had handed him, the blacksmith walked over to peer at the load in her cart. He shook his head as he gazed at the collection of pieces. "How many salt pans you want?"

"Ten. I want ten pans. They can't be too big because they'll be too heavy. They have to have loop handles for stick carrying. I'm not building a factory. I'm going for the evaporation method."

The blacksmith picked up a harness buckle from the pile in the wagon, polished it on his leather apron, and held it out to the light. He threw it back and lifted out a pot. He rubbed a side of it with his hand, then nodded.

"Miss Cecilia, you want these salt pans about so big?" He measured space in the air with his hands.

"That looks about right," she answered.

"You don't have enough here for ten pans. Eight, maybe." The blacksmith shook his head. "With the wife gone, it'll take at least two weeks to make that many. With all the men off to war, she was suppose to be my helper. She said she wouldn't. Miss Cecilia, that's why she run off like she done."

Again Cecilia choked back giggles. The blacksmith's wife was a petite woman. Cecilia could not image her working at the forge. She took a deep breath and stated a price for the work.

"Eight shillings, Mister Elliot. That's a shilling a pan and I've supplied most of the material." The dickering began.

"And I need workers, Mister Elliot."

"You ain't gonna find any men worth their salt." The blacksmith grinned.

Cecilia could tell he was beginning to enjoy himself. He'd gotten her up to eleven shillings, three pence for the work. "If you'll pardon me for saying it again, ma'am, ain't no men left in this town worth their salt who'll do that kind of work."

Rory Grace, from her basket in the cart, began to fret. Cecilia lifted the baby to her shoulder, crooning to her.

The man gazed at the infant for a moment. "Miss Cecilia, I might know somebody. When you come back to get your pans, I just might have a suggestion for you."

"Mister Elliot, it has been a pleasure doing business with you. Mister Macdougal will be coming in next week and I'll have him stop by to check with you. I'll come back the week after that to pay you and get the pans. I do thank you."

She felt the man's eyes on her as she flipped the reins across the horse's back and headed for Three Sisters.

Henrietta wrapped Cecilia and Rory in a warm hug as they came in the door. Leah whooped, "Lawdy, it be good to see you, child. Let me hold that baby."

"She's fussy right now, Leah. She wants her lunch. And so do I. What smells so delicious?"

"Goat's meat," Leah said. "We killed one of the goats yesterday. Miss Polly found a fresh bed of mint and made a jell last night. That rump's been roasting since before daylight, soaking up the mint and peppercorn and a touch of mustard. By the time you feed that baby, we'll be ready to slice up a portion."

"We have a letter from Charlotte," Henrietta said. "It's kind of sad, in a way. Would you like me to read it to you?"

Cecilia nodded and settled in a rocking chair to feed Rory Grace while Mama began to read.

> *Dearest Mama and all.*
> *Writing in haste. Must get this to the messenger.*
> *We left C Town in haste after bombardment. Came*
> *to this plantation outside Savannah. Little Jonathan fretful*
> *but took the trip without illness. Alexander had a fever,*
> *but is now better. My dear Johnny found us here. Stayed for*
> *three days with us before going back to his regiment.*
> *Now M. Reynolds says we must again move and we're*
> *packing to go west to one of her houses in upper S Carolina.*
> *I don't yet know where.*

Henrietta looked up and Cecilia saw the tears in her eyes. "Charlotte is not having an easy life."

"Mama, do you know anyone who is? At least Mistress Reynolds has servants. She has money and land. Charlotte may have to move about, but she won't be alone and she won't be hungry."

Henrietta dabbed at her eyes. "Charlotte was never as strong as you and Polly."

Cecilia put her sleeping baby in her basket. With a carving knife she cut a slice of meat and put it on a plate. Adding beans, potatoes and onions from a small pot hanging over the fire she began to eat before she spoke.

"Mama, we do what we have to do." Cecilia tore a hunk of bread from a yeast loaf and slathered butter on it. She licked her fingers. "Finish reading the letter."

"I was almost through. She just ends by saying she hopes all of us are well." Henrietta waved the paper at her. "Cecilia, you don't have to criticize your sister."

Cecilia looked at Leah and rolled her eyes. Leah threw up her hands, as if to say not to involve her in the conversation.

"Mama, tell Polly I'm sorry I missed her. I'll be back in two weeks time. I have to see the blacksmith about the salt business I'm trying to get started. If you hear of any men for hire, I need three or four good workers."

"Oh, Cecilia, you just got here. I thought you'd at least spend the night," Henrietta protested.

"Mama, I have a farm to run, with very little help to do it." She kissed Henrietta's forehead before she picked up the basket with her sleeping child. "I hope this little one will sleep till I get home."

As the horse pulled the cart north on Market Street, Henrietta and Leah waved her out of sight.

CHAPTER 21

Y ou said two weeks and that's exactly what it's been. Ain't no men available,"
Mister Elliott said, when Cecilia jumped down from the cart at the blacksmith's
shed. "The men who would be of help to you have gone to war. I do have a
woman wants the work." He began loading the salt pans and other equipment in her cart
as he talked.

"A woman?"

The blacksmith nodded toward a bench. "Evangeline Elliott, sitting over there.
She was married and he took a fever and died. Then she married my brother 'fore he
went off with the militia. My brother died of small pox while they was still in camp."
He swung the last iron pan on the cart. "Miss Cecilia, Evangeline's a good worker."

Even before Cecilia reached her, the woman was standing, pleading. "I need to
work, ma'am. I admit I need money, but I most need to be busy."

Cecilia nodded.

"I know another widow in my situation that can do the work. Eva Nixon, she is.
She's got two girls to bring along. They's named for flowers. The girls, I mean. Lily and
Lilac. Now ain't that pretty." Evangeline's words escaped in spurts. "They're big
enough - the girls is - to handle what has to be done. If you've got eight pans to work,
the four of us can do it, except maybe chopping wood. We might need help there."

Cecilia held out her hand and took Evangeline's. "You're hired. When can you
start?"

"Today, ma'am. Me and Eva can go today. We ain't got much to pack."

"Be back here in two hours, then," Cecilia said. "I'm going to visit with my mother. We'll leave for the farm when I get back."

Cecilia left the cart at the blacksmith's and, swinging Rory's basket by her side, walked to the tavern.

"Cecilia," Henrietta cried, as she came in the door. "How wonderful to see you. Now if we would just hear from Charlotte."

"No more letters?" Cecilia asked Polly.

"No, we only have rumors that drift like smoke pyramiding around the pots on the hearth." Polly lifted Rory from her basket. "Now this has validity. Sister, what are you feeding this child? How she has grown."

Mama fretted. "All the fighting last summer. Mistress Reynolds moving them all about the countryside. That's the last we've heard."

"Mama, Robert Howe was at the battles at Sullivan Island. He wrote his kin about renaming the fort there Fort Moultrie. The Moultrie family is connected to everybody, including the Reynolds. Surely if he'd heard anything about Charlotte and John he would have found a way to send word."

"Bobby Howe may be a Brigadier General. He may be a brilliant military man. He may write about battles and victories." Mama's knitting needles sawed back and forth through the deep blue yarn she was fashioning into a shawl. "He's said nothing about important things like how people were faring."

"Polly, how is shipping?" Cecilia asked, as much to change the subject as to know the answer.

Her sister laughed. "Oh, ships are getting through. You would not believe some of the merchandise that's being unloaded. Umbrellas and wigs." Polly held an imaginary shade over her head and rubbed a hand across her mobcap to plump her hair. "French wines and kegs of rum." She pretended to drink from a mug. "And folk are buying."

"What we need is sulfur, sugar and salt," Cecilia said. "Is there nothing useful in any of these shipments?"

"Frying pans and skillets, nails and molasses, some spices and medicines. I did buy some poppy extract for a dear sum. Prices are soaring on everything."

As she was leaving, Polly walked out the door with Cecilia. "Supplies of staples are dwindling, so your idea for the salt works should pay off. Did you find men to work?"

"I found women." Cecilia grinned at her sister. "Polly, you and I know women can do most of the work men can do. I'm going to have a successful business venture."

With her four new workers and their meager belongings bouncing in the cart, Cecilia drove the mare to the farm. She got them settled in the barn for the night and at daybreak they headed for her property on the water across from Topsail Sound. Cecilia drove the cart filled with equipment while Simple followed with the wagon piled high with split firewood.

Evangeline picked the site for the tents in which they would sleep. She, with Lily and Lilac, quickly drove the pegs and stretched the canvas as if they'd always been doing this kind of work. Eva began scooping out shallow sand pits in which to lay the fires. With Simple's help she set the short-legged tripods to hold the pans. Together they placed kindling in the pits. Only a few strokes on her flint were needed to get the first embers glowing.

Cecilia scouted along the edges of the sound for yucca plants to make shampoo and soft soap for bathing. She nodded to herself as she came back to see the settled camp and the women at work. She put her load of plants in the cart. "Evangeline, you've gotten quite a bit finished."

"Yes, ma'am. I told you I need to be busy. This'll be a pleasant place to spend the summer."

"I saw several downed trees nearby. If you give out of wood before we get back next week, I think you can get what you need from there. Fishing should be good. That will supplement the food you have."

Evangeline grinned. "Miss Cecilia, I'm partial to crabs. I got me a hankering to go crabbing right along that little run." She pointed to a place where water drained from a swampy area into the sound waters.

As Cecilia headed home she felt she'd really started a worthwhile business. If her world would just stay quiet for a while, she could finish planting her fields and look forward to harvest. And learn to ride.

In early spring she'd found a boy's saddle stored in the barn. With Benjamin's help, she learned to saddle the little mare. Gathering her skirts about her legs, she mounted, walking the horse around and around the yard, down the lane to the road, and finally out to the fields.

Each time she got on the horse, Lula fussed. "Miss Cecilia, a woman don't ride like a man. It just ain't done."

"You sound like my mother."

"Well, ma'am, I don't know if that be good or bad. Somebody need to tell you that sitting across that horse ain't done." Lula shook her head. "Ma'am, it just ain't done.

Mister Macdougal added his comments. "Miss Cecilia, there is a perfectly good side saddle in the tack room. If you want to ride, you can use that."

"The side saddle probably belonged to Emma Black. I'm living in her house and cooking in her kitchen. I'm wearing her old clothes and eating off of her china. Macdougal, I don't want her saddle."

"But, Miss Cecilia, you're going to hurt yourself." His face turned a deep red, a blush starting below his neck and spreading to his hairline.

She gazed out over the fields. "Appearances! I really thought you and Lula, of all people, would understand. I'm not going to hurt myself riding astride any more than hoeing corn. Or chopping wood. Or driving the cart. Or pruning limbs in that wonderful orchard we found. Or making sure we all have enough to eat. Macdougal, I'm going to make a go of this farm. I'll do anything I have to do. That includes learning to ride."

She set her foot in the stirrup and swung herself into the saddle. "When I learn how to ride this sweet little mare, I'm going to put myself on that big black stallion."

As she trotted down the lane, she heard Mister Macdougal let loose with a string of swear words before he yelled after her, "Cecilia, be careful."

CHAPTER 22

When Ricky Smith limped into the yard at noon on a late summer day, leading his horse and followed by two chained slaves, Cecilia just sat speechless on the porch steps. What would Ricky be doing here?

"I bring you gifts," Ricky stated. He gestured for the men to sit under the maple tree.

Cecilia covered her face with her hands, watching him through her separated fingers.

He came and sat beside her, putting a portmanteau on the steps at her feet.

"I'll play you a game of marbles for 'em," he said, nodding toward the men who sat under the tree.

"I always win, so what will *you* put up?" she asked.

He grinned. "Don't have much. My hunting knife?"

"Ricky, why are you here? Are Donny and Timmie in trouble?"

"Official business. I am the new deputy for Sheriff Benning. So this is very official business. It seems that Mister Alfred has finally finished getting Judge Moore's estate settled. The judge left you some letters and books. They're in this bag. Man, it's heavy. Must be the books. Those two slaves over there." He waved toward the tree. "What do you want me to do with the slaves?"

"Take off the chains." She stood and walked toward the tree. "Do you know their names?"

Ricky slid a leather thong from his belt and selected a key. As he unlocked the chains he answered. "This is Joel." He draped the chains over his arm. "This is Octavius. It'll be written in the papers."

"Do they have anything? Clothes? Blankets?"

He shook his head. "Nothing, Cecilia."

"Thank you, I think," Cecilia said. Then she called, "Lula, please bring water for these men to drink."

"Always good to see you, Cecilia." Ricky swung into his saddle and waved as he rode away.

When Mister Macdougal came up from the corn field she sent Joel and Octavius with him to the creek to bathe. "Have them scrub those rags they're wearing," she said. "I'll send Little Martin with something for them to wear." She climbed to the attic, looking for clothes. By the time Benjamin and Simple trudged in from pulling peanuts, she and Lula had cooked a hen in pastry to add to the vegetables in the constantly bubbling stew pot.

She had Benjamin and Lula move the kitchen table into the yard, where they might catch the slightest breeze while they ate their supper meal. Simple had made a tray for the high chair. Now Rory Grace pounded on the polished wood, keeping up a constant jabber. Cecilia laughed at her baby trying so hard to talk.

Then, as she'd been doing all summer, she asked each of them about the day. "We got the peanuts, Miss Cecilia," Benjamin reported. "Tonight'll be clear, so we'll get 'em into the shed in the morning. You does want 'em to stay loose whiles they dry, don't you?"

"Yes, Benjamin, I do. Good work. Good work, Simple."

Little Martin was eagerly waiting his turn. "I got several baskets of apples, Miss Cecilia. I put a basketful on the kitchen porch, like you said. And I fed a few rotty ones to the pigs. I packed the rest in the barn cellar, all covered over with straw." He frowned.

"Problem?" Cecilia asked.

"I didn't get all the apples, Miss Cecilia. There be more than we thought. At least a half a wagon load more. The plums need gathering. The figs is ripe."

"You don't have a problem. You need help." They had finished eating and Old Mart was weaving a chair bottom. Benjamin sharpened the prongs of a wooden pitchfork. Simple twisted brush for a broom. Mister Macdougal scraped on a deer hide. She looked at Joel and Octavius. "Do either of you have a special skill?"

Joel cleared his throat before he said, "I be good with a hammer."

Octavius shook his head. "No, ma'am."

"It's up to you, Little Martin. Pick your helper."

"Miss Cecilia, if I pick the person I most wants to work with, it'd be Simple. But if you needs him for the peanuts, I pick Joel."

"Tell you what, Mister Honest Martin. You take both Simple and Joel tomorrow. You hitch the little mare to the cart and you see if you can bring in the whole crop. Apples and plums and figs." Cecilia lifted the sleepy baby from her chair. "Remember how fragile the ripe figs are. You need to put moss in the bottom of the baskets for the figs."

The grin on the boy's face told her she'd made a good decision. Simple laid the finished broom aside and took out his reed flute. She carried Rory into the house, feeling a strange calm in the haunting melody that followed her.

By candlelight she dumped the contents of the portmanteau on her bed. She found the papers for the slaves. Their transfer was signed and sealed. She picked up a letter addressed to Cecilia Moore Black - Widow of Kenneth Black. She unfolded the pages and sat in her rocking chair to read.

> *Cousin Cecilia, my heart is heavy. I am so sorry that Kenneth was taken from us. It is always difficult to lose someone we love. In this case, it should not have been. Theodora Black continued to confess to striking his son and leaving him in the woods, even as he mounted the steps to the gallows. The most difficult part ~ ~ he seems to think he had provocation because Kenneth would not give him what he demanded. I suspect that the boy had always been under Dorie Black's domination and that standing up to his father was not an expected act. At my urging Dorie signed papers giving you everything. If you need his assistance my son Alfred will serve as guardian. However, the wording of these papers will not require his signature or his permission for anything you wish to do with the properties. You are a rather wealthy woman in land. The slaves belong to you. The bondage papers for Mac Macdougal, the overseer, are herein included and he will continue if you wish not to release him. He has another two years to serve out his indenture. You do not have much in coinage. The monies you will find here are from the sale of a property Dorie owned elsewhere.*
>
> *The Lord's Blessing on You and Your endeavours.*
> *Judge Maurice Moore, Kinsman*
> *Hereby set my seal **

On a separate piece of paper, Alfred had added a note.

> *Cecilia, my father wrote his letter to you just weeks before his death. He told me of his wishes for you and I have tried to carry out his instructions to the best of my ability. I have also made sure all of the papers and land documents are included. Let me know if I can ever be of assistance to you.*
>
> *Alfred Moore, Kinsman*
> *written from Eagles Island*
> *Aug 1777*

Cecilia held the letter to her heart. "Oh, dear Cousin Maurice," she whispered. She reached to pick up the books that lay scattered across the bed coverlet. The volume of William Shakespeare's *Love's Labours Lost* she tossed aside. She flipped open *As You Like It* to read aloud. " 'All the world's a stage, and all the men and women merely players: They have their exits and their entrances . . .' "

She held the book in her lap. "Yes, we do come and go. Cousin Maurice, it is Polly who loves to read," Cecilia said to the page. "I'm not sure I can get through a whole play of Shakespeare."

A leather pouch, the size of a man's shoe, was the last item on the bed. She pulled open the thong and peered inside. Coins! The candlelight gleamed on silver Spanish dollars and Portuguese gold Johannes, on French francs and worn English shillings.

She closed the pouch and stood, holding it to her chest. She was afraid to spill the coins out to count them, but she knew there had to be the value of a hundred pounds in her hands. Where could she hide this much money? Where could it possibly be safe? She knew of no hiding place in the house or the barn. The few coins she and Polly had secreted in her trunk were safe, but she didn't want to disturb their hiding place. She slipped the pouch under her pillow and stood looking at the bulge it made. Hiding this was going to take some serious thought.

One thing she didn't have to think about. She wouldn't have to borrow for next year's seed, even if the price was dear.

CHAPTER 23

I n the late fall Cecilia knew it was time to bring the women in from the salt works. Their venture had been more successful than she could have hoped, but storms were threatening. About midmorning, as they approached the camp, Simple pulled on the reins. He placed a finger to his lips, shook his head and slid down from the wagon seat. His long strides took him to the edge of the trees growing thick along the wagon path. Now she heard the sounds that had alerted him: a muffled oath, a man's whoop.

Cecilia climbed from the wagon and silently followed Simple. She caught sight of his shirt as he wound his way through the thick underbrush, following the rising cackles of merriment coming from the salt camp.

Where the last clump of yaupon bushes stopped at a sandy ridge bordering the sound's water, she froze. Two men sat just a few yards away from where she stood. They were clapping accompaniment to their licentious shouts of encouragement.

A man was holding Evangeline's tied hands while his mate tried to mount her. Evangeline was fighting. She tore her hands from the man's grasp. With a mighty blow she brought her bound fists down on the head of the man in front of her. He toppled into the sand. The man behind her grabbed for her hands, but Evangeline was on her knees, hitting at him.

Lily and Lilac sprawled across an overturned tent shelter. Their blood trickled across the heavy canvas, adding to a crimson pool in the sand. Cecilia knew, even from this distance, that they were dead. Eva was propped against one of the tent pegs, her arms clutched against her belly as she tried to push her insides back into her body.

Cecilia threaded her way through the undergrowth, heading for the wagon. She took the rifle from under the seat, stuffed paper wadding in her mouth and shoved the powder horn in her pocket. Back at the edge of the yaupon bushes she leaned against a maple tree while she dropped the ball down the barrel, poked in the wadding and sifted the powder into the firing pan. Only then did she look up.

Simple, wielding a knife, slashed at the two men who had been watching the action. Evangeline was battling the two men who were attacking her. Cecilia sighted, waited until one of the men near Evangeline drew back for a blow, and fired. The man flailed his arms in the air and with a horrible scream, pitched forward. Evangeline scooped sand in the other man's face and kicked him in the groin. He went to his knees, yelling oaths.

Cecilia was trying to reload. She dropped the first cartridge she took from her pocket. The priming horn shook as she tilted it and powder spilled down the front of her bodice. She clenched her fist to still the shaking in her hand, then tilted the horn again to fill the firing pan. She aimed toward the two men fighting with Simple. She could see blood trickling down Simple's forehead into his eyes.

One man, wielding his hunting knife, slashed out at him. Simple backed up a step and again swung his knife. The other man was moving to get behind Simple.

Cecilia fired.

The shot caught the man in the chest. The man with the hunting knife whirled to look toward the woods. Simple plunged his knife into the man's neck with a viscious thrust and ripped out the blade. Blood spurted from the wound as the man tumbled over and over down a dune.

Simple turned from the man's toppling body and ran toward Evangeline. He pushed between the woman and man she was still kicking. He stuck the knife in the man's chest and brought it out with such force that he lost his balance and fell to his knees. Cecilia saw great red blobs spray on the sand as the dying man fell backward.

Evangeline sank to the ground, rocking back and forth, her hands covering her face. Simple knelt beside her, plunging his knife over and over into the loose sand.

Cecilia took a deep breath, pushed herself away from the tree and stepped out of the bushes. She walked first to Eva, whose eyes were now dull and lifeless. She reached out to close the lids over the sightless stare.

Cecilia sat down next to Evangeline. She took the woman's hands between her own and spoke to Simple. "Cut her ropes, please."

Simple looked at the knife as if he had not been aware of what he was doing. He slowly reached up to sever the bonds. Then he crawled a few feet away and heaved.

Evangeline looked toward Simple. "Bless that man," she whispered. "Bless any man what finds hurting folks the same as sickness."

"Are *you* hurt?" Cecilia asked. "Cuts? Bones broken?"

The woman ran her hands up her arms, then peered toward her bare feet. "Miss Cecilia, I think I'm just bruised. Maybe cut up some. Soon's I catch my breath we'd best get this place cleaned up. Eva don't always leave things neat."

"Eva's dead," Cecilia blurted.

"Dead? They kill her? Miss Cecilia, what about the girls? Eva's girls?"

Cecilia shook her head. "They are dead, too. Evangeline, please tell me what happened here."

The woman heaved herself up, feet spread apart, fists on her hips, as if to give herself a platform from which she could speak. "The men rode in this morning. Said they smelled the fire smoke and ham cooking. Asked for breakfast. So we extend hospitality."

She looked toward the row of salt pans. "The girls was building up the fires. They come back and we all sat down, sort of in a circle. And those four men ate at that ham and mush like they was real hungry. And then they finished with the food and start to make remarks to the girls."

"Oh, Evangeline."

The woman kept on telling her horrible tale. "They tied me first. Staked me facing the water. Miss Cecilia, I couldn't get them ropes loose for nothing. I had to listen while they set in on Eva. Least I think they took her first. They said something about the girls need to know how it was done."

The woman's body began to shake. She waved her arms up and down to the rhythm of the words she screamed. "I couldn't do nothing. I couldn't get loose. I couldn't do nothing. I couldn't get loose."

While they talked, Simple waded into the edge of the sound water to bathe his face and arms. He picked up a bucket, dipped it full of the salty water and dumped it over Evangeline's head.

"What for you do that?" she sputtered. "What for you got me all wet?"

Instead of answering Evangeline, Simple looked at Cecilia. "M-m-m-issy, we g-go now."

"Simple, we can't leave yet. We have to take care of -" She looked at the mess of the salt camp, at the bodies lying so still.

"Get the horse hitched up to the cart. We'll put Eva and the girls -" Again she stopped. Her thoughts and her mouth didn't seem to want to work together.

She tried again. "We need to load the salt barrels. In our wagon."

He nodded.

"Load all the pans." She waved her arms to include the whole camp. She had known she could push through to make plans if she just kept trying. "Everything, Simple."

Again he nodded, then held up one finger.

"First?" Cecilia asked. "First, you and Evangeline hitch the horse to the cart. Load the bodies."

Then she stopped short, wheeling toward the woman. Evangeline's dunking had quieted her and she stood so motionless that Cecilia was alarmed. She stepped in front of her and spoke quietly. "Evangeline, how did those men get to this camp? Did they have horses?"

The woman's massive frame shuddered. Cecilia feared she would begin screaming again, but she answered in the same tone Cecilia had used.

"They got horses tied up over in the woods."

"Can you show Simple where they are? We need to take the men and tying them on the horses is the easiest way."

"Miss Cecilia, I glad to have a task to do. Want them men draped over the saddle? Or we gonna tie 'em up in canvas?"

"That will -" She choked bile as the image of another body assaulted her. She could see the men bringing their cloth-filled burden from the woods, crossing the yard, going in the house. She moaned aloud. "Oh, Kenneth. Oh, my Kenneth." She clamped both hands over her mouth to silence herself. She wouldn't go back. She had to think of *now*. She had to deal with what was happening *here*. She could not bring Kenneth back.

"Go away," she yelled at the apparition that wanted to take her over.

"Miss Cecilia? What you talking 'bout? Where you want me to go?"

Evangeline's questions drove the ghostly shadow from view.

"Yes," she managed to say. "Tie the men across their saddles."

It was full dark when Cecilia, driving the wagon, saw the torch light burning at the lane that led to the farm. She turned on the seat to look back at Evangeline driving the cart. She could see the shapes of the horses that Simple commanded.

"Almost home," Cecilia called to them. Turning back toward the light she whispered to herself, "Almost home." Even as she spoke the words she realized it was the first time she'd really felt the Black farm her home.

CHAPTER 24

Lula came running from the kitchen as their caravan pulled into the yard. "Oh, Miss Cecilia, we be so worried. Just 'bout worried out of our minds. Oh, Miss Cecilia, why you so late?" She stood opened mouthed as she looked at Evangeline driving the cart.

Mister Macdougal raced from his little house. He stood on the wheel, reached up and lifted Cecilia from the wagon seat. He didn't put her down. He stood holding her as if to let her go would be to lose her.

"Macdougal," she croaked in his ear.

He released her from the embrace and stepped back to look her up and down. He whispered, "Does the blood belong to you?"

Cecilia glanced at her stained bodice and apron. "No."

"What happened, Miss Cecilia?" Lula tugged at her arm. "You looks like you be in a war."

Cecilia nodded. She looked back toward the cart, where Evangeline sat motionless. "Mister Macdougal, please go help Simple with the bodies of the men. There are four of them and I think we'd best lock them up somewhere to keep animals or anything else from getting to them in the night. Maybe shut them in the corn crib. The horses need care. There are four riding horses and two pack horses. You can hobble them behind the barn. Make sure they have water."

"Ma'am -"

"Macdougal, I'll talk about it later," Cecilia said. "Lula, get Benjamin to help us. Then go take care of Evangeline. Take her in the kitchen and make sure she eats something."

"Miss Ce -"

"Go," Cecilia screamed. She yanked at the reins of the horse. She backed the animal to push the wagon through the barn door. She unloaded a salt pan and hung it from a peg on the wall.

Benjamin appeared at her side.

"Get the cellar door under the barn open and start taking these salt barrels down there. We'll leave three of the barrels for the sheriff to see, when he gets here. The rest we're going to hide." She lifted another pan from the wagon bed. "Benjamin, do you understand?"

"Yes, ma'am." He lifted the trap door, hefted a barrel to his shoulder and made his way down the ladder.

When he came up from the first trip, he stepped in front of her. "Miss Cecilia, I needs light down there. I gonna get a torch."

She nodded at him and went to help with the horses.

"Mister Macdougal," she said, as she bent to hobble the last horse, "as soon as it's light enough, you have to ride into Wilmington and get the sheriff."

She sank to the ground and leaned her head against the side of the barn. "I don't want to divulge to you what happened. When you tell Sheriff Benning that we need him here, you can only tell him what you've seen. You have to trust me on this."

Macdougal sat beside her and took her hand. "Miss Cecilia, I trust you."

"Please bring up several buckets of water from the creek." She shuddered. "I have to bathe before I can think about sleep."

"Yes, ma'am."

His hand felt warm and comforting. For another long moment Cecilia let herself rest before another quiver shook her. She pulled her hand from his embrace and stood.

"I'll bring the water up to the kitchen now," he said.

She nodded as she walked away.

With the first rooster crow for the sun, Cecilia swung her feet to the floor. She heard a horse neigh, as if in protest at being called to work so early. From the window she watched Mister Macdougal gallop across the yard.

The little sleep she'd had roiled with nightmares. Eva's sightless eyes stared up at her. Visions of the girls' bodies etched a pain that heaved at her stomach. Simple's repeated knife thrusts in the sand, only swooshes of sound when he'd forced the blade up and down to cleanse it, echoed like drums in her horrible fantasies.

She rubbed her temples, hoping to ease an ache that pushed from the center of her brain. "Peace," she whispered. "I killed two men. Will I ever again have peace?"

Rory Grace, asleep in her crib, stretched and turned her head toward the wall.

"You stay asleep, sweet child," she breathed.

By the time Cecilia had the fire built up in the kitchen, Lula was crossing the yard with a basket in each hand. Little Mart followed her, his arms loaded with wood for the hearth. The woman put her baskets on the kitchen porch, took down the water buckets and headed for the creek. Mart carefully stacked his load in the wood box. Without a word he went out. Through the open door Cecilia saw that he was going toward the cabins. She followed.

The men all came out on the cabin porches as she approached.

"Benjamin, did you finish the corn field yesterday?"

"Yes, ma'am," he answered.

Cecilia nodded. "Benjamin, with Mister Macdougal gone, you are in charge. Make sure Old Martin is up. I want him very visible. He can sit on his porch and weave baskets or string a fish net. But out in the open."

The slaves stared at her.

She clinched her fists. Her voice stayed calm. "When Sheriff Benning gets here I want everybody going about their business. Do you understand?"

Benjamin continued to stare at her. "You put me in charge, Miss Cecilia?"

Simple forced words. "H-h-he can d-do it."

"I know he can." Cecilia's fists knotted so tightly she felt the ends of her fingers tingle. The ache in the center of her head, threatening since she rose from her bed, throbbed. "There are seven bodies here. Lula and I laid out Eva and her daughters as best we could. The men who killed them are stacked in the corn crib. That's what Sheriff Benning is going to find. But I want him to see what else we have here."

She wanted to scream, but kept her voice soft. "We have a small farm. It's run by a woman. There are only you and an indentured servant to protect anything we have. So many rogues are riding, stealing and killing. They don't belong to the British. They don't belong to the patriot cause. They don't belong anywhere. As long as these lawless ruffians roam the country side, we will do what we have to do to defend ourselves."

She lifted her fists and beat against the side of the cabin. "You will help me." Her fists struck at the logs. Thud. "We will get in our crop." Thud. "We have to protect Simple." Thud. "Simple killed two white men. For me. I will protect him. I will."

Lula grabbed Cecilia's hands. "We understands. Benjamin and me understands. Simple do. My boy do. Joel and Octavius do. Miss Cecilia, my old uncle will behave hisself. I promise you that."

Cecilia gripped the woman's arms. "Lula, make sure to fix them food for a midday meal. I killed two men, but my people will not go hungry."

CHAPTER 25

ecilia stood on the front porch to welcome Sheriff Benning when he rode into the
yard behind Mister Macdougal. Both men had their hats tilted to their eyebrows
as the middle-of-the-day sun's glare baked down on them.

"Sheriff, I am sorry your visit to the Black farm is for such an awful reason."

He swung from his horse. "So am I, Miss Cecilia. Mac did bring disturbing
news. Are you injured?"

"No." She shook her head. "No, but there's so much lawlessness going on.
Men riding here and there, with what seems to be no purpose."

"Oh, they have a purpose. Theft is a major part of their riding raids." The
sheriff fanned his face with his hat. "You'd best show me these men Mac said you
killed. It's most warm for September. In this weather they're getting ripe, for sure.
Then you can tell me the whole of the story."

Cecilia began to gag as she approached the corn crib. The sheriff covered his
mouth with his handkerchief. Mister Macdougal opened the door to point to the canvas
wrapped bodies of the four men before he turned to heave.

"Where did the canvas come from?" Sheriff Benning asked.

"The tents the women were using. Mister Macdougal did tell you this all
happened at the salt works, didn't he?" Cecilia answered.

As the sheriff unwound the material from the head of one of the men, Cecilia
turned her back. "Sir, the two tents were torn down, the fabric cut and ripped. Several of

the salt pans were flung up-side-down in the sand. Clothing was strewn everywhere. With all the damage done around the campsite, those women fought." Her voice broke, as she remembered the scene.

"This man is Jake Tanner," the sheriff interrupted. "Lives up the river on a small farm."

Cecilia looked toward the door of the crib to see him unwrapping other bodies. He pointed. "This one's his brother, Neillie. They've both been in trouble, but nothing I've heard about before can compare with this raid, Miss Cecilia."

Mister Macdougal was peering at the faces. "Sheriff, I believe the man there jumped ship at the port a few months back. I heard something about it when I was in town buying supplies. The ship captain said he was a troublemaker and he didn't intend to spend much time trying to get him back."

"Name?" Sheriff Benning asked.

"I don't remember a name, sir. The ship was out of Charles Town. The captain nearly lost the ship running through a host of British vessels and wasn't inclined to worry too much about a deserter. Miss Cecilia, it was the last ship bringing mail from your sister, if you recall when that was."

"February, I think," she said.

"This last man? Know him?" asked the sheriff.

Both of them shook their heads.

"Sheriff, what are you going to do with these bodies?" Cecilia asked.

"We'll load them on your cart and take them into Wilmington. Bury them there. We have to present all this to a judge. Close the door, Mac," Sheriff Benning said.

He walked several paces away and spoke over his shoulder. "Where are the others? The women? Mac said three women were killed."

Cecilia led the way to the cabins. She pushed open the door, taking a step inside. Sheriff Benning came in behind her and walked over to the girls laid out on the floor. "They're so young."

"Ten and twelve," Cecilia said.

"Their necks are broken!" Sheriff Benning took off his hat and held it against his chest. "Those men broke their necks. They weren't planning to leave anybody alive. Miss Cecilia, if you had missed -"

He crushed the hat in both hands. "If you had missed your shot -" His voice faltered. "If the slave hadn't -"

He gazed down at Eva. "She's butchered. Butchered! I've been at this job a long time. I've seen a lot of knife fights. Fights on the waterfront and brawls in the taverns. Beatings and fisticuffs on the street. I've never seen a man cut up like this. Certainly never a woman."

He rushed from the cabin and sank to the ground, his forehead on his knees.

Cecilia didn't know that Lula had followed then until she handed the sheriff a gourd of water. "It be fresh from the creek, sir."

The sheriff swished the water around in his mouth and spit. He took several gulps before he handed the gourd back to Lula. She refilled it from a bucket which she handed to Macdougal. He, too, rinsed his mouth before drinking.

Sheriff Benning squared his shoulders, as if ready for blows he could not yet see. "Well, Miss Cecilia, I guess you'd best tell me what happened."

"Let's go into the parlour, Sir. There's a breeze there and we'll be more comfortable. It may take a while to tell you everything."

Sitting on the edge of her chair, Cecilia started her story with the part where Simple heard a noise, and continued through the decision to put the men's bodies in the corn crib. "Evangeline was a big help with everything. Today she's out in the field working, like it was what she did every day. We thought laying out Eva and her daughters in the cabin would be the best place for them to rest.

"Sheriff, what are we to do with Eva? Her husband was dead before she came to Wilmington. She had no family except for her daughters. I could bury them all here, I guess. It's the Black family plot, but my daughter and I seem to be the last of the Blacks." Cecilia twisted her fingers together. "Sir, that's almost the scariest thing I've yet said to you."

"Miss Cecilia, you have had a time of it. Your husband murdered. Your father-in-law hanged for the deed." Sheriff Benning stood and walked over to look out the window.

"Now you have this incident when you were trying to earn a living with the salt works. I don't think there is much permanence in anything anymore. Everybody is right. The patriots are right in their discontent with King George. The British are right in their determination to hold to the colonies and have them bow to the wishes of Parliament. The raiders are right in the belief that they're owed property of some kind, whether it be land or coin or extra food for the table. They all go off to prove their rights."

He came back to sink into his chair. "You've the right to protect what's yours and to protect your very life when it stands in the way of another's right. No legal problem there. Now I have to figure out what to do about your slave Simple."

"Simple?" Cecilia just looked at the sheriff. "There's nothing to do about Simple. You thank him for saving me. For saving Evangeline. For getting us from the sound back to the farm. For going to the field today when his head's busted open and the cuts on his arms are still raw. Sir, you leave Simple alone."

"People aren't gonna like it."

"Like what?"

"Like the fact that a slave killed white men." The sheriff sat forward in his chair. "People are worried about a slave revolt with this war going on. To learn that one of them has killed a white man is going to be most worrisome for some folk."

"He killed to protect," Cecilia stated. "Simple was protecting me and you know it. That's what you tell your worried people. You talk about permanence and property and rights like the idea doesn't translate. It does. It comes down to this. Simple saved my life. He deserves thanksgiving. Nothing less. Certainly a whole lot more if I had it to give."

She got to her feet. "Now I'll call Simple and Evangeline in from the field. You can talk with them. Then you're going to load up those ruffians -" She paused. "The bodies of those murdering men. You're going to take them away. I don't care where."

She hurried from the parlour and was calling to Lula before she cleared the porch. "Go down to the field and tell them all to come to the house."

Lula ran.

From behind her Cecilia heard Mister Macdougal speaking. "Sheriff Benning, she usually gets her way because she's usually right. She's right about Simple."

The sound of a galloping horse, turning into the lane, stopped him. A woman was driving a buggy, leaning forward, slapping the reins across the animal's back. Another woman was screaming, but Cecilia couldn't understand her words. Behind the buggy a man on a horse appeared to be chasing them.

As the buggy slid to halt in the yard, Henrietta's cries of distress were very clear. "You're going to kill us. Pauline, slow down. Pauline Moore, you're going to kill us."

The man on horse back reached to grab the reins on the buggy. "Sorry, sheriff. I couldn't stop them from coming. In fact, sir, I had trouble keeping up with them."

"Ricky?" Cecilia said. "Mama, hush. Polly's not going to kill you."

Polly leaped from the buggy and ran to Cecilia. She clutched at her sister's shoulders and held on as if one of them might fly away. "You're not hurt?"

Cecilia began to giggle. "Oh, Polly." The giggles turned into great belly guffaws that sent them both to their knees. Her laughter turned to sobs as they leaned into each other. Cecilia gasped between the sobs that shook her. "What *are* you doing here?"

Her sister was crying too hard to answer.

It was Henrietta who yelled from the buggy. "It's too dangerous for you to stay here. We're taking you back to town. You girls get off the ground. I'll not have you behaving like that."

Polly scrambled to her feet. "Cecilia, we were so worried. The news Ricky brought was jumbled. We wanted to see that you were all right. But we're not taking you anywhere you don't want to go."

"Good," Cecilia said. She crossed her arms and looked up from her seat on the ground. "Very good, because I'm not leaving home."

All the men, Lula and Evangeline with them, stood at the edge of the yard.

Sheriff Benning looked at them and then down at her. "Miss Cecilia, I'll just have your slaves load up those dead bodies. Ricky and I will get them back to town and he can bring your wagon back in a day or two."

She got to her feet and brushed at her skirt.

"As for that other matter," the sheriff said, "I think we can leave things as they are."

Cecilia curtsied. "Thank you, Sheriff Benning. I thank you with all my heart."

So the sheriff left with the bodies of the men. Benjamin, with Joel and Octavius, dug graves for Eva and her girls in the grave yard. Over cups of sassafras tea Cecilia calmed Henrietta before they went to say a prayer at the graveyard.

"You need to come home," Henrietta fussed, as she and Polly were ready to leave.

"Mama, I am home."

Cecilia waved till they were out of sight. Only then did she hide in the barn. "So senseless," she cried out in grief and rage. "Killing is so senseless."

Lula found her there. They sat, holding hands. Then they went together to get ready for the supper meal.

CHAPTER 26

The air pressure twisted at her joints and thrust bolt-like darts through her head. Cecilia endured the pain all day as she worked. The last of the corn crop was under shelter, the last sweet potatoes stored in the kitchen cellar, the horses secured in the barn, the goats penned in stout shelters.

She looked often at the sky as she directed the work of closing down every shed and outhouse. A strong gust of wind tore the corn crib door from her grasp. Benjamin leaned his weight with hers so they could latch it in place.

"It be a bad blow coming in, Miss Cecilia," he said.

"I'm afraid you're right, Benjamin." She glanced again toward the sky as the first rain drops pelted them. "Make sure everyone is inside. With Mister Macdougal in Wilmington, you're in charge. I'll send Lula down to your cabin now. Rory and I will weather it out in the kitchen."

"You ain't gonna keep Lula with you?"

"No." Her skirts wrapped around her legs like a hobble. She pulled at the fabric. "We'd best hurry, Benjamin."

A gum branch skipped across the yard and Cecilia took off running for the kitchen. She pushed Lula out the door. "Go. Go stay with your husband and child."

Cecilia watched as the couple ran for their cabin. She'd done all she could do. Whatever happened now was in the winds of the storm.

She rocked for a time with Rory Grace. She did not want her baby to feel the dread she felt with the rising winds. She knew the damage the winds and rains might cause, but the baby did not need to be afraid.

"Your Aunt Charlotte sang this song to me. 'Michael, row your boat ashore. Hallelujah. Michael, row your boat ashore. Hallelujah.' Rory, your Aunt Charlotte has the prettiest singing voice. Mine's not much good, but I try. And she has black curls just like yours. One day you're going to meet her. And your little cousins."

Rory reached to pat her mother's face.

"You like the song. Well, my precious, this one I sang to your Uncle Timmie when he was a baby. 'Big A, little A, bouncing B. Oh, the cat's in the cupboard and can't see me.' Now what do you think of that?"

Rory's eyes soon closed and Cecilia laid her on a quilt on the floor. She fed a log to the fire, more for the light than the heat. She dozed, only to wake at the sound of roaring wind. She heard the giant sucking noise of the maple roots as they tore from the ground. The tree sighed as it fell. Its massive branches embraced the kitchen porch. She could see them through the window, as if a magical forest had sprung up in a place that she had walked just a short time before. She prayed the glass panes would hold against the scraping of the wood. She waited, her head pillowed next to her child.

The sound of a crosscut saw reached her. Ax blows pounded close by. The winds were not as strong, and she knew it was early morning, but the room was still dark. She sat up on the quilt, putting her fingers against her aching temples, rubbing to ease the pain that stabbed through her head. Her chest felt as if a weight were pressing against her.

"Miss Cecilia? Is you there? Miss Cecilia?" Lula's frantic cries rose higher and higher as she called. "Little Baby Rory Grace, can you hear us out here? Oh, Miss Cecilia, if yous there, please answer."

Little Martin's calls came on the heels of his mother's. "Oh, Miss Cecilia, are you hurt? Miss Cecilia?"

"Move them limbs, boy," Benjamin shouted. "Move 'em."

A splash of water on her face made her look up. The ceiling on the front part of the room sagged toward the wall. Another drop of water dripped down and the ceiling seemed to move.

Lula was still calling. "Miss Cecilia? Miss Rory Grace? Is you there? Is you living? Can you hear?"

Benjamin yelled above the screeling of the saw. "Lula, shut your mouth and move them limbs outta my way." Screel, screel from the saw. "Joel, get that rope tied off. Where Octavius be with that horse?" Screel, screel. "Lula, you want to holler, you holler for Octavius to get that horse up here."

For a moment the saw's rasp stopped. In the quiet, she heard Simple's stammering words. "M-m-m-missy? M-missy?"

"I'm here," she called back. "I'm here."

Outside a limb thudded to the ground. Benjamin shouted, "Tie that piece to the horse. Pull when I say."

As the maple moved away from the window, she watched the porch follow.

"Stop," Benjamin shouted. Then he pushed in the door. Simple darted around him, scooped up the baby in her blanket and ran out. Benjamin caught her hand and yanked her through the door. The roof of the kitchen imploded.

Benjamin didn't stop pulling her until he reached the middle of the back yard. He dropped her arm. "Oh, ma'am, I didn't mean to be rough. Just want to get you outta there." He leaned over, his hands on his knees, his breathing harsh and labored, as if he had reached the end of his tether.

Cecilia looked at the wreck of the kitchen. The chimney was standing. The building was damaged beyond repair. She turned slowly. The house roof seemed to still be in place, but debris had smashed out windows on the dining room side of the building. The barn held. From where she stood she could see no harm to it. Trees crisscrossed the lane to the cabins. Two long leaf pines had smashed through the old cabin that she'd not gotten around to repairing. That small house was now totally gone. The other cabins seemed to have weathered and would need only minimum repair.

They were all standing, looking at her. Simple still held the baby. Rory cooed and patted his face.

"Well, we're all here," Cecilia said.

"No, ma'am," Lula said.

"Martin. Lula, where's Old Martin?"

It was Simple who answered. "D-dead."

"It were his heart, I think," Lula said. "He just closed his eyes and went real peaceful. I think he 'cided to fly and the winds was right for him to just let go."

"Winds to make you want to fly," Cecilia said. "I feel I'm trying to catch winds in a net. I feel I'm trying to harvest winds to do my bidding. I think I'm caught up. I think getting in the crops will solve problems. I think making salt will be good business. Nothing works. And Old Martin decides to fly." She swiped at the tears that traced her checks. "He was a good man, Lula. Old Martin was a good man."

"Miss Cecilia, I thinks we needs to have something to eat, 'fore we starts to clean up," Lula said. "We do got lots to clean up. My hearth got a fire. I got bacon. You come on down to my place."

Simple, still holding Rory Grace, followed Lula toward the cabins. Cecilia followed them. Her chest ached and she clutched her hands across her bodice, trying to ease her breathing as she walked.

By the full light of morning, Cecilia saw more and more damage. She did not know where to begin cleaning up. The headache that had started the morning before continued to pound against her temples. Her arms and legs felt fat and full, as if someone had stuffed them with sawdust. When she tried to eat she could not swallow.

One of the men rescued a rocking chair. Joel put it on Lula's cabin porch and Cecilia sat, numb, too tired to think, too tired to plan. She knew that Simple and Little Martin were caring for Rory Grace. She knew that Benjamin and Octavius were digging a grave. She knew that Lula was picking through what they could find in the kitchen so they could get to the cellar door for foodstuffs. Cecilia couldn't make herself move to help.

At some point, she felt Lula lay her hand across her forehead. She caught people saying words like "burning up with fever . . ."

"She burning hot."

"When Mister Macdougal gonna get back?"

". . . send for help 'fore . . ."

Then the whole world spun away from her.

CHAPTER 27

"N o. No more." Someone was trying to pour liquid down her throat. Cecilia struck at the hand that held the glass.

"Well, well, little sister. Welcome back."

Cecilia opened one eye. "Polly?"

"Yes."

"Are you trying to poison me? What is that stuff?"

"She better, Miss Polly. Thank the angels in heaven, she better than the last time she woke up." Lula leaned over the bed. "She can knock a glass outta my hand any time, if'n she gonna get better."

Cecilia scrunched her eyes closed. "The last time I woke up? I can't remember. Have I been sick?"

"Very," Polly answered.

Cecilia opened her eyes and sat upright. "Where's Rory Grace? Where's -"

"That baby fine, Miss Cecilia," Lula answered.

Polly pushed Cecilia back down on the pillows. "Rory is right across the hall in the parlour with Mama. She is just fine. In fact, they both are. I think you've had a chest inflammation. Whatever you've had does not seem to be contagious No one else is sick. No one else has fever."

Still trying to sit up, Cecilia asked, "Polly, where am I?"

"In the dining room. In your very own house. We moved furniture around a bit and brought your bed down here. You're not upstairs because there was damage from the storm to the roof and chimney, which is being repaired even as we speak. Now be a good patient and drink this medicine."

Cecilia shook her head. "That's the worse tasting mess I ever put in my mouth. You've been torturing me with it for days. What is it?"

"Why, little sister, it's Stoughton's London Bitters, advertised as a preventative against ague and fevers." Polly held out the glass. "It's supposed to be excellent. Drink."

Cecilia drank, made a face, and burrowed down in the covers.

When she woke again, Polly was sitting by her bed. For a long time she watched her sister concentrating on her book. Polly did so love to read and had never had much time to study. She remembered once finding Polly hidden in the barn loft, a newspaper held close to her nose so she could see the print in the dim light. Charlotte always teased that squinting would give her wrinkles.

Cecilia stretched and pulled up on the pillow. "How long have I been sick?"

Polly put down her book. "A week. The storm came through on a Thursday and today is a Thursday. One whole week."

"Polly, I killed two men."

"You've been moaning that over and over. The hotter your fever got the more you talked about it."

"What else did I say?"

Polly took her sister's hands in her own. "You grieved for Kenneth. You hung Mister Black over and over again. You seemed far more distressed over his death than the fact that he killed Kenneth."

"Oh, Polly."

"Your nightmares were very real. Very vivid. So precise at times an artist could have drawn pictures from your words. You mourned for Eva. You cried for Lily and Lilac. You worried over Evangeline Elliott and what she's doing this winter in Wilmington. You pleaded for the welfare of each slave on this farm. Dear sister, you killed those men at the salt works at least a hundred times."

Polly reached to brush her sister's hair up from her forehead. "The one thing you never mourned was your daughter. There were times you reached for her, gathering her into the crook of your arm to hold her close. Crooning a lullaby."

"Why am I crying now?" Cecilia sobbed. "I've lost a week and all I can do is cry like an infant."

"You're tired, sister. You're tired from fighting. You've been fighting for a long time. Fighting for food. For safety. For money to supply the needs of your family, to pay your taxes, to have something set aside for next year's seed. I've been there. Oh, have I been there. But when I was left with the burden of the tavern at Brunswick I had many people around to help me. Cecilia, you are so alone here."

Polly put the book in her chair and walked over to the boarded up window openings on the side of the dining room. She ran her hands across the drapes, letting the thick fabric fall from her fingers. She moved to the windows that overlooked the front of the house and stood, staring out.

"Cecilia, when trouble comes or problems arise, Mama and Charlotte retreat. You and I plow right in. Whatever it is, we plunge in head on. We wring solutions from the problems. We act. That is our way of dealing with life. But it tears out our insides.

Shooting those men is tearing you into little pieces. You have to let it go. I don't know how. I can't give you directions. I do know you have to let it go. Of all the things I taught you -"

Polly pressed her head against the window frame. "Cecilia, of all the things I taught you, I'm most glad, right now, that I taught you how to shoot straight."

Polly wrapped her hands in her apron. Cecilia knew that's what her sister always did when she was upset about something or when she was trying to figure out what to say next. She didn't expect what Polly did say.

"You'll recover from the fever. In fact, you're stronger now than you were when you woke a few hours ago. You'll be back at running this farm. Do you remember saying that you were going to sit and direct the work being done?"

Cecilia nodded. "Yes. I said that."

"Do you remember what I said?"

Cecilia hiccuped. "You asked me what I would do with myself if I didn't have work to do. I thought you were being mean. I thought you didn't want me to marry Kenneth and move away and be happy."

Polly picked up the book and put it on the bed. She sat in the chair and folded her hands in her lap. She bowed her head. She was crying so hard that tears dripped from her chin and spotted her bodice. "I did so want you to be happy, Cecilia," she sobbed. "I did so want that for you."

"Please don't cry. Please don't, Polly." Cecilia struggled to get out of bed.

Polly swiped at her eyes. "Don't you dare try to get up yet." She lifted her apron to dab at her bodice. "Oh, what *has* come over me."

Cecilia picked up the book that lay on the coverlet, shaking it at her. "It's all that reading you do, you know. I never did see how any good could come of so much reading."

"Girls, are you quarreling?" Henrietta stood at the dining room door.

"No, Mama," they chorused in unison before they burst into giggles.

"I never understood how you could do that," Henrietta stated.

"Do what, Mama?" Polly asked.

"Say things together. It's like you know what the other one is thinking."

Polly and Cecilia looked at each other. It was Polly who spoke. "Not always, Mama. Not always. Right now I want to know what my sister wants to eat."

"Oh, she can't have anything yet but broth," Henrietta said.

"Mama, I'll agree that she needs to start with broth or watered-down stew." Polly stirred her finger in the air, then licked it as if she were tasting batter. "But later, Cecilia, when Mama let's you eat again, what do you want?"

"Quail. I want quail basted with scuppernong wine sauce and nestled in plums all cooked with honey." Cecilia ran her tongue over her lips. "That will be a most welcome change from those horrible bitters you've been pouring down my throat."

"For now you'd best lie back and rest," Mama said.

"Yes, Mama," Cecilia and Polly said together.

CHAPTER 28

Polly went back to Three Sisters. Mama stayed at the farm. "You've got to get the Christmas gifts ready, Cecilia. You and I both know you are not the best seamstress. We have shirts and breeches to make for all the men on this place. A skirt and bodice for Lula. Something special, I think, for the boy Martin."

Cecilia's strength was coming back so slowly that she held hard to patience. "Mama, I'm glad you're staying to help me." She held up a man's shirt sleeve. "Where did you get the fabric?"

"Polly sent it. I asked her to." Mama cut a length of thread, and taking the sleeve from Cecilia's hand, began stitching it to the shirt.

"Whose money?"

Henrietta held up the shirt for inspection. "I know nothing about money. You'll have to ask your sister."

Cecilia felt that she'd lost so much time. She had to start planning for spring. A heavy frost covered the grass the morning she sent for Mister Macdougal to come to the house. She shivered from the cold, even though a fire burned on the hearth in the dining room where they sat at the large table, going over books and records.

"Miss Cecilia, I ordered glass for these windows, but I don't know if it'll come through. General Washington is having problems getting supplies for the troops. Able-bodied men with good reputations, who used to haul freight, are hard to find. It's difficult for ships to get up river with the British blockade. I don't know when we'll get panes to fix these dining room windows."

"What about the kitchen, Mister Macdougal? I need the kitchen." She sketched a rectangle on the slate that sat between them. "I want it bigger than the old one. The chimney's here." She pointed at the drawing. "The foundation stones are still in place. So the width can stay the same. Just make it longer."

Together they chalked out a design. "That's practical. Until we can get glass panes, we can use shutters on the windows," Mister Macdougal said. "If I can get the carpenters back from Wilmington, we'll start this week. They did a good job on the repair work on the house. What's next on your list of tasks?"

"Seed. Spring planting. Corn and peanuts, of course. Sweet potatoes and white potatoes. A larger garden plot. Early cabbages. Carrots and beets and radish. Beans and peas. We have to have a cash crop. Do you know anything about tobacco?"

Mister Macdougal put down the stump of charcoal he'd been using to make notes. "Where's your mother?"

He spoke so softly Cecilia wasn't sure at first what he'd asked. She frowned.

"Timothy and Donny are traveling into Virginia before Christmas." He continued to whisper. "They'll be in the tidewater area. They can bring back tobacco seed. But Timothy doesn't want Miss Henrietta to know he's leaving again so soon."

"Leaving before Christmas will be a real issue for Mama." Cecilia sat back in her chair. "How much money for how many seed, do you think?"

"Several pounds, I'm afraid. The new term is dollars. So fifty dollars to have enough seed to plant enough acreage to make a profit. That's one reason I hadn't mentioned tobacco before now. If you can purchase the seed, and if we can raise the plants, and if the weather holds out till harvest, we can make a good return. I think tobacco is the cash crop we need."

He pushed back his chair, leaning his elbows on the table. "Miss Cecilia, that is a lot of iffiness and I don't know anything about growing tobacco. It has to be cured, but I'm not sure what that means. We'll need to hire someone for all of that."

He paced around the dining table, worrying a path across the carpet. "Miss Polly paid the carpenters she brought from Wilmington. She made them all stay till they'd finished everything on the house, except for the windows in this room. She supervised the work on every cabin. She had the foreman sign a paper saying they'd come back to build the kitchen. I didn't know if *you* have the money for tobacco seed."

Mister Macdougal reversed directions, still stalking about the table. "It's like the salt works. We have the salt. We've traded some and used some. We still have salt stored. The price, it seems to me, was especially dear."

"I shot two men," Cecilia stated. "I *killed* two men. That is a very dear price, indeed. I didn't do it for salt."

The man stared at her.

"I didn't kill for salt, Mister Macdougal. Simple didn't knife two men for salt. We both did the deed to survive. I do hope Simple isn't having as many nightmares as I'm having." Cecilia pushed back her chair. "Nothing I've done since I came to this farm has been without a price. I can't seem to stop paying."

"Oh, Miss Cecilia."

"I have money for seed, Mister Macdougal. When do you need it?"

He sat and gave a huge sigh. "Your brother plans to leave early in the morning."

"All right." Cecilia stood. "Help me get into the kitchen cellar."

Going through the parlour, where she had helped Mama with the sewing, Cecilia selected several of the small cloth pouches she'd made. The overseer lit a lantern with a spark from the fire burning on the hearth. They went out together and crossed the broken floor of the ruined building. Mister Macdougal propped open the cellar door and held the light for Cecilia to climb down the ladder. He followed her and stood in the middle of the underground room, waiting.

Cecilia pried out a small stone set in the foundation. The sack she'd hidden there had not been touched with the destruction of the building above. "While I was getting over that strange fever, I knew someone else had to know about my hiding place," she said. "I couldn't think of anyone I could trust more than you, Mister Macdougal."

The lantern trembled in his hand and he reached to hang it from a peg fastened into the foundation stones.

"Now," Cecilia continued, "I've put about ten pounds value in each of these four bags. That's what? About fifty dollars? Whoever is carrying the bags can find different places to stash them away and not have to show too much money at once."

"Is all of this for the tobacco seed?" Mister Macdougal leaned against the wall. "Your land taxes are going to be due soon and you'll have taxes to pay on the slaves. You'll need coin for that."

"This is for the seed. Fill some small barrels with salt. Timmie can carry those on a pack horse. Salt is always good for bargaining. Will you see to packing? Use what we have stored here. When the carpenters begin work on the kitchen they don't need to see how much salt we have."

Mister Macdougal nodded and held the light for her to climb to the floor above.

As they reached the house, they both heard Henrietta yelling from the parlour. "Cecilia! Cecilia, come see!"

She ran, Mister Macdougal at her heels.

Rory Grace was standing in the middle of the floor. She took a tiny step and plopped on her bottom.

Henrietta clapped. "Just look, Cecilia. She's taking her very first steps. Isn't it just wonderful?"

Cecilia sat on the floor, crossed her legs and propped her elbows on her knees. The baby tugged on her mother's sleeve to pull herself to her feet. She took another step before she again abruptly plopped. For a moment she frowned. Then she looked up at the people surrounding her, nodded her head and grinned.

"Go, Miss Rory Grace," Mister Macdougal said.

Cecilia took a deep breath. "Oh, my dear little daughter. You're trying your legs much too early. But your grandmother is right. This is wonderful. This is a sight worth far more than the price of a barrel of salt."

CHAPTER 29

Mama went back to the tavern the first of the year. "You are doing so well, Cecilia. Now that I've finished up on the sewing, you don't really need me for anything else," she said. "Polly always has so much to do."

As if I don't, Cecilia thought, but she didn't argue. She knew Mama missed her circle of friends coming and going at Three Sisters. And in spite of her protests, she really did want to hear all the news. She had Macdougal hitch up the cart to drive Henrietta to Wilmington, hugged her goodbye and waved her off.

The news of British forces surrendering to General Horatio Gates at Saratoga in the fall of 1777, lifted patriot spirits for a short time. Then the speculation of a southern campaign began to circulate. With each task she started Cecilia expected disaster, startling at unexpected noises and looking over her shoulder for things that weren't there.

Mister Macdougal brought gossip from Three Sisters Tavern. "The British have to save face, Miss Cecilia. They seem to think striking the south will be easy. A drive north from Georgia and South Carolina, with forces coming down from the north to join in, could crush the rebellion. At least that's what some are saying."

Cecilia listened. "What do you think of the plan, Mister Macdougal?"

He grinned. "The south will not be the easy target many think. The British don't seem to remember Moores Creek Bridge and the licking they took there. How can they dismiss the action at Sullivan's Island, down in South Carolina? Unless their commanders can enlist good local guides, they have no idea what to do with our terrain. *Nobody* just ambles through our swamps and wetlands."

"So do you think we'll beat them? Beat the British troops?"

"I think we're in for some bitter fighting." He gazed across the yard. "I'll have to go, Miss Cecilia."

She walked away without answering him. That winter of '77, merging into a freezing January of 1778, was quiet in her little corner of the world. Too quiet, she felt.

Her cow calved. The heifer was sound of limb, skipping about in the chilly barn lot after her mother. The cow's milk was so rich and creamy that butter churned readily. Several of the nannies delivered kids. The herd was large enough now that she was studying how to make cheese. There was far too much milk to feed to the pigs, who were growing fat in their pens.

Timothy had gotten not only the tobacco seed on his trip into Virginia. He brought Urijah. "The old woman who owned him was dying, Cecilia. She was getting rid of everything she had. She gave me a smooth bore rifle. Just out and out handed it to me. She said to please take the black powder that she had hidden in the barn. There was a small keg, maybe ten pounds of it. Our militia sure can use every bit we can get. If I hadn't taken the slave, someone else was just waiting to grab him up. He'll be better off with you and you need help. Urijah knows tobacco. He didn't cost much."

"Timmie, it's not the money. I don't want more slaves."

"I know that. You and Polly have strange ideas about owning slaves. But how else are you going to run this farm?"

Cecilia got up from the kitchen table, where she'd been sitting since she'd sent the slave down to the cabins with Benjamin. She poured coffee, put the pot on a tripod near the coals, and added a split oak log to the fire.

She stood, watching the flames. "I'll run this farm with indentured servants. With hired hands for the fields. With women to work when I can't get men. Women are good workers at most any job."

She turned to look at her brother. "At least this man has clothes and a couple of blankets. The men Ricky brought last summer were in rags and had nothing. Timmie, I know you're helping me. Thank you for that. I do need someone who knows about growing tobacco, because I don't know anything, really."

"I brought something else." He dropped his knapsack on the table to dig through his possessions and pulled out a large cloth bag. He unknotted the string to pour a few seed in his hand. "Look. Just look at this, Cecilia."

"Corn? It looks like corn seed."

"But special. It's popcorn seed. See, you shell it and then you cook it." Timothy interrupted himself to again rummage through his knapsack. He held out a scrap of paper.

"What's this?" she asked.

"The recipe. The old woman wrote out the recipe for popping popcorn. You butter your pot. And you soak the corn kernels in soft salted butter. And you cook it over a hot fire while you stir and stir so it won't burn and it pops. And you eat it hot." Timothy licked his lips. "It *is* good."

"Timmie, what happened to this old woman you keep talking about?"

"She died. I buried her, just like she asked me to. I took the things I'd paid her for and came on home." He finished his coffee and stood. "I'll just put my blanket by the fire in here to sleep and head out for the tavern early. Anything you want to tell Mama and Polly?"

"Let them know I'm faring well." She turned at the door. "Timmie, thank you for the tobacco seed and the popping corn. I'll have to get used to the idea of Urijah before I thank you for him."

The next morning, with Lula busy at the hearth and Rory Grace playing on her quilt nearby, Cecilia sat again at the kitchen table to talk with this new man who had come to her farm. "Urijah, tell me about growing tobacco."

"Where would you wish me to begin?" Urijah asked.

"From planting the seed. Everything."

"Ma'am, you need to plant the seed now. In fact, it's a little late in the season to be putting the seed in the plant beds. When the weather is warm enough, you transplant the seedlings to the field. As the plants grow, they need care. You hoe and weed. You sucker. You inspect every day for worms and make sure you get rid of any worm you see. When the leaves are beginning to turn a certain shade of yellow you begin to harvest, pulling the lugs first. The lugs are the bottom leaves. Over the days, you work your way up the plant. You tie the leaves in bundles called hands, drape them on the sticks and hang them in the barn for fire curing. Unless, of course, you are one of those who wants to cure the whole plant at once. Some do that."

Cecilia held up her hand and Urijah stopped talking. When Timothy had ridden in with the man just at dark the night before, her first thought was that he carried himself like a gentleman. Listening to his cultured speech reinforced the notion. She would have to know him better before she questioned him about himself. She was already sure that her little brother had indeed gotten a bargain.

"Fire curing? Urijah, explain that."

"A tobacco barn is a special kind of building, ma'am. It should be about sixteen feet square and inside you have your tier poles spaced to accept the sticks. If you don't have a barn built, you would need to begin building now. The caulking between the logs needs to be thoroughly dry before the tobacco is placed for curing, else the odor from the caulking will penetrate the tobacco aroma and the grade will be lessened. The higher the grade and the sweeter the flavor, the better price you should get for the product."

Cecilia's thoughts were spinning. She had to plant the seed. Now! She had to build a barn. Now! She massaged her temples, trying to decide what to do first.

Lula sat down at the table. "Miss Cecilia, sounds to me like you asking for a heap of work. Maybe a heap of trouble with this 'bacco business."

"The profits can be astronomical," Urijah stated. "If the plants are cared for and the curing is done correctly, the proceeds are well worth the efforts."

Lula looked Urijah up and down. "Black man, where you go to school? Can you read, 'long with that fancy speech you got? You talk like a white man. You even act like a white man."

Urijah shifted in his chair, glancing toward Cecilia.

"Man, you can talk in front of Miss Cecilia. She believe in reading and numbers. She ain't gonna hold nothing 'gainst you." Lula shook her head. " 'Cept meanness. She don't put up with meanness."

Urijah nodded. "Yes, Miss Cecilia. I read. I can keep accounts. Miss Abigail taught me many things."

"Is Miss Abigail the woman my brother bought you from?" Cecilia asked.

"Yes, ma'am."

Cecilia knotted her fingers together on the table. "I'm thinking about planting the seeds. They have to be in a warm place, you said. That means inside the house. Lula, what if we move the furniture around in the dining room. We can fill troughs with soil. Keep a fire going day and night. Open doors if the days get too warm."

Lula looked at her as if she had lost her mind. "Grow stuff in the house?"

Urijah smiled. "I see you are a woman of action, Miss Cecilia. I have worked with folk who grew plants inside. The pursuit of diversity has many rewards. Do you have troughs ready for planting seed?"

Cecilia smiled back at him. "No, but we'll have them by the end of the day. Now what kind of soil do you suggest we fill them with?"

Lula stood and pushed her chair under the table. "We in the 'bacco business. Though I don't see how we gonna do any more work around here than we do now. Work day to night."

"Hush fussing, dear Lula. Urijah, let's go see the men and talk about building whatever we're going to build to plant our seed in."

"Work and more work." Lula was still fussing as Cecilia and Urijah went out toward the cabins.

CHAPTER 30

Her taxes were paid and the road work required by law was finished. The tobacco barn was built and the plants almost ready to set out in the field. Cecilia still felt a twinge of fear. Things were going too well. Her major surprise was Evangeline showing up on a windy March morning.

"Thought you'd want them salt works going, Miss Cecilia," Evangeline said. She settled at the table in the new kitchen and looked around. "Now this is nice. Real nice. You got elbow room."

"Evangeline, I had no idea you would ever want to go back to the sound."

"What? You found somebody else?"

"No. I haven't even thought about doing the salt again."

"Miss Cecilia, making salt was good work. It weren't your fault what happen. You can't take the blame for nothing that happen."

"What about people to help you?"

"I got some help all lined up. If you wants us to work, then I'll stay here tonight and they'll be on along in the morning. They got a ox and a cart, which'll be mighty handy. If you don't want us, I'll just take myself on back to town and that will be the end of that."

"Tell me about the help." Cecilia set out the remains of an apple pie, put cups on the table and poured fresh milk for each of them.

"Nettie's a widow. Don't you look alarm, Miss Cecilia. Her children is all boys. The oldest one just come back from the militia with a busted up arm, but he can work. Name of Earlis. She got two other boys big enough to handle the pans and carry the water and such. She's hoping that keeping that oldest boy out in the sun all summer'll heal that arm better. 'Sides keeping him away from drink, which he's developing a true fondness for."

Evangeline took a healthy bite of pie and washed it down with milk. "You can supply the wood like you done last summer. Just check on us when you can." She licked her lips. "Oh, my, that's good eating, Miss Cecilia."

Cecilia pushed the pie pan toward her. "Finish it, if you'd like."

"Thank you, ma'am. It's been a lean winter," Evangeline said between bites. "A long, lean winter."

So Cecilia set up the salt works again. Nettie turned out to be the same kind of worker that she'd found Evangeline to be. She wasn't too sure about the character of the oldest of Nettie's three boys. Earlis had a sullen attitude, but his surliness didn't seem to infect the younger children. She could only hope she was doing the right thing.

By harvest time the bounty on the farm was so overflowing that Cecilia hired extra hands to work. Mister Macdougal found four women in town to employ. They moved into the new cabin she'd had built. For two weeks they gathered corn, cut stalks and stacked fodder. They pulled peanut plants and laid the fruit out to dry on canvas stretched in the sun. They picked the last of the garden beans, stringing them on lengths of twine, hanging them from the rafters of the cabin. They were willing workers and cheerful with news. Cecilia had forgotten how merry chatter livened up a kitchen at night.

That late summer and early fall of 1778 Octavius, Joel and Benjamin, with Urijah directing, harvested the tobacco. Simple and Little Martin cared for the goats, the cow, the horses. Cecilia and Mister Macdougal were everywhere, taking turns feeding the fire at the tobacco barn, hoeing and gathering vegetables in the house garden, taking the corn to Mister Lillington's grist mill for grinding. In between other tasks, there was wood to cut to take to the salt works and someone to cart it there and bring back barrels of salt. Always there was wood to cut for the hearths in the house and kitchen.

"Lula, I helped cook at the tavern from the time I was a little girl. People coming in from early morning till after the supper meal. This is the hungriest crew I've ever kept up with."

Cecilia put down the ladle she'd been using to stir a pot of beans. With a long wooden scoop she lifted out yeast bread from the oven by the hearth and slid the loaves onto the kitchen table. She smeared the bread with butter and loosely wrapped each loaf in toweling.She leaned into the wall, trying to ease a growing pain between her shoulders.

Lula handed her a cup of coffee. "Sit down a minute, Miss Cecilia. The work ain't gonna run away if you take a minute for yourself."

Cecilia sank down on the quilt where Rory was having a tea party with her dolls.

"Mama, dat Polly," Rory said. She set one of her handkerchief dolls in a little chair that Joel had whittled out for her. "Dat Gamma Henny." She put this doll in another small chair on the other side of the doll's table.

"Polly and Gamma Henny, are they." Cecilia picked up a doll and held it to her chest. "Sweetie, I miss them, too. Maybe we can go visit as soon as all the crops are in."

She sipped her coffee. "Lula, Polly was always quoting from Shakespeare or the Bible or some other book she was reading. I'm trying to remember something she said. It went sort of like 'for what we lack we laugh. For what we have we are sorry. Let us be thankful for that which is.' " Cecilia sighed. "I am thankful, Lula. I truly am."

"Yous tired, Miss Cecilia. That's all that be the matter with you."

The next day the men gathered the popcorn. They shelled several of the dry ears. That night after supper, Cecilia popped her first batch. The exploding kernels sent them all into peels of laughter.

Rory danced about the yard, squealing. "Poppy corn. Pop, pop, pop! Poppy poppy popcorn."

Benjamin beat out a rhythm on his thighs in time with her song. Simple piped a tune on his reed flute.

They laced the hot corn with warm butter and tasted their first batch of popcorn. Martin did an imitation of Rory's squeals. "Poppy corn. This popcorn is some kind of good eating, Miss Cecilia."

Mister Macdougal sat beside her. "I thought you were barmy, planting popcorn. It's going to be a seller, if you can teach people about it."

"I could offer a recipe, I guess," she answered. "But barmy? You thought I didn't know what I was doing?"

"I don't know what you're doing half the time." He took her hand and brought it to his lips. "I always trust that you're right."

She retrieved her hand, shoving it into her pocket. Her heart was pounding so that she felt he surely could hear it. His next words were not what she'd expected.

"As soon as the harvest is finished, I'm leaving. I'm joining the militia. I have to go."

Cecilia screamed at him, "You can't leave. I depend on you. Who will make the weekly trips to Wilmington? Who will organize the work? I can't handle this farm by myself." To make herself shut up, she bit her lip so hard that she could feel a trickle of blood inside her mouth.

"I have to go," he repeated. "Please understand. I have to go. Cecilia, you can keep Evangeline here for the winter. She can go and come with freedom because she's white. I don't think you want to keep Nettie and her boys. I'm not sure I trust Earlis. There's something about him I don't like.

"Besides, Benjamin is better at judging the crops than I am. You can depend on him. With Benjamin in charge there'll be no problem with spring planting. Simple is a good man. Martin is learning fast. Joel and Octavius work hard. Now you have Urijah."

Mister Macdougal reached for her hand but she inched away. "Don't be angry, Cecilia. That is the one thing I could not bear."

"I'm not angry, Macdougal."

"You're always upset with me when you leave off the Mister to my name."

"I hadn't noticed."

"I notice, Cecilia. I notice everything about you. How you walk. How you tilt your head. How you wring your hands when you're having a hard time making a decision."

Cecilia stood. "I ask that you let me know before you ride out."

He nodded.

"Now I'll have to look over my shoulder more often. The crops have been too good. The weather has been too perfect. The pigs are getting fat and the goat herd is increasing. No one has been ill." She twisted her hands together. "There will be a disaster. There always is."

While they were talking, Lula and the men cleaned up the yard. The big table was back in the kitchen, the popping pot cleaned, the fire extinguished. Rory ran to grab Cecilia's legs in a hug.

"It's too perfect," Cecilia said.

"Think positive," Mister Macdougal said, as he walked away.

Cecilia gathered Rory in her arms and went in to bed. It was after midnight when she heard the knocking on the back door and Timothy's voice calling up to her bed chamber. "Cecilia, help. We need help."

 CHAPTER 31

By the dim light of her candle, Cecilia saw the blood tracing down from Timothy's forehead to his chin. "Oh, Timmie, what hap -"

"Not me. It's Donny. Help me with Donny. He's the one *bad* hurt."

"In the kitchen," Cecilia said. "Most of my supplies are in the kitchen."

Her brother slid his friend from his horse.

"On the table," Cecilia said. "Light a lantern and put a piece of wood on the fire." She bent to look at the boy. His left arm was bound to his chest. There was so much blood on his shirt that at first she couldn't find the wound. With scissors she began to cut away the fabric and bindings.

She swallowed to still her heaving stomach as she looked at the broken bone and shredded flesh. "Go down to the cabins and get Simple. Tell him to bring all of his basket making strips and that half-finished basket. Then get Macdougal. Tell him to bring buckets of water when he comes. Hurry, Timmie."

As her brother went out she turned to the unconscious boy and finished stripping away his shirt. Beginning at the shoulder she bathed the arm with warm water left in the bucket on the hearth. Pieces of bone, slivers of glass, bits of nails, other debris she couldn't identify, came off in cloth embedded in the wound. She'd changed the water for the second time when Simple came in. MacDougal, carrying the water buckets, followed on his heels.

The foreman stood and stared at the sight. "My God," he exclaimed.

Simple turned and ran out the door.

"Get the water over the fire to heat," Cecilia said. "Find me a pan to put this refuse in. Please check on Simple. I'm going to need both of you."

"Cecilia, how can you *do* this?" Mister Macdougal waved his hand toward Donny's mangled arm.

"I don't think about it," she said. "I just do what has to be done." She walked to the door, threw bloody water over the porch railing into the herb bed, came in to fill the pan again with warm water, and went back to work cleaning Donny's arm.

Simple, his face drawn and scared, came in the door. "S-s-sorry, Missy." He held up the cane strips he used for his basket weaving.

"I'm going to need that thin wood to make splints for Donny's arm. With this much damage, the skin will have to be able to breath. Then we need a cage to go around his whole arm. For protection. Can you weave something?"

Simple motioned from his own elbow to his wrist.

Cecilia nodded. "Yes. But now that I'm cleaning more of the wound, I think we'll need one basket from wrist to elbow and another from elbow to shoulder." She continued to give orders. "Macdougal, go find my brother. He's hurt, too. I don't know how badly. Find him and bring him back in here. Get more water. It's going to take an ocean of water to clean this wound. Oh, how I hope he stays unconscious till I'm done."

Simple sat on the floor, pressed his back against the wall, and experimented with his basket strips.

Cecilia washed and picked away another piece of metal. She washed and cleared out a sliver of glass. She washed and pulled a splinter of wood from Donny's arm. She changed the water again and again until finally she thought she'd gotten everything foreign cleansed from the gaping wound.

"Simple," she said, "please go down in the cellar and bring up a pitcher of rum." He put down his basket weaving equipment, lit a lantern and made his way down the ladder.

Cecilia poured a small portion of rum in a mug, tilted it to her mouth and sipped. She poured a similar amount into another mug and handed it to Simple. "Drink up. Now we've got to set this broken bone. Please pray with me that Donny does not wake up till we finish the task."

Simple put his cup on the sideboard without drinking. He took a position at the table beside Cecilia, his feet braced apart. Together they brought the bone in place.

As she wound the last bandage, setting the basket-like structures about Donny's arm and shoulder, faint light filtered through the window shutters. She wiped across her forehead with the back of her hand. "Simple, thank you. Thank you so much. Now please go tell Lula to cook breakfast down at her cabin. Just anything will do. I don't want to move Donny yet."

When she walked out on the porch she found Timothy sleeping in a chair. She brought him in the kitchen, dressed the cut on his forehead and went with him to the house to put him to bed. Carrying Rory, she went to the cabins and handed the child to Lula. She went back to sit by her patient.

Midmorning Mister Macdougal pushed open the kitchen door. Behind him were two men. "Miss Cecilia, I brought the doctor," he said.

Cecilia looked up from her seat in a chair next to the table. "Doctor?"

"I knew, as soon as I saw it, that arm had to come off. I went for a doctor."

The taller of the two men came over to the table and reached toward the basket coverings on Donny's arm. Grabbing a knife from the cupboard, Cecilia pointed it at him. "Do not touch that arm."

The man jerked his hand back. The brawny man who accompanied him made a growling sound deep in his throat. Cecilia pointed the knife at him. "Do not touch that arm. Do not touch that boy."

"She just needs a minute to get use to the idea," Macdougal said. "We'll talk first."

"You can talk all you want to," Cecilia said. "Do not touch him. He's no longer unconscious. He just asleep. He has no fever. The wound is clean and the bleeding is stopped. He's sipped water and willow bark tea and rum. Leave him alone."

The stout man shook a beefy finger at her. "I can take that knife. Doc, you want I should take that knife away from her?"

"No," Mister Macdougal shouted, moving to stand in front of her. "Leave Miss Cecilia alone."

"I don't think we need to interfere." The doctor's voice sounded as if he'd poured oil on his words. "The young woman has clearly made up her mind. Of course, the boy will die with that kind of wound, but we will not interfere with her treatment." He turned on his heel. "I do expect to be paid for coming this distance."

The men walked out on the porch. Mister Macdougal looked at her. "I was trying to help." His shoulders slumped. "Miss Cecilia, I was only trying to help."

"The doctor, if he really is a doctor, has the dirtiest hands I've ever seen," Cecilia said. "Where did you find him?"

"At the port in Wilmington. He'd just come in on a ship. Miss Cecilia, I wanted to help. I didn't know what else to do. How was I supposed to know you could do this kind of medicine?"

She sank down in her chair but held the knife as if she could and would hack through anything that got between her and her patient. "You have forgotten that I grew up in a tavern? That I would have seen fist fights and knife fights? Gun wounds? That my sister is skilled with herbs? Whether you remembered or not, you could have stayed and fetched water. You could have held Donny's hand while Simple and I set his broken bone. You could have gathered willow bark and steeped tea."

She brandished the knife. "Macdougal, Donny may die. I *have* killed. Donny won't die because I shot him. He won't die because the wound wasn't cleaned and stitched and the bone set. Not *this* young man."

Mister Macdougal eyes followed the shimmer of lantern light on the knife blade as Cecilia continued to turn it in her hand. "I promised the doctor and his assistant I'd pay them."

"Then you'd best do it. Send them back to wherever they came from." She rested the knife point on the table. "In fact, Mister Macdougal, escort them to the road."

Sometime during the morning she fixed a pallet for Donny and had Simple and Benjamin move him to it. Sometime during the afternoon she ate so Lula would stop fussing at her. Sometime later in the day Mister Macdougal said he was leaving.

She was lighting the lantern at dusk when she saw Donny's eyes following her movements about the room.

"Hello, Donny," she said.

"My arm," he mumbled. "Is my arm still there?"

"Oh, yes. Your arm is still there. Mighty cut up and broken. Protected by a quite clever basket woven just for you. But it's there."

Donny closed his eyes and slept.

CHAPTER 32

W e were set upon," Timothy said. That was all he would say about how he got the lick on his forehead or how Donny got the blast of lead and glass in his arm.

As soon as Henrietta knew that Timothy Charles was staying at the farm she had Polly drive her out. "I just brought a few things," she said, watching Benjamin and Martin struggle up the stairs with her trunk.

"Yes, Mama," Cecilia said.

"Really. Most of what I packed is for sewing. We have to stitch clothes for the slaves. You know they expect their new outfits at the beginning of a new year."

Henrietta had made up her mind. She continued to give her reason for being there, never mentioning Timothy. "It's been a whole year since I was here to help sew clothes. Cecilia, you do not like to sew. You know you don't."

"Yes, Mama."

"Now the parlour will be a good place to work. Send Lula in here to help me."

"Yes, Mama." Cecilia sent Lula.

She took Polly out to Macdougal's cabin, where she'd let Donny and Timothy set up their own housekeeping.

Polly nodded approval as she examined Donny's arm. "You have no fever. Your hand looks good so the bandages aren't too tight. You should mend, although how much you'll be able to use that hand and arm might be in question."

Donny grimaced as he sat up on the bed. "I have it, Polly. I have an arm. Cecilia didn't cut it off."

Walking back to the house Polly said, "Cee, I'm sorry you're going to have Mama to look after. She does want to be with Timmie."

"Yes, Polly."

Henrietta stayed through the winter. Cecilia tucked her feelings into her chest, watching, waiting for the next disaster.

Timothy had the beginning of a beard, which Henrietta reached up to stroke whenever he was near her. His voice had dropped to a baritone, which seemed to startle his mother when he spoke. He had made it very plain that he would not talk about the scouting he did for the militia, but Henrietta kept asking him questions.

As much as possible, Timothy avoided his mother. He made trips for her and for Cecilia into Wilmington. He cleaned the stalls in the barn and cared for the horses. He took loads of corn to the mill and brought back grits and meal for bread. He cut wood and kept the wood boxes filled. He sat for hours talking with Donny. Cecilia caught the two of them reading one day, which seemed to embarrass them both.

"Polly would be glad to know you remember some of your lessons," Cecilia said. "There are lots of books in the parlour and packed in trunks in the attic. If you look, you might find some interesting stories. How nice if you read to Rory. She'd love that."

Cecilia was grateful for Timmie's help, even while she knew her little brother was miserable. She knew he wanted to be scouting, but he couldn't go alone. Donny's arm was healing. They all knew it would be a long time before he could ride.

The men were planting corn the day the news came that Sir Henry Clinton had been appointed commander-in-chief of all the British forces in North America. "We're into 1779, so it's been three years since Moores Creek," Timothy said. "Don't the damn British know by now we're going to lick 'em?"

"Timothy, the word British, spoken in the correct tone, is curse enough." Henrietta's needles attacked the yarn she was knitting. "Oh, this awful war. Fighting and looting. Boys shot. Men dying."

In early spring Cecilia again set up the salt works and Timothy took on the job of going back and forth with supplies. Earlis had a horse this year, and seemed to be away from the sound more than he was there to work.

"What do you think of Earlis?" she asked Timmie, after one of his trips to bring back salt barrels.

"He's a mean cuss, Cee. He bullies those smaller boys and they are glad when he rides out. They'd rather have the extra work than have him hanging around the salt camp."

"But where does he go? What does he do?"

Timmie shook his head. And then, without a word to Henrietta or Cecilia, Timothy was gone.

Donny, from his chair in the parlour, defended his friend. "He was called. He had to ride." He made a loose fist, then straightened the fingers on his damaged hand. He closed his eyes against the pain, but again and again straightened and stretched his fingers.

"Donny, stop that. Please stop that," Henrietta pleaded.

Cecilia put her hand on his shoulder. "Count to ten, Donny. Then do five stretches. Then count ten again. Mama can tell you I'm not very good at sewing, so you do need to watch out for my stitches on your arm."

Donny gave a half grin. "At least you understand I want to get well."

******

With Timothy gone, Cecilia began the trips to Wilmington for supplies and news. A breeze from the open shutters slipped through the tavern room this early morning as she and Polly sat near the hearth.

"With all those goats, have you thought of cheesemaking, Cee?" Polly asked.

"Yes." She lifted her cup, but instead of drinking, she studied the steaming coffee. "Polly, I have to have help. Macdougal's gone. I haven't heard from him so I don't even know if he joined the militia. Timmie's gone. We're planting and all of the men are in the fields. Lula and I have our hands full with the garden and cooking. Mama's a big help with the sewing and mending. She does some dusting. She watches Rory. But you know Mama. She doesn't give much support." Cecilia put her cup on the table.

"I asked because of something I heard here last night," Polly said.

"What? Help for me?"

"A Captain Harrington brought *The MerryMaker* in to port yesterday. He has two girls aboard, but the man who paid their passage has died and the estate doesn't plan to honor the indenture papers. You might look into it."

"Polly, what do the girls have to do with cheese?"

"The man who sent for them had a large herd of goats." Polly got up to add wood to the fire. "Cee, the captain is also carrying a supply of sulfur. I'm going down to see how much I can get. We need the sulfur for gunpowder and most of the men who will be bidding and buying this morning know that. We have to go now if we want to get it. And any other supplies he might have." Polly poked at the fire and turned to grin at her sister. "Supplies, that is, that don't include French perfume and parasols."

At the docks Cecilia walked up the gangplank ahead of Polly. The captain doffed his hat to them. "Harrington's the name. The vessel on which you stand is *The MerryMaker*. How may I be of service?"

"Good morning, sir," Cecilia answered. "I'm Cecilia Black. I understand you have two young girls with indenture papers. Please tell me about them."

"Mistress Black, I'll do better than that," the captain said. Raising his voice, he called to a hand who was swabbing the deck. "Jack, fetch the Cotter girls. A lady here for them."

"I'm Pauline Moore, Captain Harrington. I have need of a great many supplies."

"Miss Polly Moore? Of Three Sisters?" the captain asked.

When Polly nodded, the captain took a dramatic step back. "Ahhh, I have heard of your establishment and the fine hospitality there. Captain Russell -" Harrington dramatically wiped his eye. "Oh, gone now, he is. But I sailed with him for several years. Russell told stories of the Moore family here. Now, for a delectable cup of wine, and perhaps a portion of venison, which I understand you cook rather well, I will be more than glad to talk with you about merchandise."

"Alas, sir, wine I have none. Venison and mutton, cooked with herbs, I can serve you. Dried apple pie, cabbage stewed with onion, perhaps baked sweet potatoes, could be side dishes for the meat. As for me, I need sulfur," Polly said. "I need needles and thread. I need cloth for shirts and skirts and pants. I need medicines, especially poppy seed or poppy extract."

The captain narrowed his eyes. "An impressive list. I'll not take your worthless Continental paper, even for a delicious meal at your establishment. Are you then buying with coin or are you bargaining?"

"We can dicker. I do have *some* coin."

Cecilia spoke up. "Sir, I have a fine grade of tobacco, grown here in the area. I have dressed buck and doe skins, which I understand sell very well in some places. I have fresh butter, which your men, long at sea, would be more than glad to taste. Between us, my sister and I have much bargaining power."

As Polly and Cecilia talked with Captain Harrington, several other men had come aboard. They joined the conversation. The two Cotter girls the captain had sent for came on deck. Everyone stopped talking to stare at them.

"Two wet hens!" Polly exclaimed.

The younger of the girls, who could not have been more than twelve, lifted a tear stained face toward the captain. The older girl, who appeared to be about sixteen, held her arms rigid at her sides and stared toward shore.

"Sir, what have you done to these young women?" Cecilia demanded.

The captain dusted his hat against his thigh before settling it firmly on his head. "We ran into some storms along the way. I'm afraid I didn't realize how much these women had suffered down below deck."

"Find the papers for them. They will be coming with me when I leave this ship."

As Captain Harrington left for his cabin, the older girl whispered to her, "Ma'am?"

Cecilia looked at her. "Yes?"

"Ma'am, 'tis several crates we have. The freight has been paid on all of it. I have the written proof of that in the cabin."

"Your name?" Cecilia asked.

"Kathleen Cotter, ma'am. Kathleen Cotter from Ireland. This is my sister, Maureen Cotter." She reached out to take her sister's hand.

"What is packed in your crates, Kathleen Cotter?"

"We were cheesemakers at home, ma'am. 'Twas why we indentured ourselves. We brought our cheesemaking equipment to start our new life with our old belongings."

"Ma'am, she even packed the buckets," Maureen said. "She didn't know what kind of buckets we'd find in this strange land."

Cecilia smiled at her. "Maureen, we have buckets, but I look forward to seeing what kind of buckets your sister packed. Go to your cabin and get all your things together. You are going home with me."

Polly threw a ha'penny to a boy on the dock to run to Three Sisters and have Rollen and Travis fetch the wagon to load supplies. It took some time to separate the crates that the Cotters had stored from other boxes in the ship's hold.

Maureen had tried to stuff her gold-red curls beneath her mobcap. She'd wrapped a woolen shawl about her shoulders, which hid most of the rents and tears in her bodice. Kathleen hadn't bothered with arranging her clothes or hiding her filthy red hair. She climbed through the bowels of the ship, pointing out boxes labeled with her name and demanding attention about how each crate should be lifted.

"Do you know what you're doing?" Polly asked Cecilia.

"No, I don't," Cecilia answered. "But I'm going to learn." She watched Kathleen arguing with one of the deck hands about how to move a crate. "Those girls have heart and backbone. That's most important to me right now."

"You're describing yourself, you know," Polly said. "And Cecilia, do please let me have two or three of those dressed deer skins you mentioned. I want to use them by the door for the men to clean their boots."

Cecilia made a check mark in the air. "Deer skins to be delivered. Polly, you can be fun. Why didn't I know that when I lived in the tavern?"

"Because you lived in the tavern. You'd best go see to your new servants."

Cecilia grinned. "Our sister Charlotte was right. You are fussy."

CHAPTER 33

The first thing Cecilia found out about cheesemaking was the need for space. The equipment that Kathleen and Maureen had packed would take up the entire kitchen if they set up operations there. She looked at the boxes and crates piled in the wagon.

"I don't know where I'm going to put all of this," she said. "We may have to build a house for you."

"At home we did have a separate house for the cheesemaking," Kathleen said.

" 'Twas a great stone house with a huge table in the center of the cobbled floor," said Maureen. "Gran complained about the cold, but it had to be cool for the cheese."

"Your grandmother taught you to make cheese?" Cecilia asked.

" 'Twas a passion with her," Maureen said.

"My sister is correct." Kathleen leaned back against the wagon seat, plucking at her water-stained skirt. "Cheese and cleanliness. Oh, to be clean again. We haven't had a bath since we left Ireland."

"Little sponges here. Little sponges there. The water never hot." Maureen said.

"Where is your grandmother now?"

"She died," Kathleen said, her tone so abrupt that Maureen started wailing.

"Sister, hush. Miss Cecilia, our parents died when we were still very young. Gran took us in to raise and work for her. She left us all she had." Kathleen gestured toward the boxes in the wagon. "The contents of the little factory we had for making cheese. A few pieces of furniture, which we sold for the money to bury her. The clothes folded in her cupboard. 'Twas all she had."

"No, Kathleen, not all." Cecilia turned the horses into the lane that led to the house. "She gave you what we call grit."

"Grit, ma'am?"

"Strength. Determination. Without that you'd have stayed where you were. Instead you signed papers of indenture to travel across the Atlantic. You brought your treasures with you. If you'll look up, you'll see where you'll be living for the next few years."

"My, 'tis a grand house," Maureen exclaimed. "Two stories, with an attic above, and porches for the late afternoon when the work is done."

"And of course we'll be in the attic," Kathleen said.

"No," Cecilia said in the same emphatic tone the girl had used. She pulled the wagon into the back yard. Benjamin ran to open the barn doors and help her back into the wide space between the stalls.

Cecilia jumped from the wagon seat. "Thank you, Benjamin. Meet Kathleen and Maureen Cotter, come all the way from across the sea from a country called Ireland. Girls, this is Benjamin. If you'll show him which trunk holds your clothes, he'll take it to the kitchen porch."

Benjamin nodded at the girls. "Miss Cecilia, you does seem to collect womens. You say you wants the trunk at the kitchen?"

"Yes, please. We'll have to wash everything before it goes in the house. I can't imagine what being at sea all these weeks, with storms coming in to splash about in the cabins, has done to the contents. All these boxes need to be stored safely. If there's not enough room in the barn, then use any of the outbuildings. It may be a few weeks before we're ready to uncrate them. Get the other men to help."

Kathleen pointed to a small trunk. Benjamin lifted it, balanced it on his shoulder and headed for the kitchen.

"Miss Cecilia?"

Cecilia was unhitching the horses. She looked up at the younger girl. "Yes?"

"He won't steal our trunk?"

"Benjamin? Steal? Whatever gave you that idea, Maureen?"

Kathleen answered. "We've heard many tales of black folk. They steal and murder. They creep up on folk in the night and scalp them. They do horrible things."

Cecilia led the horses out to the small fenced pasture behind the barn. When she came back she stood to look at these strangers she'd brought to her farm. "White men steal and murder. White men creep up on folk in the night. White men do horrible things. Not all white men, but some. Not all black men, but some. Here, on this farm, we trust each other. Now get down from the wagon and come into the kitchen, where you will meet Lula, Benjamin's wife. If he isn't working with the goats, you will also meet their son Martin."

She headed across the yard without looking back.

Kathleen hurried to catch up with her. "Why do we need to wash everything we've packed?"

"Because it's evident that everything has been soaked with sea water. I've lived on the river all my life. I've seen what comes into the port on the ships. When you open the trunk you're going to find mold and mildew and maybe other unpleasant things. I don't want that in the house." She raised her voice. "Lula, I hope you have coffee."

Lula opened the door. "I ground the beans and put that coffee pot on the fire soons I heard you drive in the yard. Should be just 'bout ready for you.

"Kathleen and Maureen Cotter, meet Lula, who is my right hand around this place."

Lula nodded at the girls.

"They're cheesemakers, Lula."

"Miss Cecilia, I do like butter. I don't know if'n I ever taste cheese."

Henrietta, holding her shawl close about Rory, hurried toward them.

"Girls, meet my mother and my daughter." Rory held out her arms and Cecilia folded her own about her child. "I did so miss you today, my sweet baby. I love you."

"Miss you," Rory said. "Love you." She buried her head in Cecilia's shoulder.

Henrietta supervised the baths, cautioning Lula about how to scrub the girls. She mixed the yucca shampoo, advising Lula about not getting soap in the girls' eyes. She heated pot after pot of water for rinsing, warning Lula not to scald the girls. She lamented over the damage to their clothes, fussing all the while that it was going to be impossible to get anything clean again.

Lula began to bicker back. "Miss Henrietta, I knows how to wash clothes. I knows how to get rid of lice, if there be any in these skirts. I knows how to bring water up from the creek. I knows how to bleach these linens to get rid of the mildew in 'em. I knows how to make 'em white. Miss Henrietta, I even knows not to pour boiling water over somebody's head." Lula got louder and louder with each "I knows" she uttered.

"A black woman speaks to her mistress like that?" Kathleen asked.

Rory, playing tea party with her dolls, answered. "Grandma Henny having fun." She held up her grandma doll. "Fussy fun."

Cecilia, stirring the stew, broke into a peal of laughter.

It was when all of the men came trouping in for the supper meal that the girls showed the most surprise. Joel and Octavius hung their lanterns on wall hooks near the door. Urijah and Simple each carried an extra chair, placing them at the end of the long table. Little Martin, who had been in and out of the room most of the day, nodded to the two girls as he dumped an armload of firewood in the box near the hearth. Donny shyly told them his name before taking his place at the table. Benjamin, working beside Lula, ladled stew into a large bowl and placed it in the center of the table.

Henrietta settled Rory in her high chair, sat beside her, then beckoned to Kathleen. "Come sit here. Maureen, come sit."

"Urijah, will you say words for us before we eat?" Cecilia asked.

"Yes, ma'am. 'Thy meat offering shalt thou season with salt. Neither shalt thou suffer the salt of the covenant of thy God to be lacking from thy meat offering. With all thine offerings thou shalt offer salt. Thou shalt offer for the meat offering of thy first fruits green ears of corn -' "

"Popping corn," Rory chanted. "Popping corn."

"Oh, yes ma'am, Miss Rory. Thanks for popping corn. Thanks for two who come across the seas to sit at this table." Urijah nodded at Kathleen and Maureen. "Thanks to Miss Cecilia, who brings us together to serve our meat with salt. Amen."

"The tales of this land did not include anything like this." Kathleen gestured to include everyone seated about the table.

"There are many tales of this land that no one has heard," Cecilia answered. "Or if they've heard the tales, they don't give them credence. King George and England's Parliament certainly haven't listened or heeded. But I will have to tell you that what we do on this farm is *not* typical. It had a strange beginning." She looked at Lula, then Benjamin. "Events happened over which we had no control. We cling together."

Donny said, "That we do."

"A storm be coming," Lula said. She rubbed her elbows. "My joints is a'flaming tonight."

CHAPTER 34

The wind rose in the night. Twice Cecilia went down to the dining room to feed logs to the fire and check on the tobacco plants. She took an extra blanket in to Kathleen and Maureen, sleeping in the bedchamber across the hall from her room. She checked to be sure Henrietta was warm under her comforter. She lifted Rory from her crib and hugged her close in her own bed.

Toward morning she heard Urijah tiptoe through the downstairs hall. He would be as concerned about the young plants as she. He'd be feeding the fire, she was sure.

Icy drizzle began mid day. "It be freezing," Lula complained.

Cecilia had gathered the girls, with Benjamin, Simple and Donny, about the kitchen table. "How much room do you need for all of the cheese equipment?" was her first question.

"A room at least the size of your kitchen," Kathleen answered.

They used a coal from the hearth to sketch out different plans for the room. Soon the table top was covered with black lines and smudged angles. "If we builds to the side of the kitchen, we save putting up one wall," Benjamin finally said.

"An **L** shaped building. Benjamin, that's a grand idea." Cecilia rubbed the table top clean and drew the plan. "A porch to wrap from the kitchen door to the cheese door." She drafted a porch, deep enough for rocking chairs and tables. "My herb garden following all along the foundations. Like this." With a flourish she planted imaginary rows of thyme and garlic and mint. She threw the coal in the fire and danced around her chair.

"It should be fine," Kathleen said, still looking at the scribblings on the table.

"A new adventure. Some enthusiasm, please," Cecilia said. "Now what tasks shall I assign to you until we begin building?"

The next day, though still freezing, the rain had stopped. Cecilia sent Donny into Wilmington with Joel and Octavius to collect ballast stones dumped at the wharf. "Gathering those stones for the foundation walls will be a good test for your arm, Donny," she told the boy. "You let the men do the heavy lifting. We'll see how your arm handles riding in the wagon."

After the storms that destroyed the kitchen and damaged the house, Polly had been the one to place orders for lumber and hire carpenters to do the work. Now, for the first time, Cecilia had the responsibility. Mister Lillington had his lumber mill set up on the same creek as his grist mill, using the dam to run water wheels for both operations. On this icy morning she rode Big Boy to Lillington's Lumber Mill to see about placing her order for the rafters and board feet of lumber she needed for the cheese room addition.

"A room built just for making cheese?" Mister Lillington asked. "Can't believe you're starting another business, Miss Cecilia. I haven't had a taste of cheese in such a long time I've most forgotten what it'd be like to bite into. It will be good to have cheese again."

"So I can count on you as a customer then?" Cecilia settled in the saddle, her feet firmly planted in the stirrups.

Mister Lillington, looking up at her, commented, "Ma'am, long as you pay your bills, I'll saw your boards. This order will be ready in a week. You make a good cheese, you have a good customer. But, ma'am, I don't like seeing a woman ride astride."

Cecilia acknowledged his comment with a nod before she rode away, heading for Mister Ashe's plantation. There she made arrangements with the overseer to hire three slave carpenters. She signed the papers and again mounted Big Boy. The overseer didn't make remarks, as Mister Lillington had. He did look disapprovingly at her in the saddle.

As she trotted toward the Swann plantation, she muttered to herself. "Cousin Maurice said Polly and I should have been boys. What difference does it make to be male or female, if we get the work done." She patted the horse's neck. "Big Boy, do you think it makes a difference?"

The stallion made a snorting noise. He did not break his long stride.

Mistress Swann invited Cecilia in for ale. "Thank you, ma'am. I do accept. Can someone put Big Boy in the barn while we talk?"

With her horse cared for, Cecilia gratefully sat in the parlor, sipping hot ale. She tried to quickly get to her reason for the visit. "I've acquired two indentured Irish girls who are skilled in cheese making," she finally inserted into the conversation.

"Cheese! Wonderful!" Mistress Swann said.

"I need to hire a cooper who also knows how to use a forge and work iron."

"Cooper? Wherever for, Cecilia?"

"I need small casks for packing the cheeses. I need larger casks for the salt works. I need barrels for the tobacco I'm growing." Cecilia knotted her fingers under the folds of her skirt. "Mister Elliot, the blacksmith in Wilmington, told me you have a skilled cooper, a slave named Gabe, here on your place. I'd like to hire him for a few weeks."

"Hire? My husband, Samuel, is away with the troops just now. He's the one who looks after that sort of business."

"Mistress Swann, with your husband gone, I'm sure you're making decisions. I know Mister Swann has let Gabe out to others for coopering jobs. I really do need to hire him."

It took five shillings, placed on the table between them, for Mistress Swann to say yes. Two more shillings, added to the pile, gave permission for Gabe to have a horse to ride so he could go with her. "And to take the tools he needs to work with," Cecilia added.

Mistress Swann looked at the coins.

"I don't have any more hard money. I can, later this week, send you ten pounds of salt." Cecilia leaned back in her chair.

"You do run a salt works. I've heard about that." The woman's eyes grew hard. "You killed a man. Or was it two?"

"Everyone knows I killed two men. The sheriff was notified as quickly as I could get word to him." Cecilia kept her voice steady. This woman would not bully her. "I came here on business. I know that not all business deals are satisfied with silver, Mistress Swann. I'll give you fifteen pounds of salt but I want it all in writing."

"We are short of salt. Twenty pounds."

"I knew we could bargain together, Mistress Swann. While you're putting our agreement on paper, so the wording is exactly to your liking, I'll just walk down to the cabins and talk with Gabe myself."

Sleet was again falling as Cecilia and the slave, Gabe, rode toward the Black farm. Hunched against the foul weather, she did not try to talk with the man. She'd only told him, when she went to his cabin, that he was to pack everything he'd need for making casks and barrels, and that he would be riding with her.

Now he moved up beside her, his horse keeping pace with the stallion. "Ma'am?"

She turned to look at him. Pellets of ice glittered as they hit the brim of his hat. He was shivering. She didn't know if it were from the cold or the unknown.

"Yes, Gabe?"

"How long I be to your place, ma'am?" he asked.

"Two or three months, probably," she answered.

He nodded, apparently satisfied. He let his horse fall back a couple of paces. They rode the remaining distance in silence.

The men had stretched boards across sawhorses to expand the kitchen table for the extra people Cecilia had suddenly gathered. She searched the trunks in the attic, looking for linens that Emma Black had stored there. She spread the longest cloth she could find, which just cleared the ends of the boards.

As they finished their meal, Kathleen took a violin from its case and began to tune the strings. "Too much water on such a long voyage," she lamented. "I need to make new strings."

"I tried my viola this afternoon, Sister," Maureen said. " 'Tis in worse shape than your instrument."

"Lula, what do your bones tell you about the weather?" Cecilia asked.

"We be having a few more days of this cold, I be thinking."

"So we'll butcher the hogs. First thing in the morning we start." She nodded toward the three carpenters. "You can't build in this weather, so I'll just put you to work with other chores. Gabe, you can help, too. We'll get your forge and supplies set up as soon as we can. Besides, look at all the help you'll have doing your work."

Benjamin clapped his hands. "We talking about some good eating, folks. If you ain't tasted Miss Cecilia's barbecue and crackling bread, you just ain't ate."

"P-p-pumpkin pie," Simple stuttered.

"Will you butcher the calf, too?" Kathleen asked. "For the rennet. We must have the rennet for curdling the goat milk."

"I'm glad you reminded me," Cecilia said. "There is so much to learn about making the curds and whey and how to process the cheese."

She turned to Donny. "I want you to go into Wilmington with the buggy tomorrow and fetch Leah for the day. She's the one who knows how to mix the sausage. She can bring all her special spices with her. Kathleen, you'll have your rennet and what you need to make strings for the violin. I want to hear you play. Simple, you shall have your pumpkin pie. We'll even try a pot of popping corn. I'm sure Rory will share that with all of us."

Simple played a scale on his flute and swung into a seaman's song.

"Oh, Kathleen, listen," Maureen exclaimed. "He's tooting 'See My Wagon.' " She began singing:

> *"See my wagon, it's well laden, Now old wives it is holding.*
> *When to market they are coming, they are quarreling and scolding.*
> *Never again I'll take, for my part, any old wives upon my horse cart.*
> *Hup, horsey, hup!"*

"Hup, horsey, hup!" Rory sang each time Maureen repeated the line.

Cecilia danced about the table as she began collecting plates to wash.

CHAPTER 35

E veryone worked at the tasks of hog killing. When the last of the six shoats were salted and the meat hanging next to the deer haunches in the smokehouse, she had the men stretch the hides on the side of the barn to cure.

"Shoes and coats and vests," she said, looking at the array of hog and deer and bear skins spread across the wall.

"I do declare, Miss Cecilia, if you don't use every single thing of a animal 'cept maybe the grunt or the squeal. You is the savingest, workingest woman I ever did know 'bout," Lula said.

Leah, who was scrubbing down the tables she'd used for the sausage making, agreed. "Miss Polly and Miss Charlotte and Miss Cecilia is always been saving. They don't asked nobody to do nothing they ain't willing to do theyselves."

Cecilia hugged Leah. "It is so good to have you here, even if it is only for a couple of days. I do so miss you. I miss the tavern. I miss people coming and going and bringing the news every day."

"Miss Cecilia, Miss Henrietta say she gonna do some spring sewing for you and all these folks. I think she wants to make clothes for them new girls you got. We done brought her quilt frame on this trip, so she planning to do some quilting. That Benjamin of yours was to set everything up in the parlour. I know she gonna stay for Miss Rory's birthday."

Cecilia sighed.

"Now you stop that, Miss Cecilia. Your mama does the very best she can."

"I know she does, Leah. I know I'd best get back to work. We have to butcher the heifer. We'll have beef stew and beef pies and beef pasties. Lula, did I ever tell you that Mary Harnett taught me how to make those mouthwatering meat pies she calls pasties? Now Kathleen can teach me how to use rennet to make junket for the cheese."

As soon as the heifer was slaughtered, Cecilia handed a bucket containing the four stomachs to Kathleen. "While the men cut up the meat, show me how to make the rennet from these disgusting organs."

Their first attempts for a soft cheese produced a mixture that Cecilia thought would turn her mouth inside-out. Lula spit her taste of cheese in the slop jar.

" 'Tis awful," Maureen said. "Simply awful."

Kathleen ran her hands through the curds. She touched her tongue to the lumps clinging to her fingers. She spread a small portion on a cloth and examined the weight and texture of the mix. She reached for the crock that held the rennet and smelled the liquid.

"The mix is good. This mess of cheese goes to the chickens," Kathleen said. "I'll start again. This time, instead of the soft, I'll try for a semi-hard batch. Miss Cecilia, your basement is cool. Plenty cool for the harder cheeses, but I fear not for the spooning kind." Her bright red curls bounced on her shoulders as she shook her head. "Maureen, let's clean this away and start again. 'Tis for sure we have a goodly supply of goat's milk."

Cecilia went to the forge to check on the casks Gabe was making. He had already finished several small hogsheads for the salt.

"Miss Cecilia," Gabe said now, "did you really want the salt barrels this small? They'll only hold you 'bout twenty pounds of salt apiece."

"You've made exactly what I want. Most of the salt workers are women, so it's hard for them to lift the larger hogsheads. Besides, it's easier to transport the smaller barrels because they can be strapped on the sides of a horse. They sell faster, too."

She picked up a stave cut for the small casks she had asked Gabe to make for the cheese and ran her fingers across the smooth wood. "I like the way you sanded this down. Keep up the good work."

Gabe looked surprised at the praise.

"I hired you because Mister Elliott told me of your good work, Gabe."

The hint of a smile played about his mouth as he stirred the coals on the forge, pressing on the billows to fan the flames. He began to turn a narrow strip of iron as a binding for the small cask. He worked the metal deftly between the tongs and for a few minutes she watched the artistry of the work.

She nodded approval and started back to the house.

With so many people here, there would be extra covers to wash. That meant more soap. She looked in the ash barrels to see how much lye was forming to mix with grease to cook soap. She climbed down into the barn cellar to see if she had enough wax berries and tallow to make candles. She had to make the soap and candles while the weather was still cold. Oh, how she longed to escape.

In the dark of the cellar room she sat on a bag of rice and let the tiredness wash over her. Tears stained her face as she let herself give way to feeling helpless. Daisy, who had followed her, pawed at her leg. She cradled the animal in her arms.

"Daisy, it never ends. There is too much to do and it never, ever ends. Soon it will be time to plant. Then the harvest. Then the winter with hog killing again. I cannot do it all."

"No, Cecilia. You can't."

Cecilia wheeled about at the sound of the voice. Donny stood at the foot of the cellar ladder. "What are you doing here?" she screamed at him.

"I saw you come in the barn and I followed you."

"Why?"

"I wanted to help. I told Timmie I'd look after you."

"Donny, I do not need looking after. I can do the work. I will do the work. I will not sit around feeling sorry for myself." She dumped the cat on the floor and wiped her face with a corner of her apron. "Get out of my way, Donny, and let me go to work."

Back in the house Cecilia mixed yeast dough for baking while she watched Kathleen and Maureen begin the new batch of cheese. They heated the goat milk, added the rennet and poured the mixture into two bowls. They each worked the mixture with a wooden mallet to break up and mush the curds. They added tiny amounts of whey into the curds. Kathleen tested the mix with her fingers, shook her head at Maureen, and went back to the stirring. When she judged it the right time, the girls poured the contents of the bowls in a pot and hung it over the fire.

Cecilia draped a towel over her dough and placed her kneading trough near the hearth. "That is a lot of work and you've just begun the whole process."

Kathleen put her hands at the small of her back and stretched. "Yes, 'tis just the beginning. But then you have to punch down your dough and let it rise again to have good bread."

"Your bread is so good," Maureen said. She washed the utensils they'd been using, turning them on a towel to dry. She stirred the heating curds in the pot. "Oh, I do hope this turns out better than that other mess we made."

The girls poured the warm liquid through cloth, trapping the curds. They tilted the bowl to slowly fill two of the wooden casks that Gabe had just finished. "Now a cool place for this to sit while it ripens," Kathleen said.

Together the three of them went down the ladder into the cellar and placed the casks on a shelf. "What kind of cheese have you made?" Cecilia said.

"I do not know," Kathleen answered. "I hope 'twill be like the Danish cheese. I hope 'twill have spaced holes and a mild taste. 'Tis only a hope."

"We'll call it the Cotter Cheese," Cecilia said. "The Cotter Cheese Manufacturing Company for the best Cotter Cheese."

"Before we name it, we'd best make sure we can eat it," Kathleen said. "We'll know in a month, when it's aged enough to taste."

Cecilia spotted her first dogwood blossom the day Urijah had the first hoeing of the tobacco plants. The corn was beginning to sprout. Her house garden was planted with peas and beans, potatoes and beets, cabbage and carrots, pumpkins and squash. She broke a branch from the dogwood tree and brought it in to lay on the table board.

"A sign of spring," she said to Maureen.

" 'Tis a pretty sign," the girl said. "Spring is always a hopeful time of year."

"Oh, please let it be a year of hope and promise," Cecilia said.

CHAPTER 36

That year of 1780 was bountiful for the Black farm. The conflicts that engulfed the nation passed them by. Urijah's prayer, as they all gathered for supper in the middle of January 1781, was from the Psalms. " 'He maketh wars to cease unto the end of the earth.' We do pray that peace comes to the land."

They all knew of the recent patriot defeat at Camden and the heavy loss of life. The whole Continental Line had surrendered to the British at Charles Town. When Mama heard of that defeat she collapsed, wailing that she'd never see Charlotte again. The prickles on the back of Cecilia's neck were actually painful as she listened to Urijah's plea for peace. She massaged the skin, trying to blot out awful premonitions.

A few day later Cecilia was kneeling over the trough in the dining room, tending the tobacco plants, when she heard a hello shouted from the yard. She brushed the dirt from her hands and hurried to the back door.

Ricky Smith jumped from his horse. "I sure could use a hot drink," he said.

"Hello to you, too. Have you come to see your brother?" Cecilia pulled her wool shawl about her shoulders against the January chill and stepped out on the porch.

"Yes. And you as well, Cecilia. I bring news I think you need to hear."

Donny looked out of the door of Macdougal's cabin, where he had been staying. "What's up, Ricky? It's sure early in the morning for you to be riding."

"Let's go in the kitchen," Cecilia said.

Before she could pour hot ale in mugs, Ricky was telling his news. "The British are here. Major James Craig has marched into Wilmington. There are eighteen ships in the harbour, loaded with provisions and munitions. He has about four hundred troops of the 82nd Regiment of Foot. The townspeople bade him welcome. There really isn't anything else to do, because our fighting men are away. We have few guns. No powder or lead. Craig's put himself up in John Burgwin's house on Market Street. Of course, you'd expect him to pick the largest house in town in the center of everything."

"Oh, my." Cecilia set the pitcher of ale on the table.

"There's more," Ricky said. "Along with a bunch of other folk, Hooper's family has been harassed out of town. Major Craig knows William Hooper signed the Declaration of Independence. Knows of the efforts he's made for the patriot cause. Craig will take his wrath out any way he can."

"William Hooper's wife? The children? Where are they?"

"Wife and children forced to leave," Ricky said. "They weren't able to take a garment or food or anything else with them. I think it was Mary Harnett who helped them, but I'm not sure. Anyway, they got out of town."

"And Mister Hooper?" Cecilia asked.

"He wasn't caught. I don't know how he got away." Ricky reached for the pitcher and poured liquid into his mug. He took a sip before he went on. "The man they want most is Cornelius Harnett. He penned our new state documents and sent them out to be read by the people. He's been in Halifax, leading the important committees since before the Battle at Moores Creek. Even King George has sent out word to capture Mister Harnett."

Cecilia nodded. "Yes, the proclamation has been out on Mister Harnett for a long time. He and Cousin Maurice were among the first leaders of this area to write to the king, trying to get the ear of men in the English Parliament. Trying to get the Stamp Act rescinded. My goodness, Ricky, that was back in 1764 and '65. King George said he would never pardon Mister Harnett for his actions against the crown. His wife must be worried sick. Dear Mary Harnett."

Donny hit the table with his good hand. "I've got to do something. Scout. Take messages."

She turned to Ricky. "Why are you here? There's more than just bringing us the news about Craig marching his British troops into Wilmington."

"The troops are already fanning out to hunt for food and other provisions. They also want boats. Anything that floats. They're talking to sympathetic people who know the lay of the land, know about the Cape Fear River, ways to get to Cross Creek."

"Ricky, how are you able to ride about? You're so patriotic it's practically written on your forehead."

He grinned at her and swept back his mop of hair. "Written right there, is it? For the time being I guess I'll have to scrub better."

The grin faded as he went on with his news. "The new sheriff is Thomas Wright. He says we'll cooperate in every way with the British. But Cecilia, *you* are very vulnerable. You have prospered. Your goat herd is talked about all over town. Your cheese - that fabulous Cotter Cheese - has become rather famous. You can be sure of raids. These men are going to need provisions and they won't care how they get them." Ricky lifted his arms as if in surrender. "I don't know what you can do."

For a long moment Cecilia worked her fingers into twisty knots. Then she clenched her fists and drew her mouth into a fake smile. "Scrub better? Ricky, what a grand idea."

Her voice took on a flirty tone. "Why, Major Craig, welcome to our little port town.   Now I do want you to try out these delicious cheeses.   Sir, I say delicious even if they are of my own making."

She stood, gave a grand curtsy, fluttered an imaginary fan. "I'll supply you and your men with just as much of this fermented delicacy as possible. That means, of course, you'll leave my goats alone. Sir, I can't make your cheese if you take my goats."

She tossed her head. "Major Craig, when you have the opportunity to correspond with the good governor of New York, do please give him my regards. Governor Tryon's daughter Margaret is a special friend."

Cecilia fluttered her imaginary fan. "How special? Why, we played dolls together at Brunswick. She stayed in my home when her baby brother was born. My sisters attended Mistress Tryon when the dear infant died. The baby is buried at St. Philips, you know, just across the river." She looked toward the wall as if she were speaking directly to the British officer. "Sir, I consider that rather special."

Ricky clapped at her performance. "I'm convinced."

"Huzzah! Huzzah, Cecilia." Donny pounded on the table. "I've heard Polly do readings and give recitations. You may be a better actress than she is."

The next morning, her buggy loaded with gifts for Major Craig, Urijah drove her into Wilmington. Rory bounced on the seat between them.

"Remember, Rory, that we have to play act."

"Mommie, you've told me over and over."

"But I cannot tell you over and over enough." Cecilia sighed. "Rory, we will not lie, but we must be very careful about what we say."

A private led her up the wide front steps of Mister Burgwin's house, where the British soldiers were headquartered. Cecilia held Rory's hand as they climbed toward the porch. The private turned them over to a lieutenant seated at a desk in the front hallway of the house.

"Your business, lady," the lieutenant snapped.

"My name, sir, is Mistress Cecilia Black. This is my daughter, Rory Grace. I request an audience with Major Craig. I've brought special cheeses for the major," Cecilia answered, in the most ladylike tone she could muster.

"If you have cheese, I'll just take it." The man stood and pushed back his chair. "Where is the cow?"

"Cow? You mean to milk for the cheese?" Cecilia fluttered her fan. "Why, sir, my cheese is made from the milk of goats. The taste has quite a good reputation in the area. It would be in your best interests to grant me an audience with your commander."

"Who is this demanding an audience with me?"

Cecilia and Rory looked up the center stairway to see who had spoken. The lieutenant spun about, stammering, "S-sir, this woman s-says she has cheese."

"Good morning, sir." Cecilia curtsied. "Welcome to our fair town of Wilmington." She smiled up at a man whose military bearing indicated he was used to giving orders. His powdered wig sat far back on his wide forehead. His black boots glistened with polish.

The major stopped on the bottom step, his eyes traveling from Cecilia's mobcap to her slippers, then up to the hand which clasped the child's. "Who are you?"

"Mistress Cecilia Black, sir. I have a small farm north of town."

"Where is your husband, then? Why is he not the one to come calling?"

Cecilia covered her face with her fan, squeezing her eyes to make them water. Fluttering the fan across her face, she could feel the tears tracing her cheeks. She bit her lip to add to the play acting. "I run the farm with a few servants. My husband is dead."

"Don't cry, Mommie," Rory said. She looked at Major Craig. "Please sir, don't make my mommie cry."

"Well," the major said. "Well, well. Lieutenant Leggett, show these two ladies upstairs to my office. And send for tea. It will never do to make the Mommie cry. I'll listen to her." He moved up one step before turning to look back. "Have the cheese brought to my office. I think I'd like to taste this product. Come, Mistress Black."

Cecilia and Rory followed the major to the second floor parlour, where he settled behind a desk, motioning them to be seated. She had been in this room so often as a girl. She had played with the Wright children who lived there after Mister Burgwin went back to England. She wanted to point out to Rory that Mistress Wright had ordered, all the way from France, the very couch on which she sat. She wanted to caress the Egyptian cotton fabric on the window hangings. When the orderly brought in the tea service she almost exclaimed over the familiar silver pieces and china cups.

Major Craig invited her to pour the tea. Before she could reach for the pot, the orderly was back with the two large baskets Cecilia had packed that morning.

"The cheese?" the major asked.

"Sir, there are several kinds. I had no way of knowing your taste, so I brought samples. There is a Camembert, which I'm sure you know came from France into England several hundred years ago. With our limited resources, it may or may not taste exactly as you might remember it from home."

"A Camembert? That is more sophisticated that I expected," the man said.

"There are several flavors we have been experimenting with. One is a yellow cheese made with garlic and another yellow with onion. Then we have a reddish cheese with spinach flavor. You will find a loaf of my bread in the basket if you'd like to sample any of them now." Cecilia poured tea, first for the major and then for herself.

"What makes the difference between the yellow and red colors?"

"The type of rennet used to clabber the milk," Cecilia said.

Major Craig took a knife from the desk to cut a small wedge from one of the cheese balls. He chewed, closed his eyes and grunted. "Garlic." He cut a piece from another of the balls and repeated the tasting, the closing of his eyes, the guttural noise. "Spinach."

Rory, staring out of the window toward the west, suddenly exclaimed, "Mommie, I can see the Market House from here. And the river. It all looks different than it does from the street."

The major looked toward the child. "I command that street, little Miss Black."

Cecilia held her breath. Rory, however, remembered. She turned from the window. She sat on a chair in the corner of the room. She folded her hands in her lap and smiled at the major.

"A bewitching child, Mistress Black. Well trained. Many of the children I've seen in this wilderness are most ill behaved. A shame." He tore off a hunk of yeast bread, smeared it with the Camembert and bit into it.

"Most delicious." He leaned back in his chair. "What do you want, Mistress Black?"

"I want you to leave me alone," Cecilia blurted.

"Leave you alone." The major's tone was dry. "We are at war. I command your city. The people of Wilmington have welcomed me. Why should I leave you alone?"

"No reason, sir. No reason at all. Except perhaps for your own gain." Cecilia sat on the very edge of her chair. "If you leave my goat herd alone, I can furnish you cheese. If you leave my small farm alone, I can furnish you vegetables by springtime. If you leave my servants alone, we will have tobacco by late summer."

"I can take any of that, Mistress Black. At any time."

"Major Craig, you can take my goats and slaughter them. Your men will have food for a week. Then you'll have to find some other place to look for rations for your troops. You can send a raiding party to tear up my fields, but then I will not be able to plant." Cecilia struck her fan against the desk. "When you destroy, you decimate property for the people who live here." She hit the desk a second time. "You also hinder your own attempts to feed your men. A strategy of peaceful coexistence is my proposal to you, sir."

"Where did you attend school, Mistress Black?"

"School? I learned lessons at my mother's kitchen table."

Major Craig strode from the room. Through the open door Cecilia heard him yelling for Lieutenant Leggett. Then he was back, the young officer behind him. "The lieutenant will ride out to your farm with you, Mistress Black. We'll see just what you have there. Then we can debate this coexistence you propose."

Cecilia stood, her hands behind her back. "Sir, I would be delighted for Lieutenant Leggett to accompany me. Do you wish for us to go now?"

"Of course, now." Turning to the officer, the major said, "Take two men with you. A full report as soon as you return. Remember, lieutenant, at this time, a reconnaissance trip only."

Cecilia hoped neither man saw the trembling in her hands as she and Rory followed them down the stairs and out to the carriage.

CHAPTER 37

As she climbed into the carriage, Cecilia saw Ricky riding toward them. Suddenly she knew how to warn everyone on the farm. "Why, Deputy Smith, you're out early this cold morning."

Ricky's eyebrows seemed to make a question mark on his face. He glanced at Lieutenant Leggett, looked beyond him to the two uniformed men seated on their horses behind the carriage, stared for a moment at Urijah, hunched over the reins.

"Good morning, Mistress Black." Ricky tugged at the brim of his hat. "You have an escort, I see. Where are you going?"

"To the farm, I think." She looked up at the lieutenant. "Is that right, sir?"

Instead of answering her, the lieutenant spoke to Ricky. "Major Craig ordered us to accompany Mistress Black home."

"Have a fair journey, then." Ricky trotted off down Third Street.

Cecilia lifted Rory into the carriage and climbed in after her. "Let's go, Urijah."

As soon as Urijah picked up the reins, she leaned toward him and whispered. "As slowly as you can, without arousing suspicion." She leaned back and put her arm about Rory. "I am so proud of you, sweet child. We'll have to go on pretending for a while longer."

Rory snuggled against her. "The major didn't offer me tea."

"My dear daughter, I do hope that is the only thing to go awry today. Right now I just trust that Ricky is riding his heart out, heading to the farm. Oh, he has to hide Big Boy. He has to. I'll not have a British soldier riding that stallion."

"Miss Cecilia," Urijah interrupted in a low voice, "worry won't mitigate circumstances." Then, speaking so the men following them had to hear, he said, "I does think that trace is loose." He stopped the carriage, climbed down and began to inspect the harness.

"Everything seems to be in order," the lieutenant barked, as he rode up to watch what Urijah was doing.

Cecilia really looked at Lieutenant Leggett. His straw-colored hair was fastened in a tight queue that hung below his red coat collar. His blue eyes were steely and she saw no warmth in the look he turned on her. He could be a formidable adversary, she thought.

Urijah climbed back in the carriage. "I thinks the man be right, Miss Cecilia. Everything do seem in order." As they moved forward, the men fell back. Urijah spoke under his breath. "Mister Ricky is well ahead, ma'am, beating a trail through the old path."

When Urijah stopped the carriage at the front at the house, the soldiers dismounted and followed Cecilia up to the front door. She led the way into the parlour, where Henrietta sat with her sewing spread in her lap.

"Mama, these men are with Major Craig's army," Cecilia said.

The lieutenant bowed slightly. "Ma'am."

"Why, how nice to have young men in the house," Henrietta said. "Gentlemen, please have a seat. Cecilia, you must tell Lula to bring drink and refreshment."

"No, thank you, ma'am." Lieutenant Leggett turned to Cecilia. "Show me where you make cheese. Show me the goat herd. Take me around this plantation of yours."

"This is no plantation, sir," Cecilia said. "A small farm is all I have. I'll be glad to show you around. Come this way."

Through the kitchen, where Lula stirred a pot in slow motion, through the cheese room, where Kathleen and Maureen washed what Cecilia knew were clean pots, through the yard to the barn, where only a lame pack horse stood munching hay, Cecilia led the three men.

Behind the barn she whistled for Pru. The dog bounded to her side and Cecilia gave her the hand signal to round up the goats. With a short bark, Pru began to gather the animals, guiding them toward the fence. When the herd was all in view, she signaled for Pru to come to her. "Good girl," she said, scratching the dog behind her ears.

"I'm impressed," the lieutenant said. He reached down to pat the dog's head. Pru's snarl stopped his hand.

"Would you like to see anything else?" Cecilia asked.

"What are the cabins down the path there?" Lieutenant Leggett pointed toward the slave dwellings. "And what is that building?" Again he pointed.

"The log building is where we cure tobacco. The cabins are where the servants live. Do you wish to inspect them?"

"I think not. I've seen enough." He took a paper from his tunic. "Major Craig wrote this out. It gives the terms of supplies you will bring to us each week. In return, we will consider your property secure from our troops. We will, of course, also expect information on any patriot movement you see in the area. You will report when you bring in the supplies."

Cecilia started to read aloud from the paper. "Beans. Potatoes. Pumpkin. Cabbages." She looked at Lieutenant Leggett. "It's wintertime. I don't have vegetables growing just now. I cannot supply most of what you've written here. As soon as we plant the garden, I'll let you know. You have to let plants grow before you can harvest."

"Ma'am, you have food for your household. You will share," the lieutenant said.

Cecilia held the paper close to her chest as she followed the men through the house, across the front porch and watched them ride down the lane. She sank down on the steps, her hands shaking so badly she was afraid she'd tear the fragile agreement she held.

Urijah found her there. "Don't give up now, Miss Cecilia. You can't give up now."

"I didn't agree to spy. Oh, I didn't agree to that." She shook the paper at him. "I didn't agree to give away all the garden produce. What will we eat?"

Benjamin had come up behind Urijah. "Why do that old rooster lift his head and crow ever morning, Miss Cecilia? 'Cause he scared if he don't, the sun won't know it got to come up. At the end of the day, that old hen knows she got to fold her head under her wing to let the sun slide on through the sky. She scared of the dark. But she got faith that old rooster gonna call the light again next morning. Now, Miss Cecilia, we knows yous scared. You can tuck your head under your wing. But I been seeing you crow for the sun ever since you come to this place. I 'spects you got some crowing left to do."

Urijah nodded. "It's called courage, ma'am."

"Courage? I don't have courage. Benjamin is right. I am sore afraid."

"That fear is what you need to give you the resolve you need now," Urijah said.

"Polly used to go in the necessary and cry. She'd come out with her shoulders squared and go back to work," Cecilia said, remembering her sister.

"Socrates thought that if -"

"Socrates? Who is that?" she asked.

"Socrates was a teacher in ancient Greece. One of the philosophies he taught was that if all our misfortunes are laid in one common heap, when everyone must take an equal portion of them, most people would be content to take their own," Urijah said. "Your sister did what she had to do. I have no doubt you will do the same. As I said, Miss Cecilia, it's called courage."

Cecilia pulled herself from the steps. "Well," she whispered. She opened the door into the front hall. "Well." This time she spoke with more assurance. In the parlour she scooped Rory from her chair and hugged her tight. "Well," she stated with firm decision. In the kitchen she took Lula's hand to hold for a long moment. In the cheese room she nodded approval at the girls.

She went to the cabin to find Donny. "Where did you hide Big Boy?"

"We tied him down in the swamp. Cecilia, we can't leave him like that."

"No, but we can build him a shed with a stout floor to keep his hooves out of mud and water. We'll have to make sure he has hay and oats every day. Make sure he can get to good water. Donny, this is going to be a long siege. I've taken on my portion of it, though I'm not sure yet what it is. But it's mine."

She leaned against the door jamb. "Donny, the enemy is closing in on us."

CHAPTER 38

Major Craig's presence in Wilmington did not stop the news from getting through. A victory for the patriots at King's Mountain; General Cornwallis marching out of the little town of Charlotte; George Washington's choice of a Major General Nathanael Greene appointed the new commander of the Southern Department. These were Ricky's hurried messages as he gobbled down the stew Cecilia served him.

"Ricky, how are you getting this information?" Cecilia asked. They were huddled by the fire in the kitchen. The girls were working in the cheese room, filling the small wooden casks with cheese which she was supposed to take to Wilmington the next day.

"Don't ask, Cecilia."

"Tell me about this General Greene, then."

Ricky finished the last of the stew, scraping the bottom of his bowl with the wooden spoon. "Greene's a Quaker, born in Rhode Island. But he's a fighter and he seems to know the South."

Cecilia slid a piece of apple pie in the empty bowl. She sliced a generous piece of cheese on top of the pastry, watching Ricky attack the food. "Is food scarce then in town?"

"Yes. Food is scarce. Salt is almost nonexistent. No one's seen sugar since the British soldiers marched up Market Street back in January." Ricky ran his finger around the edge of the bowl. "You have that crazy bargain with Craig, but I'm not sure how good it is. If his men get hungry, they'll come. Cecilia, if they do, don't fight them. You can't win."

The men were planting an early spring garden when the rumor of a battle at a place called Cowpens filtered through the town. Cecilia had delivered cheese and butter, dried apples and firewood early that morning. Now she sat in the tavern, drinking a hot ale with Polly.

"Greene retreats, then advances," Polly said. "It must be working, because he's winning battles. Timmie was with him for a few days. Then he was sent to Virginia."

"Timmie was here?"

Polly nodded. "He didn't want Mama to know. He did ask about Donny. If he could travel yet. I told him no. Cee, Timmie was only here long enough to get shoes and food."

"Our men won at King's Mountain. We won at Cowpens. The British are getting hammered in their southern campaign. Major Craig sits here in Wilmington. Polly, I can almost feel it. Cornwallis is coming here."

"Don't say that, Cecilia. I know he's coming, but don't say it."

Cecilia stood and wrapped her shawl about her shoulders. "Do I tell Mama anything about Timmie?"

"Maybe tell her that we heard he's well. He's thin enough he has to double rope his breeches." Then Polly giggled. "He's got a horrible beard. It's so scraggly that I know some officer is going to come along and make him shave."

A warm spring breeze sang across the fields the afternoon the last tobacco seedling was in the ground. Cecilia, who had been helping with the planting, stretched to ease her back. "Good job. Good job by all of you. I know it's the middle of the day in the middle of the week, but let's take the rest of the day off. As soon as the horses are fed and stabled, go fishing. Or take a nap. Or whatever you want to do."

As the men followed her toward the barn, Simple took his flute from inside his shirt and began to play a dancing tune. Octavius and Joel hummed along. She looked back to see Benjamin do a shuffle step in the path.

Urijah's urgent voice brought them all to a stop. "Good afternoon, sir."

Lieutenant Leggett sat his horse in their path. "A merry band of folk," he said.

"Lieutenant Leggett." Cecilia greeted him. "We are a hard working band, just finishing up planting a field. May we assist you in some way?"

"Where have you been hiding those horses?"

"My plow horses? They haven't been hidden, sir." She prayed her voice would not shake with the fear lurking inside her. "Perhaps when you visited before they were in the forest, pulling a wagon load of wood. Or doing some other chore. Everything and everyone here has duties, sir."

The lieutenant turned his bay toward the house. Cecilia and the men followed. In the yard several soldiers sat in the shade of the barn. An empty wagon was pulled up to the fence where the goats milled about. Lula was on the kitchen porch, standing with her feet apart, hands on her hips, as if she were on guard. Henrietta and Rory sat on the house porch, watching.

"Who else lives here?" Lieutenant Legate asked.

Cecilia looked around. Little Martin and Donny were nowhere to be seen. She wasn't about to mention either of them. "The girls who make cheese are here."

"Call them out."

Kathleen and Maureen stepped out on the kitchen porch. "We were pressing curds. 'Tis a tiresome task," Maureen said.

"Irish," jeered one of the soldiers.

Kathleen glared at him. "Yes. Irish. And 'tis proud we be of it."

Cecilia rested her hand on the bay's bridle. "Sir, why are you here?"

The lieutenant dismounted. "We need food. I want twenty of your goats."

"That's almost half my herd." Anger surged through her. "Do you want to drive them to Wilmington? Or do you want them slaughtered here?"

"It will be easier to take the bodies, I should think," he answered.

"I guess you are not used to honoring agreements, sir. You were to leave my goats alone." Cecilia tried to keep the wrath from her tone of voice. Inside she felt a burning rage that threatened to choke her. It was the same fury, the same fear, the same need to act that she'd felt so long ago at the salt works. Then, she had killed two men.

"I am not here to discuss honor or the lack thereof. Mistress Black, we will have your goats."

Cecilia picked up the shovel from the field cart, climbed the fence where the goats had gone back to their grazing and walked up to one of the nannies. She slammed the shovel into the goat's head. As the animal fell to its knees, she took her knife from its sheath and slit the goat's throat.

"Benjamin, start throwing these carcasses over the fence," she called.

Benjamin and Joel leaped over the fence as Cecilia slammed the shovel into the head of another goat.

"Mistress Black," Lieutenant Leggett yelled. "What are you doing?"

She cut the throat of the second goat before she looked up. All but one of the soldiers, who was vomiting into his hands, were staring at her.

"You requisitioned my goats, sir. You said it was easier to carry them dead. I am carrying out your orders."

Again she lifted the shovel and brought it down with a heavy blow. Again she welded her knife.

Another of the young soldiers was retching. Still another cried out, "Stop her, sir. Women aren't suppose to kill like that. Stop her."

Cecilia looked at the young man. "You don't come from a farm? You've never seen a slaughter? Too bad, really. How did you think the meat got to the table?"

A rogue gander, followed by his harem, paraded into the yard. He took a sight on the lieutenant's silver knee buckles and spread his wings. With a honk of triumph, he charged. Before the man could sidestep, the gander took a beak full of skin from his leg.

Cecilia covered her mouth so the men would not hear her snicker. She was trembling from the effort of the slaughter of her goats. Blood from their bodies covered her apron and bodice. The gander's attack was so much what *she* wanted to do that nervous giggles bubbled up and up inside her.

The lieutenant drew his bayonet and swung as the gander attacked again. The fowl's head sailed through the air as its body fluttered about on the ground. The squawking geese flew into the trees at the edge of the woods, their loud protests overriding the lieutenant's shouts.

Cecilia was laughing so hard now she had to hold on to the fence. Benjamin and Joel, Octavius and Urijah were shaking with silent glee. One of the vomiting soldiers, still leaning against the wall of the barn, wiped his mouth with the back of his hand and began to chuckle.

Rory danced around on the porch. Her singsong of merriment caused them all to look at her. "The gander's gone. The horrible gander's gone." She spun around and dropped a curtsy. "The gander's gone. The horrible gander's gone," she sang again.

Henrietta's lips twisted in a half smile, while her knitting needles darted in and out of the yarn.

The lieutenant climbed over the fence and took the shovel from Cecilia's hand. "No more, Mistress Black."

She pushed her hip against a fence post for support. "But sir, I've only killed three. You said you needed twenty."

"No more, ma'am." He threw the shovel toward the cart. He looked at his men and gestured toward the three dead goats. "Load them."

As he climbed back over the fence, Cecilia saw that blood from his shin was running into his shoe. She stood inside the fence while the solders put the dead animals in their wagon. She watched as they assumed the semblance of a parade line.

"Lieutenant, take the gander, too," she called.

"Mistress Black, I'll leave that creature for your supper. Few, man or woman, could have done what you have done here."

"Is that admiration I hear, sir?" she asked.

"I shall look forward to seeing you when you make the next delivery of cheese," he answered. "Good day, ma'am."

When she could no longer hear the creaking of the wagon or the hoofbeats of the horses, Cecilia climbed over the fence to stand in the middle of the yard. She threw back her head and yelled to the tree tops. "I'm mad. I am mad. I. Am. So. Mad."

They all looked at her.

Cecilia gazed at the herd of goats. She looked at her daughter, standing on the porch, her mouth open as if she would start wailing. "I had to get it out. I just had to. Rory, I'm all right now. I'm all right. Does anyone want to pluck and gut this fowl?" she asked.

Urijah answered. "I'll prepare it for the spit, Miss Cecilia."

Rory again was dancing about on the porch.

"I'm as glad as Rory that old gander is no longer here to menace the yard." Cecilia's voice shook now as she spoke. Whether from anger or fear she wasn't sure. To calm herself she untied her apron and held it up to look at the blood soaked into the fabric. "I hope it's always that easy to get around their orders. After all, today we only lost three goats."

CHAPTER 39

As Urijah stopped the carriage at the corner of Market and Third Streets, Cecilia heard hammering coming from close by. "What *are* they building?" she whispered.

One of the privates who had been at the farm when she killed the goats was on guard duty at Burgwin house. "Major Craig requests that you come inside, Mistress Black." The young man held his hand to steady her as she climbed from the carriage.

Cecilia found Lieutenant Leggett waiting for her in the hallway. "Major Craig is in his office, ma'am," he said.

"Ah, Mistress Black," the major said, as she walked through the open door. "Sit down, please."

She folded her hands in her lap, waiting.

"I understand events went a trifle amiss at your farm. I trust the misunderstanding is corrected." The major leaned back in his chair. "Sometimes young officers interpret orders differently than they are given."

"Major Craig, your men have to eat. I know that. I'm glad you spared my herd so that I may continue to bring you cheese. Is there anything else, sir?"

"Vegetables. I request vegetables."

Cecilia bowed her head. "Yes, sir."

"You can bring produce each week when you deliver the cheese." The major stood behind the desk. "Now, tell me what you know of your neighbors."

"Know? Of my neighbors? My house is a long way up a lane from the road and few stop in. Besides, they are all as busy as I with spring planting, with hoeing fields, with other farming duties."

"You will report any news you hear." The major sat and picked up a paper from his desk. "That's all."

She trudged down the stairs and walked the block to Three Sisters. There she sagged into a stool by the hearth.

"Lawdy, Miss Cecilia, what be wrong with you?" Leah asked.

"This war, Leah. This cursed war that takes and takes and takes. My beautiful goats. Donny's arm that's still not completely healed. Macdougal gone off to fight no one knows where. My brother. Now my crops. Major Craig is demanding my crops."

"Urijah come in here to say that major done invite you to his office." Leah sat down next to her. "What that man want?"

"Vegetables. Produce from my fields. Leah, I know they have to have food. It's much easier when they ask instead of just commandeering. But if they take all my garden crops, what will we eat? How can I prepare for winter? We have cabbage ready, and the first early peas. There's nothing else right now that's ready for harvest. And he wants to know about my neighbors. I don't know anything. What will I do? What can I tell him?"

Leah put her arm about Cecilia's waist in a warm hug. "I don't know, child. I don't know."

"What would Polly do? Leah, what would my sister do?"

"I remember when the law went out 'bout the stamps. We couldn't get trade in. We couldn't get trade out." Leah turned the spit where a ham was roasting. "Supplies got mighty low. We just hung on. What I remembers most, child, we just hung on."

Polly came down the stairs and stopped at the hearth, her hands resting on the mantle. "I heard what Leah just said. She is right that we just hung on. We were short of everything. Food. Drink. Clothes. The barrels of turpentine sat on the sleds, waiting for transport. Men acted like drunken fools, burning people in effigy, parading through town demanding impossible conditions of the government. Of the law."

"What did you *do*, Polly?"

She sighed. "I talked with Cousin Maurice. I consulted with Mister Ashe. With Mister Dry. I made soap. I made candles. Leah and I experimented with recipes." She looked at Leah and grinned. "Some of those dishes were awful. There was one where we mixed bear meat with some kind of herb that didn't blend very well."

Leah chuckled. "That was, for sure, 'bout the worstest one we tried."

"And, dear sister, I read a lot." Polly extended an arm, palm up, as if she were addressing an audience. " 'Tomorrow, and tomorrow, and tomorrow, creeps in this petty pace from day to day, to the last syllable of recorded time; and all our yesterdays have lighted fools the way to dusty death.' "

"Shakespeare?" Cecilia asked.

"Oh, yes. It's from *Macbeth*. 'Out, out, brief candle! Life's but a walking shadow, a poor player that struts and frets his hour upon the stage.' " Polly paced in front of the hearth, then brought her hands up to cover her ears. " 'And then is heard no more; it is a tale told by an idiot . . .' "

Polly stopped, her arms extended as if to ward off blows. "Oh, dear Cee, it's all a matter of survival, waiting them all out, hanging on till they're tired and will leave us alone. Their message is 'full of sound and fury, signifying nothing.' "

Cecilia stood and hugged her sister. "I love hearing you recite. It's one of the many things I miss, not being here at the tavern. When Rory is ready to start reading, I want you to teach her all about Shakespeare and the other books you know about. In the meantime, we have to eat. Instead of your 'sound and fury,' I want to hear a joyful noise. I don't know when I'll ever hear it again."

She reached for her cloak. "Now I'm going to the farm and see what else I can plant."

"Oh, before I forget," Polly said. "Did you hear all the hammering and sawing when you drove into town? The soldiers are building a prison."

"Who will be imprisoned?"

"Major Craig is rounding up any who speak out against the king."

As her garden grew so did the rumors of the armies. Cornwallis marched out of the tiny village of Charlotte. Greene zig zagged ahead of him to cross the Dan River and rest his troops in Virginia. By early February the British were in Salem, trying to outguess the elusive patriot leader, General Greene.

By March two brigades of North Carolina militia, totaling over a thousand men, had joined with the patriots. Another thousand Virginia militia and over 500 Continentals joined up as well. Nathanael Greene now had an army of over four thousand men under his command, fighting for freedom from the British. General Charles Cornwallis' ranks had shrunk to almost half that number.

When Cecilia came to the tavern on a blustery morning in late March, Polly met the wagon at the door to whisper, "Go right on to the barn. Now!"

Urijah flicked the reins across the horse's back. "Must be trouble, Miss Cecilia."

Through the window she could see several men, dressed in their Tory colors, seated for a late breakfast. Leah, in her haste to serve the meals, scuttled by a window without even looking out.

A man, the rider who had brought their latest information from the west, was buried under hay in the barn loft. He roused from sleep when Polly touched his shoulder. "You said to wake you so you could be on your way. But Mister Bennet, my sister is here and we both want to hear the news. Please tell us now."

The man sat up and pushed aside the blanket he'd wrapped about himself. Cecilia saw that his left arm was gone, his coat sleeve knotted near his shoulder.

"You're the man from Brunswick," Cecilia said. "Way back in the summer of '75, when Fort Johnston was burned."

"And you're that feisty girl who talked back to the tavern keeper, you are. Pleased it is I am to see you again."

Polly handed the man a bowl of stew she'd brought. He settled it on his lap and spooned up the food as fast as he could swallow. "I do thank you, ma'am. For the food and the safe place to hide. As for the news -"

He wiped his mouth with the back of his right hand. "The battle was the worst I've known. And ma'am, I've been in a few. 'Twas a place they call Guilford Court House. Men falling, dead and dying. The colours they wore made no never-you-mind. Then the rains started. Sheets of rain. There weren't no tents for the wounded. There weren't no food. There weren't nothing but the moans of the dying in the field and the silent crying of the living huddled under the trees. Waiting. Waiting for the light of day to come."

Mister Bennet stood, shook out his blanket and rolled it to fit his pack. "Guilford Court House will be remembered, I'm thinking. People said those damn rascal Tories won, but it shore seemed like to me there was many of them wiped out."

"Sir, do you know the names of any of the men who were there? At the battle?" Polly asked.

"Did you have a certain person in mind, ma'am?"

"Timmie Moore," Polly said. "Timothy Charles Moore. Donny Smith."

"Sorry, ma'am. Ain't names I know. But that do remind me. I got a letter here for a Pauline Moore. That's you, ain't it?"

"Oh, yes. I'm Pauline Moore." She held out her hand.

The man pulled a crumpled paper from his knapsack and handed it to her. "Now how did you say I get out of this town?"

Cecilia spoke up. "I'll take you a few miles north in my wagon. I'll get you a horse and send you on your way."

"North it is, then." Bennet shrugged his pack across his back. "Lead the way."

Mister Bennet slept in the back of the wagon from town to the farm. Cecilia gave him a slab of bacon and a small bag of cornmeal while Benjamin saddled one of the plow horses for him to ride.

"Most 'preciative, ma'am. Most 'preciative for the food and the horse and the care."

"Ride safely," Cecilia said. As he rode down the lane, headed toward New Bern, she felt the awful prickles on the back of her neck.

"Benjamin."

The man had been leaning against a stall. At the tone of her voice he came to full attention. "Ma'am?"

"We're in for something."

"Ma'am? Do you know what kind of something?"

"No." She cupped her hands, as if to hold grain. "Benjamin, we have to hide everything. Food for us. Food for the animals. Supplies of any kind." She turned her hands over, this time as if to scatter whatever she held. "Or it will all be gone."

CHAPTER 40

Polly drove the buggy out to Cecilia's farm the next day. The letter Bennet had given her was from Charlotte. "I had to share, Mama. It is so good to hear from our sister." She settled next to Henrietta on the sofa to read aloud.

> *Dear Mama, Polly, Cee & all,*
>
> *I take my pen in hand to say we are surviving. Our little house in this miserable town ~~ if this small place can be called a town ~~ is cramped & cold. I sit by the hearth with baby Richard on my lap, Jonathan & Alexander playing at my feet. Mother Reynolds lies ill, but seems ready to rally her strength if I talk of going home. Her old servant Hannah tends to her with great patience. We hired a woman who cooks & helps me with my little ones. When spring comes I hope to travel back to the plantation near Savannah. I have not heard from my Johnny in almost a year now and I must get back to the coast to find out where he is. I do so trust that all of you are well. How I miss you.*
>
> *Charlotte Reynolds*

"She doesn't tell us the name of the miserable town," Cecilia said. "She has no date on the letter, so we have no idea when she wrote this. How are we supposed to get in touch with her?"

Polly grinned. "Charlotte always did think we could read her mind!"

"Another little boy." Henrietta sighed. "Oh, my, my. Three boys to care for."

Rumors and reports, in equal measure, sailed from the west down the Cape Fear River. By the first of April, 1780, General Cornwallis was in Cross Creek. Gossip pronounced him furious that Major Craig had not arranged supplies for the army. And, said the rumors, the people of the area were not inclined to join with Cornwallis or the British troops. In spite of the fact that there were so many who had previously been supportive of the King, pronouncing themselves ardent Loyalists, Cornwallis could gather few new recruits to join his battle-weary men.

Boats, which were supposed to be ready for him to convey his men down the Cape Fear to Wilmington, were not at Cross Creek when he arrived there. An angry and hungry body of men, followed by an assortment of hangers-on, continued the trek by foot down the west bank of the Cape Fear River.

Their movement devastated the countryside. The men plundered houses and farms, stripping people of any food or valuables they could find. Those following the troops were, if possible, more savage in their pillaging than the uniformed soldiers. It took six days for Cornwallis's army to travel from Cross Creek to a bluff across from the port town of Wilmington. Waste and ruin lay in their wake.

"Mistress Black, they are savages," said a rider who stopped at her farm late one morning. "Deputy Smith asked me special to stop off here to tell you that. He said to tell you, if you got anything here you value, you'd best be sure it's hid."

He gulped down water from the gourd Lulu handed him. "They taking horses and oxen and even cows for to pull the wagons. And the women, by god." He shook his head. "Mistress Black, the women is worse than the men. Perdition on all of them!"

"Women?" Cecilia asked. "Cornwallis has women in his army?"

"They ain't in the army, ma'am. They just follow the army. They're like a swarm buzzing 'round people's heads. They mount the best horses with the best sidesaddles they can steal. They dress in the finest clothes they done took from some plantation house they robbed. They got rings on their fingers and rings in their ears. You can't fight them."

He handed the gourd to Lula. "Mistress Black, there's dead and dying all along the roads. It's gonna bring sickness. On the top of everything else, we're gonna have sickness to deal with from them corpses."

Cornwallis got his troops across the Cape Fear River. He settled into the Burgwin house on Market Street. The jail that Major Craig was building, though it did not yet have a roof, began to fill with prisoners. Anyone who spoke against the king was suspect.

The spring rains brought a humidity the soldiers did not well tolerate. They were quarrelsome. They were hungry. They sent raiding parties in all directions, indiscriminately demanding and taking food anywhere it could be found.

As she had been doing for months, Cecilia took her casks of cheese into Wilmington to deliver to Major Craig's office, even though she knew General Cornwallis had moved into Burgwin's house. She had Urijah drive the cart to the kitchen entrance and she walked around to the front steps. A sergeant she did not know stood guard at the foot of the stairs leading to the spacious porch.

"Good morning, sir," Cecilia greeted the man. "I have a delivery for Major Craig."

"I saw your man drive 'round to the back. You have no business here," the sergeant said.

"But I always visit with Major Craig when I bring the cheeses. Please let the major know that I am here. Or get word to Lieutenant Leggett."

"Lieutenant Leggett, ma'am? He's with the major and the general." The sergeant shifted his position, as if he were growing impatient with her. "You need to move along. We don't need country women hanging 'round the General's headquarters."

"Sergeant, I'm not sure you know what you need," Cecilia said. "I will leave, but I think you'll find that Major Craig *will* want to know that I was here."

She walked back to the house kitchen. Urijah was lifting the last of the small cheese casks from the cart. A corporal, who seemed to be the cook, had already sliced a wedge from one of the cheeses.

"Good," he said, as he tasted the food. "Fresh. Ma'am, I'll just keep your slave here to make cheese for me to serve the general."

Cecilia's fear gripped her stomach. She knotted her fists behind her back. This young corporal could take her cheese. He could take her slave. He could take her life. She had only her wits to use against him.

"Corporal, Urijah does not make the cheese. He just delivers for me." Cecilia realized she was talking very slowly, as if she were trying to explain something to a misbehaving child. She continued. "I don't make the cheese. I just see that the deliveries are made."

She climbed onto the wagon and sat, her hands folded in her lap. "Urijah, drive me home, please."

When Urijah climbed on the wagon seat and took the reins, the corporal did not try to stop them.

They were well out of town before Urijah spoke. "Miss Cecilia, you didn't get to visit with your sister."

"Urijah, you know the soldiers will be coming for the goats. The cheese will not be enough for them."

"Yes, ma'am. I was thinking the same thing."

"We can't hide the goats. Everyone in the whole area knows we have a large herd of goats. We have most of the horses in the swamp. We have a well hidden shed for the cow. But I'm going to lose my goats." Cecilia's fingers knotted her apron until it was a wad in her lap.

"The goats are vulnerable, Miss Cecilia."

"So are we all, Urijah." She shook out her apron. "So are we all."

CHAPTER 41

Just how vulnerable she was Cecilia found out the very next morning. A lieutenant, with about fifteen men, rode up the lane and into the yard. This was an officer she did not know and she hurried from the kitchen to meet him.

The lieutenant swung from his horse, nodded at her, pointed toward the goat enclosure and snapped his orders. "Every one. Kill every last one."

Pru gave a sharp bark to her puppies, who were yelping from their home in the barn. Then she crouched at the gate of the goat pen, ready to spring at the first soldier to approach the herd.

"Heel," Cecilia commanded. She slapped her thigh. "Come, Pru. Heel."

The dog stood beside her, a low growl rumbling in her throat.

Cecilia held tight to the fear and anger that coursed through her. She would not let these men know how much she hated them. She spoke with authority.

"Lieutenant, if your men climb the fence, instead of opening the gate, you can better contain the herd," Cecilia said. "Your work will be much more efficient."

The man looked at her. "Why should you care? We're going to take the goats."

"Yes, I know that." Cecilia put her hand on Pru's head, rubbing behind her ears, as much to comfort herself as to calm the dog. "I know you're taking my goats. But you'll take them more quickly, and be gone from my home, if you do your work properly. Sir, I do want you gone."

Cecilia, her grasp firm on Pru's collar, went to sit on the porch steps and watch the slaughter of her herd. The wagon bed was sagging with carcasses when she heard a horse galloping up the lane. Lieutenant Leggett thundered into the yard, shouting commands as if he were on a battle field.

"Stop! Stop now, I say." He leapt from the saddle. "Cease this senseless killing. Not another of these creatures."

The lieutenant turned to confront him. "General Cornwallis issued this order. We must have meat for the troops."

"You have sufficient. This meat will spoil before it can all be cooked." Lieutenant Leggett lashed his riding crop against a fence post. "I outrank you, sir. I say stop."

"You may outrank me, but I'm under orders from the general."

As the argument continued, the soldiers stopped their gruesome work. Some leaned against the fence, some sat on the ground. One took his pistol from the holster to clean. Another plaited a piece of rope.

Cecilia's anger was diverted by Leggett's arrival. Fear of what else the soldiers might do played in her thoughts. "They're just boys," Cecilia whispered to Pru. "They're just boys, like Timmie and Donny. Far from home. Far from family. Taking orders from officers who don't agree on what to do or how to do it. What if they don't listen to orders? What if two bickering lieutenants are what they need to have them turn on my household?"

Pru whimpered.

"Shhh, girl. They'll be gone soon. Maybe we're supposed to give up the cheese business. We had to stop making salt because of the British riding the countryside."

"Miss Cecilia?" Lula's voice came from behind the kitchen door, where she was trying to hide. "Miss Cecilia, is you all right?"

"No, Lula."

"Who is you talking to?"

"Just talking to the dog, Lula. Just talking to the dog."

Lieutenant Leggett and the general's lieutenant seemed to have reached an uneasy truce. The driver of the wagon climbed on the seat and whipped the reins across the horses' backs. The soldiers mounted to follow the wagon down the lane and out onto the road. The lieutenant followed his men.

Lieutenant Leggett tipped his hat to Cecilia. He seemed to be waiting for some sign from her.

She didn't move from her seat on the steps. The stink of blood, of urine and feces, made her gag. She buried her face in Pru's fur, breathing in the dog smell, feeling the heartbeat of the living animal.

A bleat from the goat pen was so surprising she gasped. Three nannies and two kids pressed against the fence. Several carcasses still lay inside the pen. Flies were buzzing about them. Overhead she heard the cawing of crows gathering in the trees.

She stood, still holding to the dog. "Pru, we have some cleaning up to do."

Lieutenant Leggett, from the back of his horse, nodded at her. "Mistress Black, you have a *little* something left."

"I had a herd of fifty-two. Now I have three nannies. That is a little something. Sir, I do thank you for your intervention."

He brought his crop down across the horse's rump. The animal reared, snorted and tore down the lane at a gallop.

She watched horse and rider out of sight before she called, "Benjamin. Simple. I know you're in the barn. Take care of these dead goats. We can save the meat. Kathleen, you and Maureen comfort the nannies. I don't know what we'll do with the milk, but milk them we will. Joel, you and Octavius start raking the yard. Sprinkle sand over the blood."

She turned to vomit, wishing she could spew up the anger that burned inside her guts. She wiped her mouth with the back of her hand, and called again. "Little Martin, we need extra wood for the smokehouse. We need to cure this meat. Martin, I want hickory for flavor."

She retched again and clutched at her stomach with her free hand. "Pru, find Rory. Guard Rory." She let go of the dog's fur. "Pru, guard Rory."

Pru bounded toward the house.

The men began to work. Kathleen and Maureen headed for the goat pen. Henrietta and Rory, hand in hand, came out on the porch of the house, Pru pressed close by the child's side.

Cecilia sank down on the porch steps, gagging bile. It was all that seemed left in her stomach except for the anger. "Damn the war." She heaved. "Damn this slaughter."

Lula handed her a cup of water.

She sloshed the liquid in her mouth and spit it out.

"Lula, please make me a cup of sassafras tea. Hot. Sweet with honey."

"I be putting the water on right this minute, Miss Cecilia." Lula disappeared into the kitchen.

Cecilia settled back on the steps, trying to calm her nausea. The fear and anger still surged through her. The hair on the back of her neck itched. Over the noise of the work in the yard, the sound of the ax splitting wood and the lullabies the girls were singing at the goat pen, she heard the creaking of what sounded like another wagon.

As Lula handed her the cup of tea, Cecilia saw a rickety carriage coming up the lane. It was driven by the oldest man she had ever seen. His black mummified-like face was set in shriveled lines. His rheumy eyes appeared blind. A wagon, piled haphazardly with boxes and barrels, followed close behind the carriage. Timothy was driving two of the sorriest horses she had ever seen. His own horse was tied behind the wagon on a lead rope.

Henrietta screamed and ran toward the carriage, her arms open. "Charlotte! Oh, my dearest Charlotte!"

The old man pulled back on the reins even as Henrietta climbed on the carriage step. "Oh, Charlotte, however did you get here? How wonderful to see you!"

"Who be Charlotte?" Lula asked.

"The other sister, Lula. Charlotte is my other sister. It looks as if she's brought her babies and her mother-in-law and her belongings." Cecilia sighed. "Lula, it looks like Charlotte has come to stay."

 CHAPTER 42

Charlotte had always described her mother-in-law as disagreeable and cantankerous. Mistress Reynolds was now scolding at her servant, Hannah, with every other breath. From the carriage her voice rang forth. "Where is my shawl? Hannah, you have misplaced my shawl."

Hannah handed Mistress Reynolds the wrap as she continued her tirade. "Where has that girl brought us? It smells like a slaughterhouse. She said we would be safe."

Henrietta hugged Charlotte. Two little boys jumped down from the carriage and began racing about the yard. Rory ran to grab their hands and pull them into a circle.

"You're my cousins," Rory yelled. "Grandma Henny says you're my cousins from Charles Town."

Cecilia walked up to the carriage. "Mistress Reynolds, I'm glad to have you here."

"Wherever *here* is," the woman exclaimed. She looked toward the goat pen, where Benjamin and Simple were butchering the goats the soldiers had killed. "Work like that should be done in private. Tell those slaves to move those -" She groped for words. "Those beasts. Why did you let them slaughter them right there in an open field?"

"The British slaughtered them, Mistress Reynolds. They didn't care where they did their work."

"And the road. That girl said we were on the Great Post Road from the north, but it didn't seem like it to me. I've never been so bumped about in all my life."

Cecilia held out her hand. "Let me help you down. A cup of tea and perhaps a slice of apple pie will help you to feel better."

"Feel better?" She gingerly put her foot on the carriage step and stumbled to the ground. "And see that? I have been seated so long I can barely move my legs. These patriots, thinking they can run a country. The very idea of rebelling against a good king like George the Third. He only wants what is best for his fellow countrymen."

Mistress Reynolds fussed her way into the house, into the parlour, into an invitation from Henrietta for a cup of herbal tea.

Charlotte looked at her sons tearing about the yard and sighed. She wrapped Cecilia in a huge hug before she stepped back to really look at her. "Timmie said we'd be safer here than at Three Sisters in town. He said that British soldiers have been billeted there. Oh, Cee, can you take us all in?"

"Take you in? Of course. Charlotte, we have so worried about you. Your last letter didn't really let us know where you were. None of your letters told us how awful your mother-in-law is. Charlotte, she is a disaster. Does she really believe in the British cause? The British invasion of our lives?"

"Yes," Charlotte said. "She is Tory to the core of her depraved, perverted heart. If she has a heart, that is."

Cecilia put her hand over her mouth to cut off her next question.

Charlotte answered anyway. "My Johnny was with the British contingent. He joined with them. He fought with them. They don't seem to know where he is. We haven't heard from him in over a year now."

She stared dry-eyed toward Mistress Reynolds. "I am worn to a frazzle trying to appease that woman. I have completely lost control of my boys. I don't know what to do."

Cecilia gave her sister another hug as she mentally counted plates and servings of beans and wondered if there were potatoes ready to dig.

Kathleen, who was helping to carry boxes from the carriage to the house, came up to them. "Ma'am, I'll look after Mistress Reynolds. She's not as much angry as she is scared. Scared of the changes. Scared of dying. My gran got quarrelsome like that the last few months of her life."

"Take her, please," Charlotte said.

"Kathleen, for better or worse, she's yours," Cecilia said. "Take charge of her." Still holding her sister's hand, she smiled. "Now I've got to figure out where to put everybody."

She sent Joel and Martin to the creek with Jonathan and Alexander. "Catch fish if you can," Cecilia said to Simple. "But take soap and get those boys bathed."

Henrietta and Rory, over tea in the parlour with Mistress Reynolds, played with baby Richard. Hannah slumped in a chair near the kitchen table while Charlotte gratefully sank into a tub, behind a screen in the kitchen, and soaked her bones.

The men salted down the goat meat and started the fire in the smokehouse for curing. Cecilia had them cut one large portion of the goat meat into small pieces. She dropped the meat in the largest cooking pot she had. She added herbs and onions and dry peas as the water began to boil, then swung the crane to the side of the fire so the mixture could simmer all afternoon.

In the garden she pulled up two cabbages. She scraped through leaves in the edge of the woods and found mushrooms to cook with them. She picked a few early strawberries, which she mashed into a pastry mix to have for spoon bread. By the time everyone gathered for the supper meal, she knew she had enough food.

With a table brought into the kitchen from the cheese room, there was space for all. Cecilia stood and looked down the expanse of faces. "Thank you. Thank you for remembering the plans we made for just such a horror as we had this afternoon. We lost most of the goats, but not one person was injured because you trusted me. We still have all of the horses. The old cow is safe. The provisions are still well concealed. Thank you for all the help you've given."

She smiled at Charlotte. "My sister and her sons, their grandmother and two of her servants, are with us. Tired and a little worn out in places, but safe. We'll wait to hear their adventure stories, for I know they will be interesting. Timmie is here, though he'll never tell us where he's been."

Cecilia sat down. "Now I'll ask Urijah to give a blessing."

"You know you are not letting that black monkey speak at table," Mistress Reynolds scolded. "It's bad enough that I have to eat with him sitting here."

Cecilia hadn't realized just how angry she was until she slammed the palms of her hands on the table board. "Ma'am!"

The force of her voice brought Henrietta to the edge of her seat. Charlotte's mouth dropped open. The little boys stopped punching at each other, sat straight in their chairs and stared at her.

"You are welcome in my home. You are welcome at my table. You are welcome to any thoughts you wish to think. But in my house you will be civil. Your speech will be circumspect."

She looked up and down the crowded table. "We are a family. We are together, no matter what the circumstances. Urijah, we would hear your blessing."

The man stood. He, too, looked down the long table. "Miss Cecilia, I thought at one time today, when the invasion of soldiers rode into the yard, that the scripture would have to be from the story of Job. I changed my mind when your sister and her household rode in. The Psalms seemed more fitting. 'Man goeth forth unto his work and to his labour until the evening. O Lord, how manifold are thy works! The earth is full of thy riches.'

"But looking at this table, with the bounty spread for us, I think Matthew told the story for tonight's blessing. The disciples said there were only five loaves and two fishes to feed a multitude gathered about them. The Master said to bring him the bread and fish. He blessed the loaves and fish and gave them to the disciples. There was enough that they all ate. Miss Cecilia, we know that if there is even so much as a crust of bread in this house, we all will eat. That is a powerful blessing. Amen."

Mistress Reynolds nodded. "Well, he does speak plainly."

Kathleen reached for a piece of meat and placed it on the old woman's plate. "Eat hearty, ma'am."

"I do intend to," she said.

When they'd finished the meal, Kathleen and Maureen brought out their string instruments, swinging first into a lively reel.

Then they played the new tune everyone was singing about a Yankee riding on a pony. Simple took out his flute to join them as everyone sang the chorus.

"Mind the music and the step and with the girls be handy."

" 'Pop, Goes the Weasel!' " demanded Rory. "I want to hear the pop!" So they sang through the verses, ending with one that had them all clapping.

"From round about the countrymen's barn the mice begin to mizzle.
For when they poke their noses out Pop! goes the weasel!
The painter works with ladder and brush, the artist with the easel,
The fiddler always snaps the strings at Pop! goes the weasel!"

Maureen snapped the strings of the viola through a scale while they all applauded each other. Simple played his flute to lead the way to the cabins. Henrietta and Rory took Charlotte and her family upstairs to bed.

In the quiet of the kitchen, Cecilia sat alone, finally able to let go her anger. She pounded on the table with her fists, crying out, "They took my goats. Why did they have to kill my goats? Why did they have to kill my goats?"

She cried for so many losses. For the death of Kenneth. For the horror at the salt works. For the callousness of the soldiers who walked about Wilmington's streets as conquerers and rode into her farm to take what they wanted. "It's not fair. It's not fair," she sobbed.

Daisy, who had been dozing by the hearth, crept into her lap, kneading Cecilia's legs as if to give comfort. She gathered the cat in her arms. "None of it is fair," she whispered. She cradled her head in the crook of her elbow. And there, with her head in her arms on the kitchen table, she sobbed herself to sleep.

CH*A*P*T*E*R 43

B efore daylight Cecilia was hoeing, moving the lantern down the rows as she worked in the vegetable garden. When she saw the smoke rising from the kitchen chimney, she blew out her light, put her hoe over her shoulder and went to Donny's cabin. She had really tried to make him leave. He would not.

"Walk into Wilmington," she said to him now. "Tell Polly -"

"Why walk, Cecilia?"

"If you're riding, the soldiers will take the horse from you. If you're on foot, it's easy to slip into the woods, if they should come after you."

Donny nodded.

"Tell Polly that Charlotte is here with all her children and her mother-in-law. Oh, that Mistress Reynolds." She bit her lip to keep from saying more about the old woman. "And I need seed."

"What kind of seed?" Donny asked.

"Anything you find. Beans. Peas. Pumpkin. Squash. Watermelon. Wouldn't you love to have a taste of watermelon?"

Donny grinned. "Watermelon would taste good."

"And cloth. Donny, we need to make skirts and breeches and aprons." She held up her hands. "Good material. Needles. They are so precious that you may not be able to find needles, but try. And thread."

"I'm supposed to carry all this on my back," Donny stated.

"Urijah will go with you. He has such good sense. You listen to him, Donny. Come eat before you go."

She gathered eggs from the hen house on her way to the kitchen. She fed Donny and Urijah, praying for their safety as they walked down the lane and out of sight.

Then, with the children seated at the table for their breakfast, she organized a school. "Charlotte, you and Maureen will teach. I think in the house, at the dining room table, would be a good place to work."

"Teach?" Charlotte complained. "I don't know how to teach."

"What can I teach the little ones?" Maureen asked.

"You both know more than the children do. Start with their letters." Cecilia began to stack plates. "Maybe Simple can make reed flutes for each of them and you can teach them music notes. Charlotte, you have a beautiful hand. Teach scripting. Your Alexander is a year older than Rory. Maybe they can learn together. Your Little Johnny should be reading by now. He's three years older than his brother." She continued to clear the table as she talked. "You can both add. Show them how to put one and one together."

She poured hot water over the dishes in the pan. "Then, when lessons are done, they can do chores." She scrubbed the first plate and set it in the rinse water. "Bring in wood." She cleaned another plate. "Pick strawberries. Feed the chickens." She added another plate to the rinse water. "Find a quail's nest and gather her eggs. Quail eggs are rich for making cake batter." She began to dry the plates. "We need the food and the children need to be busy."

Charlotte was fussing, but Cecilia pretended she could not hear. She picked up the pan, walked to the door, and tossed the dishwater into the yard. "Kathleen will be occupied with Mistress Reynolds, Charlotte. You know old Hannah cannot climb those stairs and do for her what's needed. There won't be enough milk from three nannies to make cheese, Maureen. So decide how you're going to work together."

Lula came up from the cellar, a small basket of potatoes over her arm. "Miss Cecilia do believe in work."

"You're worse than Polly," Charlotte said. "Giving assignments. Handing out tasks for everybody. I never thought I'd say it, but Cecilia, you're *far* worse than Polly."

Cecilia grinned. "My dear sister, thank you. What a wonderful compliment." She hung the dishpan on a peg on the wall. "Far worse than Polly? Well, good for me! What was that line that Polly used to quote? It was something about being furious frightens out fear. So you be angry with me, all you want. Because, Charlotte, I am furious. I'm angry at the men who killed my goats. I'm angry at Cornwallis for invading Wilmington and the whole countryside, demanding my animals and my vegetables and all my other crops. I'm angry at a war that didn't have to take place." She beat her fists against the table. "I'm furious enough that all the fear seems to be driven from me."

"Have you taken to reading Shakespeare?"

"No, Charlotte. I can't find time to read." She swept her arm out in an expansive gesture. "I was going to be the mistress of a grand plantation, caring for a rich husband who would ride out and tell the servants when to plant and harvest. I would sit and sew a fine seam and keep the keys so I could tell everyone else what to do."

Her arm dropped and she sighed. "I'm just a farmer, trying to bring in enough food to keep us from starving. I can't find time for anything but work. Now get that school organized and get your children under control."

When Donny got back, well after the supper meal, he had news from Wilmington that set Cecilia's head spinning. Major Craig's stockade, built on the north side of Market Street, was filling with men. His soldiers, and groups of Cornwallis's troops, out collecting food, brought in prisoner after prisoner. One was Colonel John Ashe, fervent patriot, who was picked up trying to leave his home on the Cape Fear. Skirmishes at Heron's Bridge, up the Cape Fear River, and patrols scouting the countryside, brought in more men.

"Cecilia, the cavalry patrols are the worse," Donny said. "The men don't question. They just arrest and throw people in that open stockade."

"Donny, how did you manage to avoid them?"

He shook his head. "I made sure my bandaged arm showed. Gained a wicked limp. Borrowed it from Ricky." He grinned at her. "You should have seen Urijah's act. He hunched, like his spine was completely out of whack, dragging his feet like he didn't have the strength to pick 'em up at all. If anybody tried to talk to us, he started drooling stuff from his mouth. If I hadn't known him before, he'd of scared me with his crazy act."

"How does Polly fare?"

"She and Leah are managing. She said she didn't know when she could get away to see Charlotte. Cecilia, the tavern is filled with British officers. They've taken over all the upstairs rooms. Polly and Leah are sleeping in the hayloft with Rollen and Travis guarding the ladder. I did get a bunch of seed and marigold plants and geranium slips and some kind of herbs. I'll put everything in the barn, so you can sort through it later." He started toward the barn, but turned back. "I forgot to tell you about Mister Hooper."

"William Hooper? Has he been captured, too?"

"Mister Hooper escaped from Masonboro Sound with the clothes on his back. He's been living there since his wife and children were chased out of town. Some said he was heading for Halifax to be with his family and work with the state committees there. He did get away."

As Donny continued toward the barn, Cecilia sat on the back steps. Just thinking of the men who might be incarcerated in a stockade was bad enough. To think of men like John Ashe, who had fought so well for the patriot cause, and William Hooper, who had the courage to sign the Declaration of Independence, was almost more than she could bear.

Even as Cornwallis, for the British, and Greene, for the Americans, worked on some semblance of prisoner exchange, the April days grew warmer. The weather was grand for growing crops, but the British troops were not used to the humidity, wrapping like wet sheets about their bodies and their equipment. Sickness crept into the camps. Rather than risk fevers, or worse illness that might come, Cornwallis marched north on April 25, 1781, with his 1400 men. They had been in Wilmington for a little more than two weeks. That had been long enough to devastate the countryside. Major James Craig was left to hold the port city.

A newspaper article stated that the resolution to march into Virginia was "bold and vigorous." The editor went on to say that the "measure, in a situation which afforded only a choice of difficulties and dangers, was undoubtedly the best that could have been adopted." It was indeed "a perilous adventure . . ."

"Perilous!" Cecilia exclaimed when Ricky told her about the article. "What isn't perilous just now. Taking a deep breath is perilous."

Then Ricky rode out a few days later with the most awful news she'd heard yet. "Cornelius Harnett has been captured, Cecilia. It is a heavy blow for the patriots. He has worked so tirelessly for the cause."

"Oh, Ricky, I remember him coming to the tavern in Brunswick with Cousin Maurice when they were writing letters about the Stamp Tax. That was in 1765, so many years ago. He's never stopped trying to address wrongs." She wiped her face with her apron. "But Ricky, I thought Mister Harnett was in Halifax or Hillsborough, or someplace to the west with the state government. That he was out of harm's way. What happened?"

"He came to Wilmington to get monies and papers and was trying to deliver them when Craig's men caught him. He was sick, or he'd have ridden 'em out and left 'em behind. You know he races to win. Sick as he was they got him. Heard one of the men laughing in the tavern last night how Mister Harnett couldn't even ride, so they just threw him over his saddle like he was a sack of 'taters and brought him into the stockade. Cecilia, they wouldn't let Mistress Harnett see him or take him medicine or food."

As Cornelius Harnett lay in the makeshift prison in Wilmington, General Cornwallis marched the British Army to the Duplin Court House, crossed the Burgaw and Rock Fish Creeks to the Neuse River, and pillaged north.

When Mister Harnett died, his wife was finally allowed to take his body. It was the end of April, 1781.

"Thou shalt be secure, because there is hope. . . . Thou shalt take thy rest in safety," Urijah said at supper that night after they'd heard of Cornelius Harnett's death.

"Urijah, there is no safety. There is no rest," Cecilia contradicted him. "It's the end of spring. It feels like the end of the world."

CHAPTER 44

Cecilia and her extended family settled into a routine that stretched from before sunup till well past dark. Food was always a major concern. She hunted at least once a week to supplement the hams and pork loins hanging in the smokehouse. Gabe, working at the forge he'd built, stayed busy with the many tasks of making casks and repairing equipment. Cecilia had him make hoes for Rory, Johnny and Alexander. Joel fitted the iron-tipped wooden pieces with short handles of hickory for the children. Each morning during the summer, before their school lessons, she took them to the vegetable garden and gave them their own short row of plants to cultivate.

The tobacco ripened early. "Thank goodness for a cash crop," Cecilia said to Urijah, as they watched the men lift a tier pole of the ripened leaf from the barn. "With the salt works shut down, I do need any money we can bring in."

"How are we fixed for salt?" he asked.

"We're low. Urijah, we're low on everything. We'll keep plugging along."

So they laboured through till harvest. Usually Lieutenant Leggett came with the men who took their share of her crops. He always took the time to sit and talk with her.

On a cool October morning, Ricky rode in with news. "There's a lot of raiding in the South Carolina back country. Timmie was just down there and said he saw one place where scalawags murdered a woman and her three children, rounded up the slaves and burned the house and fields."

"Not the British. Raiders?" asked Cecilia.

"It just can't be true," Charlotte said. "I know many of those people. Ricky, you're talking about a farm almost next door to the Reynolds Plantation. Did Timmie know anything about the Reynolds place? Oh, Ricky, did he hear anything about my Johnny?"

"The house was still standing. Timmie said he made a point to ride by there. No one was on the place, Charlotte. There was no one to ask about your husband."

"The overseer is supposed to be there," Charlotte said. "He had more than fifty slaves to work that place. Where are they all gone?"

Ricky shrugged his shoulders. "I'm sorry, Charlotte. The other reason I'm here, Cecilia, is that I have a letter for you from Lieutenant Leggett." He handed her a folded paper.

As she took the letter from him, she invited him to have a slice of pie. Charlotte walked with Ricky to the kitchen and Cecilia sat on the steps to read the message.

> *Mistress Cecilia Black,*
> *May I have the Privilege of calling on you on Tomorrow*
> *at Two o'clock in the Afternoon. I have a Matter to discuss that I*
> *think will be to our Mutual Benefit. I will hope for a Response with*
> *the messenger I sent with this short note.*
> *Your servant*
> *Richard Leggett*

"What on earth does he want now?" Cecilia asked herself. She stood, shoved the note into her pocket and went to find Ricky. "Tell the lieutenant that I will be glad to see him tomorrow. Explain that I have no paper on which to write a note. He might even think I don't know how to write." She grinned at the thought. She knew that many of the British thought of people in the colonies as ignorant and unlearned. Maybe the lieutenant would think that as well.

"I'll tell the good officer as soon as I get to town," Ricky said around the pie in his mouth. He swallowed the last of the water Lula poured for him and grinned back at her.

The message nagged at her. After supper was over and the kitchen cleaned, she asked Kathleen and Maureen to put the children to bed so she could talk with her mother and Charlotte.

"Is there trouble?" Henrietta asked.

"Mama, I do not know." She handed the note to Charlotte. "Read this and tell me."

" 'Your servant,' he signs it?" Mama asked, when Charlotte finished reading aloud. "What could the lieutenant want that would be to your mutual benefit?"

Charlotte grinned. "He's going to propose, Cee."

"Propose? Propose what?"

"Oh, Cee, don't be stupid. He's going to ask you to marry him."

Cecilia's mouth dropped open. Charlotte put a finger under her sister's chin to push it back in place. "I've seen it coming. Every time he's here he looks all moony-eyed at you. Think about all he's done to try to protect you. Think of the hours he's sat with you on the porch while his men load up the food stuffs."

"Marriage? Cecilia, do you like the man?" Mama asked.

"Of course I like him, Mama. But I never thought about *marrying* him. I've never thought about marrying anybody since Kenneth died. No, no, no." Cecilia waved her arms in the air and let them fall in her lap. "I have a farm to run. I have all these people to look after. I have a daughter to raise."

"If you marry a British officer, he'll take you to England," Charlotte said.

"*Eng*land?" Mama wailed.

Then Charlotte was saying angry things about a backwoods farm in North Carolina as opposed to castles in a foreign country and Mama was arguing that there was nothing backwoods about where they lived and England was a lifetime away.

Cecilia pushed up from her chair and went to lay a log on the fire. She stood watching the flames, thinking of Kenneth. Of his beautiful black hair he never could secure in a proper plait and his deep blue eyes that looked at her with love. He *had* loved her, even while he lied to her. He had lied about so many things. She knew she hadn't really known Kenneth at all.

She thought of Macdougal. He went after a bear waving an empty gun. He stumbled and bumbled over almost every task he undertook. But Macdougal had a good heart. She knew that heart. He might not be the right man for her and she'd never thought about marrying him. And, of course, he had gone off to war and might never come back here at all.

She thought of Ricky, who played a good game of marbles and laughed whether he won or not. He went out of his way to bring news to the farm and ask how she fared. Ricky never let his short leg interfere with what had to be done and always did a good job of whatever he went after. She had always felt a strong affection for him. His friendship meant everything to her.

She knew nothing about Richard Leggett's heart or thoughts or feelings. Until she got that note from him, she hadn't even remembered his first name.

"England? Would he really take her away?" Mama continued her wailing. "I'd never see Cecilia again. I'd never see sweet Rory Grace again."

"Hush," Cecilia said, turning back to them. "Hush, both of you. Right now."

Henrietta hiccuped, but she stopped crying.

"What will you do, Cee?" Charlotte asked.

"I will hear what Lieutenant Leggett has to say. He may not have marriage in mind at all. He may want more food for the troops. He may want to commandeer this house for some purpose. Who knows. I'll have to hear him out. Then I will think. Then I will decide," Cecilia answered.

CHAPTER 45

When the lieutenant rode up the next afternoon he stopped in the front of the house. He handed the reins to one of the two men who had ridden with him and stood for a hesitant moment by the steps.

Cecilia went out to the porch to greet him. "Come in, sir."

He carried his hat in his hands, seated himself in the gentleman's chair next to the long couch in the parlour, and fiddled with the braid on his uniform jacket.

Cecilia poured sassafras tea in his cup before she spoke. "We don't have sugar or lemon, Lieutenant Leggett. We do have honey, if you'd like a sweetener in your drink."

"Thank you. Honey would be good." He sat on the edge of his chair and reached for his cup.

Cecilia swallowed hard to keep from giggling. He looked as if he'd fly away if she so much as made another sound. She gazed at the fire, burning low on the hearth. She listened to the sounds coming from the dining room where the children were having their lessons with Maureen and Charlotte. Mama would be with them, she knew, listening for any conversation she could hear from the parlour.

Finally Cecilia looked at the lieutenant sitting so rigidly before her. She took a chance that he'd stay seated. "Sir? You wanted a word with me?"

He put his cup on the table by his chair. "Mistress Black, I have a proposition for you. I would ask for your hand." He stood and began to pace from his chair to the hearth and back. "This is usually done with the head of the house, but here you don't have a man to ask. So I have come directly to you."

"Sit down, Lieutenant Leggett. Please."

He sat, again perched on the very edge of the seat.

"Lieutenant, you *are* talking to the head of the house. I would have to know how much of my hand we're discussing. Can we start from there?"

He leaned forward. "That is one of the traits I've come to so admire about you, Mistress Black." He put his hands on his knees. "Please, may I call you Cecilia?"

He didn't wait for her answer. "Cecilia." It was as if he were trying out the sound of the name. "Cecilia. Your openness. Your courage. Such admirable qualities for a young woman. Your life here is so difficult. Your responsibilities so tremendous. I would like to take those burdens from your shoulders. Relieve you of the weight. Set you above all this drudgery. Marry me, Cecilia. Let me take care of you."

"Lieutenant Leggett, I don't particularly want to be taken care of."

He sat back in his chair, relaxing for the first time since he'd ridden up in the yard. His penetrating look seemed to bore into her skull. "Ah, love is what you want. A romantic is inside that hard head of yours. After the grinding down of labor, you want the polish of diamonds. I can give you the glitter."

He popped a knuckle. "My older brother is dying. When I return to England I will have titles and land and more money than you have ever dared to dream about." He popped another knuckle. "My father and mother are elderly and will not be around long to be looked after." For the third time the popping noise. "If you want a romantic position, you will, of course, with your title through me, be received at court. You might even be invited to serve the queen. Traveling with the royal family is an adventure in itself." The fourth knuckle cracked. "We would journey to courts all about Europe. With your tiny figure, graced in the finest clothing that I could acquire, you could set the fashion of the continent. Is that intriguing enough? Romantic enough for you?"

Romance? The images in her mind so disgusted her that she felt she might actually gag right in front of this man. His words conjured up pictures of a dying brother and elderly parents soon to be out of his way. This man thought he could cast a spell to bring her before a court that she bitterly opposed. He would command her presence before society. He wasn't even aware, in presenting his proposition, of the affront to her feelings or the indignity to the way of life she had established on this farm.

It was a proposition. He didn't love her. She bit her lip to stay silent, because she couldn't figure exactly what he did want with her. To show her off at court? To dress her in fashion and parade her about for some wild or selfish purpose? He was the enemy, now in more ways that ever before. She had known from the beginning he could be an adversary. How could she answer without having his wrath turn on her and her household?

She willed her hand steady, reached for her tea cup, made herself sip and listened as he continued.

"I have no idea why you're friends with that Moore woman who runs Three Sisters Tavern. You go there every time you come into Wilmington. We all know the Moores are enemies of the crown."

Cecilia took another sip of tea.

"Your sister, Mistress Reynolds, married a good Loyalist who understands which way this conflict will go. We will win. We will have dominion over these American colonies."

Cecilia carefully set her cup in its saucer. *He thinks I'm a British sympathizer.* Even as the thought knifed into her brain, she bit her lip to keep from correcting him.

"You yourself married into a family of Loyalists. I've heard how Mister Black argued for King George's policies. He agreed with the actions of Parliament."

Cecilia slipped her hands under her thighs. *Yes, before he killed his only son.* She bowed her head and fought to keep her thoughts from showing.

"So, then, Cecilia. Are you ready for a grand adventure?"

"Lieutenant." The word choked in her mouth and Cecilia cleared her throat. "I am overwhelmed with the honor you wish to bestow upon me. I really need some time to think about your proposition."

"We are at war, my dear. War does not allow for indecision."

"Then I must say no."

"No?"

"Think about morale, Lieutenant. Your men. What would they think? Major Craig needs your undivided leadership and attention. I've long known how he relies on you for so many things."

"No? You are saying 'no' to me?"

"Oh, dear. Lieutenant, I'm sure I'm not putting any of this very well. We must first think of winning this awful conflict. Our personal needs must come later."

" 'No,' because of what people think? 'No,' because of the war? 'No,' because of personal needs?"

Cecilia nodded.

The man stood, took time to fit his hat exactly at the correct angle, bumped against a table, rattled his sword sheath against a chair. His face was stony, mottled with anger. Without a word, he stalked from the room.

Cecilia swallowed blood, realizing that at some point she'd bitten her lip. "That's the price of play acting," she whispered. "There's really very little blood."

She leaned her aching head against the back of the couch, thinking of the look on the man's face. "Very little blood. Yet."

 CHAPTER 46

The first retaliation against her and the Black farm came the next morning. Pru's bark, and the yelping of her half-grown pups, brought Cecilia's head from the pillow. "Stay inside," she called softly down the hall. She pulled her wrapper over her gown as she raced down the stairs.

In the early morning light Cecilia saw a sergeant, six men following him, ride into the yard at the back of the house. She was still tying the ribbons on her wrapper when she reached the porch. She called first to the dog.

"Pru, quiet. Come." She slapped her thigh. "Heel, Pru."

The dog leaped across the yard to her side and leaned into her leg. Cecilia put her hand on the animal's head and looked up at the sergeant "Sir, how may I help you?"

"We are here to take your horses."

"No good morning? Why, sir, I see you each time I go to Major Craig's office. You always greet me." She gave a small curtsy.

"We have no time for pleasantries, ma'am. We were told to collect your horses. If you'll just point out where they are hidden, we'll gather them and ride on." The sergeant shifted in his saddle and Cecilia realized he was uneasy with this task.

"There is a plow horse in the barn. He can pull a wagon or carriage, but I don't think he'll make a very good riding horse. There is a pack horse in the shed next to it. He's cared for, but he's just a sorry old pack animal."

Cecilia felt an arm around her shoulders and turned to see her sister. "It's chilly this morning," Charlotte said. "I brought your shawl."

Cecilia hugged the warmth of the fabric about her shoulders, reaching to grasp Charlotte's hand in a brief embrace. She watched the men lead the two horses from the barn into the yard.

"Mistress Black," the sergeant said. "We were told that you have a stallion. A large black stallion. Where is it?"

Cecilia knotted her fingers in the shawl. Who had told? Why? Now the soldiers knew. If she didn't give up Big Boy, the men would just fan out to hunt for him. If she didn't give him up the search might lead them to the cow, to the other horses hidden in the swamp, to all the places she had stored away food stuff. If she didn't give up Big Boy, someone was bound to get hurt.

"Charlotte, will you find Benjamin, please," she whispered. "Tell him to bring Big Boy to me."

As Charlotte walked toward the cabins, Cecilia looked up at the sergeant. She could not stop the tears. "Sir, Big Boy will be here in a few minutes." She wiped at her cheeks. "It's too early for breakfast. I cannot offer you food while you wait. There is a creek just down the path there where you and your men can get water." She held back the sobs that threatened her. "I'm sorry I cannot be more hospitable on your first visit to my small farm."

The sergeant swung down from his mount and handed her a handkerchief.

She wiped at the tears that streamed down her face. "T-thank you."

"Really special horse, is he?"

Cecilia nodded. "He belonged to my husband."

The sergeant's men had come from the creek when Benjamin walked up with the stallion on a lead rope. The horse's black coat was thickening with the cooling weather and gleamed almost purple in the early morning sun. He lifted his head, snorting, pawing the ground as if ready to take off on a gallop.

Cecilia took the rope from Benjamin and nestled her cheek against the horse's neck. "You be good to him," she said to the sergeant. "You be good to him. He's never known the whip. He's never felt the spur. He'll outrun anything in this county or the next." She handed the lead rope to the sergeant. "You be good to him."

"Ma'am, I was told to get the saddle and bridle, too."

"Get them, Benjamin," Cecilia said. She was still looking at the man who was giving orders. She knew the demands were not really coming from him. Lieutenant Leggett had commanded this confiscation of her horse. Anger at the man, at the circumstances, began to burn in her stomach. "Sergeant, you'll not have much need for the saddle, I'm thinking. It's made for a boy. I do not have a man's saddle here."

The sergeant must have felt the change in her voice. He backed up a step, sawing on the lead rope. The stallion reared. The man jerked the rope. The animal reared again, his legs flailing the air.

Cecilia spoke in a singsong tone. "Big Boy. Oh my sweet Big Boy." She took the rope from the man. As his front legs hit the ground, she placed her hand on the horse's nose. "Big Boy. Sweet, sweet Big Boy."

At the sound of her crooning, the stallion shook his head, his body calming.

"I said to be good to him, sir. Be easy. Speak softly. Call him by name. He will do anything you want him to do if you treat him well." Cecilia's voice was still low, as soothing as if she could tame the soldier and the horse together.

Her words carried a weight that caused the sergeant to lift his hat and hold it against his chest.

"Sir, if you mistreat this horse, I will call my dead husband back from wherever he is. I will pray that he haunts you." She handed the rope to the sergeant. "You can tell Lieutenant Leggett exactly what I said."

She turned on her heel and walked into the house. Inside the hall Mama and Kathleen and Maureen huddled with the children.

"Oh, Cee, to lose that beautiful horse."

"Miss Cecilia, how awful."

Rory pulled at her wrapper. "Mommie, hold me."

Cecilia scooped Rory in her arms and plopped her on her hip. "Hush, all of you. The men coming is a scare, especially so early in the morning, but no one is hurt."

Mistress Reynolds yelled down from her room, "Tell me what is going on. Now. Someone come and help me dress. I cannot put on my corset without help. Where is everyone? Somebody come help me."

Cecilia began to giggle. "Well, *that* sounds normal. Kathleen, you'd best go tend to her." She slid Rory to the floor. "You children get dressed and go to the kitchen."

"How do you do it?" asked Charlotte.

"Do what?" Cecilia asked.

"Go from crying to laughing to giving orders."

"Scoot, Rory," she said to the child, who stood watching her. "Get dressed, my sweet baby. It's cold this morning. Put on your linsey-woolsey skirt and bodice."

As Rory went up the stairs, she answered her sister. "I don't know, Charlotte. I just keep going." Then, as an after thought, she said, "I stay angry much of the time. Anger is good fuel for energy."

CHAPTER 47

The next morning the sergeant was back. This time he had only one soldier with him. "A wagon load of wood for the hearths, ma'am."

Cecilia had Benjamin and Amos pull the wagon from the barn while Octavius and Martin began to load gum and maple logs from her own woodpile.

"Sergeant, you and the young private will need to get off your horses and take off the saddles." Cecilia stood, trace lines over her shoulder, waiting for the men to dismount.

"You're not going to pull the wagon with our horses, are you?" the sergeant asked.

"What creatures would you have me use? You took my pack horse and plow horse yesterday. Now you can pull the wagon."

She did not try to conceal her anger. "You can hitch up your horses. You can ride back to Wilmington and bring help. You can think of some other plan." She dropped the heavy lines on the ground. "You have your wood, sir. What else would you have me do? Haul it on my back?"

With Benjamin's help, they hitched the two horses belonging to the British soldiers to pull the wagon. Cecilia wrapped her shawl closely around her shoulders, pulled wool mittens on her hands, and walked up to speak to each horse. She had no anger toward these animals. Her voice was pleading as she addressed them.

"You're not used to pulling a load," she whispered to the sergeant's gelding.

"I know you're a smart lady," she said to the private's mare. "We have this load to take to Lieutenant Leggett and I do need your cooperation."

The gelding eyed her and shook his shoulders against the collar. The mare nodded.

"Well, then," Cecilia said, "let's get started."

She climbed up, sat on the seat and flicked the reins. The two men scrambled into the wagon as it began to move across the yard.

Cecilia's arms ached from the strain of driving horses not used to pulling a load. When she finally turned the team into the kitchen yard at the Burgwin House she sat, rubbing muscles from wrist to elbow to ease the tension. Then, with help from the sergeant and private, she began to stack the logs near the door.

"Ma'am, we can do this," the sergeant said.

She shook her head as she placed another piece of wood on the growing pile.

Lieutenant Leggett came to lean against a wall. His eyes followed her every movement.

Cecilia stacked the last piece of wood, stretched to ease her back and looked at the sergeant. "Now, sir, how do I get my wagon home?"

"Home?" Lieutenant Leggett stood with his arms folded across his chest. "You call that miserable farm home?"

Cecilia picked up a switch broom and climbed into the wagon. She started in a front corner, sweeping slowly toward the back. She scooped the debris into a wooden bucket. The private helped her lift the tailgate in place. She had her anger well under control when she spoke to the watching lieutenant.

"Sir, I have lived at the Black place now for almost six years. My husband died on that farm and is buried there. My daughter lives in the house her grandmother Black's family built. I have planted the fields and logged the woods. I have opened my door to the many who have come seeking shelter and food. Sir, it is home."

"You do not seek another?" His rigid stance did not alter.

"I do not seek another,"Cecilia said.

"You need no assistance?"

"We all need assistance, lieutenant. The price of that assistance is sometimes too dear to pay."

He looked at the sergeant. "Give her back the pack horse. That creature should be capable of pulling an empty wagon the distance to her chosen place of abode."

The lieutenant nodded to her. "Yes, Mistress Black, you have chosen." His gait was military starch as he climbed the back stairs of the big house and disappeared inside.

"Sergeant, will you please help me unharness your horses and get that old pack horse hitched up?" Cecilia asked.

He and the private switched the animals and put the extra harness equipment in the wagon bed. "You have a safe journey back, ma'am," he said.

"Sir, you had a sorry task to do, but you have been most kind. I thank you for that," Cecilia said to him.

She drove first to Three Sisters. The tavern was filled with soldiers. At two tables men played at noisy games of whist. One man was writing what seemed to be a report, papers spread out in front of him. Several loitered near the hearth, one even reaching out to spear a chuck of venison from the haunch roasting over the fire.

Leah frowned at the man, smiled at Cecilia and motioned for her to go upstairs. Polly was sitting at her desk, adding numbers.

She thumped her hand on the ledger. "I'm going deeper in debt every day with all these soldiers quartered here that I must shelter and feed. How are you, Cee? It is so good to see you."

Cecilia burst into tears. With her sister's arms wrapped about her she poured out her news. The proposition from Lieutenant Leggett. The confiscation of the horses. Big Boy taken. The demand for firewood. "I don't know what else he can do, Polly. He will try something. I know he will."

"I'm sorry you lost Big Boy. I know how you prized him." She handed Cecilia a damp washcloth. "Wipe your face. Count your blessings."

"I expected a little more sympathy," she said, as she scrubbed at her cheeks.

"If I offered you sympathy right now, you'd just keep crying. Tears will not bring the horses back or get you home again."

Cecilia stood, threw her head back and screamed.

Polly sat suddenly in her chair, kicked up her heels and waved her arms above her head. "Good for you!" Polly shouted. "Good for you."

Leah came rushing in the door. "What be wrong? Lawdy, girls, what be wrong?"

Behind Leah several soldiers crowded the upstairs hall. One waved his bayonet. Another man yelled, "Attack? Is this an attack?"

Polly laughed as she went to the door. "Shoo. Go away. Do please go away. My little sister is having a fit. Nothing, really. Thank you for coming to the rescue, but there's no need. Private Sawyer," she said to the man with the bayonet, "do put that weapon away. Who's winning that card game, Private Thomas?" With her cheery questions she soon had the hallway cleared.

"You scared me most faint, Miss Cecilia." Leah sank in a chair.

Cecilia still stood in the middle of the floor, her shoulders squared, hands on her hips.

"Cee, I have always wanted to do that," Polly said.

"What?"

"Scream. Just open my mouth and let out a screeching scream. A howling keen that would shake trees like a hurricane wind. But sister, the next time you decide to let go with such a sound, please do it from the backside of a cornfield," Polly commanded. "I think my bed chamber is still vibrating from the sound."

Cecilia giggled. "Charlotte said -" She doubled over with laughter. "Charlotte said I could give orders -" She dropped down across the bed, hugging her knees to her chest as her body shook with glee. "Give orders better than you can."

Polly, too, began to giggle. "She always did think of me as fussy."

"Lawdy, girls, you ain't growed up one bit." Leah's face blossomed into a huge smile as she pulled herself from the chair. "You just stay here and have your fun. I gotta go turn the spit and keep that young soldier down there from eating up all the meat 'fore it be time to serve a meal."

Cecilia stayed with Polly so late that she had only the moon to light the road back to the farm. When the old pack horse faltered, she walked the last mile toward home, her hand gently patting the animal's neck, whispering encouraging words near his ear. Benjamin and Simple came running to help her before she was halfway up the lane to the house.

"I'm fine, Benjamin. I'm just fine, Simple. I stayed to visit with Polly and the time got away from me."

"We was worried 'bout you, Miss Cecilia," Benjamin said, as he led the stumbling horse into the barn. "And look at *this* poor creature. He done been some mistreated."

"Do what you can for him."

"M-m-missy?"

Simple spoke so seldom that Cecilia stopped to really look at him. "Yes, Simple?"

"B-big B-boy?"

"Big Boy? Simple, I don't know. I didn't see him." She started toward the house when she remembered that Simple had been here when Kenneth had gotten the horse. She turned back. "You looked after Big Boy for Kenneth, didn't you, Simple?"

He nodded.

"Did you ride him as well?"

Simple again nodded.

"Then you miss him as much as I. Oh, so many things to miss."

CHAPTER 48

Apprehension about Leggett's next vengeful act was never out of Cecilia's mind. She was not the only one who had to worry. Someone hidden out on Eagles Island, across the river from Market Street, took random shots at soldiers as they walked near the docks. Men were afraid to go to the Market House or Court House, and women were afraid to shop at the Mercantile. Concern they'd be mistaken targets was everywhere. Children were forbidden to play in their yards, for they, too, were vulnerable. Soldiers treated everyone as a potential enemy, no longer giving polite greetings.

Any news from away, sometimes days, sometimes weeks old, seemed almost insignificant. To the north of them Cornwallis was marching his army into Virginia, ruin and destruction in his wake. He seemed to be heading toward a place called Yorktown. Raids by both the British and armed civilians in the back country of South Carolina were frequent and devastating.

Craig was invading all across the area, with sweeping attacks as far away as New Bern. Lillington, with his militia, harassed the British regulars as much as he could, though he was short of most supplies, including gunpowder.

Cecilia registered the information as riders came by the farm with news. She fed the messengers, watered their mounts, and waved them on their way. Then she went about her work, trying only to think of the next task and the next task.

Kathleen and Maureen cleaned the cheese equipment, covering it with sheets Cecilia brought down from the attic. They pushed the work tables against the wall to clear the floor. The men gathered the ripened corn and piled load after load in the middle of the cheese room. Any time anyone had a spare moment, they shucked ears, getting them ready to go to the grist mill.

"Sixty bushels to the acre this year," Cecilia chanted, as she interrupted the children's lessons in the dining room. "Sixty bushels times my twenty-three acres. Sixty bushels times twenty-three acres the British didn't steal. Johnny, do the math for us."

"I can't do that yet, Aunt Cecilia," the boy said.

"Then let me show you how it's done." With a coal from the hearth she wrote on the table top. As they worked out the numbers, Cecilia chanted again. "These numbers mean bread. These numbers mean grits. These numbers mean dumplings. Learn your numbers, my sweet babies. They translate to food for your bellies."

As she went out into the hall she heard Johnny ask, "Numbers and bellies? Mama, is Aunt Cecilia always so silly?"

She didn't wait to hear Charlotte's answer.

With Benjamin, Joel and Octavius, Cecilia made midnight trips to the grist mill. Mister Lillington always greeted them quietly. "You're not the only one who has to come at night," he said each time they drove into the mill yard. "Mistress Black, it is a fearful time."

She didn't dare risk lantern light that might draw attention to their activities. As they traveled the dark road she tried to keep the fear from her voice. She didn't always succeed.

"Benjamin, what if the soldiers come on one of their night raids?" she asked on one trip. "Or those roving bands of thieves who seem to be riding everywhere come galloping up to take everything we have?

"We can't do nothing about it, Miss Cecilia. If'n they comes, we give 'em the corn."

"We give them these plow horses we've kept so carefully hidden. We give them full stomachs while we go hungry. Benjamin, I do fear being hungry."

Benjamin slapped the reins across the horse's back. "Miss Cecilia, you ain't gonna go hungry."

As they drove into the yard on a frosty morning in October Joel spotted a man propped against a stall in the barn. "He look dead, Miss Cecilia. You stays on that wagon. I'll just hit him over the head and be shut of him."

"No, Joel. He looks sick."

"That be all the more reason to get rid of him, ma'am. We don't need no sick 'round here."

Cecilia climbed from the wagon and peered into the man's face. She took several steps back, her hand clamped to her mouth. She whispered through her fingers. "Mac Macdougal. Oh, you are in sorry shape."

"That be Mister Macdougal? Don't look like 'em." Benjamin frowned. "He dead?"

She reached to lift the man's hat from his forehead. From his hair to his chin a vivid gash oozed pus. She unwrapped his neck scarf and could see, through the torn shirt fabric, another cut across his shoulder extending down his arm.

Macdougal moaned.

"Benjamin, tell Lula and the girls to set up a table in the cheese room."

When he hesitated, she yelled, "Go! Now!"

Benjamin ran.

"Joel, get a board wide enough for a stretcher. There should be boards in the tool shed. Octavius, start unhitching those horses and get them back to their hiding place in the swamp. Get help to store the hogsheads of meal in the cellar." Again she yelled, "Go, Joel. Move, Octavius!"

Joel was already out of the barn. Octavius went, his feet making a rapid shuffle through the frosted grass. When Joel brought the board they slid Macdougal's limp frame on it. Then they each lifted an end and started for the house.

Martin raced out from the kitchen toward the barn.

"Get water, Martin," Cecilia yelled to him. "Buckets of water. Keep the fire up and boil the water. Go!" He scurried to the porch for the water buckets and took off running for the creek.

By the time they carried Macdougal through the kitchen door, Maureen had stretched an old cloth across a large table in the cheese room. She stood at the ready, a knife in her hand. As they slid the man on the hard surface, she began to cut the torn shirt from the wound on his arm.

"Help me turn him enough to see his back," Cecilia said.

Bruises and thorn scratches laced his shoulders. "He's been walking through the woods." She glanced toward the end of the table. "No shoes. We'll take care of his feet later." They eased him back and Cecilia began to exam the pus-filled cut on his face.

With each swipe of the warm soapy rag down his cheek, the man's body flinched. She began to talk to him. "You're not completely passed out, Macdougal. Let go. I'm going to hurt you to clean this cut. And, Lord willing, guiding my hand, I'll get it right enough so you'll see again. Oh, this cut is close to your eye."

His legs began to shake.

She called out, "Martin, get a fire going in this room. Maureen, warm a sheet in the kitchen and cover him."

As she again and again wiped at the wound, she continued her conversation. "Now, Macdougal, we've had some problems around here since you've been gone. We've had some good times, too. You don't know that my sister Charlotte and her family have moved in with us."

Mister Macdougal moaned.

"You might well moan over Charlotte being here." She left the wound on his face and moved to the gaping damage on his arm. "My sister has three little boys and a mother-in-law who is most quarrelsome and an old servant woman who can't work and an old carriage driver who sat down the day that got here and hasn't done a lick of work since."

Without changing her tone, she said, "Maureen, fetch me turpentine, please."

"No!" Macdougal yelled.

"Oh, hush, now. You've got enough problems with these cuts. We don't want more. Beides, you're the one who keeled over in my barn. I don't think you'd have ended up here if you hadn't been looking for help."

He opened his good eye, glaring at her.

The angry stare sent her into giggles. "Good, Mac Macdougal. Anger is good."

Donny came to stand beside her. "Hello, Mac. I see Cecilia has taken up medicine again. I sure hope she does for you what she did to mend my arm."

"Donny, get him some sassafras tea. Lace it with honey and pour in a little rum, too." She selected a thin piece of cotton yarn from her basket of supplies and began to thread a needle.

"Make her stop," Mister Macdougal pleaded. "Donny, make her stop."

"Nobody makes Cecilia do anything and you know it,"Donny replied. "Macdougal, I'm going to brew you a pot of tea. I *will* put in a goodly portion of the rum."

CHAPTER 49

Timothy Charles limped into the kitchen several days later. "Food," he said to Lula, who was tending the hearth. She spooned venison stew into a wooden bowl, sliced off a hunk of cornbread to lay on a napkin, and ran for the house.

"Miss Cecilia," she shouted to the women gathered about their sewing in the parlour. "Mister Timothy done rode in. He ask for a something to eat."

The whole contingent, the children racing ahead and Mistress Reynolds bringing up the rear, descended on the kitchen. Henrietta reached Timothy first. She hugged him so hard he pushed her away, then ran outside to vomit over the porch railing.

Charlotte handed him a wet rag to wipe his face. Maureen gave him a cup of water to rinse his mouth. Henrietta wrung her hands and wailed, "My baby. Oh, my poor baby."

"Lula," Cecilia said, "just broth and tea. Evidently Timmie hasn't eaten any solid food recently. Maybe we can cook up apples and make a thin sauce with them."

"Well, I never saw such carrying on in my life," Mistress Reynolds complained. "Pampering the boy like that. When has anyone cooked something special for me?"

"Ma'am, what if it were your son coming in the house," Kathleen said. "What if it were your son Jonathan coming home from battle."

Mistress Reynolds settled into a chair. "Well, he certainly wouldn't be hanging over the porch railing, I can tell you that. Spewing up like he'd had too much to drink. He'd show decorum, just as I taught him."

"Ma'am, I do hope you have the chance to find out how he would act," Kathleen responded. "Yes, I do hope you have the chance. Not many chances come."

With broth and sassafras tea laced with rum settling his stomach, Timothy began to talk. His voice was expressionless, as if he were too tired to understand what he was telling. "It was Yorktown. Yorktown, Virginia. Cornwallis traveled down the peninsula and Washington trapped him."

"Were you there?" Donny asked.

"At the very end, I was." Timothy held his cup with shaking hands. "I was carrying reports back and forth. But I saw the fleet." He set his cup on the table and began to arrange dishes in battle lines.

"The British were here." He pointed at a pile of saucers. "Our troops were over here." This time he swept his hand toward a stack of bowls. "The French ships started bombarding the little town. Noise! Oh, the noise was horrible. Confusion! Confusion in the ranks! Both sides. Smoke from the guns and buildings burning with fire leaping from a roof over here and a house over there. Oh, so many buildings burning. Ashes streaming like banners through the sky. Men falling and getting up and charging and falling again."

Tears traced Timothy's face, streaking through the hair on his unshaved chin. "There were times when the lines crossed. Separated. Men yelling orders. Men screaming with pain. Men dying where they fell." He reached to lift his cup. His hands were shaking so badly it slipped from his grasp.

"Enough," Cecilia said. "Timmie, I think we'll hide you in the barn loft. Donny, you go help him get settled and I'll send someone out with blankets. October nights can get chilly."

"In the barn? Cecilia, you can't put him in the barn," Henrietta protested.

"Mama, he'll be safer there. You know the sergeant will be here today for wood and anything else he can pilfer from us. Timmie has to hide."

Not an hour later the sergeant rode up the lane to the house. He had a wagon drawn by a team of horses and six soldiers with him.

"How may I help you today, sir?" Cecilia asked. She pulled her shawl about her shoulders as much to hide her trembling hands as to feel the warmth of the wool.

"Firewood, ma'am," the sergeant answered. "And food. Almost anything you've got on the place."

Cecilia clutched her arms closer to her chest. She was not about to tell that she'd shot a deer that very morning. Benjamin and Simple had already butchered the animal. The meat was hanging in the cold of the barn cellar. She certainly was not about to admit to having gun powder - not for hunting, not for anything.

"Sir, I'll call the men to help load the wood. My food supplies are low, but one of the servants did trap several rabbits this morning. They haven't been dressed yet. You can take them, fur and all. If you scrape the skins, rabbit fur can be stitched into good warm gloves. I have some winter cabbage, if one of your men would like to go with me to the garden to pull some of them."

"Corn, ma'am? Didn't you grow corn this year?"

She crossed her fingers against the lie. "No corn available, sir."

"If we search your barn we'll not find any corn? And what about cellars. You don't have a cellar anywhere on this farm?" the sergeant asked.

Simple, clutching the ears of several rabbits in his hand, walked up to them.

One of the privates jumped down from his horse. "Tell me about your traps. I could trap rabbits."

"Simple, do show him," Cecilia said. "Don't you have your box traps in the shed?"

Two of the soldiers walked through the barn, poking and prying. When one of them climbed to the loft, Cecilia was so afraid she felt she could not breathe. The men came down empty handed. "Sir, there's not an ear of corn that we could see and there's very little hay. The stalls are all fresh swept. There's no sign there have been any horses stabled here except that old pack horse. Want us to take it?"

The sergeant shook his head.

Two other soldiers rode down to the cabins, throwing open doors and snooping through the contents of the rooms. "There's a man in bed in that bigger cabin. He looks almost dead with a wound in his head," they reported. "Fires banked in two of the cabins and a really old black man sleeping in a chair."

"We work here," Cecilia said. "We don't loiter about. I think some of the folks are looking for nuts in the woods. That's something you could do to help your food supply. Someone here is always splitting wood. Everyone's working."

The man who had gone with Simple to the shed came back carrying several wooden traps. "I'm taking these, Sarg. I'm going in the rabbit business." He tied the traps to his saddle bag.

"Do you know how to skin and gut a rabbit?" Cecilia asked.

"Yes, ma'am." He mounted his horse.

As soon as the wagon turned from the lane to the road, Cecilia scampered up the ladder to the barn loft. "Timmie? Where did you hide?"

Donny swung down from a beam. He swept a bow and pointed toward the rafters. From the wide beam he was stretched out on, Timothy grinned down at them. "Cee, I've been scouting and hiding for years. I don't get caught. That's why I'm so valuable."

"Valuable! My brother is valuable, is he!" She made a face at him before she climbed down. She called back, "Are you worth lots of money? Could I turn you in for a big ransom?"

"You're laughing at me."

"Oh, yes. Yes, I am. How wonderful it is to have you here to be laughed at, dear brother."

Cecilia found Henrietta with the children in the parlour, where she was continuing their sewing lessons. Mistress Reynolds was holding forth with one of her grudges. "Teaching boys to sew. It is not a natural thing for boys to do."

"But, Mistress Reynolds," Kathleen said, "boys sometimes have to look after their own needs."

"Needs? What needs, pray tell me."

"Well, you had that harrying trip from the west. What if -"

"No 'what if' is involved," Mistress Reynolds said. "These young men will always have someone to look out for anything they need or want."

"Mistress Reynolds, do please hush," Cecilia said. "Rory, I like the way you're hemming that apron. Johnny, what a handsome pair of shoes you'll have when you finish stitching that fur. Alexander, your handkerchief looks fine enough to wear in a parade. And what is the baby doing? Richard, has my mother not given you a task as well?"

"He's too little," Johnny said.

"You'd best get used to little brothers growing up very fast." Cecilia sat on a cushion by the hearth and picked up an abandoned set of pockets. For a few moments the parlour was quiet.

Maureen's scream from the hallway upstairs brought them all from their seats.

CHAPTER 50

Kathleen was the first to reach her sister. "What's wrong?"

Cecilia, just behind, asked the same question. "Maureen, what's wrong?"

"Hannah," she sobbed. "It's Hannah. I came up to get a fresh apron and there she was all knarkled over in her chair. She wouldn't speak."

Cecilia pushed past the gathering crowd of women and children who had followed to the upstairs hall. Hannah was indeed slumped in the rocking chair. Cecilia touched the woman's hand and knew she would never again speak. She would never again listen to Mistress Reynolds's scolding. She would never again pull her painful way up the stairs to do another's bidding.

Maureen caught at Cecilia's sleeve. "How did it happen, do you suppose?"

"She was very old, Maureen. And tired. And maybe sick. I don't know. She seems peaceful."

"Well, it is very inconvenient, I must say." Mistress Reynolds stood beside the rocking chair. "Right in my very own chair. That chair came all the way from the Reynolds Plantation in South Carolina. She decides to go out on me, sitting in my chair. Just like that. Now how am I to replace her in this godforsaken colony?"

"We're not a colony, ma'am. Not any more," Cecilia said without turning around. "Kathleen, take Mistress Reynolds out of here. I really don't care where. Maureen, get two of the men to come and move Hannah down to the cheese room."

Rory pressed against Cecilia's leg. "Mommie, what can I do for Hannah?"

"Why, my precious, you can help me pick out a skirt and bodice to dress her in. We do want her to look lovely in her casket."

"Red, Mama. Old Hannah loved red. She had a red handkerchief she always carried hidden away in her pocket."

Cecilia looked at her daughter. "Rory, I did not know that Hannah loved red, but I'm so glad that you know that. We will certainly find something red for her to wear at her own laying away."

Later that day, looking through Mistress Reynolds's trunks, Cecilia and Rory found a cream colored silk bodice trimmed in red lace. "Mama, this is what Hannah should wear." So they dressed the old slave woman in the clothes of her mistress and laid her to rest in the graveyard back of the cabins.

Mistress Reynolds held her tongue during the brief service. Head bowed, she stood at the edge of the turned soil where the men had dug the hole for the casket. Even that night at supper she was quiet.

"Cecilia," Kathleen asked, "what do you think she's thinking?"

"I don't know," Cecilia answered. "I'm just glad she's not carrying on."

When Ricky rode out to check on them that week he brought more news of the surrender at Yorktown. The women and children gathered about the table, wanting to hear about the battle.

Before Ricky could launch into his story, Macdougal wandered in. He dropped into a chair and held his hands against his temples as if the pressure would relieve his pain.

Ricky nodded at him and began telling his news. "The French had been promising help. They really came through. Their ships moved into the Chesapeake Bay. Lieutenant General de Rochambeau put his French troops under George Washington's command and the Tories lost the battle."

Timothy walked in the kitchen. Ricky jumped up to give him a mighty slap on the back. "When did you get here?"

"A while back. What have you been doing?"

"Trying to keep peace and not always having much luck doing it."

Timothy sat down at the table and reached for the ever present teapot. "I left before the actual surrender. What do you know of it?"

"You were there!" Ricky exclaimed.

Timmie's cup slipped from his hand. Cecilia reached to mop up the spilled tea.

Ricky didn't seem to notice and went on talking. "What we heard was that Cornwallis wouldn't even come out to be a part of the formal surrender. Sent another British officer. The band was playing a tune called 'The World turned Upside Down.' Guess it was upside down for them. One report said that Washington's letter to Congress, after the battle, was to inform the government of a 'reduction' of the British Army."

"Which is true," Timothy said. "There was a great deal of reduction. It's a neat and tidy term for dead and dying." He put his hand under the bottom of his cup this time to raise it to his mouth.

"With Craig still here in Wilmington, his troops have just about cornered the food in the region." Ricky looked about the snug kitchen. "If Cecilia wasn't such a good hunter, this family would be as hungry as many of the other folk here about. Even with Leggett sending for foodstuff every week, she's managed to conceal enough to keep this place going. By gosh, she even has salt. That is one *precious* commodity!"

"She doing good," Lula spoke up. "Nobody here be hungry."

"We had a surrender at Yorktown. In spite of that, the war is far from over. The

British still have troops in South Carolina and Georgia." Ricky stood and shrugged on his coat. "They still ride the back country, gathering spoils."

Mistress Reynolds spoke up. "Young man, you are saying that British troops are riding through South Carolina?"

"Yes, ma'am."

"And they are not behaving?"

"No, ma'am. They are certainly not behaving."

The woman sat and put her head in her hands. "What am I to do? Will I ever be able to go home again? Oh, what am I to do?" she moaned over and over.

No one answered her.

Timothy walked out with Ricky. Cecilia, watching from the window, saw Donny join them. Henrietta said, as she looked over Cecilia's shoulder into the yard, "They're fine young men."

"Yes, Mama, they are fine young men."

As everyone began to gather for supper a few nights later, Cecilia heard horses coming up the lane. She draped her shawl about her shoulders as she ran into the yard. In the gathering dark, the torches they carried lit the faces of the men in grotesque shapes, but she recognized the man who led the group.

"Earlis?" she called out. "Nettie's son, Earlis?"

"Yes, Mistress Black. Earlis it is." He gestured behind him. "Earlis and a few of his friends come to visit you. Boys," he continued, speaking to the four men who rode with him, "spread out and see who you can round up on this place. From the news I've heard about town, there are some mighty pretty women living here now. There's a couple of redheads from Ireland. Mistress Black has a pretty little girl that ought to fit on the back of somebody's saddle."

Before she could react to the anger that boiled suddenly in her stomach, she heard the song of Simple's sling. One of the men at the edge of the yard cried out and slumped from his horse. As Earlis whirled to see what had happened, a stick of wood, thrown with enough force to rock him in his saddle, caused Earlis to make a scream of his own.

Joel and Octavius speared at the men with wooden pitchforks. Benjamin hit at them with a shovel. The sound of Simple's sling rang again through the air and another man swayed as his horse danced into the side of the barn.

One of the men took off at a gallop down the lane. Donny and Timothy raced across the yard, jumped together on the rider, and brought him to the ground.

The children pelted the horses and men with sticks and gum tree burrs. As a horse reared, Charlotte grabbed Rory from near its hooves and Henrietta scooped Alexander into her arms.

Mistress Reynolds stood on the porch with baby Richard clutched to her chest, shouting at the top of her lungs, "Monsters. You aberrations from Hades. You mutations trying to be men. Go. Get away from this place. Go, I say."

Cecilia gripped a horse's tail, making the animal rear enough to throw the rider. She held the reins, trying to calm the frightened horse even while she kicked at the man who had fallen to the ground. From the middle of the chaos all about her, she saw the torch fall.

"Fire," she screamed, racing toward the barn. Urijah and Martin were suddenly beside her, stomping at the flames from the torch. Johnny jumped up and down on sparks that twinkled between his feet. Maureen and Kathleen were there with buckets of water. Lula grabbed a pail and ran for the creek.

As they battled the blaze, Benjamin and Simple, joined by Timothy and Donny, hurled themselves on the riders. Their fury was no match for the men who had invaded the yard. They were quickly disarmed and bound.

When she knew that the fire was out and that the barn would not burn, at least not tonight, when she knew that the intruding monsters were contained and tied up in the old corn crib, when she knew that her family was still intact and no one was hurt, she stood surveying the yard full of people.

"We're still here," she called out. "We're all still here."

Rory, escaping from Charlotte's grasp, climbed on the porch railing and yelled, "My mommie is a fighter. My mommie is better than any Yankee Doodle Dandy. My mommie is the bestest fighter in the whole world!"

Surprising even herself, Cecilia threw back her head and laughed.

CHAPTER 51

Major Craig charged Cecilia with assault. When she sent Charlotte into Wilmington to tell the sheriff about Earlis and his men attacking her household, Sheriff Wright rode out to the farm with papers to arrest her. His orders were to bring her into town along with the men she held prisoner.

"They were acting under my command," Major Craig informed Cecilia, as she stood in the upstairs room in Mister Burgwin's house. The British officer sat behind his desk. In a most bold move, Sheriff Wright stood beside her. Lieutenant Leggett lounged next to the fireplace, watching.

"Earlis and his men were under my command, Mistress Black," the major repeated. "Do you understand what that means?"

"Sir, may I ask what their orders were?" Sheriff Wright asked.

"Gathering supplies. Mistress Black, I've thought for some time now that you had gunpowder," Major Craig said. "We've heard reports of occasional shooting. We've heard that you often have venison in your stew pot. It seemed a good time to test that supposition."

"Did supplies include trying to abscond with the two indentured women in my house?" Cecilia asked. "Did gathering supplies include threatening to take my daughter because she would fit well on a saddle with one of the men? My little girl is five years old. What would Earlis and his men want with her except to do her harm. Did supplies include insults to me and all those on my farm?"

"Taking women? Threatening a child?" Major Craig shook his head. "Surely not. Earlis and his men were under strict orders."

"Then why not send the sergeant? You know that since you've been here I have brought food to this house. I have followed every order you've given me directly. I have supplied food beyond the asking."

Lieutenant Leggett, to Cecilia's surprise, stood up for her. "In spite of your orders, sir, I believe Earlis and his men did trespass on Mistress Black's home and hospitality on this foray. Using civilians can be tricky. At least two of the men who were with him admitted that they threatened the women.

"These men may well have invaded her home with intent," the lieutenant continued to argue. "There is much of this kind of activity going on in the area, sir. Most of the people who are attacked have little chance against their viciousness. Mistress Black was fortunate that her family and slaves came to her aid."

"Those slaves would be freed if they joined us," Major Craig said. "Surely you've seen the proclamations that have been posted. I'd like to have a small contingent of those slaves to work for me."

Cecilia held her breath. Would the major take Benjamin and Simple? Octavius and Joel? Urijah? Little Martin? She could not bear to even think of it. And they would not be free. They would be sent into battle. As soon as the war was over they'd be sold off someplace else, to be owned by strangers. She held her hand over her mouth to keep herself quiet. She first had to be relieved of the charge of assault. Then she could debate with Major Craig.

She stood, her arms rigid at her sides, while the men talked. She tried to follow the logic of each man as they discussed her fate.

"Jail time, at least," seemed to be Major Craig's ultimate stand.

"Self defense," was Sheriff Wright's plea. "She acted in self defense."

"Reprimand. Confiscation. That would give justification for not locking her up," the lieutenant said.

"Call that man Earlis in here," the major demanded.

She hadn't been asked to sit, but suddenly Cecilia knew her knees would give way when Earlis walked into the room. She moved to a straight chair near the hearth and sank down on it. She smoothed her skirts to cover even the tips of her shoes. She folded her hands under her apron. She waited.

Earlis betrayed himself. He came in the door, looked around till his eyes lit on her and grinned. "Guess you ain't so high and mighty now, missy. Where is your little girl?"

It had to have been the tone of his voice that enraged the major. He roared up from his desk. "Out! He did try to take the child. Get this man out of my sight."

Earlis was bustled out so quickly Cecilia hardly had time to feel her hands shaking.

The major sat, picked up a quill from the blotter on his desk, and twirled it around and around in his fingers. Without looking up, he said, "Well, Mistress Black, I think you can go."

Cecilia dropped a curtsy. "Thank you, sir."

She was at the door when he spoke again. "No demands? You do not even ask for an apology?"

Cecilia put her hand on the door knob, feeling the cold surface against her palm. She addressed the wooden panels in front of her. "Just end this war. Just let it be over."

She walked to Three Sisters.

Polly was settled by the hearth with a book. "Why, Cecilia, what are you doing here!" she exclaimed.

Cecilia burst into tears. "Take me home, please Polly. Take me home."

"How did you get here?" Polly asked.

"On the back of Sheriff Wright's horse. Oh, Polly, it's been awful!" Between hugs and banking the fire and harnessing the horse to the carriage, she poured out the horrors of the raid. On the road she told of the interrogation from Major Craig and how the lieutenant had stood up for her.

"Sheriff Wright tried to be fair, Polly. He has to answer to the British or they'll put somebody else in as sheriff. But he hasn't for one minute forgotten where he comes from. He argued self defense for me. He really is in a tenuous position of loyalties."

"Many are in that same subtle place where they have to bow to the orders of the soldiers. Cee, I have heard rumors in the last few days. Craig and his troops may be pulling out soon."

"It can't be soon enough. Oh, I have been sore afraid."

Polly looked at her. "You do realize that as soon as the soldiers are gone, the looting and scavenging will get worse. It's bad now. With the few men that the sheriff has to patrol, real containment of the lawlessness is impossible. And, dear sister, you are in an isolated location."

Cecilia sighed. "Yes. I know."

Henrietta scurried about making Polly welcome when she rode in with Cecilia. Rory showed off her newest doll. Johnny had to tell of putting out the fire. Alexander shouted that the monsters were gone. The grown-ups had their own stories to tell.

Cecilia sat in the midst of the excitement, feeling so weary that it was difficult to hold up her head. She was grateful no one asked about her trip to Wilmington.

As soon as they all waved Polly from the yard, Cecilia went to the empty kitchen. She had given all the slaves the day off, asking only that they care for the animals. Now she stirred the fire and added a small log. She slumped down on a stool near the hearth and watched the flames weaving a smoke wreath about the wood.

Macdougal opened the door. His stumbling gait brought him to her side and he sat, cross legged on the floor, next to her stool. She leaned her head on his shoulder.

"Cecilia, I wish I could fix it."

"I know, Macdougal."

"My head is not healing."

"I know, Macdougal."

"I can think, sometimes. Like right now, I know what's happening. But sometimes I'm not able to think through things. I couldn't help last night. I just sat and watched."

"I know, Macdougal."

"So what are we going to do about me." She knew he wasn't asking a question.

She sat up straight to really look at him. "That blow to your head -" She stopped. "Oh, Macdougal, that is something I don't know."

Charlotte opened the door and was talking before she got it closed. "I supposed you'd be out here to see about the supper meal. I came to help." She looked at her sister and Macdougal, sitting so close together. "Did I interrupt?"

The man unfolded his lean frame and stood, holding to the mantelpiece to regain his balance. He gave a slight nod and shuffled outside.

"Cecilia, I'm sorry if I interrupted something important."

"Oh, no, Charlotte. I welcome help getting supper together. I'll do a bread mix if you want to see about the stew."

They worked together in the quiet of the kitchen.

 52

Griffin Rutherford, collecting militia along the way, set out for the relief of Wilmington. By the time the patriot general camped on the banks of the Northeast Cape Fear River, some ten miles above the port city, Major Craig was packing. On a clear, cold November morning of 1781, just weeks after Cornwallis had surrendered at Yorktown, the major began moving his small band of soldiers out of Wilmington.

Cecilia and Charlotte stood near the wharf where the British ships rode at anchor, watching as the men moved boxes and horses up the ramp to the deck. Every able-bodied man in sight was pressed into service. It was evident Craig wanted to weigh anchor and be gone as quickly as possible.

Lieutenant Leggett, leading Big Boy, came up to them and gave a half salute. "Good morning, Mistress Black. Mistress Reynolds."

"Sir." They both acknowledged him.

He looked at the line of men loading the ship before he spoke again. "Mistress Black, you will be glad to see us go. You are, after all, a Whig."

"Patriot to the bottom of my heart, sir," Cecilia answered.

"And a spy as well."

"No, Lieutenant Leggett. Never a spy. I tried to get along. I think it's called survival. I tried to please. I think it's called hospitality. I tried to hide assets from you and your army. I think it's called waiting you out. But I never spied."

"You have survived. Your tactics worked."

"Lieutenant, didn't Cornwallis know of the battle at Moores Creek? It's been six years since that conflict. Our militia routed the Scots there. We discouraged the

British fleet enough that it turned south. We turned you away at the islands off South Carolina. We harried you throughout both Carolinas. There were your awful losses at Cowpens and King's Mountain and the devastating battle at Guilford Courthouse. Who knows who won there. It seems to me your leaders, and even King George, would be aware by now that the patriot cause is not a threat. We fight not only to survive but to win the right to express our ideals."

"How do you know this news?" the lieutenant asked.

"Couriers riding back and forth stop at the farm for food. After all, I do live near the Post Road. Through news brought to the tavern, most often by your own men. Shoptalk along the waterfront and at the mercantile shops." She grinned up at him. "People love to talk, sir. I love to listen."

He grinned back. "You are a rare woman, Mistress Black." He handed Big Boy's reins to her. "I never could fit in that little saddle."

Cecilia recognized Kenneth's saddle on the stallion's back. She held the reins in one hand and patted the horse's neck with the other. "You're giving him back?" she whispered.

He stepped away from her, turned and headed for the ship.

"Thank you," Cecilia called.

He kept walking.

"Sister, what was that all about?" Charlotte asked. "Did you - Did he -"

"No, I didn't. No, he didn't. There's really nothing more to it, Charlotte."

Cecilia rode her horse back to the farm. Charlotte, driving the carriage, bickered on and on about ruining her hands on the rough leather of the reins. "I've tried so hard to keep them soft and ladylike. Now I'm driving this contraption."

"Get down and walk," Cecilia said.

Charlotte fussed about Cecilia riding astride. "It's just not done. What will people think of you. You're a widow and if you ever want to get married again there are just certain things you cannot *do*."

"So far I've done fine."

Charlotte argued about the supplies Cecilia had bought. "Why, the cost of the bean seed alone would have bought all kinds of foodstuff. Then you wouldn't have to plant and harvest and all that other hard work you seem to enjoy. I don't for a minute believe you really want to work like that."

Cecilia leaned over Big Boy's neck and whispered in his ear. "Let's race." With a leap the horse stretched out to leave the carriage far behind. Cecilia reveled in the freedom of the rush of wind in her hair, the power of the horse under her legs. Too soon, she pulled him to a trot and turned into the lane that led to the house. She was brushing the stallion's coat when Charlotte drove up to the barn.

"How dare you leave me alone!" Charlotte screamed. "How dare you ride off and leave me like that!"

"How dare you criticize me, Charlotte. You're living in my house and eating my food. A thank you every now and then would be nice." She led Big Boy into a stall, measured out a scoop of grain for his trough and came out to bar the opening.

"I'll take my children and leave, if that is what's bothering you. Polly will be glad to have me at the tavern," Charlotte said.

"Oh, yes, I remember. You and Polly get along so well." Cecilia turned over the bucket she'd used for the grain and sat down on it. "Charlotte, your being here is not the problem. What bothers me is how you tell me how to think. How to act. How to change to be some person I don't even know. Mama does it all the time. I've learned how to get around her."

The tears traced down her checks. "Charlotte, you are my sister. You're supposed to stand beside me. Not stand behind, pushing and pulling. Not criticizing everything. I know you've had a terrible time. I buried a husband, but you don't even know if yours is alive or dead. That must haunt your dreams."

Cecilia swiped at her face. "I had Mister Black to deal with before he was hanged for murder. You have Mistress Reynolds. Though she does seem to have calmed down some. I have my one little girl. There are days when she is a handful. You have three boys to care for."

"Cecilia, hush."

"And then there's the work."

"Cecilia, I'm sorry."

"What?"

"I said I am sorry." Charlotte held out her hands, palms up. "I'm sorry I fussed. I'm sorry I criticized you. Believe me, Cecilia, please."

"Charlotte, I've never heard you say those words before."

"Well, I admit I don't say them often. I am sorry. Truce? Please?"

Cecilia stood and gathered her sister in her arms. As they walked toward the house, Charlotte said, "Cecilia, I did offer my opinions for your own good, you know."

"Quit while you're ahead, sister."

CHAPTER 53

By the first of the new year Cecilia set the men to cutting firewood and clearing fields for planting. "More potatoes this year," she said. "White potatoes and sweet potatoes. I want to plant several acres of peanuts. We need more corn. More beans."

"Miss Cecilia, yous biting off a mighty big chunk of work," Benjamin said.

"The tobacco is going to require a great amount of care," Urijah cautioned. "You have more seedlings than last year growing in the troughs. You're going to be planting at least four acres of tobacco. Ma'am, you will need to hire help."

"I know." She looked out across the yard toward the field where Joel and Octavius had turned dirt to be ready, when the weather changed, to lay out rows for planting. "I know. I may have to hire men. Or women. We'll get it done."

In spite of a few raids to neighbors in the area, she dared to bring the horses and the few goats up from the swamp. The old cow mooed forlornly as she plodded at the end of her rope. "She's going to have a calf soon," Cecilia exclaimed, when she got the creature to the barn and looked her over. "Now how in the world did that happen?"

"Lots of folk been hiding stock in them swamps, ma'am," Benjamin said. "Not all of 'em was hobbled or tied. I think we be getting some kids 'bout the same time as the calf."

"Cheese! If the nanny's have their babies, we'll have milk and can start making cheese again. Benjamin, things just might be looking up."

"Yes, ma'am. I hopes so, Miss Cecilia."

Timothy Charles and Donny rode away one icy morning without giving any hint of their destination. Simple and his slingshot kept them supplied with rabbit, quail and ducks wintering on the sound shore nearby. Cecilia hunted often, taking two of the men with her to load her kill on the back of the pack horse and lead the animal home.

She set aside one cold February week to make soap and candles. All of the women had to help and she found herself acting as a referee, their bickering wearing her out more than the physical labor.

Ricky visited to check on their welfare. He had little news except to say that both South Carolina and Georgia were still occupied by the British. "How's Macdougal?" he asked.

"Mending very slowly. He has trouble keeping his balance." She knotted her fingers. "Walking from his cabin to the kitchen tires him out. He tried to ride a day or two ago, but he couldn't stay in the saddle."

"I'm sorry, Cecilia. I was hoping he could be of help for you." Ricky mounted his roan. "Like I've said, I'll come as often as I can. There are many women alone out this way who need help. Mistress Swann is one. Mistress Harnett has moved from town out to her plantation, trying to get ready for spring planting." He rode away slowly.

To make him feel a part of the ongoing work, Cecilia asked Macdougal to always be in or near his cabin, even knowing he could not be relied on in an emergency. He really could not hold a thought for very long at a time.

"I'm a burden," he said.

"Never a burden. You're going to get better. Think of how long it took Donny's arm to heal so he could even ride again. Or lift anything heavier than a spoon. Be patient."

On a warm April morning, working in the kitchen, Cecilia heard the drumming in the creek. "Lula, that alligator is going to be a problem."

"Yes, ma'am. Those children be feeding it again."

"After all the warnings I've given them? An alligator is not a pet. Especially a bull the size of that one."

"Got any work, Miss Cecilia?" Evangeline greeted her from the kitchen door.

Cecilia turned at the sound of the familiar voice. "Do come in, Evangeline. Sit. I'll spoon you up a taste of this new stew recipe I'm trying out. I put yeast pastry in it."

"Thank you," the woman said. "I am hungry." She scraped the bowl of the last drop and moistened her finger to pick up a crumb of cornbread from the plate before she began her gossiping.

"Salt is some kinda scarce in town, Miss Cecilia. I wondered did you plan to start up the works again."

"Do you have a plan in mind?"

"Well, there's several men back from battles who got problems. Like my new man. He lost his toes on one foot to frost bite. He can't walk too good but he can work. He got some friends who can't find nothing but farming and they wants something else for a while." Evangeline ran her finger around the edge of the plate, looking for another crumb.

Cecilia cut a small piece of bread for her.

Evangeline reached in her pocket. "Now I come close to forgetting 'bout this. Miss Polly give me this letter to bring when I come out here. She said it was 'dressed to Miss Charlotte."

Cecilia took the letter and read the address.

Mistress Charlotte More Reynolds
To the Care of Three Sisters Tavern
Wilmington on the Cape Fear River

The folded paper was tied with a narrow black ribbon. When she turned it over, she saw the black seal with an ornate shaped letter *L* embossed on the flap.

"Black?" Cecilia said. "Oh, my. Evangeline, you serve yourself more stew if you want. I need to find Charlotte."

In the dining room Maureen quizzed Johnny on his multiplication tables. "Seven times seven is forty-nine," the boy sang out. "Seven times eight is fifty-six."

Charlotte corrected a letter that Alexander drew on his slate and helped Rory draw a letter D. Cecilia stood watching them for a moment before she spoke.

"Charlotte, please come out on the front porch with me for a minute."

She left the children and followed her sister. "You never interrupt lessons, Cecilia. What is it?"

Cecilia handed her the letter.

Charlotte turned it over and over in her hands before she gave it back. "You open it. Please, Cecilia, you open it and see what it says."

Cecilia first looked at the signature. "It's from Lieutenant Leggett."

"Why is he writing *me*?"

"Do you want me to read this?" Cecilia asked.

"Yes." Charlotte sat, her hands folded in her lap. "The black ribbon tells me it will be terrible news. Just read."

Mistress Charlotte Reynolds,
    Ma'am, With great Sadness I take pen in hand to report that John Reynolds has been killed.

She looked up at her sister. "Do you want me to go on?"
When Charlotte nodded Cecilia began reading again.

    The news was brought to our Headquarters by A Neighbor, one Will Baker. The only Details I was given was that Reynolds is buried in the Family Plot at The Reynolds Plantation. I fear the Sad news continues. The Plantation house there burned and no one remains on the place. M. Baker did not know of the Distribution of the Slaves or household Servants. He did ask that his condolences be given to you and to John Reynolds Mother, If she is still with you. Give my Regards to those of your family. I sail in a few days for England and will not again return to these shores.

                        Richard Leggett

Charlotte took the paper from Cecilia's hands and held it in her lap. "I knew John would find me, if he lived. I had to keep on hoping."

"I'm so sorry. I'm so sorry," Cecilia said.

"Oh, what am I to do!" Charlotte wailed. "Cecilia, you have to help me."

Rory screams tore through the morning stillness. "Mommie! Mommie! Come quick!"

"Go, Alexander," Johnny shouted. "Go! Go! Go!"

Cecilia ran down the hall and skidded into the dining room. No one was there.

Rory's screams and Johnny's shouts lifted till it seemed they would tear a hole in the very sky. Cecilia raced for the back yard, Charlotte treading on her heels.

CHAPTER 54

An alligator, mouth stretched wide and tail thrashing, advanced across the back yard. Rory, backed against a tree, seemed to be trying to push her way inside the trunk. Her screams hung in the air, faded, and rose again louder than before.

The closest child to the alligator was Jonathan. Cecilia grabbed him by the arm and flung him behind her. Joel ran up to slam a chunk of firewood down the creature's throat. Octavius and Benjamin advanced, shoulder to shoulder as if for support, yelling as they beat the reptile over the head and back with pitchforks. Martin ran up with a thick tree branch to add to their killing blows. Henrietta, her knitting needles held like knives, trailed yarn behind her as she ran in circles, trying to reach the screaming Rory.

Mistress Reynolds, from behind the railings on the porch, waved her apron and shouted at the alligator. "Get away from my grandbabies. What fiend from the nether reaches of an underworld dredged you up to threaten my babies." She continued to flap her apron, as it she could shoo the reptile away. "You leave my grandbabies alone."

Alexander swung a basket toward the alligator. With each swoop of his little basket bread spilled on the ground. The boy was singsonging, "Nice 'gator. Nice 'gator. Come get your dinner, 'gator."

Rory, backed against the maple tree, screamed, gurgled in her throat as she caught a breath, then screamed again.

Cecilia seized her, handed her to Lula and reached for Alexander. The boy fought at her clasp. "Feed the 'gator. Let me go, Auntie Cee. I want to feed the 'gator."

"That 'gator is going to feed on you," Charlotte screeched at him, and plucked him from Cecilia's arms.

Jonathan jumped up from where he'd landed on the ground. "I told him not to. Auntie Cecilia. Mama. I told him not to feed that alligator."

"You did not, Jonathan Reynolds. You dared him," Rory hollered. "You dared Alex and you dared me. You yelled 'go' over and over and over. 'Go!' That's what you yelled. So there, Johnny Reynolds." She glared at her cousin, lifted her head and let out another cutting scream.

The men flipped the dying but still thrashing reptile on its back. Macdougal had come limping from his cabin. He sat suddenly on the ground as if his legs could not hold his weight.

"How'd I dare you?" Johnny yelled back at Rory. "Nobody's gonna believe you anyway, you baby."

"Jonathan, come here," Charlotte said. "Come here. Sit on the steps. Alexander, come here and sit ."

"But, Mama -"

"Not another word, Jonathan Reynolds. Sit." She pointed at the steps. Both boys sat, Jonathan in sullen silence, Alexander in sad resignation.

"Lula, is Rory all right?" Cecilia asked.

Lula answered, "Yes, ma'am. She scared, but she ain't hurt."

Cecilia stood, head bowed.

From the porch steps she heard Charlotte lecturing Jonathan. She heard Rory's accusations. "Johnny dared Alex to feed the alligator. He said Alex could have him for a pet. He did, Aunt Charlotte."

Alexander pleaded with the creature. "Get up, 'gator. Get up and eat your bread."

She heard Mama and Mistress Reynolds squabbling about whose fault it was that an alligator could just walk up from the creek into the back yard.

Benjamin spoke up. "Miss Cecilia, we all right now. It be dead."

She looked at the great scaly creature lying so close to where she stood. "I bet there are several pair of shoes in that tough hide, Benjamin. Maybe even a good pair of boots."

"Yes, ma'am. Probably is."

"Go ahead and skin him."

"Missy Cecilia, I is heard that 'gator meat be good to eat."

"Benjamin, if you want to cook that thing, you go right ahead. I've had about all the alligator I want for one day."

She had to get away. Far away. No refereeing quarrels between Charlotte's children. No settling problems two old women cooked up. No one asking her advice about food or seed or when there would be enough milk to make cheese. She had to think. She had to be by herself for just a little while. Without a word to anyone, she left the children to Charlotte and their grandmothers. In the barn she saddled Big Boy and walked him down the lane. On the road she swung into the saddle and leaned into his neck. "Go, Big Boy. Race!"

She didn't stop till she reached the lapping waters of the sound. She slipped from the saddle and walked the horse to quiet his breathing. "Big Boy, I am so tired. I am tired of being strong. I am tired of everyone looking to me for answers. I am tired of the constant quarreling and the constant bickering and the constant noise. And now an alligator."

The stallion nodded his head hard enough to clank the metal on his bridle.

"You know what I'm talking about, big fellow."

Again he shook his head.

"But we can't stop, now can we? What would happen to my sweet Rory if I stopped?" She looked the stallion in the eye. "My daughter dared an alligator. She did an awful lot of screaming. It was a very foolish thing to do. There is nothing brave about daring an alligator."

The stallion pawed the ground.

"If I don't teach her when to dare and when to back away, who will teach her? Big Boy, alligators come in many forms. Some are even two-legged."

The horse stretched to the end of the reins she held loosely in her hands and cropped sea grass that grew at the edge of the water. She watched him, imagining Kenneth on his back, wondering what her husband would have done when their daughter was in danger. "Would you have run to the rescue, Kenneth?"

At the sound of the name, the horse pricked up his ears and looked toward her. "I'm sorry, Big Boy. Kenneth isn't here." She repeated herself. "Kenneth isn't here. He's been gone now for seven years. That is such a long, long time. And I'm not sure he would have run *toward* that creature."

Suddenly she knew it was true. He would have made excuses. He would have called for the slaves to do something. Anything. He might have gone to the kitchen to get the rifle, but he would not have fired it. No. Kenneth would not have run to the rescue.

She caressed the stallion's neck. "He did look good riding you. Yes, he did. So handsome. So full of life and living. I'm not sure anymore which of you I first fell in love with. You were always a part of each other. Did he lie to you too, Big Boy?"

In her heart Cecilia knew she was finally saying good-by. She'd never said those words. Now she spoke them aloud. "Good-by, Kenneth. With your black curls and your blue-green eyes. You bequeathed them to your daughter. Good-by, Kenneth. With your sweet kisses and your horrible lies. You endowed me with those. Good-by, Kenneth."

She gathered the reins. "It's time to go home before a search party comes looking for us. This time we'll travel a little more sedately. Big Boy, if you're not going to answer me back, I'll just not talk to you any more." She swung into the saddle, nothing resolved, nothing settled. Even as she jogged down the road she felt her burdens were lighter than they had been since Kenneth died. She had finally said good-by.

At supper Cecilia watched a silent, chastened Johnny take his place at the table before she turned to Urijah. "What words do you have tonight?" she asked.

"My first words for all of us, Miss Cecilia, would be of thanksgiving. Our children are seated round our table. But there are other words from the psalmist that I would share. These words are just for you, Miss Cecilia. 'She goeth forth unto her work and to her labour until the evening. She works wondrous miracles every day. Some small, some large, but always with caring.' And that message is from every person who sits gathered here.

"A little further in that psalm of meditation the poet speaks of the great sea, where there are creeping things innumerable, both small and great beasts. These creatures wait upon the time that they may have their meat in due season. The time of feeding for one of those great creeping things is past."

Urijah lifted his hands above his head. "Thanksgiving! With exhortation! Hallelujah!" He lowered his hands and sat. "The children are safe. Amen!"

"Amen, Urijah," Mistress Reynolds whispered.

CHAPTER 55

C ecilia watched the sky that late September afternoon of 1782. The weather had been almost too perfect. The harvest of potatoes and peas, bountiful beyond measure, was stored in the cellar. Cured tobacco, bundled in canvas tarps, waited for transport to market. The ripened corn was ready for shucking and milling. The British were gone from the Cape Fear, although they still occupied parts of South Carolina and Georgia.

"Storm's coming," Lula said.

"Are your bones telling you that?" Cecilia asked.

"Yes, ma'am. Is you gonna get the folks from the salt works?"

"They should be watching for weather, especially this time of year. Evangeline knows what to do and she has men from this area working with her. They'll recognize approaching storms."

Cecilia pushed the wooden paddle into the oven and took out two loaves of yeast bread. The aroma filled the kitchen. For a moment, before she put in the next pans to bake, she savored the fragrance.

"Do smell delicious, Miss Cecilia."

"I'm so glad to have flour again for baking. We have butter from the cow's milk. Cheese from the goats. Vegetables in abundance. Ducks and geese and chickens to eat. Venison and bear meat hanging in the smokehouse. Hogs fattening in the pen." She sat at the table and propped her chin on her hands. "Lula, I'm so afraid."

"What you feared *of?*"

"Of not having enough. Of losing what I have. Of disasters coming." She wiped angrily at her eyes. "Every time things go right, something comes along to mess it up."

Lula sat down across from her. "Miss Cecilia, I done been on this earth fifty years. My firstborn child was sold away from me 'fore she could walk. My second died from measles. I never figure out which was the worst taking. My massa sent me from the low country up to this place and give me to Mister Black. It were to cover some debt."

Lula took Cecilia's hands in hers. "I done seen lots of the good and lots of the bad. Miss Emma was a good woman. She treat me fair. Mister Black was a cruel man. Cruel to everybody, even that son of his. But I found my Benjamin here.I had my little Martin. Though he ain't a little boy no more. My, he done growed up fine."

She squeezed Cecilia's hands. "Ma'am, you can onlys do your best. You got to stop thinking about things that be wrong. You got to meet up your mind on things that be right. Oh, ma'am, you got so many blessings they spilling out all over this place."

Lula stood and pushed her chair under the table. "Now, if a storm be coming, we got fixings to do 'round here."

Cecilia hugged her. "How did you get so wise in only fifty years?"

Lula grinned. "Just living, ma'am. Just living. Oh, Miss Cecilia, if'n I had the freedom you has, what kind of living I would *do*!"

Cecilia walked to the creek with the water buckets and sat on the deck, thinking. Freedom. That's what the Declaration was about. The document declared all men equal. "All *men* equal" a man had written. No mention of women. No mention of slaves or indentured servants. Did "men" mean people? If it did, why hadn't that word been used?

It said to pursue happiness. Did that mean to seek out those things that made you feel wonderful? What was happy? To find work that gave contentment while it put coins in your pocket and food in your stomach? To love someone? To care about some one? Some thing?

She watched a great blue heron, standing on the other side of the water, grooming her feathers. "Mistress Heron, what do you think? I'm not used to asking myself these kinds of questions. I'd really like an opinion."

The bird took a step toward the creek bank. She craned her neck to peer in the direction of the voice.

"Yes, ma'am," she said. "I'm talking to you. Are you happy, Mistress Heron? Do you feel free, wading in my creek? Who says the creek is mine, anyway? Who gave it to me? Oh, Mistress Heron, this creek was bought at a terrible price. There's never been much freedom given with it. Unless you call hard work freedom."

The heron walked her stilted way up the creek bank, lifted her wings and flew away.

"Miss Cecilia?" Urijah's quiet voice spoke from behind her.

She nodded.

"I need to discuss two things with you, ma'am. Do you have the time just now?"

"Sit, Urijah." She patted the wooden deck beside her. "Talk."

"Ma'am, Mister Macdougal is worse every day. He's having seizures. He is in constant pain. I was wondering if you're familiar with the poppy plant. An elixir cooked from the poppy can ease pain and sometimes it's been known to help restore health."

"Thank you for telling me. Macdougal tries to hide his feelings from me. I'll see what I can do. I remember Polly buying some poppy seed. Was there something else?"

"Yes, ma'am. The old man who drove for Miss Charlotte is missing."

Cecilia raised her eyebrows. "Missing?"

"When he settled in the cabin with Joel and Octavius, I do mean he settled. Some days he never moved from his pallet. He had no teeth, so Lula mashed up food for him. He seemed especially fond of sweet potatoes. Then, about three days ago, he walked out in the yard and down toward the fresh water pond where we used to have the animals hidden. The old man hasn't come back."

"You've looked?"

"We have. We could trail him to the pens where we hid Big Boy and the mare while the British were here. After that, there is no sign."

"Let him go, Urijah. He probably went to seek out a peaceful place to die. When winter comes, and the trees are bare, we'll find his body. We'll bury him where he's fallen."

She stood, shaking out her skirts. Urijah took the water buckets for her. As they walked toward the house, she said, "I'll find out about the poppy plant. Or find other ways we might help Macdougal. Urijah, there is so much I don't know. There is so much to learn. There is so much to think about."

"Yes, ma'am." Urijah set the buckets on the table and went back to his labors.

Evangeline and her crew of men brought a wagon load of salt barrels to the farm just hours ahead of a nor'easter that lasted for several days. They unloaded the barrels in the barn as the rain pelted the roof. They scrubbed down the huge salt pans and hung them to dry.

"Sure is nice to have coins jingling in my pocket," Evangeline said, as she left for Wilmington. "We'll be back early spring."

Cecilia waved to them from the porch before going in to see about the next meal she'd have to prepare. Watching Lula working at the hearth brought back the remark the woman had made about freedom. Cecilia knew she had a lot more thinking to do. She needed advice.

It took her three days to compose the letter to Cousin Alfred. She made notes on one of the school slates. She tried to organize what she wanted to say. She even brushed off Charlotte's remarks about her poor penmanship.

"What *are* you writing anyway?" Charlotte finally asked. "If it's that hard to do, just tell me and I'll write it for you."

"The only writing I've done in the last several years is to keep the farm ledgers. How much seed cost. How much a barrel of salt brought at market. How many deer I shot. When the Cotter girls came to the farm. Charlotte, I haven't put pen to paper for a letter in so long I need to practice," Cecilia said. "Thank you for offering, but I want to do this by myself."

She hadn't seen her cousin Alfred since he'd gone off to war. She'd heard little about his movements in the last year, but she did know he was living at his plantation on Eagles Island. She wanted to be polite, so she put in her greeting and asked about his family. Her request for Alfred's help she wrote in one sentence.

Tell me Please how I can free my Slaves.

She signed it Cecilia Moore Black. Holding it carefully she read and reread what she'd written to this lawyer cousin. Alfred's concern, in the first few months she'd been so alone on the farm, showed he cared about family. Surely he would answer.

She folded the letter, lit a candle to burn long enough to drip wax to seal the paper closed, and propped it on the mantel in the dining room. She'd send it to Wilmington with the first passing. Someone there would get it over to Eagles Island to Cousin Alfred.

Right or wrong, she'd asked for advice. Right or wrong, someone else would now know about her jumbled thoughts.

 CHAPTER 56

Timothy Charles and Donny rode into the yard on a bright October morning. Cecilia, baking pumpkin seed over embers in the fire, rushed to give them hugs.

"Those ready to eat?" Timmie asked, nodding toward the hearth.

"I'll feed you!" she exclaimed. "How good it is to have you here to feed."

In the next few days, Charlotte huddled with Timothy. "She up to something," Lula said, watching them.

"We'll find out when she wants to tell us," Cecilia answered.

Then Charlotte came out to the barn where Cecilia was mucking stalls and stood, arms folded across her chest as if to resist argument. "I'm going to Charles Town. Timmie and Donny are going to drive the wagon. It will be so much easier to travel now, before cold weather. Cee, I have to find out about the Reynolds property. There's the town house and the warehouses on the docks. The plantation. The slaves. Timmie says there are still British in Savannah, but Charles Town is free of them. I have to go."

"Of course you do, Charlotte."

"I have a tremendous request, Cecilia."

Cecilia forked manure into the wheelbarrow and pushed it out of the stall.

"Cecilia, can I leave Mistress Reynolds and my Richard here with you?" The words spilled in a rush, as if she had repeatedly rehearsed them.

"What?" Cecilia stuck the pitchfork into a pile of fresh hay and gripped the handle. "Mistress Reynolds? Your baby?"

"Oh, Cecilia, I don't know what I'm going to find. The town house may be gone. We know the plantation house is burned. If Mistress Reynolds is there, she'll hamper me at every turn. And fuss about everything. You know that. With Jonathan and Alexander I can do whatever I have to do. In fact, they're old enough now -"

Charlotte took a gulp of air. "But I cannot look after a baby as well. Please help me, Cee. Please."

Cecilia lifted a fork-full of hay and tossed it into the stall. She thought of the care a small boy would need. Richard was walking everywhere and getting into everything. She plunged the pitchfork into the pile and again pitched fresh hay. She thought of the bite of Mistress Reynolds's tongue, although since the alligator attack it seemed less vile. She tossed the next bundle of hay and began to spread it out in the stall.

She thought of how much help she had been given when she was hungry, and except for the few bewildered slaves, so alone. If Cousin Maurice had not helped she did not know how she would have survived. If Polly and Mama had not come to support her, she would have been hard pressed to carry on with what had to be done.

She took a bucket from its peg on the wall, turned it upside down and sat. One of Pru's puppies put its paws on her lap and she scratched behind its ears. "When will you leave?" she asked.

Charlotte was still hugging her arms close to her chest. "As soon as possible. While the weather is good. While Timmie and Donny can drive for me."

"Charlotte, do you have any money?"

"Money? A few coins. Maybe five dollars. A few worthless Continental papers. Why?" Charlotte asked.

"Sister, I will care for your son. I will care for your mother-in-law. I will give you some money for your trip. Hard money instead of paper. Continental money isn't worth the paper it's printed on because there isn't anything to back it. Our new state of North Carolina is financially broke. So is everyone else."

She reached to take Charlotte's hand. "Yes, you'll need coins in any town you go through. I will give you small pokes of salt, which you can use for barter. Salt will help you more out in the countryside than coins."

"Oh, Cee, thank you," Charlotte said. "I'll go tell Timmie." She ran from the barn.

Cecilia whispered to the puppy, "Oh, what *have* I promised to do."

At dawn the next morning Timothy drove a wagon, loaded with trunks, from the yard, Charlotte and Donny beside him on the bouncy seat. Jonathan and Alexander sat behind them in the wagon bed.

"You are an ungrateful wench," Mistress Reynolds screamed after them. "You will suffer for leaving me here. You will suffer."

"Mommie. Mommie," little Richard cried. He waved his arms frantically as the wagon disappeared from view. "Want Mommie."

"Peace!" Cecilia whispered. "I want peace."

Alfred stopped his carriage on the road by the churchyard on All Saint's Eve where Cecilia, with Kathleen and Maureen, were decorating the graves with flowers and candles. She introduced the indentured girls to her cousin.

"I haven't seen this done since I left Boston," Alfred said. He stepped from the carriage to walk about the small graveyard and inspect the flower arrangements.

" 'Tis our custom, sir," Kathleen said. "We'll light candles and say prayers for the dear departed. Since we can no longer do this for our own in Ireland, we do it here. Perhaps the prayers will wing their way across the great ocean."

Later, seated at the dining table, Alfred looked about the room before he spread out papers and books. "I'm glad you finally got the glass for your windows."

"So am I," Cecilia answered. "In fact, most things about the place are repaired. The harvest was good. The tobacco sold well. The salt is a high quality. We have meat in the smokehouse and meal in barrels in the cellar. Now glass panes in my windows. All in all, Alfred, a good year."

"In his letters to me, while I was in Boston, my father often mentioned how well Polly fared at the tavern in Brunswick. He always bragged about her stewardship at Three Sisters in Wilmington. You are cut from the same cloth as your sister."

"Thank you, Alfred," she said.

"Speaking of being a steward, how do you intend to run this farm without your slaves?" he asked.

"I will hire them back," Cecilia answered.

"If they do not wish to stay?"

"Then I will hire others." Cecilia picked up a law book from the pile Alfred had placed on the table. "It is wrong to try to own a person, no matter what is written here. The men who wrote the Declaration said that men should be free."

"That is very literal, Cecilia."

"Is there some other way to interpret it besides literally?"

Alfred took the book from her hands and sat for a long moment before he spoke. "If you free your slaves, they are only free in the state of North Carolina for a matter of months. They must then remove to another state. Safe conduct is not safe. Most states will not receive them. If they are apprehended during the move, the papers are really worthless. The slave can then be sold, imprisoned or hung. That is the law."

Cecilia took the book back from Alfred and weighted it in her hands. "The law is wrong. I can run this farm because I'm a widow. Polly can run the tavern because she has never married. We are single women, which gives us a little freedom from these laws. When we marry, everything belongs to the man.

"We don't often have the chance for the same education as a man. Some don't think women should even be taught to read. At the same time, we're cursed because we cannot teach our sons and daughters. We aren't supposed to think. Then we're accused of not using good judgment. Rather paradoxical, isn't it. Very literal. The law is wrong, Alfred."

She set the book on the table. "Tell me how to free my slaves."

Alfred wrote out the papers, signed them and placed his seal on each paper. "You are taking on a great deal of responsibility, Cecilia. The paradoxes are real. You will have to acknowledge the fact that they are real."

She walked Alfred to his carriage. Only after he was driving down the lane did she realize she had not offered him even a sip of tea. "You can be a businesswoman and be polite at the same time," she said to herself.

"Who is you talking to?" Lula asked from the porch.

"I'm muttering to myself. Muttering to myself. Lula, do we have an empty metal box in the cellar? I have some papers to keep safe."

"Yes, ma'am. I get it for you. Miss Cecilia, little Richard is fussing for his nap and Mistress Reynolds is fussing to be fussing. With your mama back in Wilmington there ain't a body to entertain that woman 'cept the girls. The girls ain't got back from the churchyard and I got too much to do 'round here. We needs *help* on this place."

Cecilia picked Richard up from the highchair. Rory had been spooning him apple sauce and mashed potatoes for his noon meal. She washed the baby's face and brushed his brown locks from his forehead. Still holding him, she sat down beside Rory.

"Mama, I miss Jonathan and Alexander. There's nothing to do."

"Oh, my sweet child, if for an hour I could say I had nothing to do." She shifted Richard on her lap and placed his sleepy head against her chest. "I have to pay a visit to Mistress Swann this afternoon. You can ride with me. Then we can plan for a trip into Wilmington to see Granny Henny and Aunt Polly. Would you like that?"

Rory beamed up at her.

CHAPTER 57

Going to Granny's house. Going to Granny Henny's," Rory sang all the way to Wilmington.

Richard tried out the words. "Gam Hemmy. Gam Hemmy."

The clear November day lifted Cecilia's spirits as well. They pulled into the stable yard laughing and singing. Henrietta and Leah rushed to greet them, hugging and kissing the children.

"How did you get away without Mistress Reynolds?" Henrietta asked.

"We didn't tell her where we were going," Cecilia answered.

Polly ran down from upstairs to greet them all. Finally Henrietta got the children settled at a table with their dolls and books, while they all talked.

Then Polly motioned to Cecilia to follow her upstairs. She closed the bedchamber door and sat behind her desk. A ledger, with columns of figures for the tavern, was open.

"One of the hardest parts of farming is the records," Cecilia said. "I'm so glad you taught me how to add and subtract."

"This ledger is from 1776," Polly said.

"The year I was married. Almost seven years ago. Why? Is there a problem?"

Polly leafed through pages in the front of the book, stopping at March. She placed her hand on the open page. "I put coins worth two hundred pounds in a specially carved wooden box. On the night before your marriage I handed the dowry box to Cousin Maurice. He and Kenneth read through the marriage contract. Cousin Maurice handed the box to Kenneth. He left with it."

Cecilia sank down on the bed. Bile rose in her throat and she could hear her own ragged breathing. Kenneth had been murdered for the contents of that box. That dowry. She had hoped never to hear of it again.

Polly's voice sounded as if she were reciting words from a book written in a language not her own. Cecilia wanted to hush her sister. Wanted to say that she did not want to know. She could not speak.

Polly continued talking in the same dry tone. "Yesterday I had some repair work done in the stable. We replaced some of the flooring in the stalls. One of the workmen dug up a box."

She rose from her chair, opened a trunk in the corner of the room and lifted out a quilt wrapped around another wrapping. She pulled the quilt aside, drew heavy waxed sail canvas aside and picked up a wooden box.

"Your dowry box, Cecilia. Rollen and Travis saw Kenneth bury it, but they didn't know what they had seen. When there were questions about the box, or questions about the money, they never connected them with what they saw Kenneth do. It's been under the floor of the tavern barn, all this time, protected and safe."

"That is what Mister Black wanted?" Cecilia croaked around the pain welling in her throat and chest. "Mister Black killed Kenneth for that box and what it holds?"

Polly set the box on the floor. "Kenneth must have had a reason for hiding it. I don't know if we'll ever know that reason. But Cecilia, I think he was trying to protect you. I never really liked Kenneth. I have to admit I never fully trusted him. But he loved you, Cecilia. Of that I have no doubt."

Cecilia crawled to the chamber pot and threw up. Sitting there on the floor, tears running down her cheeks, she sobbed, "I wanted his horse."

"W-what?" Polly stammered.

"I wanted Kenneth's horse. Polly, I think in fell in love with a horse."

"Sister, you fell in love with a horse," Polly said in the most sarcastic voice Cecilia had ever heard.

Cecilia began sobbing again. "It is so ridiculous. So stupid to kill for money."

When she threw up again, Polly sat beside her, hugging her tight. "Shhh. Shhh."

Cecilia leaned against her sister, fighting to calm her breathing. Finally she got up, went to the water basin, wet a cloth and washed her face. She looked in the mirror to push wisps of hair under her mobcap. Still looking at herself, she sighed. "Who am I, Polly? A silly girl who married a man to get away from the tavern and Mama's fussing? A stupid girl who tries to run a farm with a handful of men and women for help? A girl who takes her sister's child to raise? Who am I, Polly?"

Polly came to stand beside her. "Not a girl, Cecilia. The girl who married Kenneth doesn't exist any more. She has walked through every tragedy that could be dredged up for her. She killed two men. She built a successful business with salt. She is building another with cheese. She is raising a loving daughter and caring for a little boy as if he were her very own. Cecilia, you are a strong woman capable of doing anything."

Polly turned Cecilia to face her. "I believe Kenneth saved that money for you because he loved you and wanted to provide for you, no matter what. Take the money and use it."

Cecilia wiped the cloth across her face again, then hung it on the towel rod on the side of the water cabinet. "For now, hold it for me. I'll know it's safe. Maybe, when the last British soldier has left this continent, and we can think peaceful thoughts,

I'll know what to do with the money. Polly, I never want to see that wooden dowry box again."

When they came down to the tavern the huge room was filling up with afternoon patrons. Leah cut venison from the haunch she had cooking on a spit. Rory carried a mug of ale to one of the men. She held out her hand for the payment coin. Richard, his still unsteady steps carrying him across the room, took a scroll of tobacco to another man. The baby, too, held out his hand for payment. Each of the children took their pennies to Leah.

"Cecilia, that's the way you learned," Polly said. "You were no bigger than Rory when you started waiting tables."

"Oh, I do remember," she answered. "Waiting tables and standing on a stool to stir the mush. Pouring drinks and collecting coins. I do remember very well. I thought I was getting away from it all, but I'm still doing it. Come, children. There might be rowdy riders on the road. We want to be home before dark."

"Mama, I know we're still at war. I know that not all the bad men are British soldiers," Rory said.

"And you're not scared?" Polly asked her.

"No, Aunt Polly." Rory put her hands on her hips. "They make me mad. They don't make me scared 'cause Mommie can take care of them. She can even stop an alligator."

"Well, Cecilia Moore Black, does that statement help you to define who you are?" Polly said.

"Cecilia, I'll plan to be out in the next few days to help you with the sewing," Henrietta said. "Polly found some lovely material for skirts and bodices for Kathleen and Maureen. A pretty muslin in a flower print for Lula. I found out how much she likes colors, so the cloth is purple and red. It's not the British red, but more a crimson."

"Mama, you come as soon as you can. Please. Get Mistress Reynolds busy so she'll leave me alone."

"I think I'll give her quilt squares to do," Henrietta said.

Cecilia climbed in the wagon to tie Richard to the seat so he wouldn't bounce too much. "Polly," she said as she checked the fastening on the child, "I'm glad you found the box. It has caused pain since the first day I heard of it. It is painful now to think about. All the same, I'm glad it's found."

"You stay safe," Polly said. She waved good-bye.

Cecilia looked to make sure Rory was sitting before she picked up the reins. They could still see the Market Street Courthouse when Richard put his head in Rory's lap and closed his eyes.

"Mommie, it was a nice visit." Rory's voice sounded so grown-up that Cecilia bit her lip to keep from crying.

Trying to sound as formal as her daughter, Cecilia said, "Yes, it was a very nice visit, Rory Grace. I hope there are many more visits like today."

With Richard nodding and Rory singing softly to herself, Cecilia gathered her thoughts. Mama would be there to do the sewing and keep Mistress Reynolds busy. Christmas gifts to prepare for everyone would take time and care. If a ship came in from the islands, there might be fresh oranges. She had a few poppy seed she'd gotten from

Polly's supply of medicines, but she wanted to buy more for Macdougal. On and on, in her mind, she made lists of what she needed to do before the end of the year.

The first week in January. Where had the time gone? It would be January of 1783. She needed to start her tobacco seed. Before the plants could be set out in the fields, it would be time to start the salt works. Would she need the money from the box?

"Hush," she said aloud.

"Mommie, I'm not making any noise." Rory sounded indignant.

Cecilia laughed. "I was thinking in circles, Rory. I was telling myself to hush my worrisome thoughts. Let's sing 'Pop goes the Weasel.' I bet that old weasel running around the cobbler's bench will send my worries just spinning away."

So she sang with her daughter.

All around the cobbler's bench the monkey chased the weasel.
The monkey thought 'twas all in fun. Pop! goes the weasel.

Richard lifted his sleepy head to sing pop each time they reached the chorus. Cecilia pushed the bedeviling worries from her mind.

 CHAPTER 58

It is almost the end of 1782, Cecilia constantly reminded herself. As she went about the multitude of seasonal tasks, preparing for the winter ahead, she thought of all she had done in the last seven years. The time had seemed endless, but looking back, it had passed far too quickly.

I've been married and widowed, she thought. I've borne a child. Just saying the name of her daughter - Rory Grace, my blessed Rory Grace - made her want to wrap her arms about herself, as if she could keep them both safe with her love.

As she gathered the last of the fall beans from the garden, her thoughts were of how she'd brought a neglected farm to fruition. "I did a good job of it, too," she whispered to a cardinal, perched in a tree near the bean row. "You saucy bird, you. Come on down from your branch and help yourself to whatever I leave."

She thought of running the salt works. Her guts always roiled with the memory of the slaughter at Topsail Sound. In her mind she could still hear the screams of the men as they fell. She could see the girls lying dead on the torn tent canvas. Then she would think of Simple's actions in saving her. Of Evangeline's determination to continue working. Her stomach would ease and her mind would quiet.

As she worked with Pru's pups, teaching them to look after the goats, she thought of how she'd developed her herd, lost most of it, and brought it back. "I'm naming you Mittens. You look like you pulled a pair right over your front paws," she said to one of the little dogs. "You are Gruffy, because your bark sounds thick," she said to another. For the runt of the litter she shook her head. "You're my Scrapper, you are."

As she fed Richard, she talked to him of his mother. "I sheltered your mother, Charlotte. You will have sanctuary with me as long as I can keep you."

Richard nodded as if he understood.

"Now," she told a catfish swimming near her bucket, as she got water from the creek, "I am ready to take another leap."

The catfish flipped its tail and swam away.

The week before Christmas, that year of 1782, Cecilia asked Lula and the men to stay in the kitchen after the supper meal. She made sure, ahead of time, to have chores for Kathleen and Maureen in the house. She had asked Henrietta to see to the children and Mistress Reynolds.

Now she stood at the end of the table and looked at the metal box in front of her. What she was about to do scared her so badly she felt frozen. She was setting a precedent. Once done, there would be no turning back.

"Miss Cecilia?" Urijah spoke softly. "Miss Cecilia, what can we do for you?"

She sat and pushed the box toward the center of the table. "Benjamin. Lula. Martin. Simple. You were here when I first came to this farm. When I was abandoned you cared for me. You listened to me. You worked for me. There are not enough words to say the proper thank you.

"Joel. Octavius. You were sent to me because of a debt owned to Mister Black. You did your work with never a complaint. You used your skills to better everything you touched. Thank you.

"Gabe. You came to me to make cheese casks and set up a forge. I thought you'd be here a short time, but Mistress Swann never sent for you. I've made arrangements to purchase you. I need a blacksmith.

"Urijah. My brother brought you here for your expertise in tobacco. You taught me well. You recited scripture for me and for all of us. For that, and many other tasks you have done, you have my heartfelt gratitude. Thank you."

Cecilia placed her hands on the top of the box. "I have never believed that one person can own another. I have the papers here to free each of you."

"Free?" Benjamin was the first to speak. "Yous freeing us, Miss Cecilia?"

"Miss Cecilia, you done wants us no more?" Lula asked.

"Let's hear her out," Urijah said. "I think our Miss Cecilia has a plan."

Cecilia nodded. "Let me tell you first about the law." Carefully, she explained what Alfred had told her. Everyone looked scared except Urijah.

"Now, what I want to do is hire you to work for me. Hire you as free people. Benjamin, I want you to be my foreman. Martin, Maureen has been teaching you to read and write. I suspect Urijah has been adding to those lessons. I want you to be your father's assistant. You would keep the books, make the seed lists, write what has to be bought and what will be sold. You will have to learn a great deal about weights and measures and keeping accounts, but I've seen that you learn quickly.

"Lula, you will continue to have the kitchen as your kingdom. You need help. I want to find a servant to work with you, but the final choice of who works at the kitchen hearth will be yours. I will sign the indenture papers. You will train the girl."

Benjamin turned his palms up on the table, staring at them. Martin grinned so wide his face looked as if it would split. Lula threw her hands in the air and screamed. "Oh, Miss Cecilia, ma'am. Oh, Miss Cecilia, ma'am."

"Hush," Urijah scolded. "Miss Cecilia is not through."

"Simple, you are an artist. I need you to work in the fields, as you've been doing. But I want you to have time for your basket weaving. Your baskets are most unique. You can make extra money selling them. The flutes you make are wonderful. Again I think there could be a market for the flutes. Your time can be easily divided."

Tears traced Simon's cheeks. "T-t-thank you."

"Joel, you are skilled in carpentry. I need you to work the fields, but I want you to have time for building. You can do much here. You can also hire yourself out to build for others. Octavius, you are a worthy workman. Any task you begin will be finished, well done and on time. That is a very rare quality. I need that here."

The two men grinned as Martin had. Lula began clapping her hands in a rhythm that Cecilia felt, in her bones, went back to some celebration thousands of years old. She nodded her head to the cadence, letting Lula's joy spread around the room before she continued.

"Gabe, I want to hire you as a blacksmith. You will need an assistant. You will need a larger forge. We can discuss that.

"So my proposal is to free you and hire you back. The only thing that would change is that you will work as free people. You will be paid for your labour. It is something that you will need to think about and talk with each other about."

She turned to Urijah. "I'm negotiating to buy twenty acres of land from the Swann estate. About half the land is good farmland. There is a two room house on the property. It needs some work, but it's a neat little building. You would have room for your books and papers. You can grow tobacco there and we could work out share terms. The hands you would need to work the fields is something else we would need to plan."

Cecilia opened the box and handed each person his freedom paper.

Urijah clasped the paper between his palms and bowed his head. "When they moved out of bondage, they ate bitter bread."

"The papers need to be kept safe," Cecilia said. "This metal box will be a good place to store them. You can put it wherever you want to. The barn cellar would be one hiding place. For each of you, may your bread be covered with butter and honey. May you eat it in peace. May you never go to bed hungry."

"Oh, Miss Cecilia, ma'am." Lula began the clapping again. Benjamin collected the papers and put them in the box. Octavius lit a torch to guide them on the path to the cabins.

Cecilia blew out the candles and stared at the fire for a long moment before she wrapped her shawl closely around her shoulders. A glow of exhilaration brought a smile to her face. Was this happiness? Giving to someone what should have been theirs in the first place? She reached for the poker and pushed the logs together to bank the fire. The kitchen would be warm and welcoming in the morning. She ran across the yard to the house.

CHAPTER 59

P olly and Leah closed the tavern the last week of that year, 1782. Rollen drove the carriage into the yard at noon on Christmas Eve. Leah picked up a small basket of lemons to take to the kitchen. Travis lifted out a large basket of oranges and set it on the ground.

"Wherever did you get oranges, Polly?" Cecilia asked. "My mouth has been begging for a taste of orange."

"What's orange?" Rory asked.

Polly handed her a piece of the fruit. "Now that the British blockade has disbanded, we have shipping again. There was a brig from France, a sloop from Connecticut and a brig from the islands anchored at the docks this morning. Cecilia, I even bought coffee beans! Oh, the grand taste of fresh coffee!"

"Rory, you come with me," Henrietta said. "I'll show you how to eat an orange." Taking Richard by the hand, she led the children toward the house.

"Mama, save the peelings," Cecilia called after her. "Save the peelings and seeds. I can use them in baking."

Mistress Reynolds complained as she followed Henrietta and the children. "Did anyone bring *me* an orange? Did anyone think about me?"

"Ma'am, there is a small crate of pineapples on that wagon. I hope you enjoy eating fresh pineapple. We can certainly slice one or two for our supper meal."

The woman actually smiled. "Why, thank you, Polly. I do like pineapple." She hurried to catch up with Henrietta.

"Where to put this?" Travis asked, holding out a pottery crock.

"In the kitchen," Polly answered. "It's my scuppernong wine, Cecilia. The vines were heavy with grapes this fall and made a tasty drink."

They sat in the dining room for the Christmas Eve supper. There were so many gathered together that Cecilia shared the head of the table with Polly and Rory. Looking down the long board, weighted with food and drink, she silently counted the many blessings in her life.

The laughter was contagious. When Mistress Reynolds stopped fussing about the way the ham was served and complimented the oyster dressing, Cecilia knew her meal was more than a success. It had become a celebration.

Urijah stood from his place at the foot of the table. He raised his glass. Everyone quieted.

"A toast to Miss Cecilia and to this place we call home. To 'the green groves of the dwelling of the blest.' "

"Quoting Virgil, are you, Urijah," Polly said. "Most apt." She lifted her glass toward Cecilia. "I would add to your blessing. To the warm hearts and hearths that inhabit this dwelling."

"What a fuss," scolded Mistress Reynolds.

When everyone else had gone to bed, Cecilia and Polly pulled their chairs up to the fire in the parlour.

"I miss Charlotte. I wonder if she's doing well."

Polly snorted. "She will toss those black curls, blink those dark eyes, plead helplessness and get all the assistance she needs. She has Timmie with her, but you know Charlotte always comes out on top."

"Have you heard? Have the British soldiers left Georgia?"

"Cee, I don't know. There are still troops in New York. This war is still going on, even with the surrender of Cornwallis and his troops at Yorktown over a year ago." Polly reached to put a piece of wood on the fire. "There are negotiations in France for a peace treaty. Maybe, soon, we'll get word about some kind of settlement."

"This afternoon, long before the sun had set, I saw a waxing moon high on the horizon. It was like a ghost shape lifting in the sky. Leah always said it was a good sign to see the moon in the daytime," Cecilia said. "In one week we have a brand new beginning. The new year 1783. Polly, I predict a good year."

"A good year? Cecilia, we have weak state and federal governments. Continental money not worth the price of the paper. Nothing to pay a standing army. Food scarce. Salt scarce. Medicines nonexistent. Men like Cousins Maurice and James Moore, John Ashe and Cornelius Harnett, backbones of the rebellion, buried without fanfare. Men like William Hooper ill, not able to give the services they once did." Polly's voice faltered.

Cecilia pointed to sparkles spitting from a log. "Sister, those men started a fire. See. The blaze bursts out everywhere. What they kindled will not be stopped."

She settled deeper into her chair before she continued. "Polly, I have another project I'm thinking about."

"What now, little sister?"

"I'm going to ask Ricky Smith to marry me."

"Oh! Cecilia, you never cease to amaze me. Well, the only thing I can think to answer that is what Leah always says when she's surprised. 'Lawdy, Miss Cecilia. Lawdy, lawdy.' "

Polly reached out her hand. Cecilia twined her fingers about her sister's. They watched for the future in the warm glow of the hearth.

About the Author

Blonnie Bunn Wyche

was born and raised in North Carolina, and holds dear the traditions and history of the state. Her first published story appeared in *The Biblical Recorder* when she was nine. Her first novel for young adults, *The Anchor - P. Moore, Proprietor*, won the Juvenile Fiction Award from the American Association of University Women and the N.C. Historical Society of Sherrills Ford's Clark Cox Fiction Award. *Cecilia's Harvest* is the sequel to that award winning first novel. Blonnie taught elementary school in North Carolina for thirty years. Her sons tease her about the different centuries in which she lives, for she does - on paper - move back and forth through time. Blonnie lives in Wilmington, N.C., where her resident ghost checks on her writing progress.

Printed in the United States
212745BV00004B/4/P

9 780978 526566